SEEDFALL

Robert M. Campbell

Dedicated to the everyday people doing hard things.

Preface

The following is an excerpt from an infomercial brochure for prospective new colonists heading to Mars on the first Ark ship, the *Exodus*.

The Tharsis Region of Mars is an elevated, volcanic crustal area covering nearly thirty million square kilometers: roughly the same size as the North American continental land mass. It is dominated by three extinct volcanoes, Arsia, Pavonis and Ascraeus Mons. A fourth smaller volcano, Tharsis Tholus, lies nearly five hundred kilometers to the north-east. The region is composed primarily of volcanic basalt, with a smaller percentage of more developed feldspars, quartzes and granites making up the remainder of the thick crust. Due to intense convection during volcanic activity, the region is strewn with large fissures of metals brought up from deep within the mantle, leaving vast quantities of iron, nickel, titanium and other metals relatively accessible. The volcanic activity also produced large amounts of carbon dioxide and liquid water, some of which became trapped within the crust in vast pools and underground lakes. Some of these drained, leaving pre-existing networks of caves and tunnels. Others remain filled and pressurized from the surrounding rock, absorbing large quantities of minerals and gasses.

Other features under the surface include laccoliths and sills of volcanic compounds – bands and tubes of lighter, porous material trapped within the denser rock formations. These features can be easily excavated to produce caverns and tunnels beneath the surface. With proper reinforcement, these will form the basis for sub-surface colonies and networks of sub-surface connections. Requiring minimal material to produce, large colonies could exist in relative comfort, shielded from the radiation of the surface in underground cities.

Orbital scans with deep penetrating radar have already located several candidate sites, with a particular interest in one large laccolith at W102°30' by

N8°50'. *Scans show a high concentration of basaltic rock in a two kilometer radius beneath the south eastern base of Ascraeus Mons. The region appears devoid of any interesting surface features from space, but analysis shows that there is a deep layer of dust at the base of the volcano due to the prevailing winds traveling up slope and depositing it there. It is expected that the surface is relatively featureless with only minor deformations due to liquid and atmospheric erosion.*

We feel that this is an ideal location for a surface dome and colony. The analysis of surrounding rock structures indicate high metal content as well as a complex of rocky materials that includes high levels of potassium and nitrogens, both essential for supporting life and growing things on the Red Planet. Salts and chlorides on the surface can provide additional important building blocks.

The Ark ship Exodus *is nearing final completion in dock at the International Space Station. As the greatest engineering project ever attempted by human kind,* Exodus *is composed of four main sections: the Dome, The Assembly, The Core and the Command Module. The ship is ready to begin taking passengers aboard for her one year trip to Mars, scheduled to depart in Spring of 2044. Her sister ship,* Draco, *has begun construction aboard the United States Space Platform, and is expected to be completed for launch in 2050.*

Introduction

"It is of vital importance that we create a foothold on another world. A reserve for a future should our home, the Earth, become the unintended victim of a global disaster. It might be an asteroid strike, or a nuclear catastrophe by a rogue state. It could come about from climate or ecological disaster. Any number of things could create a tipping point that would render our planet inhospitable to life in a very short time. I'm talking about the span of less than a human generation. We must hedge against that all-too-possible outcome, with courage and innovation. This station will be the first step towards building a colony on Mars that will provide our own planet with the presence in space that will begin a new era in orbital construction and industry. We will overcome the dangers and tame the hostile environment of outer space itself."
- Rainer Koenig, Lighthouse Project Commencement,
July 12, 2024

"We, the people of New Providence, are tired of living beneath the surface. We live in caves, scrabbling around in the dirt and rocks, digging for metal, and water, and materials. We live in the cold, dead ground, when there is sky and land and the potential to live and grow outside. Mars is not our tomb. We are not meant for this bleak existence. We must take the surface. The domes can't be just for growing things. We need to grow too. If we are truly to become Martians, we must begin to spread out and take our place upon the surface and in every nook and cranny on this godforsaken planet.
"It's what the First Seven would have wanted."
- Zander Bale, Mars First Community Leader, R65.344

Previously

LTHS ORBITAL SIGCOM
PRI1 XMISSION, ALOG VICTOR

Attn: Henry Grayson
City Hall
New Providence
R69.174

Esteemed ladies and gentlemen of the Council:

Following is a short recap of recent events prior to our meeting in a day's time. I will have more detail for you then, but for reasons that will be apparent, I do not want to transmit sensitive data over our network. Indeed, we have disabled networking with the colony and I am sending this through encoded radio.

On sol 155 of this rotation, our first discovery of the object came from a university student, Emma Franklin, who discovered a series of flashes in a sequence of telescope images during her school project. She and her friends, Greg Pohl and Tamra Wheeler traced the path to an intercept course with their parents' mining ships on return path from the Mars-Jupiter asteroid belt. Warning the Council, Emma and eventually Greg, were granted passage to Lighthouse Orbital Station to help our small science team study the object and help return their ships safely home.

The first ship, MSS13 *Pandora* encountered the object on sol 160. All hands were lost. There was no communication.

The second ship, MSS18 *Calypso*, piloted by Emma's father, Captain Edson Franklin, saw her crew succumb to panic and a mutiny broke out. The ship's second in command, Carl Lambert attacked Captain Franklin, critically injuring him. We believe it was a head injury. Crewman Lambert attempted to fashion a bomb out of their plasma mining feeder and the ship's remote sensor platform, but failed during his EVA and was separated from the ship. Presumed lost in space. Unable to unlock the controls, the remaining crew member, Ben Jordan worked with engineering here on Lighthouse to establish a remote connection and bring the ship home. It is believed that the unidentified object over-rode the remote protocols, and performed an overload on the ship's engine, destroying it and her crew. All hands were lost on sol 162.

Regrettably, at this time, our station's long-serving commander, David Mancuso, took his own life. We are still attempting to recover his body. I, Bryce Nolan have been promoted to Acting Commander of Lighthouse until a permanent replacement can be appointed.

A fifth ship, and our only fully-functioning spare, MSS12 *Happenstance* under command of Captain Joseph Randall was dispatched with her crew with a medic (Doctor Vela Banks) with the hope that they might provide assistance in the event they were needed and could reach the next ships.

Ship three, MSS27 *Making Time*, piloted by Captain Hal Wheeler and his son Jerem were on a slower return trajectory. They attempted a decoy maneuver with their ship's cargo module, jettisoning it and sending it ahead in an attempt to confuse the object. The onboard camera took what is believed to be the only successful image of the object as it boosted away. Details unclear. Hal and Jerem rigged their ship to fire its engines on an optical trigger, initiated from their remote sensor platform. Their engine fired, but the resulting blast crippled their ship's systems. Last telemetry from them was on sol 166.

Ship four, MSS02-heavy, the *Terror* had suffered a communications failure due to antenna damage from a wandering debris field. [Location tagged for scans and orbital plot] Captain Francine Pohl and her crew of three managed to repair their antenna and through intermittent comms, pieced together what was happening. They made fast track for MSS27 in the hopes they could provide assistance if needed.

On sol 167, MSS02H arrived in vicinity of MSS27 and attempted a corrective maneuver to stop a hard rotation. It appears MSS02H was damaged in the maneuver, but were able to perform a rescue operation, retrieving Captain Wheeler and his son from *Making Time*.

Happenstance arrived on scene within 48 hours of the impact and reported a medical emergency aboard the ship. *Terror* and *Making Time* were no longer able to perform hard burns and were going to miss Mars insertion. Captain Randall decided to abandon the ships and their crews as the injured were unable to make the transfer in suits.

Sweeps of the belt have so far found no traces of unidentified object, but we are continuing the search with all available resources. The station's food supplies have become critical and without a resupply in the next few days, we are going to have to break into hard rations. Our water reserves are getting low and we have instituted conservation protocols. I should remind the Council that the *Terror* was hauling our month's water supply in her hold.

Any and all assistance you can provide the station will be appreciated during the interim.

I look forward to speaking with you all soon, in person.

Yours Truly,
    Bryce Nolan
    A-CMDR LIGHTHOUSE STATION

001

HAPPENSTANCE AND THE TERROR

"Maneuvering in five minutes. Get those lines cut." Captain Randall's voice resonated through Vanessa Macgregor's helmet. She took one last look around the galley of the *Happenstance* then grabbed another handful of ration packs from the cupboard and stuffed them into her duffel.

"Come on, Reggie!" Her voice was frantic in her ears, wavering panic as she closed her bag full of food and hurried to the ladder that would take her down to the airlock. She took one last look above, up through the decks of the ship. Past the bunks of the crew section, through the tiny porthole of the cockpit and through the windows high above. The stars slowly turning outside as the two ships rotated about one another.

Reggie grabbed the first aid kit off the wall beside her and scrabbled through it. He pulled out a silver packet and stuffed that into his own duffel, along with the hastily assembled dry rations. "Yeah. I'm coming."

He replaced the kit on the wall in its harness. Grace Fielding watched him, concerned.

"For the kid," Reggie explained with his visor up, before he pushed himself past Vanessa to the equipment room below.

Vanessa followed him, with one last look at Grace before she kicked herself through the accessway. She'd only been on *Happenstance* for fifteen minutes. It was barely enough time to process that their rescue was going to leave them falling through space, away from home on an ever-expanding arc through the solar system.

Abandoning them on a crippled ship.

She joined Reggie and Winston in the equipment room. Connor Stevens was waiting for them in the airlock, the inner door open. He waved, urging them in. "Come on!"

Reggie shoved Winston's helmet into his bandaged and bloody hands – ragged skin where he'd torn one of his gloves open.

Winston looked at the helmet, then back up at Reggie, shaking his head. "I can't."

Reggie was half turned away from him, beginning to lower his visor as the bigger man hung there in the equipment room near an empty suit locker. "What?"

Vanessa's mouth fell open in incredulity.

"I...can't! We just had a baby. She's only three months... She can't lose her daddy now." Winston's lip quivered and a tear squeezed out of his eye, sticking to his eyelid and cheek.

Reggie's shoulders bunched up in his suit and he lunged at Winston. "Put on your fucking helmet and get in the airlock!"

Vanessa grabbed one of the hand-holds on Reggie's shoulder and pulled. He spun around towards her and for a second she thought he might hit her.

"Reg, come on," she implored him.

The intercom in the equipment room broke their standoff. Captain Randall from the cockpit above. "Three minutes until maneuvers. We're moving whether those lines are unhooked or not."

"Gotta be fucking kidding me," Reg said to Vanessa, his face working through the betrayal and hurt he was feeling. He took one last look at Winston, eyes bulging with tears. He opened his duffel bag and pulled the silver packet of opioids out of it. "You're gonna have an uncomfortable trip back, you mutinous junkie."

Winston's eyes grew wide and his sweat and tear-sheened face blanched as he recognized the bag of painkillers. He reached forward, beginning to plead but Reggie was lowering his visor now, the bag returned to the duffel on his shoulder.

"Hurry up, move!" Connor waving in the airlock, hanging by one of the hand grips in the ceiling.

Reggie pulled himself through the doorway and Vanessa followed. She turned, taking one last look at Winston, floating by the locker in his half-opened suit. She shook her head sadly. She couldn't believe he'd leave them. After all they'd been through on this trip, all the crises they'd survived together. Because of him. He was a part of them. He was crew.

She felt her own tears welling as she lowered the reflective outer visor, hiding her face as the airlock door closed behind her, the rush of air cycling out, red light flashing.

She was jealous. Annoyed he'd done it first. It could have been her.

No. She'd never do that to her crew mates. Her stomach knotted and she felt disgusted with herself for even thinking it. She could never do that to her captain, who was willing to stay on board her crippled ship and watch them all leave without her. She was the co-pilot. Second in command of this free-falling wreck.

Solid red light. "Vacuum. Opening outer door." Connor hit the switch and the door swung open into space.

The *Terror* hung suspended across from them, her airlock door agape. The starboard fuel pod was crumpled and hanging incorrectly on its moorings – the only visible damage from her collision with *Making Time*. Two steel cables hooked into the eye rings outside *Happenstance*'s door converged between the two ships, holding them together as they spun gently beneath the stars.

"Sixty seconds until maneuvers. Cut the lines, Connor."

Connor held onto Vanessa's arm, his own face reflected in her visor. "I'm going to hook these onto you directly. You can pull yourselves across."

Vanessa nodded, her face hidden by her visor as Connor detached the first guy-wire and hooked it onto her shoulder ring. Reggie took one last look through the inner door and gave Winston the finger. Not easy in a pressurized suit glove, but he got the message through.

Connor hooked the second line onto Reggie's shoulder and pushed him out, away from the airlock, without a word. They were barely outside as the door closed and the red light flashed in the porthole. Vanessa floated away, hanging on her cable in space, rejected from the safety of *Happenstance* fifteen meters from the *Terror*'s entrance.

"They're outside. Clear." Connor's clipped voice on the helmet radio.

"Roger. Firing above thrusters." Captain Randall, voice devoid of expression as the jets fired on the spine of the ship, *Happenstance* easing away, dropping out of reach. The ship's big, reflective dome shield dome blotting out the sun and casting her in shadow. "We will come back for you. Godspeed."

Captain Pohl, silent for the duration of the separation, finally spoke. "Roger that, *Happenstance*. You'd better. *Terror* out."

"*Happenstance* out."

Vanessa and Reggie hung in space, the ends of the lines coiling behind them, watching *Happenstance* fall away, thrusters firing along the outside of its hull, turning the ship, one of the huge fuel pods blocking her view of the airlock as it rolled about. Vanessa's vision blurred as the tears filled her eyes and she tried to blink them away, shaking her head inside her helmet.

A hand on her shoulder tugged on her and she turned around to face Reggie, his visor blocking his own face. "Let's get inside."

She nodded and they pulled themselves toward the airlock, hand over hand, along the trailing safety lines. They floated into the airlock in a daze.

So close. For a few fleeting minutes, she'd been safe.

Reggie unhooked their lines and closed the hatch. He began the cycle to pressurize the airlock. Flashing red light illuminated them both in the confined metal space.

A face appeared in the inner door's window: Vela Banks, the doctor, her eyes wide as she cupped her hands around the door to peer inside the airlock at them. She lit up in green as the cycle finished, air pressure stabilized.

The inner door opened and Vanessa pulled herself through into the messy equipment room. Deck panels floated above their normal resting places. Tools and debris littered the air around them as Vanessa popped the seals on her helmet, stale air rushing inside as she lifted it over her head.

"They left us?" Vela looked like she was near panic, her face a silent scream.

"Yep," Reggie answered, his helmet flying through the room to bounce off a panel, ricocheting into one of the suit lockers with a bang. He pushed up through the accessway, hauling his duffel bag after him.

"They left us," Vanessa replied, matter-of-factly.

Vela hung there surrounded by the remnants of the equipment room. Suit parts, tools and debris floated around her in a slow spiral.

Vanessa wiped her eyes with one gloved hand. "Help me get this mess cleaned up." She was the co-pilot.

002

THE REEF

Aden weaved through the crowd back to the table, four drinks balanced precariously in his hands. The noise was deafening, a remixed incomprehensible slurry of drumbeats and vocalizations, sampled and altered beyond recognition. Someone bumped him and he spilled some of the clear liquid on the floor and his hands. He half-turned to give them a piece of his mind, but the place was too crowded and he didn't want to spill any more.

Maneuvering carefully, he set the drinks down on the long table, and squeezed into his seat between the people crammed in around him. He slid each a drink to Dan, Jason and Ray. Jason waved his hands helplessly. "No more. We gotta drive tomorrow."

"Ah, come on, one more won't kill you." Aden held his drink up under the pink and blue lights, encouraging the others to do a shot with him. "Ray! Come on!"

Ray turned away from the long-haired man beside him, eyes lidded and heavy. He looked at the drink sitting in front of him on the table and a slow smile formed.

Jason reluctantly picked his up and they all downed the drinks together, slamming the glasses down on the table with a splash. Jason made a face.

Aden pulled a capsule out of his jacket and attempted to load it into the chamber of his vaporizer, the lights in the club flashing off the small glass cartridge as he loaded it into the slot.

"You're not doing that in here." Jason leaned over.

"Why the hell not? I just got it."

"Don't be an asshole, man." Dan leaned back in his chair, look of disgust on his face. The pretty girl beside him watched with something resembling interest. She leaned forward and took the glass from Dan and finished the contents for him with a smile.

"Don't gimme that. If you weren't trying to impress yer friend here, you'd be all over it." Aden raised the vaporizer to his lips and pressed the ignition, taking a long hit. His eyes closed as he felt the cool steam hit his lungs, his head tingling.

Ray turned away from the guy beside him and leaned on the table, into the bubble-gum-scented cloud of vapor Aden released through his nose and mouth and breathed in. "What's in it?"

"Cannabinoids," Aden wheezed thickly, passing the device to Ray, who turned it over in his hands. "Who's yer friend?" He gestured with a hand at the black-clad, tattooed face beside his crewman.

Ray raised the vaporizer and took a hit, blowing the cooling vapor across the table. He exhaled again and more of the white smoke puffed out of him. "This guy? I dunno."

The man leaned forward, the piercings in his nose and eyebrows glinting in the lights. What Aden thought were tattoos were revealed to be circuits embedded in his skin. They looked red and infected. "Do you believe that we are extinct?"

"Oh, fuck. Ray, get that outta here."

Jason backed up in his seat, putting his chair down on a woman's foot behind him, causing her to shriek and flail her arms at him. Jason stood up and tried to fend her off, apologizing, but the girl's male friend stepped forward and started yelling.

Dan's female companion stood up and walked into the crowd, and he got up to follow her. "Wait!" he yelled, and dug into the people blocking his path, unwilling to lose her. Someone from the crowd sat down and pulled another person into the newly-vacated seat.

The man with the bad implants leaned in closer, elbows on the table. "We are obsolete! Inefficient!" Flecks of saliva fell from his mouth. "We are disposable waste used for pointless projects – the only reason for our existence is keeping the deciders alive. And for what? We're already dead!" The man's eyes goggled in his head, possibly from too many chemicals, or possibly because he was deranged.

Aden took his vaporizer back and put it in his jacket.

Ray mumbled something under his breath but nobody heard him.

The Machine Worshipper beside him pulled on Ray's arm. "Don't you understand?" He stared into Ray's face more insistently.

Aden stood up. "I think we're done here. C'mon, Ray. Say goodbye to your buddy."

Jason had given up placating the man who'd stood up for his girlfriend. He was yelling into the other man's face, nose-to-nose. Aden leaned in and put a hand on his friend's shoulder and said, "We're gonna go, bud. Talk to you tomorrow." He looked at the other man's bent nose and laughed. "Hey, buddy. It's cool."

The man frowned, unsure where to direct his ire after being interrupted.

"My buddy's sorry. We're leaving. C'mon, Jayse." Aden made what he thought was a calming gesture to the limping woman and she waved her bag at him threateningly. He guided Jason out through the mob – not really resisting, but not too happy about it either – past the bouncers and into the cool air of Main Street. Street lamps illuminated the road in harsh white light circles. The bouncer sitting outside on his stool, looked up from his tablet and nodded at them. A few late night partiers milled around the front entrance trying to get in, but the bouncer ignored them.

Ray followed, trying to get away from the man with the scarred face. Some of the late night crowd backed away when they saw him and the bouncer perked up. "We don't want his kind in here! Beat it!" The Machine Worshipper pulled his coat around him and skulked away into the night.

Aden didn't care. He laughed, the cannabinoids making everything seem amusing.

A female figure walked towards them through the small crowd as Ray caught up. "Hey, Erika."

"Hey, I thought I'd catch you guys here."

Aden stuck a toothpick in his mouth. "We was just leavin'. Up early tomorrow. Gotta hit Dome 5 first thing." He pointed at her. "Don't stay up too late!"

Her smile dropped. "Uh, OK. See you guys tomorrow, I guess."

"0700 sharp!" Aden laughed and walked down the street, Ray in tow.

"Was she wearing makeup?" Ray asked.

003

SHUTTLE 5

Bryce Nolan hooked his suit into the bindings of the copilot's seat aboard Shuttle 5. He belted in and checked his straps before going over the console. It had been two years since he had flown one of these himself, but he was still checked out to ride shotgun on the Switchblade Class surface-to-orbit shuttles.

"Radio check." Captain Jun Nagaoka was strapped into the pilot's seat running the checklist.

"Roger, Shuttle Five, over," the reply came back from docking control.

"Check. Fuel?"

Nolan verified the gauge on his console. "Twenty-five percent. Check."

They ran through it together with occasional punctuations from docking control, Bryce reacquainting himself with the ship's systems, unchanged since he'd started flying eight years ago.

He felt guilty leaving the station like this, but he had no choice. Pradeep could handle things in his absence. He'd given them strict orders to listen only. No outgoing transmissions. Keep eyes on Watchtower. Monitor the belt.

The ships were out there on their own now and there wasn't a damned thing any of them could do. *Happenstance* was coming home, looping back through L1, leaving the *Terror* behind to fend for herself. They needed more provisions and more fuel to attempt the rescue, and there was no way they were getting Francine off her ship. Bryce wasn't sure how he felt about the call to leave the other ship's crew behind, but it wasn't his decision to make. Leave it behind. Focus on the drop.

"This is your Captain speaking. We will be detaching from the station in five minutes. Please secure all your cargo and make sure you are securely locked in. This will be a depressurized drop, estimated total transit time, 87 minutes. Weather in the caldera in Ascraeus Mons is... mostly airless and a nippy 125 kelvin. The worst of the dust storm has passed, but we are expecting a little chop on re-entry so we will be holding off on beverage service for the duration of this flight." He looked over and smiled at Nolan, who was barely paying attention to him. "Captain out." He killed the channel with less mirth than he'd started with.

Normally they wouldn't be risking a drop into the tail-end of a Martian dust storm, but this was important. Even at the altitude of Ascraeus Mons' caldera, the thin wind and particulates could wreak havoc on a rocket shuttle attempting a vertical landing. But he had to make this trip. He'd warned the Chairman they'd be coming down with important information and that they were terminating orbital communications effective immediately until further notice. He'd gotten his attention with that. He couldn't risk saying anymore over their compromised network.

"Docking control, release clamps."

"Releasing clamps, aye."

A distant bump relayed through the hull of the ship. There was a slight shift in the weightless cabin.

"You are free, Shuttle Five. Good drop. Control out."

"Thank you, Control. See you soon. Shuttle Five out."

The shuttle moved away from the station, maneuvering thrusters firing them sideways and downwards towards the dark brown ball below. The station receded on their forward camera, the shuttle's nose thrusters flashing on the sides of the screen. The giant hab ring spun gracefully above, sunlight glinting off the glass and steel, giant solar collectors fanning out along the hub. Nolan felt a pang at the sight of it. He'd considered asking Jill to come with him down to the city, but it would've left the station even more short-handed. Pradeep needed someone to back him up on comms now.

Nolan watched their distance. "Approaching three thousand meters, ready for deorbit burn."

The Captain gripped the controls. "Roger. Lining us up for atmospheric insertion." Jun flicked the radio on. "Crew, prepare for deorbit maneuvers." He nudged the stick forward and the station slid up above, pointing their nose down towards the ruddy brown planet rolling by below. A couple of smaller dabs on the controls put their ship into the correct orientation. "We're in the box. Burning in three, two, one. Burn."

Throttle forward. The main engine lit up in chemical fire, braking the shuttle out of its orbit with steady pressure. The cabin shook the crew, their seats unable to absorb the full shock of the big rocket.

And just as suddenly, it was over. The ship burned for nearly ten seconds then extinguished the engine, falling toward the red planet below. Gravity would do the rest, pulling them closer and closer. The Captain held their nose up pointed towards space, one last glimpse of the station racing away from them as they fell on a long slow arc.

For fifty minutes their ship fell through space, until a faint rumble alerted the occupants to their arrival in the upper fringes of the thin Martian atmosphere. The rumble became a steady buffeting, a shriek transmitted through the ship's hull into the passengers' bones through their suit connections.

Captain Nagaoka reached for the wing control stick and pulled it back, deploying the shuttle's fins. The four vanes at the tail of the cylindrical shuttle eased out and spread into spade-shaped petals at the back of the ship, pushing everyone back in their seats. The fins created drag to slow the shuttle and gave the pilot some control in the thin upper atmosphere. The rumbling inside the shuttle increased and became steadily more violent as the Captain wrestled with the controls.

"Off mark by two... no, three degrees, north-northwest. Steady," Nolan called out, watching the navigational displays on screen as Nagaoka fought the shuttle. "Forty thousand meters."

"Aye. Pitching." Nagaoka pulled back on the stick, thrusters firing raising the nose against the atmosphere, using the full length of the control vanes as air brakes. "Engine ignition." He pushed forward on the throttle and the engine roared to life. The shuttle continued pitching up past vertical until it was pointing away from its direction of travel, engine firing back ahead of them into the dusty sky. The vanes on the sides of the ship flared and adjusted, spewing trails of carbon dioxide, trying to keep the shuttle steady but not gaining much purchase.

"Ascraeus. Shuttle Five on approach. Over."

"Roger, Five, we have you on scope. You are cleared for landing. Over."

The crew inside the shuttle were pressed back into their seats as the engines began to rapidly slow their descent. The powerful rocket engine fought against their massive velocity as the high altitude wind heated the shuttle's hull. Maneuvering thrusters fired, keeping the ship pointed up and away from where they were headed.

"Maneuvering fuel at 68 percent. Main engine, 15 percent."

"Plenty of room."

"Fifteen thousand meters."

The shuttle's pitch became closer to vertical as they slowed their lateral velocity. The rear camera showed the dark crater of Ascraeus Mons shimmering below them through the dusty haze and rocket flare. Jun eased up on the throttle and they descended, lowering into the caldera towards their hexagonal landing pad. Number five. The shuttle's four landing legs folded out, mantis-like from the sides of the ship, waiting to extend to take the weight.

Jun brought them down into the crater, the walls of the dead volcano sheltering them from the hundred kilometer an hour winds outside.

"Shuttle Five, you are at one hundred meters. Gantry's ready."

"Ascraeus. Landing computer looks good. Touchdown in five, ..."

Bryce was home.

004

FRANKLIN RESIDENCE

Tamra Wheeler woke up with a start, disoriented. She had been dreaming about an afternoon at home. Her father and Jerem sitting at the table, playing a game of backgammon on a tablet. Mom in the kitchen baking a casserole, humming that little tune she sang when she didn't think anybody could hear her. Greg was there too, sitting on the couch beside her, holding her hand in his. The dream started as a happy one, surrounded by her family and her boyfriend. There was a knock on the door. Suddenly the apartment was empty and dark. The smells of cooking were gone, replaced with empty food wrappers and a frayed couch. Was she in Greg's apartment? Had someone knocked?

She looked at the tablet propped up on the night table beside her: 0530. She sighed and flopped back onto her pillow, looking up at the dimly-lit ceiling. Drawings of Phobos and Deimos on the walls, covering earlier sketches of people. One that looked distinctly like her brother, Jerem.

She was in her friend Emma's room, and suddenly felt self-conscious being here. Sleeping in her friend's bed. An intruder. In the last two weeks, all their lives had been upended. Emma had been sent up to the station, then lost her father. Now Tamra was stuck down here and living with Emma's mom in the same apartment building off Moffett Boulevard, a few floors down from her own place, now empty. Her boyfriend Greg was also gone – taken up to the station too. He used to live one floor up from her. She stared at the ceiling, imagining his living room, still full of discarded ration packs and empty bottles.

Tamra sighed and swung her legs over the side of the bed and got up. She pulled her mother's old sweater on and padded to the bathroom to wash up.

It had been almost two years since her mom Nancy had passed away. Her pregnancy had been an unexpected surprise and, Tamra had gathered, maybe not an altogether welcome one at first. Her mom and dad were still excited, though, and they had been so cute together after the initial announcement. It was like they were a younger couple all of a sudden. Dad helping out more, doing little things for her. Lots of laughing and touching, to the point that it made her and Jerem embarrassed to be around them.

And then Mom got sick. They hadn't detected it earlier, but when she went in for a routine test, they found the lump in her breast. Worse, it had spread. They decided not to treat it in the hopes they could bring the baby to full term.

The worst part of it was, the cancer would have been prevented with the anti-virals they had on Old Earth. The second Ark ship that was supposed to bring the next load of colonists and medical specialists never made it to Mars. All that was lost.

The doctors said that working in the domes was what killed her. The higher surface radiation they all absorbed up there was the cruel price for growing food to feed everyone. The colonists had been from modified Earth stock. Radiation-hardened genes had drifted back towards baseline over the generations that followed, without additional checkups and treatments no longer available to them.

Tamra washed her face in the sink, splashing water on her cheeks, running her fingers through her long blond hair, pulling it back away from her face. She looked at herself in the mirror. Dark circles under her eyes, still rimmed with sleep. She thought she still looked pale from her recent flu. She pulled her hair into thick bundles and started braiding, staring at her face in the mirror. She looked older somehow. More drawn. Maybe she'd lost more weight than she thought she had. She pulled her hair tighter, feeling it in her forehead and eyes.

In the last four weeks everyone she knew and cared about had left. They'd taken Greg away, first to the mines, then to space. Emma had already gone up to the station to help track whatever was following their mining ships. Jerem and her father were still out there… she hoped. Over, under, over, under. She pulled the last strands of her braid together and tied it off.

She didn't know. After they'd lost *Calypso*, MARSnet had stopped reporting on what was happening in space. Most of the colony didn't seem to care. The routine mining operations in the asteroid belt were of no more interest than the efforts in the tunnels down here, deep beneath the surface. In some ways, people found the operations in space less interesting. It was a common complaint of many of the residents that it was a waste of resources to send people up. Now that their ships were in actual danger, there was even less sympathy for the space program. Worse, it was becoming a central issue for the People of Mars First movement – the Firsters, sometimes called Fisters by those less tolerant of their signature salute. During the food riots last week, there were protestors calling for the wholesale dismantling of the space program to focus more on the people in New Providence, the people who really needed it.

Tamra finished cleaning up and pulled her long sweater back on, padding back to her room. *Emma's room*, she corrected herself. Julie, Em's mom, met her on the way by.

"Hey, sweetie. You want some breakfast before heading in?"

"That's all right, Mrs. Franklin… Julie." Old habits. "I'll just grab a breakfast bar and some coffee when I get to school."

"You sure? I got some eggs yesterday. We should eat 'em."

Eggs did sound good, but Tamra was still feeling a bit queasy. "Yeah, that's OK. I have to head in early to check my plants before heading up to the Dome with the guys." She hadn't fully recovered from her flu yet. "We should have the eggs for dinner. Maybe I'll make a stir fry?"

"That'd be lovely, hon." Julie smiled at her affectionately and gave her a squeeze on the arm.

Tamra did her best to smile back. She guessed they were family now. "I'm going to swing by my place on my way back and pick up a few things from the kitchen. Maybe some stuff for Em's room."

"Whatever you need." Julie smiled and turned away back to her own room, shoulders hunching in her green bathrobe, a hint of sadness at the mention of her daughter, Emma.

Tamra sighed, took a deep breath and went to her room to get dressed.

005

WILLOW PARK

Sean Tay sat cross-legged on the grass in Willow Park. He leaned back against his favorite tree, watching the chattering students meandering along the pathways in twos and threes on their way to class. He put the last of his breakfast bar into his mouth and chewed it carefully to soften it, the hard, packed cereal and soy rectangles were processed and packaged in plastic, and had a shelf-life of two years. They never lasted that long, usually being one of the first items to go from the Store shelves, everyone getting their allotment. But some that never made it to the Stores. They'd slip out the backs of the trolleys, or off the packaging line at the Fab and into the hands of those who had enough chits to pay for them, who otherwise didn't have access to the Stores. This one was two and a half years old. He had three left in the box for the rest of the week.

Sean drank some of his soy milk in an attempt to moisten the sharp, dried-out cereal in his mouth. He'd scraped his palate on a bar from this box yesterday and wanted to avoid a repeat of that unpleasantness.

On the curved stage of the amphitheatre, a man in a long coat called out at the passing people on the paths wandering through the park. "Do you believe we're extinct? Do you think we could have gotten here, to this place, without the Machines? No! Do you think we can survive without them? We cannot! We need them to progress, to move past this beginning stage of our meagre lives and enter the next phase of our evolution! We are stranded here. Prisoners beneath the rock…"

As if on cue, someone threw a rock and hit the man in the temple, drawing a gash of red. A beefy-looking boy at the edge of the stage laughed and pointed as the Machine Worshipper stumbled. Another one helped him up and waved a finger at the boy.

Sean looked away. He poked at the worn tablet on his lap, messages scrolling past. Close inspection of his tablet revealed a non-standard metal housing around the back of the device that didn't hold the screen quite firmly enough. Tape held the screen in place, barely. Scratches on the screen and chips around the edges suggested this wasn't the screen's first tour of duty. The feeds of the day, Kaylee Baker reporting for MARSnet from City Hall muted in the corner. She was recounting the aftermath of last week's food riots. Several injured. The instigators rounded up and detained for reasons of safety, theirs and the public's.

He heard crunching on the path behind him and he turned his head slightly, hood obscuring one of his eyes, to look at the source. Black boots, black jeans, a woman's legs. A blonde girl strode past him, braid bouncing on her shoulder, pack on her back, barely glancing at him as he clutched his tablet in his hands. Another student on her way to class, he figured.

From here he could just reach the school's network. He'd been using the credentials of a generous donor for the past three years and nobody'd ever complained about it. He worried that one day this connection would stop working when the student graduated or the IT staff at the school recognized the strange connection patterns, but they hadn't yet. He would have.

He wadded up the breakfast bar wrapper and placed it beside him on the ground. His oversized boots dug into his calves under his legs and he shifted to prevent his leg from falling asleep. Deft fingers switched screens on his tablet, bringing up the Observatory – his name for the suite of network traffic monitors and databases he'd been assembling. He watched the traffic flow by in graphical visualization, eyes flickering across the web of nodes, recognizing patterns he'd seen before. The morning news. Students and teachers logging on for the first time this morning. City Hall, a vast black box absorbing everything around it, broadcasting very little.

He tapped the screen and zoomed out. He'd been mapping the city's network for two years now. It had begun as an exercise in keeping his connection alive in case he ever lost the one he'd borrowed. He'd found an old network analysis program in the school's computer science archives and managed to get it running on his makeshift tablet. Old host files and server lists still held active machines he could look up. With that, he'd generated a map of the city's network infrastructure, or what he could see of it at least. Pinging remote systems lit up the intervening nodes, tracing the routes his packets took, presenting paths through the network. From different locations in the city he could see the different pathways his packets took. Over time, he updated his database as the network changed, but was surprised to see how infrequently that happened. He'd augmented his database with the radio traffic he could see walking around the city. Access points upon access points. Ad hoc networks installed in the inhabitants' apartments. Darknet nodes hidden in plain sight. All of it broadcasting invisibly all around them – but only if you knew how to look for it.

And he was collecting a good portion of all this traffic on the observatory node he had installed at his friend's stall in the East Side. Splicing a line in was a simple matter for him, and his node was a little more than just a dumb repeater with some storage.

He watched the graphs glowing in green and red, traffic shunting between the web of nodes and access points around the city from under his tree in the park.

"What are you doing, grub?"

Sean turned his head to see a pair of thick booted legs beside him. He looked up, the broad torso attached to the legs supported an oversized head sneering down at him. He recognized his shape as the boy who'd thrown the rock.

"Yer not supposed to be here."

Sean hastily shut off his tablet and began stuffing it into his bag, scrambling to his knees. He stood up, ready to run if he had to.

"Leave him alone, Derek." Another voice. A group of three students walked up behind the bigger boy.

Derek, wide eyes and broad mouth, scowled at Sean, not looking away. "You leaving that here?" He pointed at the wrapper on the ground beside him. "Pick that up."

Sean hesitated, stooped over, the other boy was easily forty centimeters taller than he was. Sean was small for his age. His growth had been stunted by the operations on his spine he'd had as a child. He considered bolting, looked around to see if anyone was blocking his path out.

"I said pick that up!" Derek pointed at the wrapper with a stubby finger.

Sean cautiously bent over to pick up the wrapper and Derek kicked him in the side with a heavy boot. Sean felt something crunch in his backpack and he rolled over onto the grass, clutching his bag beside him.

"That's for littering, grub." Derek cracked a knuckle and the boys behind him started booing and jeering.

"Cut it out, you jerk." One of the other boys stepped forward, defiant look on his face.

Derek turned on him. "You want some too?" He smacked a fist into his other hand and the other boy's toughness dropped away. He shrunk back into his group of friends. "Yeah, I didn't think so, Rory." Derek turned back to Sean, who snatched up the breakfast bar wrapper and stuffed it into a pocket, backing up on his hands and knees. "I don't wanna see you hanging around here again. You get me?"

Sean nodded, not looking at him.

Derek punched his fist into his hand again to emphasize his point before laughing and continuing on to school.

The other boys stepped forward as Derek walked away. "You alright?" another one of them asked.

Sean nodded, not really looking at them directly, his straight black hair hiding half his face under his hood.

Rory, the boy who'd stepped up, said, "That guy's a jerk. Don't worry about him." But Sean noted he didn't say this with the same bravado he'd shown earlier.

Sean stood up, as straight as he could. "Thanks." He brushed himself off and felt something in his bag rattle. "I have to get to work."

"What's your name? I haven't seen you around school before."

"Boots." Sean stalked away, oversized boots crunching on the gravel pathway towards the Fab.

006

LIGHTHOUSE

Greg and Emma sat on opposite sides of the table in the small boardroom off the Control Deck.

Greg had his hat pulled down over his eyes, his back to the windows, shades drawn obscuring the view. He was arranging a small tub of peanuts into a line in front of him on the smooth glass table. His fingers were shaking.

"I can't believe he just left." Greg batted the small tub the peanuts had previously occupied down the table. It sailed off the edge onto the floor with a light plop. He stood up and walked down the length of the table to retrieve it, Emma watching him. "I had a return solution and he wouldn't let us use it. I couldn't even relay it to them!"

"I'm sure he had his reasons," Emma offered helplessly. She took a bite of the small carrot she'd been fidgeting with. She was worried too, scared if she let herself think about it, but right now Greg was acting a bit erratically and she wasn't sure where he was going with this.

Greg picked up the empty peanut tub and set it down beside his soy milk. "Reasons? That's my mom and your dad out there. And Jerem! We don't even know what kind of shape they're in or if they're even alive!" He banged his fist on the table, the peanuts jumping in response.

"Take it easy. *Happenstance* made it and is looping back to us. Hopefully they have your mom on board." *And the rest of them.* Not knowing was agony for her, but she was trying to stay positive. They were no longer getting imagery of the falling ships from Watchtower. The remote station, aimed away from the inner system, was back on duty looking for targets of interest. Ortega had taken over control of the big telescope and was using it to look for traces of the Object. He wouldn't let them turn it, claiming this was priority, which it probably was.

"Not that we know. Without comms we can't even get pictures from Olympus, let alone radio the ships." He plunked down in his chair again. "We're cut off."

"It's just temporary." Emma wished she'd been allowed to go back down to the colony. She was worried about her mom and Tamra, and Jerem. She wrung her hands, and felt her chest tighten up. Not now. She blinked to try to stop herself from crying.

Silence.

Greg was watching her from under his hat. "I'm sorry. This is fucked."

"Yeah." She sniffed.

They sat in silence for a few minutes, Greg absent-mindedly picking up peanuts and popping them into his mouth. The door slid open and Dan Wilkins stuck his head in.

"Wide field scans are in. I could use your help going through them." He waited in the doorway, looking at the array of snacks on the table.

Greg stood. "Alright. That's something useful I can do, at least." He looked at Emma. "You coming?"

"Sure." It was a one-person job, but she didn't care. She didn't want to be alone in here. She stood up and walked to the door, following Dan and Greg through it onto the Control Deck.

Emma looked around on her way to the science station, banks of screens surrounded four chairs with a divider splitting the two stations. Sunil Pradeep was sitting in the Commander's chair, reading his tablet. He blinked and looked up as they walked in, barely acknowledging their return. A faint smile started to cross his face before it was replaced by concern and he quickly looked back down at his screen.

Jill Sanchez looked like she was sleeping at the Comms station, eyes closed and head tilted back against the headrest. Her headphones were on and Emma could see her fingers moving, as if in time to whatever it was she was listening to. Probably another language training program from the station's archives. She didn't have a lot to do without any active communications from the planet or space. The station was still using local radio for operations channels, but listening to Engineering chatter got old fast. Emma sighed and sat down at her station.

She looked through the tall floor-to-ceiling windows along the planet-side wall of the room. Mars rotated past them, three thousand kilometers below. She squinted, spotting Olympus Mons and the

Tharsis volcanoes east of it, and grey-brown blobs on the dusty surface of the Tharsis plateau. The dust cloud was receding, moving north and east across the planum but Ascraeus Mons was still partially obscured by the twenty kilometer high ball of dust.

"It's still out there." Wilkins smiled at her with that awkward grin of his. "Clearing up. Hopefully Bryce had a good drop."

Greg grunted as he sat down next to Ortega on the other side of the divider. "What've you got, Nelson?" Wilkins' grin changed into a frown and he sat down beside them.

"Initial analysis came back with eighteen points of interest. I was able to get that down to four." Ortega brought up a star field on his monitor and zoomed in on a red-circled dot on the screen. "I've tagged this as 052-167-01." He moved onto the next three, named in sequence. "Cross-check these against our databases and see if you can identify them. None look like they're in the right place to be our object, but they're within reach, given the right push."

Greg frowned, pulling in and setting up his station to do the work, loading the observation data and a map of the asteroid belt on his screens. Emma rolled her seat over and sat beside him, bringing up the Near Mars Catalog on her tablet. Small asteroids didn't always stay where they were supposed to. Sometimes they got pulled out of their orbits and shifted into new positions. It wasn't common, but it happened. Sometimes comets showed up here, or bits of rock from further out in the solar system. Identifying them was a largely automatic process, until it wasn't.

Emma enjoyed the detective work. Her mom, Julie, used to bring home charts of space from school when she was little. She would show Emma the map of the asteroid field where her father was going and they would play a game of figuring out what each of the rocks might have in them. She thought about doing this with her mom as a kid. They'd go through the nearby asteroids and figure out which one was likely to have the most metal. They were able to guess where her father's ship, *Calypso,* would be going with him and the crew.

It was over a week since the Object had taken her father away from her forever. She shuddered, remembering that sound they'd broadcast before the bright light obliterated their ship.

"I'll take oh-two and oh-four," Emma said, loading the data on her tablet.

Greg sucked air through his teeth. "Fill your boots."

She rolled back around the divider to her station, and set to work.

007

GAGARIN TERMINAL

Bryce walked down the tunnel with the rest of the flight crew to the main terminal, their helmets still on, suits still sealed. They turned the corner, walked into the final airlock and it fast-cycled to pressure, sliding doors hissing open onto the brightly lit waiting area of Arrivals beyond.

Bryce and Jun unlocked their helmets and lifted them over their heads on their way inside. A couple of families were waiting for their sons or daughters and perked up as they walked in with the rest of the shuttle's passengers. One of them ran forward to a man waiting for her. Bryce breathed in the terminal's air, not smelling much different from that of Lighthouse. Clean and filtered, freshly recycled. "Nice landing, Jun."

"Good to know you can still handle yourself at the controls. Can always use more pilots." Jun stuffed his helmet into its bag, gloves on top before closing it up. They walked away from the small group of people leaving the shuttle through the hall to the crew lockers.

"You know anything about what's going on out there?" Jun asked quietly. Bryce could tell he'd been waiting to talk about it. Like everyone else, he was curious about what was going on with their ships.

"Sorry. Can't really talk about it." Bryce shut down the power to his suit's comm systems and backpack, already in standby mode since his helmet came off.

Jun tutted and shook his head. "It's all very strange. Losing two ships in a week. Talk around Pancho's is that there's something out there.

Maybe a ship."

Bryce set his jaw. "I wish I could talk about it, I really do, but I can't. I'm going to meet up with the Council and they'll decide what we can say. If anything." He hated not being able to say anything to his friend.

Jun looked disappointed. "Man, they really did a number on you up there."

"It's the job. Look, I'll catch up with you later. Maybe we can go for a drink or something." Bryce had no intention of it, but thought it might placate the other man. And who could say? Maybe he would.

"Yeah, sure thing."

After changing into his street clothes, Bryce walked down the tunnel to the main terminal area. Bryce's father Robert was waiting for him on one of the benches. He stood up and walked over to greet him, arms open and gave him a big hug. The grizzled engineer clapped him on the back.

"Good to have you back, kid. Didn't expect you to be wearing your old pilot's uniform." He tapped the patch on his jacket with a finger.

"I only have the one jacket." Bryce smiled. "Don't get too used to it. Just down for a quick trip." He looked around at the small group of people leaving with them. One of the passengers, Vicki from Personnel, smiled and waved at him. He nodded and looked away. People were watching him. His newfound status as Commander of the Station had already gotten around. He had to watch what he said.

"Well, it's nice just the same." They walked in silence for a moment down the long tunnel, the moving walkway doubling their speed, bright white and blue LEDs casting moving shadows of themselves around their feet.

*

On the train his father started up his old tune. "When are you going to move back to the city permanently?"

"Come on, Dad."

"Well, I'm just saying, space isn't easy on anybody. All that radiation." He hesitated for a moment. "What happened to Commander Mancuso?" He said this last quietly then trailed off.

Bryce frowned and shook his head. He rifled through his duffel bag looking for something to distract himself.

"Nobody lives to old age up there. All I'm saying."

"I know, Dad. I've heard it before." Bryce stopped digging through his duffel and zipped it back up, not finding anything useful. He looked back up at his father. The older man looked tired. A little greyer, like he'd aged since he last saw him two months ago. "How are things down here?"

"Oh, you know. Same ol'... There was a riot last week. People are worried about the food supply. We didn't get a lot of information about what was going on up where you are, and they think it's a waste of resources. The Witnesses are all preaching about the machines coming for us. The End is Nigh. All that doomsday crap." He cleared his throat, thick eyebrows furrowing. "They're not, are they?"

Bryce shook his head. "I don't think so."

He looked over across the aisle and caught Vicki looking away from him.

"How are the food supplies doing?"

"Down here? Word is, we're going to be short. We lost a lot of chickens to the flu, a lot of eggs on the vaccines. Still finishing up our spring harvest in the domes though, so there's a bunch of new food to process. Market's been running in the park every couple of days, so there's been some fresh fruit for everybody." His father smiled, eyes crinkling above the jowled cheeks.

Bryce closed his eyes and dozed for a spell, the smooth ride lulling him to sleep after the early morning departure. He woke up as they pulled into the station, wiping his eyes, suddenly alert. His father smiled at him again. "We're here. You coming home when you're done?"

"Yeah, might be late."

"I'll save you some dinner."

CITY HALL

Bryce spent most of the tram-ride to City Hall in silence, blending in with the after-work crowd riding the lines homeward. He wasn't sure how this meeting was going to go. He was nervous.

City Hall was one of two buildings in the city that had a "lawn," Nikola Tesla University being the other, just down and across the street. A pair of tall cedar trees bracketed the walkway leading up to the curved building. The facade had raised rectangular surfaces in the concrete, suggesting columns in front of the main dome-like building. The spire in the middle climbed up above, reaching up to the vaulted roof of the cavern overlooking the city. Bryce climbed the black stone steps up to the main entrance, walking through the open doors. A sleepy-looking, middle-aged security guard raised his head from behind his desk on the other side.

Bryce walked across the polished grey stone tiles inside the lobby. A soft bubbling water feature fed the trees in their planters. Walls of smooth grey and yellow concrete curved up and over to the round ceiling, arrays of LED lights shining down through lenses, giving the impression of a bright blue sky. Curved staircases on either side of the space wound up the outside walls to a circular mezzanine above, glassed-in offices looking down over the entrance below. Half were occupied with city officials tending to the day's work of keeping everything running. Bryce walked past the large circular desk in the center with receptionists directing people to their destinations. At the back of the space, he passed the directory, walked under a tall pair of ficus trees and entered a short hallway with four elevators.

It had been nearly two years since Bryce had been here last. The hum of government always made him uncomfortable. Bureaucratic authority that seemed to require pointless precision in the most mundane matters. He remembered coming here to sign the paperwork when they'd made him a junior officer for the station – a surreal experience for him. Riding in the elevator brought it all back. The lifeless ceremony, formal dress and self-conscious feeling that he was out of place the whole time. He adjusted his jacket over his flight suit and ran a hand through his hair, cursing himself that he hadn't gotten it cut.

Top floor. Bryce walked the hallway to the end, past the offices of the City Councillors to the heavy double doors of Henry Grayson's office. They were marked with a gold plaque engraved with *Office of the Chief Councillor,* and *Henry Grayson* underneath. Bryce knocked. A gruff voice from inside called for him to enter.

Light washed over him as he opened the doors onto a lush vista stretching out into the distance. It took him a moment to realize the room was immersed in a holographic projection showing a pastoral setting, green fields lined with trees. Grayson stood hunched forward, silhouetted against the virtual grass, knees slightly bent, holding a long thin-shafted implement with a flat blade on the end. As Bryce's eyes adjusted, he could see Grayson wore a pair of khaki pants and a short sleeved, tight-fitting collared shirt. "Come on in. Make yourself a drink." He indicated the bar on the other side of the office, incongruously outside the projection, with his head.

He drew the club back and then swung down, hitting the ball at his feet with a loud crack. It covered the short distance to the screen in a fraction of a second, hit the fabric with a whack and fell to the floor with a few dozen others, rolling among them. On screen, a virtual ball continued sailing away from them.

"Lights up." The lights in the room came on and Grayson turned to face Bryce, the club still in his hand. "Glad you could make it. I was just getting a few holes in while I waited. Good drop?"

Bryce tried to keep the look of amazement off his face as Grayson returned the club to a rack on the wall next to a dozen others like it. "Is that... golf?"

"Ever played? It's a relaxing game."

Bryce heard chirping sounds from speakers hidden within the room. "No." Nobody had.

"I saw this setup in a movie once and I had to have one for the office. Took the software guys quite a while to get the physics right." Grayson walked to the bar and poured himself a glass of brown liquid, picked up an ice cube with a pair of tongs and dropped it in with a plop. He took a sip. "Our distiller's been working on this bourbon for almost twenty years now. No idea if it tastes right, but it is getting better. This one's a five-year-old. Try some." He plodded over behind his desk and sat down with a grunt. Bryce got himself some water from the jug. He picked up the glass, admiring the way the light played in the cut surfaces along the sides.

Grayson gestured with his drink. "Kid down in the Stacks made those for me. Genius with glass." He took another sip, the ice cube tinkling. "Have a seat." He indicated one of the chairs on the other side of his desk. Bryce took it and sat down, suddenly feeling foolish in his flight suit and pilot's jacket. Grayson watched him with steel grey eyes. He was at least sixty Earth years old but looked tough as hell. His arms were lean and muscled. An intimidating man.

"I think we're in deep shit." Not the words Bryce had intended to speak here this meeting, but that was where he started it.

Grayson took a bigger swig this time. "Alright. Let's hear it."

Bryce took a breath, leaned forward. "Watchtower's been compromised. I'm almost certain. Not only did it fail to send the object as a point of interest, it hid the files. It didn't show up at all until our student found it. When *Happenstance* showed up to run a systems check, they couldn't get near it. It seemed like it was defending itself."

"But how? All our machines are secured. Everything's encrypted, according to our IT people."

"Encrypted with Earth technology." He hesitated for a second. "I... we think all of our comms have been monitored since before this started. It's paranoid and crazy but it's the only thing that makes sense. There's no way the object could've tracked our ships without inside knowledge."

Grayson scratched his neck, stuck his chin out. "It *is* paranoid and crazy. Those ships light up like Christmas out there. They're visible with basic optics."

"It was the other stuff. Flashing in front of our decoy. Broadcasting engine signatures. It was playing with us." Bryce took a gulp of water, wishing he'd tried the bourbon.

"And now we've shut down all external comms because of this theory." Grayson finished his drink and put it down with a thump. "We had a riot down here this weekend the likes of which we haven't seen in twenty years. People are scared shitless. We've been spinning the ships as accidents, but it's starting to leak. They don't believe it. And now we've lost five…"

"Two!"

"Five!" Grayson banged his hand on his desk. "Five ships. Until they're back in dock, they're gone, you hear me? We can't even talk to them because you've shut down our antennas." The Councillor pointed a finger at Bryce then leaned back in his chair and folded his hands on his belly. "Sixteen spacers' lives. Fucking hell. You don't get to sugar coat that, Nolan."

Mancuso made seventeen. Bryce stayed quiet, hoping the storm would pass. He finished his water.

"You really think our comms are compromised?"

"After Watchtower, it seems likely. Not sure if it's widespread or not, but I'm worried and want to minimize the vectors. What if it's a virus?" Bryce winced as he said it. The words sounded ridiculous to him.

Grayson leaned forward and started typing on his desk. "We're going to have to run this by the rest of the Council. I expect we'll want to send a team out to Watchtower for a full rebuild. Probably have to junk all our comms gear and start from scratch. We'll need to get engineering and IT on board. They're going to want to reinvent the whole thing. What a fucking mess." He hit enter and looked up, pointing at Bryce again. "God help you if you're wrong, Commander."

Bryce groaned inwardly. "There's… one other thing."

Grayson reached for his glass and drained it, sat back in his chair. "What else could there possibly be?" He stood up and walked to the decanter, poured another for himself. He brought the decanter back with him to the desk and set it in front of Bryce.

Bryce drained his own glass of water and replaced it with some of the brown liquor.

"It's *Hope*, sir. Our long-range science ship. She's on her way back from the deep." He took a swig, savouring the sweetness and the burn. "She's hauling *ARK II*. We found her out past Neptune over eight years ago."

Grayson stared at Bryce for a moment, for the first time a look of incredulity on his face. "They found it?"

008

DOME 3

Tamra left the "farmhouse," the metal and concrete structure in the middle of the dome that served as a staging and recreation area for the people working the fields and beds. She walked past the slapdash outbuildings housing tools and equipment, along the stone path to the dimly-lit surrounding field. LED towers cast yellow-white light down onto the walkways between the flat rows of waiting earth surrounded by a small forest of trees, towards the edges of the glass and steel dome.

She'd been up here most days in the past couple of weeks. The spring harvest was nothing like the Earth season it was named for. With the approach of summer, the seasonal dust storms brought a darkening of the sky that cut off a lot of their growing light, the mirrors above reflecting a diffused grey luminance down to the surface. The exterior solar panels didn't draw enough power for the banks of LEDs they used as supplements. The air circulation systems were running in "winter" mode for the trees, moving the air quickly with artificial wind. Professor Chandler said that helped the bigger trees grow stronger, kept them from breaking.

Zipping up the front of her pressure suit against the chill, she walked through the tall stand of evergreens and hardwood, the sparse canopy overhead letting even less light inside. Dome 3 was an attempt at a recreation of a temperate Earth climate, though there were exceptions everywhere. A small citrus grove and coffee beans, sweet potatoes and rice were in the hot section to the west. This small patch of forest was considered the ideal for this Dome. The deciduous trees had all gone to sleep when the storms came. Some changed color and had dropped most of their leaves onto the soft earth below. Tamra crunched through the leaves as a gust of wind whipped the maple and birch leaves around her. A speck of green caught her eye and she carefully stepped through the earth to see the delicate curve of a frond poking up through the humus. She smiled and reached down to brush it with her fingers and saw others poking up nearby. The small early ferns were a delicacy if cooked properly. Mosses and lichens lined the trees. One old pine looked like it was ready to be cut down to become a mushroom incubator. She lifted a fallen log and beetles scurried away, earthworms burrowing into the soft earth. The decayed wood would be converted into feed for chickens through enzymatic processes and combined with grains, grasses and vegetables. Nothing was wasted here.

Tamra adjusted the hood on her suit against her neck, her braid tucked inside over her shoulder. She hugged herself in an attempt to warm up, wishing she'd brought a jacket. Last week, she had discovered that she could close up the hood with her hair like this and keep it in while she worked. She liked her hair long, but it got in the way up here. Still, it was how her mother wore hers and Tamra thought she looked like her in the old pictures she had on her tablet.

She looked up at the sky, shielding her eyes against the still-bright reflections from the mirrors. High above, three hundred meters up, a line of bright sky shone through where one of the scrubber robots had cleaned a track. Another was arcing up towards it from the other direction. There was a crew out there somewhere, deploying the little robots that would clear off their collectors and glass. She couldn't imagine why someone would choose to do that over working inside this magical environment.

She turned and walked back towards the small group of students gathering at the edge of the field around Hector Rashid, the dome's groundskeeper. Hector waved to her as she approached. "Hey, Tamra. Ready to get to work?"

"Oh yeah," she smiled. Hector was a nice man. He seemed to always have a smile on his face, and she found his positivity almost surprising in light of the long hours he put in every day. It was a common joke among the students, wondering if he just lived up here. Old Man Rashid living up in his shed with his beans.

"Good. We're going to be doing some planting today. Going to start on this batch of soy beans for our first crop. When this is done, in about a month we can plant some corn." He held up a bag and handed it to her. She noticed the rest of the team were already carrying theirs. "You'll want to plant the seeds about this far down" – he held up his index finger and pointed between the first and second knuckles – "and about this far apart." He held his two index fingers up, a gap between them of about fifteen centimeters. "Each person should plant their own row, just less than a meter between them. Any questions?"

Joe Price stuck his hand up. "Don't you have machines for this?"

"You're my machines. You're cheap and don't break down."

Joe groaned and rolled his eyes. Rory punched him in the arm. "Don't be an ass." He turned to Hector. "How come we always start with soy beans?"

"That's a better question. Bacteria in the soy plants' roots stick nitrogen to the earth. Makes it better for growing afterwards. So we rotate soy, corn, soy, and some other grain like wheat or barley. Sometimes alfalfa or grass for chickens." He smiled and boosted his hat up on his head. "Anything else? I'll come back and check up on you in an hour. Have fun!" Hector walked off leaving the students holding their bags of seeds.

Joe said, a little loudly, "I'm just gonna stick this bag in the ground and then go for a bound. See if I can catch Helen tanning again."

Rory crouched down in the dirt, sticking his hands in it. "You'll get a failing grade if you ruin those beans and you'll never see the sun again."

Tamra moved towards her patch of soil, fresh recently-converted compost, smelling rich and loamy under the heat lamps shining down on it. She'd spent the last couple of days spreading these plots out, dumping compost out of wheelbarrows and sprinkling worms into them from buckets. She got to the nearest corner and got ready to start her row as Nils Lam walked up behind her. "Sorry to hear about Jane. How's she doing?" He crouched, took a step away and crouched again, dug into his bag and started pushing seeds into the earth.

Tamra dug out a seed and stuck it into the ground, soft dirt coming away. A big earthworm rolled away and back into the ground nearby. "She's... pretty messed up. Hard to say." She planted another seed. Her friend had gotten badly hurt during the riots last week, trampled in the rush to get away from the gas and stun sticks. She couldn't talk yet, but Tamra suspected something had happened. Someone did something to cause it.

It made her mad. The Mars Firsters were fighting for the right to choose how everyone lived. They wanted to start building another colony of people who could live off the land, a surface colony under a dome. But some of the more militant members scared her. She worried about what they were willing to do to their home in order to create a new one. They were dangerous and Jane had gotten wrapped up with them and their protest.

Nils was quiet, planting as Rory and Joe started arguing about how far apart they should be. Tamra thought about visiting her friend in the hospital. She shuddered at the memory of her broken arms lifted above her, pins protruding from the casts where they'd put her back together.

Nils broke their silence and snapped her out of her dark thoughts. "Well, I'm sorry anyway. That sucks."

"Yeah. Thanks."

Some chickens started flailing around, fighting over a worm they found in the dirt in the plot next to theirs and one of them flapped away with its prize. For a flightless bird, they flew pretty well up here. Nils grinned. "Someone's going to have to go get her."

"Ah, let her enjoy her freedom for a while."

009

ROVER 2

Erika Rin unloaded the last of the Scrubbers and placed it onto the entrance track leading up the surface of the big glass and steel agridome curving away above. The little machine rolled forward on its soft, grippy wheels, carrying its brush aloft like a confused jouster, its blower fan a shield. Eleven others were already getting to work high above on the slippery, dust-covered glass, running through the tracked, tessellated framework built into the super-structure.

"That's the last of them," Erika reported, closing the doors on the RV's now empty trailer with a light bang. She stood there watching the little machine drag itself up the track, scrubber dropping onto the glass, dust blowing away behind it. She looked up at the sun, grey and faint in the dusty air, covering the top of her faceplate with a gloved hand. "We're going to have to come back in here in a few days and do this all over again. There's still a shit ton of dust blowing around," she said to no one in particular.

"Alright, you two. Get inside and we'll swing by Dome 2 on our way back." A sudden gust blew against the two maintenance workers and blasted sand against the dirty side of the RV with a hiss. "Get moving, ladies. It's gonna be a howler."

Erika, face obscured under her mirrored visor, planted her feet and nodded towards her coworker, Ray Becker. He gave her a thumbs-up and trudged back to the airlock on the big six-wheeled vehicle. "Shotgun," he called over the radio.

"Whatever, Beck. You sit up front with sugar boy. I'm looking forward to some couch time." She nearly tripped over a rock, recovered from her stumble and bounced forward gracelessly, but stayed upright. "Damnit!"

"You OK?"

"Yeah, yeah. Thanks." She shrugged off Ray's attempts to help her and gestured to the steps. "Go ahead."

"Oh, no." Becker held out his gloved hand to the door, covered in dust. "Age before beauty."

"Such a gentleman!" Erika climbed up the two steps, opened the door at the rear of the big vehicle and entered. She began the cycle and a jet of hard air blasted her suit from above and from the sides, filling the tiny entrance with dust. Another set of fans under the floor grids sucked the dust back out through vents, air reserves adding positive pressure to the tiny airlock. The cycle repeated as she raised her arms, then turned around and patted herself down to try to get as much of the damaging silicates and dirt off her suit as she could. The sand on Mars was filled with tiny knife-like blades of glass that wreaked havoc with the delicate seals of their pressurized environments. The airlock filled with breathable air and the light turned green. She entered the RV and popped her helmet seals, lifting it over her head.

"What're you doing tonight?" Aden Reed asked from up front, sitting in the driver's seat, feet up on the dash. He reached into the side pocket beside his seat and pulled out a coiled length of black rubber tubing. He pulled out a knife from his pocket and cut off a stubby chunk from the tube before stowing the rest back beside his seat. He leaned back and looked around behind him at Erika, sticking the piece of black rubber between his teeth.

"Oh, I thought I'd put on something nice and go out on the town." Erika stowed her helmet in its case, started undoing the seals on her gloves.

"Uh huh. Yeah, I'll be down for that after the game." Reed ignored her and continued his conversation over his headset, oblivious to Erika's attempt to distract him.

"Then maybe I'll bring a man home. Maybe a woman. Or both!" She undid her boots as the airlock turned green again and Ray entered the increasingly-cramped RV's locker area.

"Didn't think that thing was going to let me in here. Wasn't sure we had enough air left in the tanks." Ray took off his helmet as Erika undid her suit's waist seals. The rover's compressors kicked in with a hum as they replenished their stored air supply.

"I tried to lock you out but Reed changed the codes."

Ray grunted and started pulling his gloves off.

Erika backed into the locker harness and raised the torso piece over her head into its storage position on the ceiling, then pushed the legs down, wriggling out of them. When she came up, Ray blushed, averting his gaze with an exaggerated movement of his head.

"Like you've never seen me in my underwear," she said.

"Oh, everybody's seen you in your underwear." Grinning, he flung his gloves into their bag and started popping more seals.

Reed yelled back from the front, "You sandworms all settled in? I'm gonna start rolling in one minute." Erika and Ray exchanged a look of exasperation at their driver taking interest in his vehicle all of a sudden.

"Yeah, Dad!" Erika stooped and stepped through the divider into the crew section and climbed onto the couch, pulling a thick poly blanket over her legs. She flipped the windows open so she could look outside at the dark tan terrain around them. "Make some coffee, Beck?"

Ray ducked his head and stepped into the crew area wearing a stained and grubby one-piece suit liner. He opened a drawer and tossed Erika her water bottle. "Here ya go, princess. Just add crystals." He pulled his orange overalls off the hook beside the lavatory and climbed into them.

Reed signalled for them to be quiet with a jab of his hand. "Go ahead, control." Pause, as he listened. "Roger. We'll go check it out."

The RV started rolling and Ray lurched through the cabin into the cockpit, dropping into the passenger seat. Six big, flexible carbon-steel mesh wheels slipped in the dust and sand of the Tharsis plateau. Through the cockpit window, beyond the glittering domes and solar collectors, they could see the long gentle slope of Ascraeus Mons rising above them, the caldera obscured by haze and distance.

"Still pretty damned dusty out here. We're going to have to do this again in a week." Ray took a swig out of his own water bottle.

"That's the job, son." Reed steered them around a big boulder and pushed forward on the throttle, electric engine whining as the tires dug in, the rover picking up speed. "We have to go back to Dome 4. One of the scrubs is stuck in its track."

"Not it!" Erika called from her seat on the couch, settling in with her tablet.

"Goddamnit." Ray never remembered the rules of the game.

010

MACHINE PARTS

Sean sat on the floor of the control shed, leaning against the back wall by the door, his bag on the floor beside him and his damaged tablet on his lap. The screen was cracked and separated from its housing, ribbon wire snaking away, half off the connector. He grimaced and stuffed the broken tablet back into his bag, banging his head back against the corrugated steel wall behind him.

"Don't hurt yourself." Mike Allen didn't turn around, keeping his focus on the screens in front of him. There were screens and a keyboard on his console, banks of override switches along either side on the long desk, flashing lights illuminating him irregularly on all sides. "You going to be around this weekend? I could use an extra pair of hands to help out with the refit. Could learn some new machines."

"Sure, boss."

"That's what I like to hear." A buzzer went off beside him and Mike exhaled through his teeth. Sean stood up and looked at the board, watching instructions rolling past on the screens in front of his foreman. Mike leaned forward and spoke into the microphone on his desk. "Perkins, you see any problems around our favorite bender?"

A pause. Mike looked around at Sean, his eyes glued to the screens and their constant spew of code. He could almost read it, but it was too fast. For every line on the screen, one of the machines out there beyond the reinforced tempered glass was performing a job. Even in the control hut, the din was loud and constant from the machines outside. Their purpose was to build the raw parts for other machines: gears, pipes, specifically-shaped pieces of metal that were either too commonplace to tie up the printers or had particular material requirements they couldn't replicate. The denser core of the parts factory produced nuts, bolts and fasteners from the discards. Most of these machines were old, among the oldest in the fab, part of the original boot-strapping machinery the colony needed to get started. Machines that built other machines.

The radio crackled and a burst of noise came back over the speaker. "Yeah, it's MP510. Blew its hose off again. You want me to fix?"

The noise died. Mike turned around and looked at Sean, then back at the mic on his desk. "Naw, we'll let Boots do it. He's gotta learn all this stuff. Just keep an eye on him, would you?"

"Alright, boss."

Mike turned back. "This is about as simple a fix as there is. Nothing to it. Just put the hose back on the pipe and cinch it down. You ready to get back out there?"

"OK. Boss." The word sounded funny in his head, but they all called their foreman that. There was a funny dynamic between the unionized workers and their foreman that Sean hadn't figured out yet. He'd only been there two weeks and still wasn't part of the crew, but was eager to learn how to become permanent.

Sean stuffed his earphones into his ears and grabbed his helmet off the hook on the wall before opening the door onto the hot, loud volume beyond. The space was huge, but it was impossible to see past the first stack of machines that ran the full height from floor to ceiling, twenty meters tall and fifty on each side. Each level had a steel gantry for workers to walk along and access the equipment housed there. The entire block was filled, yellow flashing lights and whirring robotic arms moving between the cacophonous engines so fast you could barely see them.

Sean walked up the steps to level three, passing Perkins on the gantry beside him. Perkins leaned over, sweat sheen and grease masking the tattoos on his face and neck, and yelled in Sean's ear, "You know where to go? You're up there on level four. Three ranks back. Right?" Hot breath on his cheek.

"Got it," Sean shouted and nodded back. Perkins seemed satisfied and unblocked his path.

Sean walked down the gangway and up the mesh steel stairs, trying not to look through them down below. Coolant lines and hoses carrying fluids for the various machines ran up the wall beside him, some of it dripping water from condensation formed along the outside. Massive fans in the ceiling above carried heat away from the factory and distributed it back out where it was needed.

Level four. He moved along the outer wall, past three layers of machines, and worked his way in. The ramp here was narrow. The big metal stampers and benders needed a lot of room. Above him, the arms were whirring past, carrying pieces to and from their destinations along some program only they knew.

"There. That's the one." The voice of his foreman in his ears. Sean could see which one needed help, red lights and gushing air blowing out like smoke. He crawled between the bulky equipment, the noise deafening through his earphones. A loose air hose flailed ahead, blowing gas into his face, making him flinch, arm raised.

"Careful, Boots. Keep your hands away from that lathe," Mike warned him over his headset.

Degloved. A word he hadn't known before coming to work here only two weeks earlier. The big equipment that produced parts for other machines had some fast-moving hardware that could separate a man from his skin in the blink of an eye. He pulled his arms back in close, the wind from MP230 buffeting him with hot air.

His small size made him the new favorite for the shop foreman to crawl into the tight spaces between the machines. It was exciting work, but dangerous.

He'd only been here for two weeks but had learned a lot in that short time. He was quick that way. He learned how metal moved from Material Supply into Sizing, then into Shaping and Final Treatment, transferred between each phase by whirling robotic arms. Leavings from each stage were collected and shunted back to Supply for reuse. When everything was working properly, it was very efficient. They lost very little.

He still didn't understand what the parts they made were being used for. The orders came in over their computer network from other sections. The orders would be completed by the machinery and the new parts sent down the line to whatever source requested it. Somewhere in the one-kilometer cube of The Fab, a borer vehicle, a new rail car, some piece of finished equipment would roll off the line and report for duty. Order fulfilled.

Sometimes the machinery broke down, thanks to wear and tear from the constant use. Then the machinists would have to take it offline and diagnose the problem. Sometimes that meant replacing a part. All of the machines had copies of themselves throughout the tower, in case they needed to replace a piece of themselves that only they could make. None of the parts were really made by hand in here. Order a part, put a rush on it, and that part showed up some fifteen to twenty minutes later. He looked forward to the next time that happened so he could try to see the new part getting made from scratch. Maybe during the refit this weekend, he'd figure that out.

He wasn't sure any one person really understood the whole process anymore. The Fab had been started seventy revs earlier, during the bootstrap phase of the colony. Five generations of Martians. It began with mining robots sent from Earth. The initial teams of colonists had set up the smelters and the first of the domes. Then the Ark ship arrived and the Primer began building the machines that would become the Fab from the surrounding materials. The resulting hole became the city, New Providence.

Why didn't they use mining robots anymore?

Sean, feet apart, crept forward with his hands in front of him, reaching towards the flailing air hose. *Wait... Keep your eyes on it, watch it move...* He caught the air hose whipping in front of him with his left hand, recoiling as the end nearly lashed his face. "Got it." He held it away from his face but it continued spraying gas at him. He grabbed the nozzle with his right hand to minimize its motion.

"Good. Get it plugged in," Mike's disembodied voice advised him.

Red lights flashed on MP510. Hydraulic Pipe Bender. Its whole job was to bend pipes into different shapes. Above him, a multi-segmented arm held a steel pipe in its grip. Cameras like eyes flashed as it waited for the machine to open. Yellow lights flashed above it through the smoke and haze of the parts block as more machines finished their jobs, waiting for the pipeline to open up.

Sean dragged the air hose towards the bender, warning klaxons blaring at him. He plugged the air hose onto the regulator and screwed it in, the worn brass fittings turning easily in his gloved hands. He slapped the Restart button and the sirens stopped screeching, and the red light turned green. He backed away in a hurry as the doors opened on MP510 and the arm stabbed the pipe into its jaws, releasing it before flying away. The doors slammed shut around its payload as the robotic arm whirled up above him to its next available piece.

"Alright, get out of there, Boots."

Sean didn't need to be told. He was already crouch-walking back to the relative safety of the platform alongside the leavings conveyor that rattled with bits of metal. He was weaving between the computer-controlled machines going about their daily routine, ignoring the pain in his back around his fused vertebrae. Eight hour shifts. Three per day. He was approaching the end of this shift. Mike would record the fault on MP510 in the log for the next shift. Only three faults today. No accidents.

It was a good day.

011

FRANKLIN RESIDENCE

Tamra stopped by her old apartment on the sixth floor first, brushing her card over the lock and sliding the door open. The lights came on and she stepped inside, sniffing the air as she walked across the carpet to her room. She gathered up a couple of things from her closet, some clothes she hadn't worn in a while that she suddenly missed, then grabbed a hairbrush from her dresser. She picked up a picture of her and her mother from nearly four revs ago, when she was just a kid on a field trip up to the dome and put it into the bag she was assembling.

Next stop, the kitchen. She opened the refrigerator and grabbed everything she could that was still good or even questionable and tossed the contents into a shopping bag they kept in the cupboard.

She lingered for a moment, looking around the apartment she'd grown up in, now empty. Her brother and father floated through space somewhere, she hoped. Another picture on the shelf in the wall of her father, Jerem and herself at Jerem's flight school graduation found its way into her bag.

She left the apartment, locking the door behind her.

Tamra ran down the stairs to Julie Franklin's apartment and let herself in. The apartment had the same layout as the one she'd just left but with different things on the walls. A picture of Emma and her father smiled out at her from the shelf.

"Hey, Mrs. Franklin," she called. "I brought some stuff from home. Some food. Where do you want me to put it?"

"Just leave it," she answered over sounds of cleaning in the kitchen.

"I'll pick it up and put it away while you get cleaned up."

She went to Emma's room and stripped out of her clothes, tossing them on the floor and pulling on the robe she took from the hook behind her door. She padded into the washroom, pulling her hair out of its braid. After a day in the domes wearing the pressure suit, she was ready for a shower.

After drying off and brushing her hair, she put on some old comfortable clothes, grabbed her tablet and plopped down on the couch in the living room. She flipped through the feeds rolling in from MARSnet. More aftermath from last week's riot. Projected food shortfalls for this season. An interview with Zander Bale, the leader of the Mars First movement, was interrupted by a member of the Witnesses of the Automata yelling in the background and getting escorted out by a team of Safety and Security Officers, holding him with stun sticks at the ready.

It made her angry. She believed in what the Firsters were about, in principle. If people were going to thrive on Mars, they needed to focus on expansion. They needed a new government if they were going to get any further. They needed to start building the next colonies on Mars instead of hunkering down here in the tunnels under the old volcano, afraid of the surface.

The Mars First group were big advocates of moving out of the underground and into the domes as a first step. It had been thirty revs since Dome 5 had finished construction and they hadn't had a breach in that whole time. They were stable, given the constant maintenance and inspections by city engineering. Having people up there would make it much easier to get casual labor around the farms. It would be great for everyone to take part in producing their own food. They'd understand better what it took to grow food for a population this size. She believed it might cut down on the anger that seemed to pervade every conversation about food that happened all-too-frequently when talking to people outside the agricultural program.

Another problem she had with the Firsters was their position on the space program. They felt it wasteful, a needless expense, and that attitude had a strong pull for the conservative elders on the Council. The administration was a bunch of old Earther cranks too stuck in their ways to think of doing anything differently.

The Witnesses, on the other hand, or Machine Worshippers, or Machinists, were a bunch of idiots, in her opinion. A splinter group from the Fabricator Unions, they believed in the all-out embrace of technology. They advocated for massive automation. Over the years, they'd become more extreme, calling for people to rise up and let the machines come to wipe them out, claiming humans were already extinct. Of course, most people wrote them off as crazy, and rightly so. Their presence on the feeds was typically by some unkempt representative with illegal implants, frothing at the mouth about human extinction.

She shuddered at the thought.

Tamra flipped open the messages on her tablet and considered writing one to Emma. She missed their lively discussions about how to fix the government, how to change it into something new and more forward-thinking than the stodgy old autocracy they were stuck with. But mostly, she missed her friend and was desperate for news of her brother and father.

The sounds and smells of cooking coming from the kitchen distracted her. She tossed her tablet onto the couch and went to see what was going on. Julie's voice met her at the entrance. "Are you almost ready to eat?"

Tamra peeked into the kitchen, leaning into the small space. Emma's mom was tossing something sizzling in a hot pan. "Hey, what're you cooking? This smells great."

"It came from one of my students – do you know Henry Wong?"

Tamra nodded. Everybody knew the Wong clan. Henry's father, Jimmy, was the colony's leading mycologist. They'd been growing mushrooms for the colony for generations in the hot caves past Tartarus.

"He brought me some oyster mushrooms today. I found some eggplant at the market on the way home from work. Seemed like a good idea to make a stir fry." She looked over from her wok and smiled at Tamra. The sadness around her eyes was still there, but she was doing her best to hide it. Julie cracked a couple of eggs and swished them around in the wok.

Tamra squeezed her arm and smiled. "That looks great."

Julie turned off the heat and lifted the heavy steel wok off the burner. "Careful. This is hot." The smell of rice hit Tamra's nose when Julie opened the pot on the back of the stove. "It's all ready. Go sit down and I'll bring you a plate."

Tamra backed out of the kitchen and went to the table. She gathered some place mats from the cupboard and set them. Julie came out a second later with two steaming plates of food, which she put down on the placemats. She went back to the kitchen, humming to herself, and grabbed the jug of water and some forks, set them on the table.

Julie smiled. "Eat before it gets cold."

Tamra took a forkful of eggplant and rice and blew on it. "I think we have a dozen revs before that happens." She popped the food into her mouth and chewed, the eggplant bursting with heat, then flavor in her mouth. "It's good." She chewed and smiled.

They ate quietly. Tamra had been living here for more than a week now. The mushrooms reminded her of Greg and his squeamish attitude towards them. She hadn't heard from him or Emma since she'd moved here, and she didn't know what was happening anymore. They said there was a communications problem with the station, but she knew it was deliberate. They'd been locked out.

Julie interrupted her thoughts. "I've got a present for you after dinner."

"Really? You didn't have to." Tamra wiped her mouth on her napkin.

"I did." Julie got up and went to the table in the living room, bringing her tablet with her. "I guess I can show it to you now. Keep eating." She poked at the tablet while Tamra soaked up some of the sauce on her plate with a mushroom and some rice. "I'm just happy you've been spending some time here with me. I really appreciate it." Julie smiled.

"What is it?" Tamra watched, chewing her food.

"I've been requesting more time on Olympus' ten-meter array. This is a detail in Hydra, near Twenty-One Hya." She turned the tablet around and showed Tamra a region of space, one bright star dominating the screen.

"What am I looking at?" She put her fork down and leaned forward.

"Here." Julie zoomed in on a region beside the bright star. A fuzzy blob emerged on the screen.

Tamra leaned forward and squinted at it. "What is it?"

Julie smiled a sad little smile, her eyes crinkling. "That's your father and brother."

012

NOLAN RESIDENCE

Bryce walked the streets around Fabtown to his father's apartment, passing cyclists and pedestrians along the way. The tram rattled by a block away overhead along St. Joseph Drive. He could've taken it from City Hall but felt like walking. The air was cool and damp on his face. You never really forgot you were living in a cave down here, despite the attempts at a fake sky on the ceiling. Still, it felt good after the dry sterile air of Lighthouse. The vast caverns of New Providence housing apartments and green spaces under LEDs and light pipes from above felt like outside to him.

He cut across Progress Way, long strides and a steady lope, his boots digging into the hard black rock of the road. The Fab grew up on his right, extruded over a century ago by the big ship *Exodus'* assembler section. People stood along the dark grey walls vaping and hanging around on their breaks, waiting for the next shift, shooting the breeze. He didn't stick around. This corner was a known hot spot for crime. The Metal Clans from the smelters had an ongoing turf war with the Fabricator Unions, and he wasn't interested in anything they were offering.

His head was still buzzing from the bourbon. It had taken them almost three hours to go over the contents of *Hope*'s mission, and he still didn't know much about it. Eight years beyond the belt. It was the furthest any humans had ever ventured. And they'd received almost no communications from them since they'd acquired *Ark II* nearly four years ago.

Package Acquired. Full stop.

Shivering in the damp air, Bryce ducked down Spring Avenue. He walked up the steps to his father's place and swiped his card, unused for over a year. The door buzzed and he opened it and walked in, half amazed that it still worked. Well, why wouldn't it, he wondered. It wasn't like anyone was going to deactivate it. He wasn't dead.

He trudged up the flight of stairs to the second floor and down the hall to his dad's place. He knocked then tried the door, and found it opened.

Inside, the living room was dimly lit with strings of LED lighting draped along the walls. Light jazz played on the speakers. There were sounds from the kitchen of water splashing, of the clinking of plates and cutlery. His father poked his head through the door. "Hey. Just cleaning up a bit." He disappeared again and was replaced with the sound of running water.

"It's after ten, Dad." Bryce took off his boots and flopped onto the couch. He felt something sharp digging into his back and pulled a fork out of the cushions behind him. He placed it on the table next to what appeared to be a mechanical clock, disassembled. He looked at the finely-machined gears locked into the mechanism. The largest visible was about ten centimeters in diameter. The body of the clock, nearly sixty centimeters across.

"Are you building this?"

His father padded out of the kitchen wearing an old cardigan sweater over a thread-bare American Patriots tee-shirt and grubby sweat pants. He sat down in his chair, a crippled old thing patched with duct tape and tilting dangerously back on one damaged foot. "Yeah, that's my latest project."

"Where'd you get the parts for it?"

"Scavenged most of 'em. Had to requisition a few others."

Salvaging parts destined for recycling was technically illegal. "Dad…"

"What? Man's gotta have a hobby. I'm making it for your mother…"

Bryce stared at his father, waiting for him to continue.

"So she can see how much time she's wasting."

"Ah, there it is." Bryce nodded and leaned back on the couch again. "How's work?"

"Oh, same as always. Fills the hours."

"Anything new?"

His father picked up his tablet and started poking at it, breathing noisily. "There's some food left in the kitchen."

Bryce considered it, but decided he wasn't hungry. "I'm OK."

His father looked up from the tablet. "Are you?"

Bryce shrugged. "Sure."

Putting the tablet back into his chair's duct-taped pocket, Robert Nolan leaned forward as best as the chair would let him. "What happened up there? Can you talk about it? We don't get any details – they're not telling us a goddamned thing."

"Not really." Bryce let out a sigh. "We lost two ships. Most of a third," he started, then started again. "Two more intercepted *Making Time*, they have their crew, but the rescue ship had to abandon them. *Terror* and what's left of *Making Time* are headed in-system, taking the long route back."

"Jesus. They have enough supplies for that?"

"Nope." Bryce got up and went over to the old cabinet, his buzz had worn off. "You got any liquor in here?"

Robert got up, plodded into the kitchen again. He came back with a frosted bottle and two glasses. He set them on the cabinet and popped the top off the bottle, pouring them each a drink. He took his back to his chair and sat down, the old frame creaking under him. He took a sip as Bryce took his over to the couch.

"So what caused it?"

Bryce swallowed a big gulp and blew through his mouth, the alcohol burning his throat. "It was robotic, we think." He stood up and went to the kitchen, pulled the water jug out of the mostly empty refrigerator and poured some into his glass, turning the liquid blue-white. His father was still sitting, watching him when he came back.

"Say again?"

"Some kind of robot. Black body. Probably small." Bryce tried another sip of the harsh spirits.

"From Earth?" Bryce's father asked, his voice hoarse.

"Don't know. Maybe? Probably." Bryce looked at his glass in his hands, swirling the milky white liquid around in there. "Look, you can't tell anybody any of this, ok?"

His father nodded.

"Our kids… we have these students on board the station, helping out with the science team. Anyway. They found this thing first in some images that came off Olympus." He took a sip.

"The telescope, you mean."

"Yeah." Bryce's stomach growled and he realized he was suddenly very hungry. "Anyway, they did some more digging. They found our timelapse footage of Earth. Also from Olympus."

"And they found something, didn't they?"

Bryce nodded. "Yeah. We think maybe they did. It isn't much, just a single hot pixel, but it lit up the cloud layer." He ran a hand over his head through his short hair. "Looks like Earth launched something a few weeks back."

Robert Nolan slumped back in his chair and whistled. "And you think this is the thing that's been chasing your ships."

"It's the best explanation."

"I see."

Bryce's stomach growled again and his dad stood up.

"I guess I should make you some food before your belly crawls out your mouth."

Bryce made to get up, but his father waved a hand at him to stay seated.

"Don't worry about it. I've got some tofu and rice in here. Can of beans somewhere. You want rice'n'beans?"

"You need any help?" Bryce was feeling sleepy, but the idea of food sounded too good.

"Nah. I got it. You make yourself comfortable."

The music changed, switching to some old electric blues. Sounds of cooking prep preceded the smell of garlic and onions. Bryce leaned back and poked at his tablet. Kaylee Baker was on MARSnet reading the news.

Before long, Bryce was asleep.

013

CITY HALL

"Bryce!" Daniel Perkins extended an age-freckled hand towards him. "I'm not used to seeing you on this side of the screen." Bryce shook his hand and smiled briefly at the Chief of Mining Operations for New Providence.

"Good to see you too, Daniel."

Fred Darabont from City Planning looked up from his position at the snack table, a plate balanced precariously in one hand, heaped with fruit and pastries, a glass of juice in the other. "Shouldn't you be running our space station, young man?"

Bryce ignored him, stifling a sigh. He spotted an actual friendly face and walked over to Dr. Tadeuz Powell, smiling broadly. "Tad!"

"Hello, Bryce." The old astronomer returned the smile, his moustache scrunching into his nose, eyes wrinkling under his bushy brows. He stopped Bryce from a hug. "Don't get too close. I think I'm still getting over this damned flu."

"It got you too?"

"All the damned kids sneezing in my office. Filthy animals."

Heads turned towards a tinkling sound to see Chairman Henry Grayson tapping a glass with his pen. "Shall we get to business, everyone? Take your seats, please." He moved to the head of the table, placing his glass there. Fred Darabont carried his haul over to his seat beside him. The rest of the room organized themselves and took their seats. Bryce sat down in the empty spot set aside for him as two aides left the chamber, amidst the sounds of throats clearing and coughing.

"Commence Recording. Ladies and gentlemen of the Council, we call to order this…" Henry checked his notes. "4795th meeting on Day 172 of Mars Revolution Six Nine, Post Earth. This is an emergency session outside regular schedule. For the record, please state your names and office, starting with," Henry indicated Fred Darabont on his right.

"Fred Darabont, City Planning," he began, then picked up a warm bun from his tray and stuffed it in his mouth.

"Daniel Perkins, Mining."

"Muriel Turner, Agriculture…"

Bryce stood fractionally and announced himself. "Bryce Nolan, Commander of Lighthouse Station." Then Doctor Powell, then Kanan Soma, information architecture, then Natalie Park-Sheehan, Keith Turnbull, and penultimately, Maude Richardson, areology.

"Henry Grayson, Chief Councillor of New Providence." Henry thumbed his tablet and leaned back, adjusting his view. There was some shuffling in the room while everyone waited for him to proceed. "We'll skip the reading of minutes and reports and move straight to our emergency business. Mr. Nolan, if you would enlighten us as to why we are here today."

Bryce stood at the end of the table. The room was dark, save for three saucer-like lights above the table, casting a white glow on the faces around the oblong slab. "Ladies and gentlemen of the Council, we're here today to discuss a matter of grave danger to our colony. Maybe to our continued existence on Mars." He paused for effect, worrying he was laying it on too thick. No, he reminded himself, this was about as serious as it could be. "As you know, last week, our ships came under attack from what appeared to be a robotic entity of unknown origin, but presumed to be from Earth. We have had no contact with the object since it encountered *Making Time* some six days ago."

Fred Darabont muttered something unintelligible from his seat beside Henry, who grunted in response.

Ignoring them, Doctor Richardson spoke up. "But you are looking for it, right? Your people, I mean?" The chief areologist was watching Bryce over her glasses, perched low on her nose. Bryce could feel the unasked questions bubbling up from the assembled Council members and hurried to answer.

"Yes, and that brings me to the point of this meeting." He paused briefly, gathering his thoughts. He didn't want to get deflected from the real reason he was here. "We believe our sensors and communications systems may have been compromised by this entity. I've come here to ask you all for help in coming up with a plan to fix this and develop a course of action to deal with this threat. I believe we are in great danger."

The muttering around the table grew louder and Henry banged on the table for order. "Let's keep it organized, people. Questions."

Doctor Kanan Soma took the lead. "Could you explain what you mean by 'compromised'? These systems are all encrypted."

Bryce nodded. "I don't have specifics, that's what I need experts such as yourself to explain. Members of my science team brought me this theory that our systems have possibly been tampered with." He didn't mention that it was the junior members on loan from the university that had brought this to his attention. Before the everyone in the room started arguing, he spoke up. "I've seen evidence of it myself. Things I can't explain away as bugs or human error. Watchtower was initially responsible for missing the object when it should have brought it to our attention. We sent up a crew to replace the hardware on board and they couldn't get near it. It prevented them from gaining access."

More muttering around the table.

"Watchtower is responsible for relaying all of our communication from Mars out to our ships." Dr. Powell frowned.

Bryce sighed. The memory and stress of the last weeks of tracking this thing never far from the surface. "That's right, Watchtower acts like a network repeater. The object seemed to know everything that was happening the whole time. Its predictions were perfect. Watchtower seemed to be the most likely culprit. We haven't seen any indication of tampering on board Lighthouse." The table had quieted. He had their attention.

"Couldn't we just shutdown Watchtower? Reboot it?" Natalie asked.

"We tried. The crew of *Happenstance* were unable to gain physical access to the platform. We did manage to do a remote reset eventually, but there's no guarantee we got whatever was infecting it." Bryce looked from her to the other faces around the table watching him and he straightened up. "I think it's worse than just that. If this thing infected Watchtower, we have to consider that all of our systems have been compromised. Lighthouse. Maybe the whole colony."

"Ludicrous!" Keith Turnbull from Resource Control blurted.

Natalie looked up from her tablet and said, "What exactly are we dealing with here? What is this 'object'? Why did it attack our ships?"

"We don't know much about it, unfortunately. We're assuming it's some kind of machine intelligence from Earth. Maybe a probe of some sort."

"Have we heard anything at all from Earth?" Turnbull had regained his composure somewhat and turned his bulbous head to the others around the table. "I think we should take a good look. Point all our antennas that way. Maybe they've been trying to reach us."

"It's…" Bryce faltered for a moment and more voices rose up around him. He was losing their attention. Grayson banged his hand on the table again and shouted them back down. Natalie recoiled at the sudden violence but composed herself quickly. The other faces around the table looked at one another in surprise.

Doctor Powell answered for him. "We've been monitoring Earth for the past sixty revolutions and have seen no indication that there's anyone alive back there. Our radio antennas haven't heard so much as a beep."

Bryce smiled at the old astronomer, grateful for some backup. "That's right. Going through some of our time-lapse footage, we found just one frame – one frame in three hundred thousand – that could be our probe. Is it concrete evidence? I wouldn't say that. It's just a blurry pixel in the cloud top, but it's the best evidence we've got of a launch."

"Right." Henry interrupted the proceedings before they could devolve into more questions. "Back to the problem of our computer networks. What did you want us to do?"

Bryce shrugged. "I think we should swap out all of our comms systems and do a full reboot. I mean everything."

Keith shook his head violently. "We can't."

"It's impossible! We have too many critical systems…" Fred Darabont was trying to interject.

Soma had been thinking about the possibility. "That is not an easy problem. You're describing a type of computer virus. If it is such a thing, it might reside in the computers and tablets around the colony." He held his hands out. "Do we replace all of those too? What little we know about the Event on Earth suggests it was a massive take-over of consumer electronics. We don't even know what we have here. Some of these systems have been in operation for forty years or more. We don't know what would happen if we shut everything down at once. What do we do with the systems running the colony's environmentals, for example? What if they don't start up again?"

The table erupted in excited arguments and Henry had to use his gavel. "Order!" He banged again, nearly knocking his water glass over and raised his voice. "Look, this is all theory and conjecture. We can't go ripping out all the computers and systems in the colony without analyzing the problem first. Unplugging the wrong thing might shut down our lights or our air filtration."

"Or the air pressure locks," Soma reminded him.

The councillors steadied themselves. Natalie raised her hand. "Motion to create a team to investigate and analyze the possibility of communications tampering. Second?"

Soma raised his hand. "Seconded. Volunteer to lead the task force."

Henry looked around the room. "Motion carries." He gavelled once and looked down the table at Nolan, slumped in his chair.

Bryce shook his head. "That's going to take too long," he said to no one in particular. Powell raised an eyebrow. Soma was already deep in thought, a look of concern on his face.

"What about contact?" Fred Darabont at the other end of the table asked, opening his hands on the table, palms up. "Has anyone tried contacting Earth? Sending a contact ping?"

Bryce was about to answer when Doctor Powell spoke up. "That might not be wise."

Darabont persisted. "But what if there's someone there?"

Powell frowned. "We've been broadcasting the whole time, just not directly at Earth. It's all the same old tech they had on Earth pre-Collapse. If there's anyone there, they know how to get in touch with us."

Natalie and Henry exchanged a look before he said, "Alright, I think it's worth testing some of these theories. Can we shut down the orbital network while we investigate how to get everything rebooted in the city?"

Soma nodded. "Commander Nolan will have to manage that from the station. They have control of our space network. As for our remote stations on Olympus, Arsia and Fesenkov, we can shut those down from here."

Powell jumped up in his seat. "We can't shut down Olympus. That's the best monitoring station we have!"

Henry made the calm down gesture, hands hovering above the table. "It should only be for a few days, Tad. Just until we can assess any problems with the network."

"A few days is a pretty big window. Are you comfortable missing another hostile? Or a bolide?"

"No, but we still have Lighthouse and Watchtower for that, ostensibly."

"Watchtower missed the first one," Powell grumbled.

Henry ignored him. "Alright. Anything else?" Collective shaking of heads, some eyes turning to Bryce to see if he was going to lay anything else on them today. He wasn't. "Good. You all have work to do. Kanan, I need you to coordinate with the other department heads to begin scheduled network shutdowns. Figure out what we need to do this quickly, but smoothly. You have three days."

Doctor Soma's eyes bugged at him. "Chairman, I don't even know where most of this equipment is. The machines running the Fab... the environmentals are scattered all over the city. The reclamation systems are all underneath. It's going to take weeks."

"Three days for your initial report. Thank you all. Adjourned." Grayson banged his gavel and stood up. Natalie stood with him and they left the room together, the rest of the council devolving into jabbered conversation as Nolan slumped into his seat.

014

THE STACKS

Sean walked down the grey and white concrete hallway in silence. He was propelled along in a stream of other workers leaving the facility as their shifts ended. He reached the heavy outer doors and spilled out onto Industrial Avenue, the cooling evening air of New Providence a welcome change to the hot temperatures of Machine Parts and the press of people in the hallway. The other people dispersed in both directions, some heading down Main Street for an after work drink. The next group of workers were lined up along the southern wall of the concrete block, ready to start their shifts.

Sean didn't really know anyone in his team other than his foreman. Perkins and Steel he'd exchanged maybe a dozen words with since he started working here, and those were given reluctantly. The workers seemed to not get too close to newcomers and that suited Sean fine. He tried to keep to himself and stay out of everyone's way.

Riders on bicycles rolled past in the street, occasionally ringing a bell to let someone know they were about to get run into. He made his way to the corner and turned left onto Mechanic Street, the neon lights of the stalls shining through the buildings. The vendors were setting up for the dinner rush of the after work crowds, merchants pulling up their shops and converting to makeshift noodle stands and dumpling shacks. Ropes of unmatched LED lights lit the little spaces in yellow and blue pools of light. Sean hopped over a shining puddle from one of the vendors' stalls, remnants of ice still on the ground melting into the city drains.

The smell from Wong's noodle stand made Sean's mouth water and his stomach tense up. He stopped at the counter and looked at the bubbling pot of broth behind. The array of addons sat in two rows of metal containers beside the stacks of bowls. Jimmy Wong came through the curtain carrying a plate of sliced mushrooms and saw Sean leaning over the counter.

"Hey, Sean. You want a mushroom soup?" Mister Wong put a bowl down and waved to him.

Sean considered it for a moment. "Can't now, but tell Henry I'll be by later."

"OK, but I think Henry's got class. Come by anyway."

Sean smiled. "OK!" He patted the counter and continued maneuvering through the after-work crowd on his way through the stalls. Sparks flew past his face, and he bobbed in the other direction. One of the vendors was shaking his hand after getting jolted from the bad connection on the homegrown chemical battery he was using to power his stall. The man cursed and sucked on his burned finger.

The festive lights soon gave way to darker stalls and grim alleys. The tram overhead marked the end of the city proper and the beginning of the slums. Lean-tos and shacks were built around the concrete uprights of the rail line used to transfer raw material from the smelters to Fabtown. Shadows moved in the smoke from figures hunched over their camp fires, smouldering from whatever consumables they could burn. Sean hurried through, for once trying to conceal the stomping from his over-sized boots. He stuck to the shadows as he crossed through the Underpass.

Nearly home. Built into the walls of the huge cavern were the converted storage containers of the Stacks. Earth-standard shipping containers had been among the first things built by the Fab for moving materials and machinery. They had accumulated and were discarded over the decades after the colony was formed, and the ones deemed unfit for use got dumped here, outside the city, ostensibly to be recycled. Now, a century later, it was a city unto itself.

Cables strung overhead carried illegal power or network connections from the city proper. Some of the cables ran along the ground and became obstacles to avoid, sometimes getting frayed or cut and causing yelling from the inhabitants as their services vanished, usually in a flash of sparks. Twisted piping and plastic tubes carried water and waste up and down the layers of stacked metal boxes, many of them leaking onto the walls of the containers below.

There was some order imposed on the chaos. Most of the containers were stacked eight high into wandering rows. Some of the more wealthy or industrious families had built their containers into the side of the cavern wall. Some well-off families managed to hold onto two containers instead of just one, usually having either paid or fought for the extra space.

Living in the Stacks wasn't necessarily condoned by the city, but they had no better place to put these people. They fell outside the normal accommodations granted to working citizens. Worse, because they didn't benefit from most of the city's services, many of the residents didn't feel it was worth registering or participating in the industries of New Providence. Over the generations, this led to a group of disconnected people living outside the system. The city did its best to survey with census taking and inventory, but their records were incomplete. They were still citizens and everybody made the best of a bad situation.

He avoided the people outside, watching before he entered the lots. Kitten was plying her trade in front of his stack and he carefully skirted around her and her prospective client. She was selling to someone setup on a stoop, either in a stupor or injecting himself into one. "You want meow-meow?" she offered, bored, but he paid no attention as she fondled her crotch.

Sean hurried through the tangled mess of wires and garbage, avoiding a shambling figure wearing several coats and a thick mane of hair and stomped up the metal steps to his home, dreading what might be waiting for him inside. "Hi, Mrs. Simone." He waved to the lady leaning on the window as he passed by, dim light from inside illuminating her wrinkled face. She waved and smiled at him briefly.

He opened his door, entering the cluttered kitchen area. Tina was sitting at the counter, a stack of dishes piled beside her. "What do you want?" she sneered at him as he walked past into the living room. Little Bun was playing with some spoons on the floor. Jeb spoke from the floor in the corner. "Where you been?"

"Work."

Bun flung a spoon into the pile with a loud ding. Ava, their foster mother, grumbled for quiet from her den, a two-by-two box separated from the space by stacked boxes and curtains. The glow from her monitor shone through the seams. She didn't like anyone interrupting her "stories".

Jeb got up from his couch and came toward Sean. "What'd you bring?"

Sean backed away, sensing menace. He had hoped his brother wouldn't be here when he got home. He often wasn't. "Nothing. I just got home."

"Liar. You were supposed to bring something to eat."

Bun started crying.

"OK, OK. Just let me get my bag."

"Now!" Jeb cuffed him on ear and Sean shrank away and scuttled through the mess to his corner, grabbing a bag of clothes off the floor. Empty breakfast bar wrappers fell out of it onto the floor. He raced past his brother, who lunged and tried to land another blow on his head but missed somehow. Sean had learned to make up for his lack of size with speed. He raced back out the door and down the stairs, his sister Tina yelling after him.

"Bye, Mrs. Simone."

She waved as he made his way down, back into the grimy streets below, angry hollering following him from above.

015

LIGHTHOUSE

"Your serve." Emma tossed the small rubber ball across the court to Greg.

Greg caught it in the air as he stepped into the service area. "Five serving six." He squared up his feet and bounced the ball off the floor, arm swinging back, he slapped the ball forward off his gloved open palm as he swung through it. The ball fired off the forward wall at an angle, bouncing off the floor heading towards the sidewall at left.

Emma lunged forward, swinging through the ball with a backhanded glove, the tips of her fingers almost catching the wall. She bounced back towards the service area, ready for the return.

Greg hopped back, the ball flying over his head after the bounce. He didn't have enough time to jump for it, so waited for the ball to come to him off the back wall. It bounced near his feet and he swung but missed, the ball dribbling forward along the floor.

Emma skipped forward and picked it up, a grin on her face. "Six serving five." She walked back to the service line and set up. "I still can't believe we haven't found anything. I've been over the footage from *Making Time*'s contact with the object a thousand times, run the patterns and haven't found a damned thing."

"I don't know what to tell you, Em. Maybe they got it." Greg shrugged, watching her with the ball, waiting for the serve.

"I just think we should've seen something. Anything." Emma slapped the ball off the front wall and it came back, hard at Greg's feet. He hopped sideways, but not in enough time to make the return, the ball rebounding into the sidewall and off the back corner.

"God!"

"Seven serving five. Gimme the ball." Emma gave him a come-at-me gesture with her hands and Greg tossed it at her. She picked the ball out of the air and they switched spots at the service line, Greg setting up to receive the serve.

Crack! Emma's serve bounced hard off the front wall into the short line, threatening to dribble along the ground. Greg lunged forward and snapped it with his backhand, the ball caromed off the front wall, then the right wall's corner, flying right back towards him. Emma kicked off the sidewall and flew straight at Greg, hands out in front of her. She flicked the ball off her fingers back towards the front of the court before bouncing off the wall in front of Greg, landing on her feet.

Greg collided with her trying to get around at the ball as it bounced along the floor, rolling to the back wall.

"No fair. You blocked me."

Emma shrugged, walking back to the rolling ball, picking it up. "Was I supposed to get out of your way? This your first time?" She winked at him and crouched, getting ready to serve. She brushed a strand of sweaty hair out of her face, trying to tuck it back into her hairband without success. She wiped some sweat off her forehead that threatened to get under her goggles. "Eight serving five."

Greg braced himself, slightly forward this time as Emma bounced the ball at her feet, slapping it lightly into the front wall. Greg jumped forward, catching the ball off its bounce at the short line and drilled it hard off the front wall towards the back of the court. He skipped backwards to center court as Emma fell back to the rear wall, the ball bouncing off the floor before hitting the glass and flying up in front of her. She grunted and swung hard at the rubber ball, sending it hurtling past Greg's ducking head into the forward wall.

Greg recovered and waited for the bounce. The ball jounced off the right forward corner, dying and dropping to the floor. He swung, connecting with it, and lightly dumped it into the front wall.

Emma, charging forward to pick up the light return, had to contend with Greg standing in center court, his arms out blocking her. She tried to get around him but he slid sideways and she barrelled into him, knocking them both forward, falling in a heap on the smooth court. The ball rolled past them along the floor.

"You dick! That was blatant!"

Greg got up and extended a gloved hand to help Emma up, a big grin on his face. "Just my game, sister."

She swatted his hand away and kipped up onto her feet, sneakers squeaking on the surface. She went to the side of the service area, tucking her hair back in its hair band unsuccessfully. "Damnit. My hair is pissing me off."

Greg picked up the ball and returned to his box. "Excuses. What is it? Five serving eight?"

She nodded, hair flopping in her face.

"I could shave your head for you if you want." Greg bounced the ball and slapped it. The ball trickled off the front wall in front of the short line.

"That was short. Take it again." Emma reached for the ball and tossed it back to Greg. "I think I'd have to be plenty drunk for that."

Greg bounced the ball a couple of times. "I know where we can get some vodka."

Emma bit her lip. "Really?"

*

"This is where you thought we could get a drink?" Emma hissed as Greg slid Bryce's cabin door open and walked inside. They were both still wearing their gym clothes, but Greg had his hat on, low over his eyes. He was carrying a case they'd borrowed from the gym with a set of clippers in it. Emma had a towel around her shoulders and her headband pushed back, holding her hair away from her face.

"Well, I didn't figure he'd lock it while he's away."

"You're nuts."

"We'll just grab the bottle and go back to your room." Greg stepped to Bryce's desk and opened the drawer he'd seen him take the bottle from on their last visit. He pulled out the clear bottle and held it up to his face. Empty.

"Would you hurry up, I don't want anybody to see us in here."

Greg eyed the brown and gold box on the desk. The words Glenmorangie 21 were in gilt lettering along the front of it. He picked it up. "Come on. You have glasses in your room?"

"No."

Greg pushed her back out of the cabin and slid the door shut behind them. He looked down the hall and broke into a run, bounding down the padded hall of the crew section to Emma's room.

She caught up to him, crashing into his side to slow herself down, and slid her door open, pulling Greg inside with a giggle. She kicked some clothes under her messy bed and flopped down on the floor, leaning against the mattress.

Greg sat down in front of her and began unwrapping the box. He opened the top and pulled the bottle of brown liquor out.

"Don't laugh, OK?" Emma took her headband off and shook her hair out. It flopped out in a mass around her, tight curls and loopy strands floating in the air.

"Wow." Greg grinned as he picked at the metal foil around the stopper on the bottle.

"This is what I have to deal with up here." Emma leaned back against the bed, running her hands through the tangles, pulling it back away from her face without much success. Greg watched her, her light t-shirt, still damp with sweat, clung to her. The stopper came out of the bottle with a light pop and Greg caught a whiff of the alcohol inside. He frowned and sniffed at it, making a face.

Emma bent forward and scrunched up her nose. "What is that, anyway? It smells terrible."

Greg took his hat off and scrutinized the bottle. Without a thought, he took a swig from it, and his eyes went buggy as he choked it down with a gasp. "What the fuck?" he wheezed, his throat burning. "I think it's gone bad."

"Let me try." Emma grabbed the bottle and took a sniff, wincing at the odor. She tried a small sip and almost choked on it, but she managed to swallow. "It tastes like iodine."

Greg recovered from his first taste and was considering what he'd just experienced. "Has kind of a sweet aftertaste, though." He thought about it. "Like burnt sugar." He reached for the bottle and tried another swig, more carefully this time. "Blah!"

Emma sighed and took the bottle back. She took a bigger gulp and made a face. "Ew! That is terrible." She shook her head, hair flopping around. "Who drinks this stuff?"

"I have no idea." He smacked his lips. "Still, there's something there." He couldn't put his finger on it.

Emma was staring at him.

"Um." Greg blushed. "Do you want to do this?" He indicated the clippers with an inclination of his head.

Emma took a deep breath. "Do you think you can?" She pulled her feet in and sat cross-legged, hands crossed on her ankles, sitting up straight.

Greg extracted the clippers from their box as Emma took another swig from the bottle. He checked the indicator and found they were charged. "Yeah, I think we're good." He turned it on and it made a buzzing sound like an angry insect. "We should do this in the bathroom."

Emma nodded. "Probably." She stood up, bringing the bottle with her she walked into the bathroom. Greg gulped, watching her bare legs, and stood up, following after her. Complicated feelings rushed through his brain as he imagined the ramifications of what he was about to do. What would Tamra think? What would Jerem think? What the hell were they doing? He walked into the small washroom, shower in one corner sink and toilet in the other.

Emma stood in the center. There was barely enough room for both of them in the cramped space. She took a drink of scotch and made that face again, but the pink in her cheeks suggested she was getting something out of it. "I'll sit here." She laid out a towel on the cold floor and knelt down on it. She arranged herself, crossing her legs and sitting with her back to him.

Greg knelt down behind her and felt the clippers in his hand, testing the weight. "I've, uh, never done this before."

Emma smirked. "Tam doesn't let you cut her hair?"

"Uh, no. She'd kill me." He reached around beside her and picked up the bottle, their bodies brushing together. "I'm going to need another shot." He took a big gulp and felt the burn as it went down. He put the bottle beside them with a clink. "OK. You ready?"

Emma nodded. "I want it buzzed. Short."

"OK." Greg adjusted the blade, setting it close, then flicked the switch and the clippers came buzzing to life. He knelt behind her. "Tilt your head forward." She did, closing her eyes as he ran the clippers forward up the back of her head towards the front. The blades ripped through her dense curls, a mass of brown hair dropping to the floor in front of her.

She giggled. "That tickles."

Greg grinned. "Be still. I don't want to screw this up." He leaned into her, holding her head in his other hand, and with another zip, a new pile of hair fell beside her.

Emma closed her eyes as Greg worked, enjoying the buzzing on her scalp, the scotch warming her from the inside. Greg's hands on her neck and shoulders, tilting her head as he shaved it. Before long the buzzing stopped as Greg turned off the clippers, leaving her scalp tingling, brushing the remnants off her head with his hands.

She got up and faced him, raising her hands to her head and rubbing her fingers over the stubble. "It feels… weird."

"Take a look," Greg said, looking at her intently.

She turned and looked at herself in the mirror, head bald except for a thin layer of stubble. She ran her hands over her scalp again, stray strands falling around her as she felt the short stubble under her fingers. She smiled at herself, her face seeming somehow different without her familiar nest of curls.

Greg was close behind her. He leaned on the sink, arms on either side of her, looking over her head at her face in the mirror. "How do you like it?"

"It feels good. Weird." She turned around, pushing Greg away from her, hands on his chest. "Your turn."

016

THE TERROR

The pain in the remnants of Jerem's arm was constant. He gritted his teeth and checked the bandage again, unable to get used to the missing section just below his elbow. The ball of gauze and tape holding him together was a blunt terminus where his forearm used to extend into a hand. He felt like he was making a fist, clenching and holding onto something that wasn't there. Try as he might to relax it, the fist wouldn't let go. The bones and taut flesh sutured together ached dully; raw and itchy beneath the wrapping.

He hadn't been able to sleep since the operation except for short drifting naps. The doctor had given him morphine after the surgery, and he had slept fitfully then, but his overtired and medicated brain was taunting him. Auditory buzzing and dark shapes in the corners of his vision threatened to attack him if he verged too close to sleep, jolting him awake.

He dropped his head back onto the pillow in his bunk, but it lifted back up again, floating in the negligible gravity of the drifting ship.

"How you doing, kiddo?" His father Hal was hooked in beside him, hanging in the dimly-lit accessway between the bunks.

"It hurts."

"I know." He didn't. He could only imagine. "You need some more drugs?"

Jerem shook his head. "Not now." He blinked. He'd have to get used to this and the drugs made him groggy and vaguely nauseous.

Hal nodded. "Can I get you anything? Some water? You want to use my tablet?"

"Maybe some water." Jerem's own tablet was nearly ten million kilometers away from them by now. He wondered if it was still broadcasting and wished he still had his music collection. Maybe the *Terror* had some movies he could watch in her storage array. Anything to distract his mind.

Dr. Vela Banks pulled herself into the accessway from below, hearing their voices. "How's my patient?" She smiled at Jerem as she pulled up to his bunk. She was in her full space suit again, helmet and gloves in her bunk below his.

Hal steadied her, holding onto her suit's shoulder handle as she wobbled in the small space. "He's in pain," he told her, then said to his son, "I'll get you some water." He pushed below into the galley.

Vela checked his dressings and seemed satisfied with their condition. "These look good. We'll change them again later today. You want something for the pain?"

"No."

She nodded. "OK. But you need to get some rest. Just some ibuprofen for now. For the swelling."

Hal returned with his son's water bottle and Vela gave Jerem a pill from the bag strapped around her. Jerem took it and drank.

"I hope we got everything," Hal wondered aloud. His stomach grumbled and Vela turned her attention to him.

"You hungry?"

Hal shrugged. "Somewhat." He'd been busy helping with the salvage and reconfiguration of their broken ship. He was burning more calories than he was taking in. Everyone was, but they were on strict rations now and the EVAs were harder.

Voices drifted down from the cockpit above, echoing on the intercom speaker set into the wall beside them. Vanessa's voice said, "I think he's almost finished."

*

Captain Francine Pohl sat at the controls arrayed around her in the cramped cockpit, strapped into the pilot's seat in her full suit. Vanessa turned her head towards her, face obscured by the remote visor inside her helmet. "Looks like he's finishing up." Maintenance panels hung open, wires hanging out of them from the recent repair work they'd performed while accessing the thruster control relays.

"How you doing out there, Reg?" Francine asked into the radio. He'd been outside the ship for ten hours yesterday. Today he was EVA for six. He must be exhausted. She looked up through the windows above and saw a piece of metal drift by from the wreck below.

"Levers are all set. Just about ready. Getting my tools secured."

Vanessa panned the drone over the broken cargo module below, inspecting the wreckage of *Making Time*'s hab, still crushed into the nose of their cargo module, but now looking like an extra cockpit bolted on to the front of the bulbous cargo module. The cargo module that connected to the main hull of the *Terror* by its array of struts and cross-braces was now sprouting a pair of arms sticking out from both sides: metal extensions robbed from *Making Time*'s reinforced hull, wedged between the hab and cargo modules to form a pair of levers. Steel cables, coiled around the ends and secured with winches, formed the machine they'd use to reposition the cargo module back into its proper orientation. "He's waiting for Hal."

Francine watched the arrangement with a critical eye, gauging how much damage the extraction of the broken cargo module would inflict on her ship when they pulled it away. It didn't matter. It would be fixable. The *Terror*'s attitude control thrusters were partially obstructed by the invading cargo module, and they didn't have the maneuverability they needed to steer the ship properly. The added bulk of *Making Time*'s crumpled hab module hanging off the nose of the cargo module made the ship twice as hard to control. It was a beast to turn, and they had a burn coming up.

Reggie clambered around the side of the ship along their tether lines out to the makeshift lever he'd constructed. "Is he coming out? We need to get this finished."

"He's on his way," Vanessa reported. Francine watched them on her screen. Reggie collapsed in the airlock, waiting for the inner door to let him inside.

They heard the airlock door hiss and bang shut below in the equipment room. Francine announced over the intercom, "Reggie, go nice and easy. Keep the channel open in case we need you to stop. Dr. Banks, suit up, please. All hands, brace." She didn't know what was going to happen when they pulled the cargo module away, but she wanted to be prepared for the worst. It was possible one of the damaged struts had punctured the hull and would cause a breach when they moved it.

Helmet seals and gloves snapped from below as Vela closed her suit up, accompanied by the sounds of the crew securing themselves into their bunks. It bothered her that Jerem wasn't wearing a suit, but they couldn't get his arm inside, so she'd agreed to let him go without. She couldn't worry about that now.

She watched Hal floating out of the airlock and crawling up the spine of the ship on the exterior camera. Vanessa, piloting their remote sensor drone Spot, just off the nose of the ship, watched the two spacers getting ready.

"I hope we got those numbers right," Reg said over the intercom, referring to the amount of force they'd calculated to separate the wreck from their ship. "I'm no mining engineer."

"They'd better be," Francine replied. She hoped the cargo module and its contents weren't going to break under the stresses they were about to put on it. Of course, that was minor compared to the risks of losing pressure inside the hab.

"Almost in position." Hal was climbing out along the end of the starboard lever. His tether line trailed behind him, running from the airlock to just above the starboard fuel pod's attachment point.

Once everyone was in place, Francine said, "Alright, nice and easy, boys."

Reggie counted down from three, then began racking the lever on his winch back and forth. "Turn." Rack. "Turn." Rack... He called out each time he cranked the winch, to keep Hal in sync. The gearing made the movement relatively easy. It took a few turns until the cables on each side tightened up. "OK. Stop a second. Are you tight?"

"Just about." Hal gave his side another couple of turns until the cable became taut.

"Not seeing any leaks yet," Vanessa confirmed from her virtual vantage point off the prow.

"Alright. Ready... Turn." Rack. "Turn." Rack...

They continued tightening the winches, the cables stretching and pulling the curved pieces of *Making Time*'s frame down against the bent steel blobs they'd wedged against the cargo module as fulcrums. The spare metal they'd cut from *Making Time*'s broken hab was useful material for building parts. Hal had fought hard to keep the broken remnants of his ship. Reggie wanted to blow it off into space, but the idea of building levers and winches out of spare ship parts had sold Francine on the usefulness of the old capsule. While cutting the parts off *Making Time*'s crumpled dome shield, they'd managed to reinforce the sections of the cargo module that had gotten damaged in their rescue. Who knew what other uses they might have for the old ship on their long journey into the solar system?

"Definitely seeing movement now," Vanessa informed them.

"Reggie, looks like your side's moving a little faster, slow it down a bit."

"Got it." He lessened his turns on the winch handle, waiting for Hal's side to catch up again. They felt a pinging through the metal, relayed along the cables, as the stressed metals popped and bent under the force of the levers.

"Hold it!" Francine ordered. "Vanessa, can you get in there and give us a look?"

"Aye, mam."

A gap had grown between the cargo module and the nose of the *Terror*'s hab module. Vanessa edged Spot forward, turning her drone's lights on in the shadows between the two sections. "I don't see any leaks."

"OK," Francine said. "Let's check out the supports. Make sure nothing's coming loose, then we can shim up and add the next pair of levers and start on those." She was about to click off, then added, "Watch yourselves."

"Aye, skip," Reggie replied with a click.

Francine surveyed the screen for a moment, then became aware of a reflection behind her. She turned as best as she could in her suit. Jerem was floating above the acceleration couch behind her and her co-pilot, watching, his arm bandaged up like a ball in front of him.

Vanessa raised her goggles, turned and smiled at him. "Hey you."

"It looks good," he said. "I wish I could help."

Reggie groaned over his open mic. "Some of these struts are pretty bent up. We're going to have to take them apart and straighten everything out."

Francine responded, "Plenty of time for that."

Hal grunted. "It's good to have a hobby."

017

NOLAN RESIDENCE

Bryce Nolan woke up on the couch in his father's apartment to the smells and sounds of cooking. He blearily wiped his eyes and checked his watch. 06:30.

"Figured you'd have time for a little breakfast before you go," his father called from the kitchen.

"Yeah, I've got time." Just. His flight wasn't until noon, but he still had to meet Grayson before heading to the terminal. He wasn't sure why he was bothering, all he'd managed to accomplish was the formation of a new sub-committee, sure to run at the meagre cruising speed of bureaucracy. Still, he had to try. Maybe he could get through to the old Chairman. Maybe it didn't matter and he was making a big deal out of nothing.

Bryce got up from the couch and went to the washroom. Faint sewage smell and tiny flies buzzed in the corner. He turned up his nose and wondered if the lines were working properly. He showered quickly, making the most of the available facilities before he had to travel back up into orbit. He was looking forward to getting back up there. Back to his station. He missed his crew and smiled at the thought of them. They were under strict ration controls now, but his shuttle should bring some needed relief. Water and food supplies. At least the Council had given them that much.

He ran his head under the hot water and scrubbed his neck. Maybe he'd ask Jill out when he got back. Take her to the Cape Bar for dinner and a drink. He was pretty sure there was something there between them and had been for the past few months. Before his promotion.

He sighed and rinsed off the remnants of soap. He was her Commander now. It wouldn't be appropriate.

He shut off the water and reached outside the stall for a suspicious smelling towel and dried himself off. He dressed, tossing his toiletries and clothes into his duffel bag when finished. The shower still dripping water behind him as he left.

Walking to the kitchen entrance he surveyed the years of grime covering the walls and cupboards. "Dad, I think your toilet needs a tech. Doesn't smell right."

"I know. Been trying to get someone over to look at it for weeks. I think it's something down line." A tiny fly flew past Bryce's head and he swatted at it ineffectually.

"This place is a mess. You should get somebody in to clean it."

"Yeah, yeah." His father grabbed a couple of plates from the cupboard and scraped out some burnt omelette from his black frying pan onto them. He handed the least burnt-looking piece to his son who took it out to the table.

"You don't have to go back up today, do you? Why don't you stay a bit longer. Help your old man for a bit."

Bryce chewed a mouthful of egg, alarmed at the amount of crunching involved. "You know I can't. I have to get back up and get the station back online." He hesitated. "Comms are down." He swallowed and took a drink of water, had a crazy idea. "Y'know, we could use some more engineers. Why don't you come up?"

His father looked at him, stopped chewing. "You serious?"

"Yeah, why not? We've got room on the shuttle and one more mouth isn't going to make a huge dent in our food and water." He grinned, masking the slightly nervous feeling he got thinking about his father getting in the way up there. Would he be able to work with the crews? Would he try to take everything over? Form a coup? He could be brash, but was thoughtful. Generally worked well with others. "I could use someone smart who isn't going to try and bullshit me. You know. Acting as a consultant with the rest of the engineers. I don't know what those egg heads are telling me half the time."

His father took another bite. Chewed for a moment. "I could do that. Yeah, but what about my job? They need me at the Fab."

"I'm pretty sure we can justify it. I'll have Grayson write you a note."

Bryce's father grinned at his son around a mouthful of egg and toast.

"Look, I can't promise you anything, but I'm meeting with Grayson this morning. Why don't you get packed, and meet me at the terminal at ten? We'll go from there."

Robert looked at his son like he'd just been given a winning lottery ticket.

018

MACHINE PARTS

Sean entered the control shed at 0756, scanning his ID card on his way in. The scanner turned green allowing him access and he let out his held breath. It still worked. He was hoping to get access to one of the requisition terminals scattered around the Fab. He needed a new screen for his tablet and might be able to find one in the system, but he still didn't want to push his luck. It had been over a day since he'd checked in on the Observatory and he was getting antsy not knowing what was going on. He was the first to arrive after his foreman, Mike Allen.

Worse, he hadn't had access to his message board, Chicago, in over a day. It was an important part of his life: his online friends were more real than many of the people he interacted with in the city every day. He missed them.

"Hey, Sean," Mike greeted him. "Right on time, nice to see it." He smiled, Sean looking up at him under his mop of hair. Mike thought he saw a bruise over Sean's eye, but wasn't sure. Maybe it was the poor light in the control shed, or maybe just dirt. He wasn't about to ask.

Some more voices from the hallway outside drifted into the shed and Sean turned to see who it was. Blake Perkins and Dinah Steel entered the shed. The tops of Perkins' coveralls hung behind him like a cape. He stopped talking to the woman beside him and stood in front of Sean, staring down at him. "You punch in already?"

Sean fidgeted. "I'm here, so I guess so."

Perkins extended a bony finger at him. "You don't punch in early, you don't punch in late. You show up on time and not before. Got it?"

"Yessir."

"I'm no 'sir'." Perkins looked pointedly at Mike, dragging out the word.

Mike sighed. "Knock it off, Perkins."

"We have rules. He wants to get his card, he'd better start stickin' to them."

A union card. Sean smiled, despite the verbal abuse. Getting his union card meant he'd be a permanent worker in the Fab. A full citizen. He'd be able to apply for housing and move out of the Stacks.

The woman he came in with rasped out a chuckle. Maybe they were a couple – they seemed comfortable together, but Sean couldn't really tell. She had the partial metal teeth of the Steel Clans and had the last name and attitude to go with it. "There's worse places than here, kid. Don't mess it up."

Mike interrupted them. "Alright. Perkins, Steel, MP238 has a stuck job. I need you two to get in there and free it up."

Perkins hooked his thumbs in the loops of his tank top, stretching it. "Why don't you send Boots in there? He was here first."

"Because I got another job for Boots and this is a two person job. Get out there and fix it!"

Perkins looked surprised, then covered it up. "Come on, we're gonna be out there already. We can take care of it."

"Make up yer mind, Wade." Mike grimaced at him, then turned back to Sean. "We're sending Boots out there. Good opportunity to get skilled up on the CNC machine."

"Whatever, Boss." Perkins ushered Steel towards the door, and she sneered at Mike on her way by, metal teeth picking up the yellow lights in the shed.

Mike ignored them as they left the shed. "I don't know what that was all about, but don't worry about them. For you, we've got a blown hydraulic piston on MP318. Need you to replace it. Part's here." He indicated it on the floor, the label still clean and white, fresh off the grid.

Sean was disappointed he hadn't seen the request come through. He could recognize at least three of the machines needed to build this part and could have followed it through construction.

"OK." He grabbed his helmet and tool belt off the wall and put them on. He picked up the heavy piston and slung it over his shoulder, balancing it.

"You want to see a schematic or anything first?" Mike indicated the screen on his desk: a wireframe version of the CNC mill, with a highlighted piece near the top of the articulated control arm. Sean leaned in and studied it, spun the wireframe around with a trackball on the console and stood back up.

"I think I got it." Sean slung the piston over his shoulder.

"All right then. Be careful up there. Keep yer eyes open."

"OK." He put in the earphones hanging from the line around his neck and went out onto the floor, the noise still deafening around him. He climbed up the ladder to the gangway that would bring him to the 311-319 row of machinery. Steam hissed at him as he walked along the narrow metal ramp. Through the tracks the robotic arms ran along beneath the stairs and walkway, he could see Steel and Perkins squeezing between the rows of benders and folders to their destination. He idly wondered what job was stuck in the big stamper they were going to clear out. Its job was crushing steel sheets into new shapes. His view was obscured as an arm carrying a curved metal case rolled by underneath. It turned left, catching a track that dropped two more levels, then disappeared into one of the exit tunnels underneath. Some machine in another part of the facility was getting a new shell.

He arrived at MP318, a big CNC mill near the end of the line used to carve solid blocks of metal into new forms. The big yellow light flashed, its arm raised and hanging at an angle, limp and powerless. Sean hit the shut-down switch and it hissed into a relaxed state, the control arm sagging as an air hose deflated. He opened a side panel beside the door and inspected the machine. The faulty piston was connected to the mill head, which contained an array of different bits for carving metal. He looked at the connectors holding the piston in place and pulled a twenty millimeter wrench out of his tool belt, and went to work on the bolts.

It took some effort, but he managed to loosen and turn the bolts, then was able to pull the piston out of the arm, hydraulic fluid leaking out onto his arm, further staining his dirty coveralls. The mill head dropped onto the plinth, still connected to the articulated arm via the wiring harness and smaller yoke which he held onto. He was about to lift the new piston into place when a panicked voice broke in over his headset. "Sean! Look out!" He barely registered the voice when he ducked, vaguely aware of a flashing motion beside him in his peripheral vision.

One of the robotic arms whizzed past and dropped onto a track below, whipping around at impossible speed. He sensed an impact and then the arm whirled back up and above him. Drops of something red fell on his hand and face as it flew by. He wiped one of them, smearing it on his hand.

Sirens blared as red emergency lights came on and cast the machines in ruddy shadows. All around him the machines began shutting down. He thumbed the mic switch. "Uh, just about done here."

Sean lifted the piston up to the mill as Mike's shaky, strident voice came back over the line. "Sean, get back here! Be careful."

He looked over the ramp, down to the shed to see Mike holding his head beside the shed, illuminated in red and amber flashing lights. Something had happened. He'd hit the switch. Shutdown.

Sean crouch-walked back to the stairs, occasionally leaning over the side of the gangway, trying to see what had happened below. The arm was raising and lowering itself in its track, apparently stuck in some kind of loop. He reached the stairs and clattered down to the main level. Yellow lights and buzzers blared.

Mike yelled over the din. "You OK? That arm... Did it get you?" The foreman grabbed Sean and pulled him over to the shed away from machinery.

Sean shook his head. "No." Mike was checking him over, handling him like a piece of chicken. Sean looked back up at the machines. Red smeared across one of the big rollers on level two. The faulty arm still swung up and down, metal gripper opening and closing in mid-air. "What? What happened?"

Mike swallowed. "Get inside. Clean-up crew's on its way."

Unable to look away, Sean snuck a glance back at the scene of the accident and saw Perkins emerge from the shadows, covered in blood, whites of his eyes shining out of a red face in the ruddy light as the mechanical arm came to a stop beside him.

019

LIGHTHOUSE

Greta Patrick, Chief Ship's Engineer, watched from her perch high up in the scaffolding atop the lip of the dome shield. She looked down over her team in the engine bay performing the refit on *MSS11*.

Banshee was still awaiting assignment of her new crew, she was most-recently Captained by Lori Harrison. She took good care of her ship, Greta thought to herself. She was a good captain.

She turned on her perch, looking down the length of the ship over her nose, the huge blades of the station's solar collectors running alongside the ship, Mars rolling past three thousand kilometers below, bright clouds of dust reaching high above the Tharsis Plateau. Barely visible from here, the domes glittered like jewels beneath the edge of Ascraeus Mons, the three big volcanoes casting long dark shadows west in the morning sun.

Greta was tethered to the supports running along the ship's open engine section. The engine casing was folded open, panels splayed like the petals of a flower, racks of LED lighting illuminated the glittering fusion core and machinery that powered the big supercapacitors her crew was replacing today. It was a big job that required careful precision to make it all work. The supercaps themselves needed to be kept sealed and isolated in their insulating layer, sealed off from the heat and radiation of the core itself. Exotic ceramics and layers of special foam acted as heat shielding around the coils to protect the sensitive equipment.

"Danko, can you check the coupling near conduit three-eighteen? We had a coolant leak, make sure it's tight."

"On it," came the reply over her headset.

Greta looked up over the rest of the dockyards. One empty bay. Two more ships in disarray beyond *MSS11*: *MSS08* and their last heavy, *MSS04H*. She'd taken a beating on her last outing, rounding up a chunk of stray comet, engines over-worked. Greta sighed. MSS13 and MSS18 were never coming back. *MSS12* was totalled. *MSS02H* was adrift in-system. This was going to be all they had for a while and her engineers were going to have to work overtime getting these hulks ready for whatever came next. It wasn't likely they'd have a ship ready to go out to Watchtower for the refit anytime soon. They'd be riding a shuttle. Maybe she'd bid on the job. It had been a while since she'd left the station.

She looked out into space, shielding her eyes against the sun, imagining where the *Terror* and her crew must be. Deimos, just a tiny speck from out here, passed beyond the hazy atmosphere over the edge of the planet below

*

Acting Commander Sunil Pradeep looked up from his tablet as the two junior science team members walked onto the Control Deck at 0756. Greg Pohl, cap down low over his face, fresh buzzcut just visible on the sides over his ears. His hair was no longer hanging in his face. Emma Franklin beamed as she walked to her station also sporting a freshly-shaved head. Heads lifted up and turned, watching their arrival with interest.

Dan Wilkins rolled back in his chair, turning fully to meet them. "Well look at you two. You look like proper spacers now." His big smile did nothing to mask the hint of sarcasm in his voice.

Greg and Emma sat down in silence. Sunil thought Emma might be blushing.

Sunil returned to the station reports on his tablet, scanning through the list of supplies they were running out of when a harsh buzzer sounded on the deck's speakers, jolting him in his seat. "Proximity alert!" A junior tech in station ops hollered as the buzzer stopped. It was so quick, just half a second, but it left a ringing in his ears.

"Commander, we have a surface impact!" Wilkins announced from across the room. A scramble of activity broke out as Emma and Greg began shuffling cameras and screens.

Sunil stood up from his seat. The updated station inventory had him dozing off in his chair when the buzzer snapped him out of it. He looked back at his tablet, still in his hand, and flipped to the morning's incident reports. He skimmed through the list, looking for any incoming meteors or asteroids. Nothing. Watchtower should have spotted anything on a direct line and tagged it priority immediate. Maybe it had come in obliquely?

"Control? This is Patrick in Engineering." Patrick was a crackling voice over the local station channel on speakers. "What was that on the surface just now?"

Jill Sanchez flicked her mic open and replied, "Hold, please." She turned around, first stealing a quick glance through the windows at the planet rolling below, then to her Commander.

Sunil watched the plume growing on the surface with an increasing sense of foreboding. Word traveled quickly around the station. The doors from the crew section slid open and the chief science officer, Nelson Ortega, loped onto the deck to get a better look through the big windows as the view wheeled away from Mars.

"What was that? Do we have any footage?" Nelson asked around the room on his way to the science station. His hair was disheveled, his shirt untucked.

Jill Sanchez was still watching him from comms, expecting an answer, headset hanging over one ear. "Sunil? What should I tell Patrick? Should we turn on the network?"

He sat back down in the commander's chair. He was under orders not to activate the station's network, and Nelson was running the team working on hardening the station's networking components. He wasn't going to turn it back on until he'd been given the all-clear from his systems people.

"Tell her to standby. We're looking into it. Do not turn on the network. Anything coming in on Victor?" He used the short code for VHF, their analog frequencies.

"We're moving away from Ascraeus. Nothing but static on land radio," Jill reported. She turned back around to her station and spoke quietly into her headset. "Standby, Engineering. We are investigating. Will advise with update. Over."

Emma and Greg were flipping through the video inventory on the station's computers.

"They saw it in Engineering. What do we have in the Dockyards?" Emma asked, looking over the big station's networking schematics.

"I have video from Materials' overlook," Greg announced, and without waiting for instruction, put it on the main screen overhead.

Heads turned and looked up at the monitor showing the view over the storage containers, Mars small but visible in between the spherical pods. The image zoomed in, grainy pixels showing a blurry streak through the thin atmosphere that brightened through its descent until it struck the surface with a bright white flash. It took less than two seconds to reach the ground from space.

Nelson Ortega asked, "Is that our only camera view?"

"Only one I could find," Greg answered. He'd become quite familiar with the external views the station had on offer in the short time he'd been on the station.

Emma opened her plotting tools. She brought up the video in a section of her screen and said, "It looks like it hit about a hundred and fifty kilometers east-northeast of Ascraeus, towards Tharsis Crater." More plotting. "Based on the footage, I'm guessing it was travelling around" – she paused, checked again – "forty kilometers per second." She frowned at her screen.

"That was close," Wilkins said, joining the scrum behind Greg. "If that had hit us…"

Sanchez was still waiting for some kind of answer from Pradeep. "Sunil? Engineering's asking what we should do."

He sat there for a long moment, the voices around him turning into a rush of sound in his head. He took a deep breath and tried to quiet his nerves. "Science, do we have any indication that there is anything else inbound?"

Wilkins and Emma started poring through camera logs. Wilkins spoke first. "Nothing yet. Still looking. Not a peep from Watchtower, either."

Pradeep turned back to Jill. "Tell them to keep working. We'll keep looking."

"OK. Relaying." She did.

The windows on the control deck became dark and filled with stars as the station passed behind Mars, the Sun occulted.

020

DOME 3

Tamra arrived at the Dome early this morning. Julie woke her up at 6:30, some rusks and soy milk already on the table. A big orange had been cut in half and placed in bowls for each of them.

Tamra smiled at the thought of Emma's mom taking care of her, then sighed at the thought of her missing friend. She'd checked the news feeds this morning, MARSnet dutifully providing opinions from around the city about the recent turmoil, much of it injecting theories about a Mars First agenda and the government attempting to shut them down. Still no news about the station or her father's ship. Reading the feeds just made her feel ill.

A chicken ran in front of her, distracting her from her morbid thoughts. She laughed in spite of herself as it flew past, clucking idiotically in its bid for freedom from the other hens in its coop. It landed and pecked at the ground, looking for something to eat. She threw a couple of seeds into the dirt away from her planting, and it scrabbled towards her, sensing it might get some more.

"Hi there," she said. "Are you the girl we saw yesterday?" The brown hen cocked its head, watching her with one eye as it scratched the ground looking for bugs.

She stooped and planted a seed from her basket in the freshly-tilled soil, the first of hundreds of the day, then looked up through the hazy light filtering through the dust-blanketed dome above. The Sun was low on the glass and steel horizon, casting long faint shadows across the ground from the buildings and taller trees. When she was done, this patch would be covered with a solar blanket to be kept warm, the seeds kept moist by tubules in the blanket until they germinated.

Tamra stared at the light from their sun, the dusky star a small indistinct disc straining through the dirty glass high above. She remembered the blurry picture Julie had shown her. Her father and brother were out there, falling deeper into the solar system away from home. She wondered if it was warmer now that they were closer to the Sun. She shuddered at the thought of the extra radiation they'd be subjected to up there and hoped they had enough shielding.

"Hey. You OK?"

She turned her head. Rory stood close, staring down at her kneeling in the dirt.

"Yeah. Just kind of… spaced-out." She smiled at her own inside joke and brushed a strand of hair out of her face with a gloved hand.

Rory was a nice kid. Small compared to most of her class, but kind and with an infectious enthusiasm. He and Nils were inseparable and she didn't have to look far past him to find his friend. She waved to Nils and he nodded back at her. "Just thinking about my family. They're out there, somewhere."

Rory sat down beside her. "Yeah. You miss them."

"Obviously. And Emma. And Greg…" She looked at Rory beside her, the strand of blonde hair falling over her face again. She felt the breeze on her face from the ventilation fans. "Everyone's gone." And Jane. Poor Jane. Still in hospital, bandaged and broken after the accident in the riots. "I wish they'd come back."

Rory grunted. "Spacers, right? They get all the good stuff then leave their friends and families behind," he said, echoing a familiar refrain of the Firsters. He scratched at the dirt and the chicken flapped a couple of meters away.

"It's not that. It just seems kind of pointless." She looked up at the dusty dome above them again.

The Sun seemed to flare and her surroundings darkened as her eyes adjusted, the shadows gained contrast in the brighter light and Tamra and Rory turned their heads to the East. "What was that?"

The light faded, then the sky grew darker, the sun dimming as the rising cloud from the surface blocked it out. Tamra stood up as the lights inside the dome came on in response to the change in luminosity. She looked around, the others from her class looking similarly confused, standing up to look to the dome's edge and beyond. A low rumble shook through the ground and then a loud crack, and Tamra's ears popped. A siren blared. Yellow warning lights began flashing on the the farmhouse.

The ground shifted, seemed to roll beneath the students' feet. The dome's pressure seals, weakened after decades of sandstorms and weather, cracked in a line from the ground up the wall, stretching meters high above them in a cascade of erupting glass. Dust and sand lifted off the interior surface and blew through the new opening, the dome's air rushing out in a deafening gale all but drowning out the blaring sirens, shifting pitch and becoming thin and reedy in the dropping pressure.

Without thinking, Tamra grabbed the hood on her pressure suit and pulled it over her head as she fumbled for the zip seals on her chest and neck. She felt the suit tighten up around her as the pressure sensors detected the drop and the suit's internal air bladders inflated. Her face felt the chill wind of the pressure drop as her hood closed over her face. "Get to the elevator, Rory," she yelled, hoping her neck mic was working, hoping he could hear her. She grabbed his wrist and started jogging towards the farmhouse, yellow lights flashing in her face.

Nils ran towards them, fumbling with his neck seals, before grabbing her and Rory's arms and pushing them towards the elevators. She glanced over her shoulder to see her other classmates following them at full run. She stopped long enough to help Joe get his neck seal closed and the other students ran past, heads down and arms out against the strong wind of evacuating air.

She was halfway to the Station Building when a blast of air knocked her to her knees and a plume of dust blew out of the entrance tunnel of the station building. Rory almost bowled into her. "What happened?" His face twisted in fear under his suit's bubble. The wailing sirens grew higher and fainter as the pressure readout in Tamra's suit dropped by almost half.

"Come on." She got up and continued running toward the Station, into the ballooning dust cloud ahead. The chicken she'd seen earlier flapped its wings hard, eyes bulging, beak wide open, and then fell over, feet kicking feebly in the dirt. She didn't have a lot of time. Without an air canister, the suit's rebreather was only good for about fifteen minutes before the system ran out of fresh air, then she'd be on whatever was left in her lungs. The suits had just enough air to reach the Station from anywhere in the dome – the designers had figured that would be enough for any breach.

The doors were open, a pile of sand and dust on the threshold at her feet. Tamra stepped inside the entrance tunnel to the farmhouse, squinting into the dark haze. Lights guttered above. Tamra waved a hand in front of her face, peering through the cloud of dust floating at the entrance to the station, looking down the flickering hallway. She walked in and froze. The elevator doors were open but there was no elevator. Red lights were spinning over the elevator doors, adding to the madness. Skipping forward, she peered over the edge and down into the dark shaft, dust billowing out and around her suit.

"There's no elevator." She looked around to see Rory and the others still standing in the building's entrance. "We're cut off."

021

ROVER 2

Erika set the scrubber bot into the track at the base of Dome 5. They were wrapping up here, this being the last of the active domes. The next job was going to be to loop back to Dome 1 to start over, a thin layer of dust having settled since they'd deployed there last week.

Erika nodded inside her helmet. "Uh huh." She looked out over the dome. The half-meter robots crawled up the surface in their tracks on soft, grippy wheels. She turned around and walked back to the trailer to get the next one, boots crunching on the rocky sand underneath. Her hands were sore and taped up inside her gloves. She was sweating despite the external temperature hovering around one hundred and ninety Kelvin.

"… I told this bot-head to get out of my face," Ray Becker continued.

"What'd he do?" Erika Rin unloaded the next scrubber and hauled it over to the tracks, Becker passing her on his way back to the trailer.

"What do you think? People all around. He just kind of backed off. I was hoping he'd try something, though. Man, they piss me off with their paranoid crazy shit. All that metal shit in their faces gives me the creeps." He hauled a scrubber off the trailer and walked it over to the rails. "Surprised the Council hasn't shut them down. It's not like they do anything useful. Rejects."

Erika let him rant, only half paying attention to the story of Ray versus the Machine Worshipper. Half the time, she suspected he made up these encounters to sound tough around Aden.

The burst of static in her headset broke her out of her daze. She turned as she was about to pass Ray on her way back to the trailer when she saw a glint reflecting in Becker's visor. She turned around and scanned the hazy distance. A brighter flash lit the sky and a long thin line burned through the upper atmosphere in a graceful arc, followed by a bigger flash, brighter than the sun casting stark shadows across the Martian plain. "What the fuck?"

Ray Becker just stared straight ahead, transfixed, dropping the scrubber bot to the ground at his feet. From the RV, Aden Reed crackled in over their radio through a wave of static. "You guys see that?"

Erika. "Yeah. What the hell was it?"

"Maybe a bolide? I'm checking with control, but radio's breaking up."

More crackling radio. Ray still just stood there, stock-still, face obscured by the reflective visor.

Erika looked from Ray back to the RV. "How close do you think that was?"

Ignoring the immediate question, Ray pointed into the distance. "What is that?" He squinted into the haze across the Tharsis Plateau. A column rose up from the dusty plain.

"Yo, everybody get inside!" Aden's voice had an edge to it that surprised Erika. She'd never heard him sound anything but over-confident before.

Erika turned back in the direction of the flare and saw a thin brownish-grey line blurring the horizon under the column of dust rising into the sky. "Move, Beck! Now!" She grabbed his arm and broke him out of the spell. They turned and ran for the airlock door of the RV. Normally, they went through one at a time, the cramped entrance at the back of the vehicle not really big enough for two. This was not a normal time. They squeezed inside the cramped airlock and pulled the hatch closed after them, dogging it shut.

Blasts of air buffeted their suits as the cleaning cycle ran. "Reed! Kill the cleaning cycle, get us inside!" Erika yelled into her mic, crushed against Ray in his suit in the tiny space.

"Whoa, check that out!" Aden came back over their headsets as the cleaning cycle continued.

"What the fuck just happened?" Ray wasn't sure what he had just seen, but he didn't like it. He was facing Erika, his mirrored visor reflected in hers, their suits pressed together in the small space. Air filled the lock with a whoosh that turned into a howling roar.

"I don't know. Something just fell. A meteor?" They fell on Mars all the time, strays from the asteroid belt and beyond, but they usually had warnings. Erika had never seen one strike the surface before. The inner airlock door swung open and they both fell inside, unsnapping the seals on their helmets, Erika flinging hers onto the couch. Aden was silhouetted, sitting in the driver's seat, staring out the window at a bright blooming cloud rising into the sky. The wall of sand and dust raced toward them, blurring the horizon and blotting out the sky.

Erika scrambled forward to the cockpit, ignoring the sand and dust falling off her suit as she moved. Ray followed, squeezing in to get a better look.

Aden turned, realizing they were inside suddenly. "Look at that," he said, voice hushed in awe.

She hit the back of his seat and looked out the window at the ballooning cloud racing towards them at two hundred and fifty meters per second.

The RV was shaken by a boom as the first shockwave hit them, then was covered in dust and blasted by a fierce wind. The entire cabin rattled as the rover was buffeted in the wind howling around them.

Erika held onto Aden's seat in front of her, listening as small rocks and sand battered the outside and bounced off the thick plastic windshield bubble. The sky turned dark around them, blurring into a dull red streak.

Aden shook his head to clear it and spoke into his headset. "Control, control. This is Rover 2. Visibility's shot. Please come in and advise. Over." He sounded calm but Erika could tell he was on edge. The RV rocked around them, Ray hanging onto the handles behind her, struggling to stay on his feet.

Aden listened hard into his headset, then turned to look at Erika, his forehead creased with concern. "Just static."

Erika knelt on the floor behind the cockpit staring into the window, picking at the seals on her gloves. She wasn't sure if she should get out of her suit or seal herself back up. "There was a radio burst just before we saw the… whatever that was."

"Could've been an airburst," Ray said through the radio's speakers, standing behind her, still looking into the darkness beyond the rover's windshield. There was a loud ping as something heavy bounced off the side of the vehicle. "Particulates on the meteor, getting vaporized at high energy give off radio waves."

Aden turned around in his seat to look at Ray with a raised eyebrow. "The hell you on about?"

"Or something…" Ray's voice was a verbal shrug through the radio. His helmet was still on.

Erika spoke from her spot between the two seats on the floor. "I guess we're going to have to start over with the scrubbers," she said.

*

The RV continued rocking in the wind, sand and small rocks spraying off the windshield, occasional pings as pieces of debris struck the metal chassis inside the wheel wells. Erika was still kneeling on the floor, dirt and sand pooling in small piles on the deck around her, gloves on the floor in front of her. She looked back at Becker, who was standing stock still behind her in the crew compartment towards the air lock door, mirrored visor still down covering his face. His suit was covered in dirt and sand, just like hers.

"Beck? You alright in there?" She stood up and walked to him. She looked at her own reflection in his helmet briefly. Hair stuck to her forehead above her dark eyes. She rapped him on his helmet and he started moving again, gloved hands reaching up to his helmet release.

"There's a good boy." Erika picked up her gloves and turned around to face the cockpit again. Aden was flipping switches on the console trying to get the radio to work.

"Control? What the fuck was that?" he demanded of his headset, still turning a dial looking for any local traffic. The speakers crackled and a voice broke through.

"Rover 2, what's happening up there, over?"

"Control! This is Rover 2. Looked like a meteor impact? Felt close. Over?"

"Standby, Rover 2." The channel clicked off.

"Alright." Aden turned around to look sidelong at Erika in her dirty suit. He picked up the mangled piece of black rubber tubing off the control surface in front of him and stuck it in his mouth between his teeth, jaw working as he chewed on it.

Becker dropped his helmet on the deck and stomped forward behind Erika leaving a trail of sandy footprints on the deck. "What the fuck, man?" They both looked at him, his face was ghost white, eyes wide.

"Easy, Ray." Erika tried to sound comforting. "Just some space rock."

"That could've been way closer. What if it hit a dome? Or us?"

"Pipe down, Beck." Reed leaned on his console, looking a little worn out. "Get a grip, man."

"Could've hit us, is all." Ray shook his head and flopped down onto the couch with a puff of dust, Erika's helmet threatening to roll off onto the floor.

The radio crackled and the voice of Control came back over the line. "Rover 2, come in, over."

Aden thumbed his headset back on, chewing. "This is Rover 2. Go ahead. Over."

"Rover 2, looks like the impact's about a hundred klicks from your position, East-North-East. We want you to check it out. Over."

Reed looked back at Erika, an eyebrow raised, "Come again, Control? You want us to roll a hundred kilometers to check in on a space rock? Over?"

"That's affirmative, Rover 2. Any problem?"

Reed cocked an eyebrow and Erika nodded at him. She was OK with the trip and didn't think Ray had any useful opinion at the moment.

"No problem, Control."

Reed was about to get up when the radio crackled again. "Wait, Rover 2. Can you swing by Dome 3 on your way out? Board looks like there was a pressure drop up there. They might need some help."

"Goddamnit." He flicked his mic back on. "Why can't you send Rover 1?"

Static then the line crackled again. "Because Rover 1's inside. You drew the short straw, Reed. Control out."

Aden stood up, tossing the headset onto his controls and stepped around Erika, walking back into the cabin. "Beck, you've still got most of your suit on. I need you back out there to unhook our trailer and do a walk-around."

Ray looked up. "You want me to go back out there?"

Aden poked Ray in the chest with the black tubing he'd been chewing on, leaving a spot in the dirt. "Yeah, I do. You're a surface tech, aren't you?" He shot Erika a look. "Either that or Rin can do it, if you're too scared."

"Not it," Erika said quietly.

Ray stood up and walked back to where he'd dropped his helmet on the deck, stooping awkwardly in his suit to pick it up. He grumbled, put his helmet on over his head.

"What's that? Didn't hear you." Reed put a hand to his ear like he was listening for a response. "I didn't think so." Aden returned to his seat up front and flopped into it, cracking his knuckles loudly. He brushed off the tube and stuck it back in his mouth, chewing on it with renewed vigor.

Erika stuck out her tongue at the back of his head, but Aden couldn't see her.

"Rin, you're my navigator." He patted the seat beside him. "Why don't you put on somethin' nice and come on up here."

Seals clicked as Ray put his helmet back on and headed for the airlock. Erika gave him a quick check when he was sealed up and patted him on the helmet. "Do it quick and get back inside. Be careful, OK?"

"Yeah."

Ray entered the airlock and closed the door behind him.

Erika began undoing her waist seals and stepped back onto the locker. She leaned back, her torso locking into its bindings and she raised her arms, the chest-piece rising up over her head. She pushed the legs down over her hips and wriggled out of them, leaving them behind in a dusty pile. She opened the overhead bin, grabbed her boots and pulled out her overalls, climbing into them, zipping up halfway before climbing into her seat in the forward compartment.

"Why you gotta be such a dick to him?" she asked as she brushed the sand and dirt off her socks, then stuffed her feet into her soft boots.

"Sometimes you gotta remind the crew who's in charge," Aden drawled, watching Ray outside from the external cameras. He chewed.

Erika hissed with exasperation.

Aden regarded her for a moment, then took the tube out of his mouth and pointed it at her. "I'm a dick to him because he's a loser." He returned the tube to his mouth like the stub of a cigar. They watched Ray struggle with the trailer hitch in silence for a while. Dust blew past the camera, obscuring him from view.

"Guys?" Ray said over the radio. "I could use some help with this."

022

CITY HALL

"What the hell is going on in here? Shut that damned siren off. Are you trying to panic the whole city?" Henry Grayson stormed into City Control, wiping a thin sheen of sweat off his brow with a handkerchief. Bryce followed him in, still breathing hard after their rush to City Hall when the pressure warnings sounded.

"Yes sir. Shutting it down, sir." Leigh Henderson killed the sirens abruptly, mid-announcement.

Bryce took stock in the big circular room, dome lights overhead projecting white circles onto the work stations covered in colorful floating displays around the room. The monitor wall showed closed-circuit cameras from around the city, crowds forming in front of the hospital, church, and university. Security teams pushed back against the press of people trying to get to the promised safety of pressure-secure buildings. An overhead map of the city showed blobs of color where people were congregating.

"This whole thing's part of the original Ark ship, isn't it?" Bryce asked, taking in the big room, the aging technology repurposed to form the hub of the city's information center.

"What hasn't broken down and been replaced. The command module ended up here. It became the core of City Hall." Grayson bunched up his forehead. "Sorry I don't have time to give you the full tour."

Natalie Park-Sheehan walked over from the observation area.

"What happened?" Grayson asked her.

95

"The Council's convening in chambers. We should probably join them," she answered curtly. Bryce noticed her touch the Chief Councillor's arm with light fingers.

"We'd get more direct information here in the Command Center. Let them wait." He trudged over to the ranking officer on duty. "Henderson. Give me a rundown on what happened."

"Yes, sir. At 0812, seismic sensors registered a low-grade tremor. It was followed by a smaller aftershock thirty seconds later. At roughly the same time, we detected a fifteen-millibar drop in pressure inside the city, but it appears to be holding." Natalie regarded the officer with a sour look on her face. "The warnings sounded automatically."

Grayson nodded. "Anything else?"

Henderson shifted uncomfortably under the Chairman's gaze. "Dome 3 lost pressure. The emergency cut-off blew and we had an elevator crash. We have teams on the ground trying to get in."

"How many people up there?"

"Not sure yet. It was early and they're on a light duty schedule this time of year. I'd say no more than a hundred, but we're still waiting on a log report from Systems."

Bryce watched the exchange in shock. Losing an entire dome would be a catastrophe for the city.

"Get in there and help anybody inside. Top priority. But keep a lid on it. We don't need that getting out before we have a handle on the damage."

"Yes, sir."

Grayson surveyed the monitors again. The black box of the Fab in the center of New Providence was suspiciously devoid of activity. "What's going on in the Fab?"

"Power fluctuations occurred at around the same time. The Fab's gone into lockdown. Also getting reports from reclamation that water pressure is down." The officer cleared his throat, unused to such direct contact with the leader of their city.

"Do we know what caused it?"

"One of our Rover teams reported seeing a meteor strike about a hundred klicks from the domes. We've sent them to investigate."

Grayson raised an eyebrow. "Let me guess. Impact at 0812." Not a question.

"Yessir."

"Holy Hannah. Thank you, Officer. If you get anything else – anything – message me directly. I'll be in Chambers. Ms. Park-Sheehan?" He turned and began walking out of the room, Natalie trailing behind him. He stopped abruptly and turned back to

Henderson. "Get Kaylee on the feeds. Have her spin up something about a faulty pressure sensor."

Henderson gulped and nodded. "What kind of pressure sensor?"

Grayson turned back on him, Bryce watching his shoulders bunch up like he was getting ready to throw a punch. "I don't give a shit! Make something up! Just get her to spin it as nothing major." He relaxed again, regaining his composure. "The goal is to relax people. We don't want mass panic on our hands. Understand?"

"Yes, sir. Sorry, sir." Henderson shifted uncomfortably.

"No word from Lighthouse?" Bryce asked the officer, trying to deflect some of the hostility from Grayson.

Henderson looked to Grayson with a raised eyebrow, not sure if he should answer. The chairman nodded and Henderson turned to Bryce to answer.

"Nothing. Orbital communications are still down."

Grayson grunted. "You've taken care of that, Bryce."

Bryce winced and faced the Chairman. "I've got to get back up there. I'm no use down here, but up there... We can get the station comms back up and running again. Get some eyes on whatever this is." He remembered that he was supposed to meet his father at the Terminal soon. Would he have gone there without him?

Grayson looked at him like he had lost his mind. "There won't be any trains running outside the city today. You'd best settle in. Figure out how to be of use down here." He guided Bryce towards the doors of the Command Center. "Look, the last thing we want to do is panic people. Right now, it's just a meteor strike. Nothing more. Let's treat it as such until we know any differently, got it?"

Bryce nodded, unconvinced.

Natalie was waiting for them in the hall. They made their way to the elevators, passing two ancient space suits standing guard at the end of the hallway. The name patch on his right read Cavanaugh. The mission patch on the other side held the complex trefoil and wings of the Ark ship *Exodus*.

Grayson asked Natalie, "Heard from your husband and kids yet?"

She shook her head and pressed the button to call an elevator. The doors opened and they stepped inside. Bryce followed, turned around and faced the doors.

"Eighth floor, please," Grayson requested and the elevator began climbing.

After an awkward silence, the elevator chimed and the doors slid open onto another hallway like the one they'd just left. They walked to the Council Chambers, Henry adjusting his jacket.

They entered the Chambers, eyes looking up from the table at the three of them as they walked in together and went to their seats. Bryce sat down at the far end of the table along the side. Henry looked around the table, eyes resting on the empty chair belonging to Dr. Powell, his science advisor. "Where's Tadeuz?"

"I'm here, Henry." Doctor Powell's voice spoke over the room's speakers. "I got locked in at the school when the pressure doors came down."

Grayson nodded. "Fine. What can you tell me about what happened?"

A brief pause and a noise that sounded like static, probably from someone breathing through their nose into a microphone. "Not much. Yet. Still waiting on imagery from Olympus." There was rustling on the microphone and then he continued. "We have word of a bolide entering the atmosphere and *probably* impacting somewhere north east of us towards Tharsis Tholus. If I had contact with Lighthouse…"

"You don't." Grayson clenched his teeth, shooting a glance towards Bryce. "Let me know when you have something, please. Can anyone tell me what's going on?"

Daniel Perkins cleared his throat. "I lost contact with one of our mining teams this morning. Just outside of Hades Terminal in tunnel twelve, section twenty nine." His voice was gruff but Bryce could sense his nervousness. He was concerned.

"Do you think there was a collapse?" Natalie asked the Mining Director.

"Don't know yet. I hope not. We have a lot of people based out of Hades."

"Not to mention equipment," Keith Turnbull from Resources observed.

Grayson ignored them. "Anything else?"

Dr. Muriel Tanner, the head of Agriculture, waited to see if anyone else was going to say anything and when they didn't, she sat forward. "The domes have gone into lockdown. They sealed themselves when the pressure warning activated."

Grayson pinched the bridge of his nose, a headache forming. "All of them?"

"All five. Yes."

There was murmuring around the table. Natalie pursed her lips.

Grayson held up a hand, spoke over the babble. "We lost pressure in Dome 3. Can we get inside the others?"

"We're working on it with the city's engineering teams."

"Marvellous."

Bryce stood up. "I need to get in contact with Lighthouse. If I can't get up there today, we need to at least find out if they saw anything."

Doctor Kanan Soma regarded him from across the table. "You shut off your station comms. How do you propose we talk to them?"

Bryce shook his head. "I don't know yet."

023

LIGHTHOUSE

Emma rubbed her newly-shaved head, looking out the windows in the small boardroom, anti-spinward from the Command Deck. She was seated at the table, her tablet in front of her. The large monitors on the wall showed Mars and a tracery of curves indicating possible trajectories with numeric call-outs corresponding to the different calculations she and Greg had run.

Mars rolled past below as the hab section revolved in space. They were moving across the dark side now, the Tharsis Highlands with Ascraeus Mons and smaller Pavonis Mons on the edge of the planet, brightly backlit against the setting Sun. The mushroom cloud from the impact had spread out and dissipated into a sea of dust, obscuring the surface when they'd last seen it an hour ago.

"Gah!" Greg, sitting on the floor with his back to the windows, tossed his tablet onto the carpet in front of him. "I can't make any of this work. Want some breakfast?"

"Not hungry," Emma replied. One of the trajectories she was working on was starting to make sense: T05. She looked at the monitor and the almost straight line radiating up from the surface into space.

"Well, I'm gonna get something." Greg stood up, stomped to the door onto the Command Deck.

"OK." Emma was barely aware she'd just answered him.

She stood up and dragged her tablet off the shiny table top and walked onto the deck, low lights and quiet beeping from the workstations surrounding her as she walked to her desk at the science station.

Dr. Nelson Ortega was in his seat, frowning and rocking his chair rhythmically.

Emma cleared her throat. "Nelson, I think I have an origin for the projectile."

He looked up at her, expressionless. "Let me see."

Emma sat down and transferred the contents of her tablet to his screen. She rolled through the back-trace, starting from the impact point indicated by a red dot on the surface, a line arcing up from the planet into space and then curving back into the asteroid belt. She stopped the animation when the timecode read 177:18:54:13.008.

Ortega blinked at her. She explained, "This solution is possible with a projectile mass of about two hundred kilograms and a force consistent with the anti-matter propulsions we saw in the Object. About sixty megajoules, I figure." Ortega shook his head in disbelief. The numbers didn't make sense to him, even though they had plenty of supporting evidence.

She ran the animation forward again. The transit took two days to reach the surface.

"I'd like to verify this. Can I have Watchtower for the afternoon? I need to run some scans."

Ortega nodded. "No. No contact, remember?"

She frowned and rolled over to her station, frustrated. "How are we supposed to do anything if we can't get access to our telescopes?"

"We have to wait for the reboot."

Emma sighed and poked at her tablet, frustrated.

Sunil Pradeep sat awkwardly in the Commander's chair drumming his fingers on the arm rest. Emma felt sorry for him for some reason. She felt like he'd been put into this position when Bryce left. Worse, he'd left in the middle of an emergency. She didn't really understand the need to go below and talk to the council when he could've done the same from up here. They were cut off and crippled.

"Keep the station running," he'd told Sunil.

And now something had struck the surface and they weren't even able to do anything about it or find out what was going on. She looked at her station, the timelapse video of Earth rolling in a corner of the screen.

She watched Sunil, staring intently out the windows onto Mars below. Ascraeus Mons rolled into the shadow of the Sun.

"Radio silence," he said aloud.

He stood up and walked over to the comm station. Jill Sanchez had her headphones on, listening to the voices from engineering on VHF.

He tapped her shoulder and she flinched, pushing one of the cups back off her ear, pulling her hair with it.

"Sorry?" she said with a start, worried she'd been ignoring the acting Commander's voice.

Sunil smiled at her. "I just had an idea. Are you picking up anything from the Colony's ground crew communications? They're all still using analog radios, aren't they?"

"Sure. Land Mobile VHF. I pick them up every time we pass over, but it's faint. Why?"

"We should be able to broadcast on their band too, should we not?"

She thought about it. "Yeah, sure. We've got plenty of signal power to reach them."

He grinned. "Next pass, I want you to open a channel with them. Say hello and see how they're doing. That impact was awfully close to the colony."

Jill smiled back at him, excited to be able to do something useful. "I'll get a transmitter ready."

"Excellent."

The next pass was in two hours.

024

DOME 3

"Don't panic!" Tamra yelled, her suit's microphone clipping in the ears of the other students.

Rory collapsed to his knees, tearing at his neck. "Can't breathe," he wheezed as Joe grabbed his hands and checked his hood seals, making sure his rebreather was connected and working.

"You're just freaking out! Relax and breathe. In and out..." Nils held his friend's wrists and stared into his face through the clear, thin hood, willing him to calm down. Rory followed and his breathing relaxed.

Tamra paced on the floor of the farmhouse lobby as Joe ran in from outside. "Any contact from below?"

Nils shook his head. "Don't know." He gestured to the half-open elevator doors and shrugged.

Tamra looked down through the open elevator doors again, the empty shaft descending into darkness. "Elevator crashed." She turned to Joe. "Have you seen Doctor Chandler or Hector?" She could hear the fear in her own voice and squeezed her hands together to try to ground herself. Her heart was fluttering in her chest. Was she low on oxygen already? She shivered and rubbed her arms, the station lobby was already cooling down rapidly.

Joe, looking uncomfortable and shaken, cast his eyes to the ground. Dust swirled around his feet. "I saw Hector." He looked up and shook his head.

She'd never seen Hector wear a pressure suit. Most of the workers never did. If Doctor Chandler hadn't threatened the students with a failing grade, they wouldn't be wearing them either. It was usually too hot under the magnified sunlight and they hadn't had a pressure leak in fifty years. She felt the panic rising up in her again and fought it back down. What would Greg do? she asked herself, then almost started laughing at the thought. He would never be able to be up here in the first place, his agoraphobia – or whatever it was – kept him underground. Except now, he was aboard Lighthouse. She struggled with her thoughts, trying to focus herself on the present.

"OK, what have we got? Our suits are good for about thirty minutes, tops, of recycled air."

Nils stood up and Rory had regained control of himself. "We should have some extra air bottles in the kitchen."

Tamra nodded, remembering her emergency training. "Hey, that's right. Let's get an inventory."

The four students walked into the "kitchen" area – a combination storage area, harvest station and recreation room. A rack of suits and air bottles lined one wall opposite a monitor and couches. Nils took a couple of bottles off the rack and slid them into the pockets on his legs. Joe and Rory did the same.

Tamra inspected the wall and grabbed a couple of bottles. "OK, this buys us a lot more time. Gives us some options." She still had seventy-five percent of her first air bottle left. "Don't start switching air until we need to."

Joe did anyway, popping and unscrewing his suit's bottle on his left leg and replacing it with one of the fresh ones from the wall.

"What did I just say?" Tamra walked over to him, annoyed.

Joe grinned at her and plugged his bottle back into a receptacle on the wall. It began recharging. "The air reclaimer's still running. There's probably still enough oxygen inside the dome, even with the pressure drop, for this thing to keep us in air for... I don't know. Months."

"Doubt it." Nils shook his head. "We're probably filling up on stored oxygen. Not sure there's enough pressure left to run the reclaimer. We usually have to vent extra oxygen outside or down to the city to prevent the domes from over-filling. Plants are pretty good at stripping O2."

Tamra grimaced. "Whatever. We've got enough air for now. We need to figure out what we're going to do."

Just then, a man ran into the room wearing a pressure suit, followed by three others, gasping for air. "Oh, thank God. We thought we were the only ones."

The four students looked at one another. Tamra stepped forward and put her hand on the lead man's arm. "Are you OK? Are there any others?"

The men were all breathing hard. They must have run from far out, a couple of hundred meters, anyway, the weaker pressure inside their suits making physical exertion that much harder on them. The man shook his head. "We looked. These were all I found. Nobody wears their damned suits anymore." His suit's name badge read SHORE, K.

One of the other men regained his breath. "Everyone's dead. The plants are dead." He shook his head, his eyes wide. "We're dead."

Tamra held out her hands, pleading for calm despite her returning panic. She handed Shore an air bottle from the wall. "Look, we've got air here. We should be fine until the elevator's repaired. We'll be OK."

Another one of the men, CARSON, G., turned on her. "'OK?' My wife was out there! I watched her die because her suit didn't work. Oh God, her face." Carson dropped to his knees. "She was always telling me to wear a suit."

This was too much for Tamra to deal with. She turned away and sat down on one of the benches.

Joe sat next to her. You couldn't whisper in a pressure suit, your voice was broadcast over radio, but he lowered his voice anyway. "We could wait for the elevator and a rescue team. Or we could try to rescue ourselves."

Tamra turned her head to look at him. Rory and Nils were watching.

"You were asking us what we should do. I think we've got three options."

Rory didn't know where his friend was going with this. "I like the 'wait to be rescued' option."

"That's number one," Joe acknowledged, raising a finger. "Number two is we go down the elevator shaft ourselves and see what the problem is." He noticed the three newcomers were watching them.

The third man stepped forward, KEATING, D. "You know how stupid that is?"

Rory turned to see who was talking. "It sure sounds stupid."

The man joined the group of students. "Don Keating. Engineering," he introduced himself and continued as if reading from memory: "In the event of a pressure drop, the elevator shaft closes itself from below to prevent loss of seal in the colony. It's 'broken' because of the fail-safe. They'll need to repair it and they can't do that until pressure's restored up here."

"But that's..." Joe started.

"That's going to be hard. Yes," Keating finished for him.

"Oh, God." Carson sank to his knees.

A quiet descended on the room.

Nils broke the silence. "Joe, what was the third option?"

Joe nodded. "Option three: We go outside."

025

ROVER 2

The drive across the sand and rock outside Dome 5 had been made more treacherous than usual by the fierce winds and limited visibility. More than once Erika had to warn Aden to watch out for a boulder that could have damaged one of their wheels or worse, broken an axle. That left her on edge in her seat as Aden, cavalier as ever, continued driving the heavy rover as if it were indestructible, grinning and chewing the rubber hose between his teeth.

It was only two kilometers between each of the domes, but there wasn't exactly a smooth surface to drive on. They had no roads. At one time, the Dome Planning committee had proposed tube tunnels between each dome on the surface, but that was deemed too expensive, the materials were put to better use on building another dome. So they drove across the sand. The tracks the rovers dug with their big carbon mesh wheels were obscured a day later by the Martian winds. Visibility was another problem. Statically charged particles of sand and dust clung to the windshield and had to be wiped off. After more than a year in service, the windshield of Rover 2 was pitted and scratched nearly white.

They were rolling alongside Dome 4 on their right, lit up from inside, the windows glowing in the gloomy afternoon light. Erika turned and peered through the side window from her seat, risking a moment to look away from the terrain ahead. Inside the five domes, arranged as points on a hexagon, Dome 6 was under still construction after nearly two revolutions. A shell of steel grew up from the sand floor at the base of the dead volcano. The cranes and support towers around the structure were all but invisible in the dusty gloom. Another storm would set them back another month, the construction crews would have to clean everything off again.

Aden hit a rock that jolted the rover, bouncing Ray off the couch behind them and Erika against her belts, the suspension buckling underneath.

"Whoa!" Ray yelled from the floor as he scrambled back up onto the couch.

"You should have your belt on with Reed driving," Erika advised.

"Hey, you don't like it, feel free to take a walk. The exercise would do you some good." Aden shot a glance over at Erika sitting beside him as he steered around another boulder. They passed the edge of Dome 4 and rolled out onto the open sand. Dome 3 was merely a grey suggestion on the horizon two kilometers ahead.

"What the hell is that supposed to mean?"

Aden glanced over again. "Just sayin', you could tone up a bit, is all."

Erika's eyes narrowed. "Asshole." She resumed scanning the terrain in front of them for a second, then stood up and made her way to the back. "Your turn to copilot, Ray. Our driver's being a dick. Again."

Erika waited while Ray got up and awkwardly made his way forward, hand over hand on the hand-rails along the cabin. She flopped down onto the couch and pulled the belts over her, then covered up in the dirty blanket they all shared.

"What're we looking for, anyway?" Ray asked as he buckled himself in.

"I dunno. Check for damage or some shit."

Aden hit another rock and Erika was nearly ejected from the couch. "Watch the wheels!" Erika yelled.

It took them nearly twenty minutes to drive the two kilometers to Dome 3. Aden managed to not break anything along the way.

Erika crept forward from the couch to look through the scratched-up glass of the cockpit bubble. Aden edged their vehicle forward, the big rover rocking on its suspension.

The glass and steel dome rising up overhead before them was opaque in the dust storm. The interior was dark. "Shouldn't there be lights on inside?" Erika asked from behind the seats.

"Yeah, probably," Ray answered, not really knowing.

Aden thumbed his mic on. "Control, what are we looking for out here, over?"

Static on the radio.

"Control? This is Rover 2, do you copy, over?"

More static.

"Must be a lot of interference from this dust storm. Lotta charged particles," Ray offered.

The radio crackled, and this time a female voice broke through. "Ground vehicle, this is Lighthouse Station, do you read, over?"

Aden and Ray looked at each other. Aden flipped his mic on. "Lighthouse, this is Aden Reed aboard Rover 2. We copy, over."

Some crackling and a high-pitched whine on the radio. "Rover 2, it's good to hear your voice. We've been cut off for days now. Did you see the meteor strike? Over."

"Lighthouse, we saw it. Is this dust storm some kind of fallout from that? Over?"

The radio crackled. "The impact appeared to be near Tharsis Crater, 80 klicks East-north-east. Over…"

More crackling. Then. "Rover 2, who are you talking to? Over?"

Aden looked at Ray again, about to respond when Lighthouse answered for him. "Ground control, this is Lighthouse Station. We only have a few more minutes, but will be passing by again in another 23 minutes. Requesting permission to use this channel as relay. Over."

More crackling. "Affirmative, Lighthouse. Good to hear from you. Please advise with any information about…" The channel fizzled as the wind blew up again and the sky darkened.

The Rover crew waited but no reply was forthcoming. Aden thumbed his mic on again. "Ground control, what are we looking for out here, over?"

More crackling.

Erika still leaned on the backs of the seats. "Well, I guess that was that. Too much interference."

Aden gripped the butterfly-shaped steering wheel, pulling the steering column back into position in front of him. "Ray, hit the floods, make sure we're recording. I'm going to do a pass around the outside of Dome 3. See if we can see anything."

The lights snapped on, shining brightly against the wall of particles around them. "We're live."

Erika flopped back on the couch and pulled the monitor closer to her, watching the view from outside as the Rover began rolling around the base of Dome 3.

026

DOME 3

She was getting cold.

Tamra could see her breath inside her pressure suit's clear bubble. Frost was forming near the sides of her vision on the clear material. Warm air from her breathing was causing condensation to run down the inside of the inflated helmet. The combination of cold compressed air mixed with the heat and moisture from her body made it impossible to stay warm.

Joe and Nils were busy gathering the gear they thought they'd need to make the trek to the next dome: blankets, overalls, various pieces of clothing, air bottles all gathered together in a pile on the concrete floor. Tamra and Rory huddled close, his arm around her shoulders under a shiny polyester blanket.

"Temperature's dropping fast." Kevin Shore, one of the workers who'd joined their group, grabbed a set of coveralls out of a locker and climbed into them, zipping them up over his suit. He snatched a blanket and wrapped it around himself, jogging in place to keep warm.

"Look, this is a really terrible idea." Don Keating, the engineer, was watching Nils and Joe going through their equipment. "These suits aren't designed for surface excursions. We've got limited air with us. What if we can't get into the other dome?"

The third man who'd joined them, Gerald Carson said, "There's no way I'm going outside. I'll take my chances here." Kevin and Don looked at him, weighing the option in their heads. Joe handed Tamra and Rory each a set of coveralls and a heavy jacket.

Nils was going through lockers looking for work boots big enough to fit over their feet in the pressure suits. He looked up at the men standing around in the grey equipment room, green pressure suits obscured by bits of found clothing and blankets. He shook his head. "You guys are going to freeze in here. Or run out of air."

"We can figure out a way to stay warm." Carson was walking along the walls, looking at the inactive electric heaters.

"No you can't," Nils countered. "There's not enough atmosphere in here to hold temperature. You'll freeze to death."

Keating held up a finger. "Actually, vacuum's a pretty good insulator. It's all the concrete and stone that's going to suck the heat out of you. It's minus twenty Celsius outside. It'll be close to that in here when the concrete radiates the last of its heat away. But nighttime is going to get much colder."

Shore, still jogging in place and breathing hard, stopped and rubbed his arms. He walked to the wall and grabbed another air bottle, replaced the one on his hip. He took a big gulp of air. "He's right, Gerald. No way we can survive in here if it takes them a day to get in here. No telling how long they'll be reopening the elevators."

"I'm not going out there." Carson didn't sound like he was going to argue with anyone about it.

Keating put a hand on Carson's shoulder and pointed at the floor. "If you stay off the floors and walls, let the thin atmosphere give you some insulation, you should be ok for a while."

"I'll stay with him," Kevin said.

Tamra and Rory looked at each other, horrified.

"We'll be OK. People will come soon," Kevin reassured the room and himself.

"You don't have to," Joe told him. "It's only a couple of kilometers to the next dome. We can make it."

"I know. We'd rather stay here," Kevin answered.

Gerald nodded. "Thanks, Kevin. We've got air, blankets and clothing. We'll be fine for a few hours, at least."

"Alright, we all ready?" Joe asked the rest of the crew. "We've got four air bottles each. Two should get us there." He slung his four bottles in their slings over his shoulders. He was wrapped up in a heavy coat and mylar blanket. He gave Tamra a knitted hat to add to her ensemble.

She squeezed the hat over her bubble and felt it collapse against her head and ears. She hoped it would keep her head from freezing. Rory had a hoodie he'd pulled over his helmet. The other two wrapped blankets over their heads like robes.

Tamra stood up. She was ready. "Alright. We get outside, then head for Dome 2. That's northwest, left of the entrance. Got it?"

Rory took a breath. "Let's do this."

Joe nodded. "We hurry, but don't run. Try not to burn oxygen. And don't get separated. Outside we link up. Let's go."

The four students and the engineer all gave a solemn nod and a wave to Gerald and Kevin as they left the locker room.

The team was silent until they were outside the building. Don said, "I'm glad Kevin's staying with him. Pretty sure Carson was going back outside to his wife."

Inside the dome was eerily silent. Gone was the constant buzzing of drones and workers talking and yelling, or the chunking sounds of shovels in dirt or rustling of leaves. Tamra looked at one of the sweet potato plants sticking out of its bed and fought back a tear at the sight of the leaves already frozen and cracking. The big trees in the distance glistened with frost as the moisture was sucked out of them onto their surface, turning instantly to ice in the decreased atmosphere. One had split down the middle. Dead. Tamra didn't know if any of them could be saved.

Then she saw the first body. It was contorted in an arched, twisted position on the ground, hands curled into claws, eyes wide and frozen. Red splotches on exposed skin. Mouth baring teeth and a swollen tongue. She realized it was Hector and suddenly felt like she was going to throw up. Rory grabbed her and pushed her forward. "Keep moving. Don't look at them."

They hurried forward across the floor of the dome. All of the carefully cultured soil in here was lost, Tamra knew. Tonnes of wasted compost. They might be able to salvage some of the root plants if they dug them out in time, but they'd have to get them within hours before they became completely desiccated.

And the bodies. They moved through the different plots, past the soy plants. The coffee plantation. The citrus groves. Banana trees. All around were bodies of the workers who were tending and caring for these plants. Hundreds of them.

"Why didn't you wear your suits?" Tamra asked the rigid bodies. She was numb, looking around at the devastation like she was watching a film, detached from herself.

"Come on. Keep moving." Rory held her arm, pulling her forward behind Joe and Nils.

"We're almost to the airlock," Joe announced.

Keating was behind them, trudging along in his multiple layers like a big inflated pillow. "What a waste."

The team arrived at the airlock, a big metal door with a tiny window set into a box under the edge of the glass and steel dome. The terrain outside beyond the glass was an indistinct brown and grey. Dust from the surface whipped against the dome from the gale-force winds.

Nils turned and faced everyone. "We should be about halfway through our current air bottles. We can either switch now or risk doing it outside. I suggest a switch."

Keating nodded. "Good idea. The less we have to change outside the better." He reached inside his coat and dug out an air bottle. "Are you all sure about this? It could be pretty rough out there. We're not going to be able to move very fast, so it could take a while."

Nils shrugged. "What choice have we got? If they don't get this dome opened before sundown, we're all going to die anyway."

They all nodded, murmuring assent before unscrewing quick-release valves from their current air bottles and replacing them with full ones. Tamra struggled to get hers lined up in the receptacle on her hip, the teeth refusing to line up. "I can't get mine."

Rory grabbed her hands and twisted the bottle until the teeth found their purchase, then pushed down and turned until the bottle locked into place. "And this is why we did this here." He smiled at Tamra, pulled her jacket closed over her sweater and overalls and zipped her up.

"OK, Don. Can you open this for us?" Nils pointed at the keypad on the airlock.

Don stepped forward and mashed his hand onto the pad and both doors swung open, wind and dust billowing in from outside. "It's on override. We're at equilibrium with the surface now."

"That's convenient," Joe observed.

They pulled their hoods and blankets tighter against their heads and walked through the airlock into the maelstrom outside. One hundred and forty kilometer per hour winds blasted them with dust and sand, catching their bulky clothes and blankets like flags. Tamra's hat blew away almost instantly, exposing her head, and she tried to hoist up her jacket around her helmet. She felt the freezing wind whipping against her body through the thick layers of clothing.

Joe turned around and faced the team, hunkered down, face obscured by sand gusting past. "Everybody stay low and hold on!" He extended a hand and Tamra grabbed it as he turned and began crab walking through the dust and dirt. He hauled Tamra behind him and she reached back and grabbed hold of Rory. Nils and Don linked up behind them, the wind at their backs.

Nils hollered over the howling wind, "Keep low! Hang onto each other!"

The five crawled forward half a meter at a time, feet and knees digging into the soft sand, those in the middle of the chain stumbling without a free hand to balance themselves in the dirt. Dome 2 was invisible two kilometers distant. Beyond that, the dead volcano of Ascraeus Mons stood like a larger version of the domes, stretching off into the sky, a red-black mound that filled the hazy horizon. The flat caldera was lost beyond the curve of the planet fifty kilometers away.

027

MACHINE PARTS

Sean sat on the warm metal floor of the control shed, knees bent, his back propped against the wall by the door. He was getting hungry, but didn't want to eat the stale breakfast bar he was saving for dinner.

Mike was still in the shed with him, waiting for the management team and cleaners to arrive. An emergency team had arrived on the scene shortly after the incident. Perkins had been taken away to get cleaned up and hopefully receive some help. Sean would never forget the look on his face, his wide eyes staring out of a face covered in Steel's blood. The face haunted him. Steel's access card was on the desk beside him, still smeared in blood.

It had been nearly two hours since the shutdown and they hadn't received any word from outside. Attempts to login to the control terminals were met with "System Lockout" screens.

Instead, he dug into his backpack and brought out his broken tablet. He spread the cracked screen, attached to the main body by ribbon connectors, on his knees.

"Whatcha doin' there?" Mike asked him, bored without anything to do.

Sean looked up from the mess in front of him. "Trying to reconnect this screen. It got broken." Sensing this was an unsatisfactory summary, he added, "When I fell on it."

Mike leaned over in his chair. "Looks pretty bad. Mind if I try?"

Sean hesitated for a second, then passed the broken mess in a stack across the short distance. "It's reconnected but doesn't seem to get any power. It's toast." He leaned on Mike's control desk and his hand brushed Steel's card. He looked down at it and picked it up. Her face looked up at him, expressionless eyes and a slight curl at the corner of her mouth. He picked at the encrusted blood on one of the corners and it scraped off under his thumbnail.

Mike picked up the screen and tablet gingerly, making sure not to put any stress on the connector. He swivelled his chair around and placed the screen facedown on his bench, the tablet still facing up. "Y'know, I used to work in Electronics Assembly. Used to put together ten to twenty of these things a day." He peeled back the layer of insulation from the tablet's circuit board, a thin sheet of blue shock-absorbent material that isolated the screen from the battery and electronics. He turned his head back to look at Sean. "Where'd you get this? I never saw one of these before." He squinted at the board, scanning the edge for a model and serial number. None of these pieces seemed to belong together.

"I built it. From parts." Sean flapped Steel's card against the desk.

"No shit?" Mike pried the board away from the casing, sticky resin-like glue trailing away in strands. He looked at the back for a moment, sniffed it briefly, then pressed it back into its case. "I don't see any damage. Doesn't smell like anything's fried."

"I'm hoping it's just the screen."

"Could be." Mike pressed the screen back over the control board and thumbed the power stud on the side. Nothing. "Can't tell if it's got a charge or not. Yer gonna need a new screen anyway. Want me to req one?"

Sean's eyes widened. "I don't think..."

Mike wheeled over to the requisition terminal in the corner and activated it with his card. The terminal beeped as it let him in. "Don't worry about it. I've still got access to electronics." He descended through the menus, tapping on the icons that took him into tablets, then components. "We'll get you fixed up with a new battery while we're in here. Still not sure about that board, but it's probably got all your stuff on it."

Sean nodded.

Mike checked over the parts list one last time, flagged it for pickup, then hit the Submit button. "Done. You can go down and pick it up. You know how to get to Electronics Assembly?"

"Just down the hall, isn't it?"

"It's in Southwest block. Can't really miss it. Ask for Gabe."

"I can just go there... now?"

"Yeah, why not? We're not doing anything here. Whole system's locked down while we wait for the cleanup." He winced, remembering the source of the outage. Mike looked back out through the windows at the idle machines hissing outside the shed. "Just check back in here before going outside. Resource Management might have some questions for you."

Sean gulped, not enthusiastic about any attention. "OK."

"Just procedure. Nothing to worry about."

"OK."

"Go on." Mike was about to wheel back to his station when a thought struck him. "Hey, swing by the commissary on your way back. Bring me a coffee and something to eat."

Sean gulped again. "Um." He felt uncomfortable using the commissary. He knew he shouldn't but it still felt weird having unfettered access to food. What if someone recognized him? What if someone asked him what he was doing there? If he was allowed to be there?

"I don't care what. Just whatever. Go on. Take Steel's card there. Should get you into electronics if you need it."

"OK." Sean pocketed the card and opened the shed door, entering the outer hall. Yellow lights were cycling in the hallway, apparently warning whoever approached that the Machine Parts facility was in lockdown. He turned right at the end of the hallway and followed the signs west. He'd normally go the other way to leave. Another exit to Industrial Avenue came up on his left and a group of workers he didn't recognize were gathered around it.

"How long are we gonna be stuck here? I gotta check on my kid," one of the workers was saying.

"Can't keep us in here like this. This is bullshit."

Sean pushed through them and passed the entrance to the commissary. People were milling inside, or sitting around tables talking. He'd go in later, on his way back.

He continued down the long hallway, smooth concrete walls running on into the distance. There were doors to a gymnasium and locker rooms. A library of technical manuals. One entrance was flanked by a felt board covered in posters. He glanced at one of them on his way past, a man wearing a Fabricators' Union jacket standing by the doorway giving him the eyeball. "You don't look like you got the revs for those." The board was covered in job postings for different positions, with lists of technical requirements and seniority measured in months or revs at the end. He knew it bordered the road outside, but without any windows, it felt like he was in another world, cut off from the city. He passed another dark corridor on his right with white on black signage pointing to *PLASTICS, MATERIALS,* and *TEXTILES.* Eventually he reached a pair of double doors, signs reading *ELECTRONICS ASSEMBLY.* He tried the door, but it was locked. He took out Steel's access card and waved it over the lock and surprised himself that it opened for him. He walked in.

Inside was a long space, maybe a hundred meters in length and fifty meters wide. Rows of benches and tables with overhead task-lighting ran along the space, each row occupying maybe five meters. Electric buggies with trailers rolled through the aisles on the sides, carting parts or finished products away from the benches. Each work station had a set of tools, parts bins and various accoutrements specific to each job.

Nothing was moving. The rows of assembly stations were mostly empty. Yellow lights flashed.

"You supposed to be in here?"

Sean snapped out of his daze and turned to look at the woman standing beside him. "Um. I'm looking for Gabe."

"Yer lookin' at her." She thrust her chin out, appraising the visitor with mock seriousness. Dermal implants in her nose and cheeks flashed in the lights. "What can I do you for?"

"Oh. Uh. Mike sent me. From Machine Parts."

"Right!" She brightened up and started walking along the edge of the workstations. "Come on over here. I'll get your parts."

Gabe was tall and took big strides through the huge open space. Sean had to jog to keep up with her. "Why is it so empty?"

"Huh? Oh, it's always like this. We don't have a lot to do most days. Most tech gets recycled or repaired. We don't make new tech very often. Not to mention, we haven't been getting any new silicon, er, semiconductors for a couple of months now. They say the production's all tied up? I don't know what they're talking about... Still getting some good replacement parts, though."

Sean nodded along, not really understanding what she was talking about, trying to keep up. He noticed something on the task station he was passing and without even thinking about it, reached down and picked it up, stashing it in his pocket, holding it there.

Gabe turned down one of the aisles and walked past an older man with white hair soldering a connection on a board. He looked up, magnifying glass on his face over a pair of bulging lenses and he regarded Sean with a gigantic eye. She walked past him to another station and started rifling through the bins on the desk. "Screen, battery. Here you go. Need anything else?"

"Um. I don't think so." He thought for a second, feeling the weight of the card writer in his pocket. He considered asking for a couple of network repeaters, but didn't want to push his luck. He looked longingly at the assembly station and its collection of soldering tools and supplies. "That's it." He wished he'd brought his tablet with him to complete the repairs here.

"Well, alright. Tell Mike to give me a call. You guys on lock down too?"

"Uh, yeah."

"Damn. No idea what's going on... What's your name?"

"Sean."

"Sean," she repeated. "Nice to meet you. Come see me if you ever need a change of scenery. Can always use a pair of steady hands on a soldering iron."

The man with the magnifying glass over his eye frowned and bent back down to his work.

028

ROVER 2

They were a quarter of the way around the perimeter of Dome 3 when Erika spotted the crack in the dome on her screen. "Guys? Are you seeing this?" On her monitor, a dark fissure ran from the base of the dome up the side, along the steel support structure. The seals split along the seams in a jagged line running fifteen meters up the wall. Thick broken glass hung like teeth in the frames and scattered around the base where it had blown out. "It's like the dome split from expansion."

Ray whistled. "That's not good."

Aden brought them to a stop and backed up, churning sand in front of the rover, making it hard to see through the lights and cameras. He flicked his mic on and spoke into it. "Control, Rover 2. We found the source of the breach in Dome 3. Well, one of them anyway. Over." Static crackled back over the radio. "Damned interference." He turned in his seat and looked at the damage through the side window, thumbing his mic back on. "Control? Do you copy?"

Erika. "Ray, can you move the lights around inside? See if that's all the way through." She knew it was. They could all tell even in the dusty afternoon gloom.

"Yup." Ray moved the lights on the roof with his controller, panning them back and forth across the fissure. A dark shadow on the ground in the concrete base showed under the lights. "Oh…"

Erika squinted at her screen. "How the hell are they going to repair this?"

"I don't know. It's going to be a big job. Too big for us today. Need a full engineering crew," Aden replied, still waiting for instructions on his radio. He tried again. "Control, this is Rover 2. We have found a breach in Dome 3. Please advise, over."

Static.

Erika pushed her monitor aside and stood up, moving forward in the cabin. "Maybe we should we get out and take a look."

Ray visibly tensed up. "Not it," he said from the front seat.

Aden shook his head. "Nah, I don't think so. Let's keep doing our circuit. Might have better reception on the other side, closer to base." He pulled the steering column back into position and the big machine woke up.

"Alright." Erika flopped back down on the couch, pulling her monitor back into position.

Ray pulled a bag of cereal out of the side pocket in his chair and pushed a handful into his mouth. "How much food have we got in here, anyway?"

Aden, watching the terrain ahead of them, answered with mild annoyance, "The usual. About a week's worth."

Erika sighed. "Got a cupboard full of brotein and hashbrowns back here."

Ray continued munching on his granola. "Check the dates?"

"Fucksakes, Ray. No." Erika stared daggers into the back of his head from the couch. "Keep your eyes on the dome."

"What are we even looking for? We found the breach."

"Dunno. Maybe more damage?" Aden asked. He swerved to avoid a rock. "Looks like we're comin' up on the north airlock." He pointed ahead of them and they focused on the windows and monitors. He eased back on the throttle and they slowed down. The wind whipped sand at the front of the RV, pelting the windshield with small stones.

"Looks like the door's open," Ray said, squinting into the storm.

"Control. Rover 2. Dome 3's airlock door is open. Can you confirm, over?"

Erika scanned the scene on her monitor, then got up and peered through the glass bubble in the cockpit. "I can't see anything from in here. I'm going outside."

Ray crunched at her, mouth full of granola. "Not it?"

She sighed. "Be ready if I need you." She swatted his arm for punctuation and turned, stooping as she made her way to the back of the RV and her suit.

She climbed in and fixed her seals. Helmet and gloves, all locking into place with clicks. She felt her left wrist seal grind and pulled her glove back off, raising her visor and blowing on the ring around the glove. She checked her wrist seal as best she could on the arm of her suit, wiping it with one of the fingers of her detached glove before putting it back on with a crunch. "You read me, Aden?"

"Yeah, I hear you."

"Next time I come back in, I'm staying for the cleaning cycle. We've got sand all over the place in here."

"That's a good idea."

"Ok, going out." She entered the airlock and cycled out. The outer door swung open and she bounced down to the sand below. As soon as she left the lee of the rover, she was blasted by wind and sand. "Woo! It's still blowin' out here!"

Her radio crackled. "Just be careful. Visibility's shit."

"Roger that." She walked forward between the rover and the dome, boots crunching in the grainy sand underfoot. She wasn't in any risk of blowing away, despite the one hundred and forty kilometer per hour winds. There wasn't enough air pressure for that. But it did make waking somewhat more difficult and the particulates were getting into every nook and cranny of her suit, turning it a tawny brown.

She approached the dome's open airlock, sand already blowing a small dune inside the room-sized cubical space. The inner door was open to the interior. A dust devil churned inside the airlock. "Aden, you seeing this?"

"Yeah. Get a look inside for control?"

"Yep." She checked her helmet cam and turned on her lights just for good measure, making sure she was recording. She stepped forward and peered into the gloom inside the dome. Plants and trees had leaves hanging off them, already covered in dust, some trees were split in half and fallen over, the sudden freeze combined with the drop in pressure blowing them apart like bombs. She scanned back and forth for a moment, taking it all in. "I don't see anything moving." In the fields, she could see immobile forms on the ground. She stepped forward and almost tripped over a dead chicken, its eyes bulging and frozen. "This isn't good."

029

THARSIS: DUNE 12

"Are we going in the right direction?" Tamra yelled over the high-pitched whistle of wind buffeting her face. Her jacket was hoisted up around her head in an attempt to keep her ears from freezing. The collar flapped around her suit's hood in the minus eighty degree Celsius wind. She could barely see Joe ahead of her, even though he was holding her hand and dragging her forward through the cold sand around her ankles.

Joe turned back and she could see him yelling but couldn't hear anything on her suit's radio. She shook her head, mouthed the word "headset". He turned back around and continued dragging her; she in turn pulled on Rory's hand.

They were walking in a line along the ridge of Dune 12, informally named Hilda. In the nearly seventy revolutions humans had been on Mars, Hilda had moved almost a full kilometer across the Tharsis plateau on a slow march between Dome 2 and 3. In another seventy revolutions it would be on the base of Dome 6, assuming the dome had finished construction by then. The loose sand was prone to shifting and walking along it was precarious. Moving carefully along the ridge, half crawling, half crouching, in clearer moments, they could just make out the bulge of Dome 2 in the distance before the sand rose up off the side of the dune into their faces again. The wind buffeted and pressed the loose clear hoods into their cheeks and faces, threatening to suffocate them.

She'd lost track of time. Had they been out for an hour yet? She pulled back on Joe, jerking his hand and he turned around, face partly obscured by the dust and sand stuck to his face mask. She pointed at her hip and the air bottle dangling there under the blanket she wore like a parka. Rory bumped into her from behind, the tiny train bunching up on the dune.

Everyone huddled together, crouching down in the sand. Tamra could see Nils talking but couldn't hear anything. She punched the side of her head and heard her headset crackle, a single word, "freeze," made it through. Tamra pointed at her head again and Rory shook his, mouthed or yelled something at her through his hood under a thick woollen hat. It looked like he said he couldn't understand. She wiped some of the sand off her face mask, leaving a streak of scratches in the soft flexible bubble. Her visibility was getting worse by the minute.

She yelled, senselessly and incoherently, a ragged howl of rage trapped inside the bubble of her protective head-covering. Rory recoiled slightly, surprised and afraid, possibly hearing her through the thin Martian atmosphere.

Tamra took a breath of stale air and looked down at her hip, uncovered the air bottle under her wrap-around blanket. The gauge was reading empty through the thin layer of dust caked onto the display. She waved her hands at the group, made an O in the air, pointed at her air bottle, then slashed her hand in front of her throat: *dead* as the wind whipped a blast of sand at them. Joe's blanket and overalls flapped around and he tied the corners into a tighter knot around his neck. Nils checked his own bottle and proceeded to pull it out with a hiss.

Tamra took out one of her four bottles and held it upside down to her chest. She twisted the spent bottle in the fitting and popped it out, then dropped the replacement into the slot, turning it to lock it in, feeling the grit crunching in the seal. Sand had worked its way into the socket. She heard a hiss in her helmet and took a breath of cold air. She put the spent bottle into the newly vacated spot on her harness.

She helped Rory do the same with his air bottle, Joe helping Nils, while Don the engineer took care of his own. Lots of gesturing and yelling at one another took place during the replacements. Were everyone's headsets out? Rory dropped his new bottle in the sand and reached down to get it, knocking it on his hand before putting it into the socket on his hip. He tried twisting it in and for a moment it wouldn't turn. A look of panic crossed his face and Tamra took the bottle in her hands and gave it a hard turn, feeling it crunch into place. She watched his face through his clear hood as he took a breath, then gave her a thumbs up. She smiled and patted his head before huddling back inside her blanket.

Joe and Nils finished getting their bottles into place and Nils made the whirly gesture indicating they should get moving again. They were all talking still, Tamra the only one without a working radio.

One air bottle. That meant they'd been walking for at least 30 minutes, maybe as many as 45. Less than an hour outside and she was freezing, shivering under her three extra layers. She windmilled her arms around about her shoulders trying to force warm blood to her numb hands.

She had no idea how far they'd come but they were making slow progress. She looked back down the hill they'd just come from, barely able to see the trough of their tracks in the sandy dune behind them. Dome 3 was all but invisible in the blowing dust.

Were they going in the right direction? She tried to get a bearing when Joe started tugging on her hand, jerking his head, saying "Let's go" in his visor. She looked for Rory and found him close behind her. She reached out and took his hand and they continued up the gentle slope along the ridge, sinking to their knees and clambering forward in an awkward procession. Five Martians in makeshift surface suits.

She didn't know how long they trudged, their motions had become mechanical: walk, slip, scramble. Her hands were numb but she couldn't bring them in to warm them up. She pulled free of Joe and Rory and tucked her hands into her armpits just as a thin gust of wind whipped a fresh wave of dust into her visor and she stumbled backwards, sinking into the thick sand. She fought back, pulled forward and felt Rory let go and she went down into the dune head first.

She felt a weight crash into her and then arms around her: Rory helping her up. Joe was stopped nearby, crouching down to help. Confused, she looked around. Don was standing, his jackets and blanket whipping around him. He seemed to be yelling and pointed ahead of them. Then he pointed again, harder and trudged forward in the sand.

"Wait, don't get separated," Tamra said, doubting anyone could hear her with her frayed electronics. Her voice sounded tiny in her head.

Where was Nils?

Rory was yelling in his helmet and she looked at Joe. His nose was bleeding. His eyebrows had a thin layer of frost on them. Rory grabbed her by the elbow and tried to lever her to her feet. Instead, she stood up and helped him, then grabbed Joe's elbow, urging him up. She led Joe and Rory forward, following after Don's shadow trudging forward in the sand.

Rory pulled back, wrenching her arm and she turned on him, half-expecting herself to punch him. He was yelling at her, she could see.

She pressed her forehead against his through the thin bubble of their hoods and he hollered. "Nils is missing! I have to go back!"

No. "You can't!"

She was feeling panicky now. Joe reached for her and grabbed her arm, towing her along after Don who kept trudging forward. He was mouthing something at her but she couldn't see his face well enough to make out the words. Rory pulled back, but she held onto him somehow, dragging him along after her and Joe. After Don.

She tugged on Joe's arm twice. Two short pulls got his attention. She pressed into his face. "Nils is missing!"

Joe looked behind her, over her shoulder at Rory and around, peering into the gloomy, dust-filled landscape. They couldn't see more than a meter or two beyond their faces.

"We can't go back! He'll follow us!" he yelled back, forehead against hers. "Come on. We have to keep up."

He pulled her along after him then and she resigned herself to follow. Rory fell in behind, looking back over his shoulder at the way they'd come.

030

LIGHTHOUSE

"We are coming into view," Jill announced as the station curved around its orbit into the light side of Mars, sunlight shining down on them in space. They were currently eight hundred and sixty kilometers above the surface, descending towards the lowest point in their orbit, nearly two thousand kilometers from Ascraeus Mons.

"SURFer's online and capturing," Greg said. He put the unprocessed stream from the station's surface scanning imager up on the main screen. The dark grey, high-contrast terrain filled the screen and rapidly brightened as they crossed over the terminator line between night and day. Greg adjusted the parameters and the feed changed from black and white, near infrared to visible color, tawny grey sand and black and blue rock filling the view. His stomach grumbled, but he ignored it, hoping nobody heard the noise.

"Thank you, Science. That is a big dust storm," Sunil observed. "It appears to be radiating out from the central point of impact." The cloud ballooned across the surface, obscuring and filling in the deep canyons of Valles Marineris on the edge of the horizon.

They were still far away from the estimated collision site, but approaching rapidly. They only had about thirty minutes of visibility and then they'd be around the planet again, sweeping back up above the surface on the long pass out.

Emma chewed a nail, sitting beside Greg at her terminal, but turned around, facing the windows. She held her other hand in front of her, over her stomach, clenching it into a fist. She looked nervous.

Dan leaned forward beside her. She ignored him, despite sensing he was looking at her. She slid back and turned around beside Greg, looking at the screen in front of him. Olympus slowly rolled past underneath. The imaging station on her northeast slope glinted as it reflected the Sun's rays back up at them.

"It would be nice to get some imaging back from Olympus again," Greg mused.

Emma nodded.

"Sunil, I'm picking up mobile VHF chatter," Jill announced. "Want me to put it on speakers?"

"Yes, please. No need to ask." He listened, standing behind Jill. The acting commander was a comms officer at heart and had to resist the urge to take over the radio controls.

Brief burst of static on the speakers. "Control, this is Rover 2. Still awaiting instructions. Over."

"Hail them. Ask for status." Sunil.

Jill nodded and leaned into her station, holding her headset to her ear. "Rover 2, this is Lighthouse. We read you. What is your status, over?"

More crackling on the speakers, then a buzzing voice from Rover 2. "Lighthouse! We are outside Dome 3, just completed a circuit around it. We found a blow-out on the eastern side and the north airlock is hanging open." There was a pause. "We haven't seen any survivors. Over."

Jill, trying to concentrate, looked over her shoulder at Sunil. "Did he say the airlock was open?"

Emma leaned closer to Greg, whispering, "That's Tam's dome."

"I know." Greg flinched, looked at her, eyes wide, a growing feeling of sickness in his gut. He turned back to the screen. Ascraeus was coming into view. He worked the controls on his station. "Zooming in." He increased the magnification on their camera, the optics sliding in. Twelve times magnification. Fifteen. The surface rolled past the screen quickly now, turbulence and dust obscuring the surface. Then the domes appeared, shining in the diffuse sunlight for the briefest of moments and then they were gone. The station continued its flight past across the Tharsis Plateau, the Lunae Planum noticeably darker ahead.

Sunil watched, taking it all in. His normally reserved face creased in a frown. "Jill, see if you can raise Ground Control. Maybe we can relay for them."

"Aye."

"Ground control, this is Lighthouse station, do you read? Rover 2 requesting instruction. Over." Jill turned around to look at Sunil while they listened.

"Lighthouse, Rover 2 again. We haven't been able to reach ground control. Wondering if their radio's FUBAR. Over."

Greg rolled back the recording of the surface they'd just made. He stepped through it, frame by frame on his screen, zooming in around the domes. Construction vehicles and equipment dotted the middle, incomplete Dome 6. Domes 2 and 3 were visible east and northeast. Shiny circles in the sand distorted from the turbulent atmosphere. He zoomed in again. Pixels resolved into squares as he crossed over thirty times magnification. A dark line appeared along the edge of Dome 3, radiating outward. "That must be the blow-out. Darker sand and dirt from inside."

"There's the Rover." Emma pointed.

"Why would the airlock be open?" Sunil wondered aloud, that particular detail worrying at him. "Is it some kind of emergency protocol or did someone use it?"

Jill shrugged in her seat. "Do you want me to ask them?"

"No, I don't think so." Sunil scratched his ear. "That airlock's on the north side, in line with Dome 2. Ask them to drive to Dome 2 and keep their eyes open. There might be people out there."

"OK." Jill switched her radio on. "Rover 2, Lighthouse. Recommend heading to Dome 2. Eyes peeled for survivors, over."

The static and crackling on the radio increased as they moved further away from the colony and the source of the transmissions.

"Copy that, Lighthouse. Rover 2 out."

"Good luck, Rover 2. Lighthouse out."

Greg looked at Emma again, still worrying at the nail on her ring finger. He put a hand on her leg and squeezed her knee. "Hey, she'll be alright. She's tough."

She turned her head and looked at him with her big brown eyes. All the guilt he was feeling for leaving her alone down there, his time with Emma on the station, it was too much and it roared up at him and he looked away, ashamed of himself. Emma pushed his hand off her knee and returned to her station. "I hope you're right."

031

CITY HALL

The Council chambers had been turned into a war room. A steady stream of officers, relaying information to the members of the Council from the Control Room, were going back and forth, keeping the elevators running. Screens had been setup and connected to the displays from Control so the assembled officials could watch what was going on in the city. Operations team members filtered in and out through the main doors with hurried intensity, bringing new information to their people inside the room, relieving others for breaks and generally adding to the frenzied feeling felt be the tired onlookers.

The streets were mostly empty now. The previously-busy heat maps around the pressurized safe zones had cooled as people moved inside. Small pockets of stragglers were met by roving security teams and ushered to safety areas. Those who resisted were taken into custody. The holding areas filled up with troublemakers.

"We have most of the citizens contained while we investigate the pressure drop," Officer Henderson informed the Council. "The citizens are under control," he added, regretting his choice of words. "We've got people trying to get into Dome 3. We're still locked out and reading a total loss of pressure inside. Crews are trying to gain access. There's an MF group on site getting the way."

"Well get them out of there." Grayson gave his security officer a stern look. "Move in some emergency vehicles if you have to. Set up barricades. We don't need them getting in the way and making things more difficult."

The engineering reports that were coming in already made it sound like the elevator access point to Dome 3 was a dangerous place. The positive pressure they were pumping in meant they could have some blow-back when they finally got the bottom section opened. There could be debris and contaminants they didn't necessarily want getting sucked into the city's air systems.

"Any word from the Fab?" Fred Darabont asked, his face a permanent wrinkled frown.

Henderson looked relieved for a deflection. "Locked down and mostly offline, sir. We're getting reports from the different section chiefs, but slowly. No word from the Smelters yet."

Grayson grunted. "That's not good. We'd better hope nothing happened to the core. Send someone to check on them." He stretched, stifling a yawn. "Anything else?"

"We received word that Lighthouse was in contact with ground control over mobile land radio, but we're having trouble transmitting out. Getting a lot of scatter around our transmitter."

Bryce perked up in his seat at mention of the station. He'd been trying to get in touch with his father for the past several hours without any luck. Communications in the city were overburdened.

"Interesting. What'd they say?" Grayson asked.

"Just a hello, as far as we know. They broke up after making contact." Henderson fidgeted on his feet, edging closer to the door.

"Just a sec." Bryce stood up. "If you get them again, ask if they saw anything useful about the impact. Figure out if we can use land radio to transmit visuals. Could be useful to get some eyes outside while we're stuck in here."

"I'll, uh, do my best, Commander."

Grayson waved the man out and he made a hasty exit.

The tinny voice of Tadeuz Powell addressed the room from his office at the university. "You're worried, aren't you, Bryce?"

He sighed. Decorum had left the room hours ago. "Well, yes, I'm worried. Given what happened to our ships these last weeks, I think we should all consider that this might be an attack."

"From what? Your space object?" Grayson asked testily.

"That or another one like it. Possibly. We need to get a team out to the impact site and see what it is. Figuring out a non-networked means of communications with Lighthouse should be a top priority," he said, registering the looks of displeasure on the council members around him. "In my opinion."

The room was chilled silent. Bryce seized this as an opportunity to dig out his tablet. "Look. This is what our science team found last week.

Seems to be as good a time as any to show you all." He spent a moment digging around on the network for the new displays standing around the table. Kanan stepped forward to help, but Bryce shooed him away. Eventually, one of the screens showing a view overlooking the near-empty vehicle yards north of the Fab was replaced with a time-lapse video of Earth. "Here. The timecode at the bottom shows the dates. This is from two months ago." He let the video roll, the Earth transitioning from a three-quarter gibbous blob to a half disc in blue and white.

The video froze, square callouts highlighting a spot in the clouds at the edge between day and night. A bright white spot.

"Let me zoom in on that." Bryce stepped the video forward and the scene zoomed in. The bright spot turned into a white pixel, the clouds underneath reflecting the illumination. "We believe this is the Object that attacked our ships."

The Council collectively leaned forward to look at the bright patch on the screen before them.

"We've heard nothing from Earth in one hundred and thirty years," Natalie said. "We've been listening. Telescopes, optical and radio haven't picked up so much as a blip. Images show most of the northern hemisphere's been wiped out. Unrecognizable."

"We've only been able to see through the cloud deck in the past twenty years. It's... uninhabitable by all accounts." Dr. Richardson waved a hand through the air.

"By humans," the remote voice of Tadeuz Powell reminded her.

"Can we send a probe to investigate?" Grayson asked, leaning on the table as he reached for his water glass.

"I suppose we could, but I think we just missed our close-approach window." Bryce cleared his throat. "Although, the *Terror*'s going to be passing Earth orbit on her way back. Hopefully they'll take some pictures." *If they're still alive,* he thought to himself.

The room quieted again.

"But what is it?" Keith Turnbull asked. "If this is an attack, did it miss us? Was that just a warning shot?"

"We won't know until we can investigate the impact site. Hopefully we'll be able to get some details then." For the first time, Henry Grayson looked like he was out of his element. "Think about what you want to do. I'm going to my office to take care of some messages. I'll be back within the hour."

The voices rose up around the table as the Chairman stood up and walked out of the room.

032

ROVER 2

"Control? Rover 2 here. We're rolling to investigate that impact site now. Nothing much we can do here. Over." Aden looked back around into the cabin, Erika was just coming forward after climbing out of her suit again. She had a towel and her water bottle and was just wearing shorts and a tank top. He looked a little longer than was strictly necessary before snapping back to reality. "Buckle up, we're rollin'."

Erika squatted down behind the two seats up front, holding onto the hand holds on the back of the chairs. She smelled vaguely of plastic and sweat from the suit. "Where we headed?"

Aden turned the lights forward and pulled back on the yoke, easing the big vehicle forward on its wheels.

Ray turned his head to answer. "Headin' out to the impact."

Erika saw her own reflection in the forward bubble looking surprised. "What? We can't. There could be survivors out here!"

Aden tried to keep his eyes on the rock-strewn path ahead. "Did you see any signs of survivors?"

"No, but I didn't have much time to look."

"What are we gonna do? Look, I'm not waiting around for new orders in this mess. We're wasting time if we're just gonna park outside the dome waiting for instructions. I say we fall back to our original orders. Investigate the impact site." Aden tried to keep the uncertainty out of his voice. He didn't like being second-guessed out here.

"There could be people who need our help."

Silence. The steady rocking of the RV as it rolled forward over the uneven terrain was making Aden sleepy. He'd been in the driver's seat all day and avoiding obstacles in the terrain required more concentration than he really had to give it. He wished he hadn't had that last drink last night. A blast of sand hit the window and the wheels turned, digging into a small dune that was making its way across the floor of the plateau. The sky was getting darker as the Sun passed into the afternoon between Ascreaus and Pavonis Mons further south behind them.

"We've got no comms. Not much we can do about it." He wasn't going to wait around for a message that wasn't coming. Worse, he didn't want to get written up for not following their primary objective. He'd already been given a negative review for not having the scrubber detail finished. It wasn't like it was his fault they were smack in the middle of another dust storm. And now this. It was going to set them back weeks.

Aden picked up the rubber tube off the console and turned it over in his hands, not liking the look of the bits of dirt and dust that had accumulated. He stuck the stub into the seat pocket beside him and fished around for the longer length of black rubber it came from. He steered with one hand while he dug his knife out of his pants and flicked it open with a thumb. "Besides, it's not like they don't have other drivers out here. If they get word somebody's missing out here, they'll send a team. They already think we're gone."

Still steering with one hand, he held the rubber tube against the wheel and cut off a new chunk of it before stowing the longer, curled up length back in the side pocket of his seat. He stowed his knife and stuck the new piece of tubing between his teeth, biting down and chewing. It squeaked in his mouth and he sucked in a bit of spit.

Another negative review and he risked losing command of the Rover. Who was he going to report to? Ray? Unlikely. Getting assigned to Jason in Rover 1 wouldn't be so bad though. He remembered they were supposed to go to the fights tonight in Pooky's Alley. He had money riding on it too, ten chits on Vargas in four. Maybe if they did this impact site investigation, they'd wipe the negative review from his file, or at least get him some kind of commendation. It was a rare thing traveling out past the spillways, and this would be his longest run yet. The terrain was rough. Hard on the vehicles.

He heard Erika rattling something around in the kitchenette behind them and he turned around, catching a glimpse of her bending over, her shorts showing more skin than was strictly necessary on duty.

"Shit." Aden swerved, avoiding a rock, then glanced away from the ground in front of them, looking over at Ray, engrossed in his tablet. He was awake now at least. "I thought you were watching out for us." He chewed on the tube with renewed intensity.

Ray looked up and blinked. "Uh, sorry."

"This is wrong, Aden." Erika recovered from almost being knocked over by his steering and walked back near the lockers, grabbing her loose-fitting overalls and dropping onto the couch with them. She stuck her legs in and her socked feet popped out of the ends. "Goddamned sand everywhere."

"You should clean it up then." Aden eased forward on the throttle and the big rover's wheels dug in and spun sand. Erika tumbled sideways on the couch, almost ending up on the floor.

"Hey!"

"He did say to buckle up." Ray got out of his seat and tried to help her up and she swatted his hand away. Aden didn't really like the way Ray acted around her, but there wasn't a lot he could do about it. He was a weird and awkward guy, in his opinion, but one of his crew. Erika added an uncomfortable dynamic to the rover team, strutting around in her underwear like she was at home. Hell, neither of them would have been his first choice but he didn't exactly get his pick of the litter.

Erika got herself upright and finished zipping up her suit. "Yeah, just take it easy, will ya?"

"I'll do my best." Aden squeezed the wheel and drove on, heading east along the base of Dune 12. The rough deck of the plateau turned to washboard under their wheels.

They'd already lost two-and-a-half hours of daylight out here around the domes. If they pushed, they could make it twenty klicks before nightfall. They'd have to rest then and charge the batteries anyway. No point running the generator and wasting fuel until they had to.

"Hey, Erika, what's for lunch?"

"Eat me."

"How about a bean stew, then?"

Rummaging from behind, then Erika was beside them. "Here you go." She handed Ray a silver ration pack.

"Oh, thank you." He smiled at her and gave it a squeeze, breaking the inner seal, the chemical reaction that would heat it began and he set the packet on the console while it cooked.

"Here's yours." Aden saw stars as the package hit him in the side of the head. His ears rang as the seal broke and Erika let the bag fall to the floor. "There ya go."

"Thanks, sweetie." Aden reached down and picked it up, putting it on the center console while he drove. He placed his tube down beside it.

"I don't think I'll ask her for water."

033

THARSIS: DUNE 12

Keating hauled on Tamra's wrist, pulling her after him in his low crouch walk along the dune's ridge line. It had been a struggle getting the kids to move after they lost one. Nils, they'd said his name was. They'd all wanted to stay behind and look for him, but he knew that would've been suicide. They were already down one bottle and his second was almost empty. He'd have to stop soon to replace it, but had to delay as long as he could. The suits' rebreathers would keep them going, but might not have enough pressure to keep the air bladders inflated in his lower legs. His feet hurt, the cold temperatures of the sand leeching pressure away from the suit, which in turn was causing painful muscle cramps and numbness.

This damned suit. He was going to have some words with provisions when he got back. Why build a suit that didn't have enough insulation to withstand typical Mars ambient surface temperatures? The workers complained they were too hot in the domes? Worse, the compressed air bottles they used added more cold air to the system, robbing them of heat. The first litre of air in the bottles was used to recharge the pressure in the suit's air bladders and unavailable for breathing. Ironically, the temperature was most comfortable when their air ran out and his extremities started aching. What a joke. He glanced back, breaking a line of ice inside his hood that had formed around his neck and ears. The girl he was dragging behind him looked half frozen, her lips were blue and she had ice on her face. She looked like she was mumbling something, probably to herself. Her lips moving…

Her lips were blue.

He stopped and turned around. "Bottle change," he said, hoping the mic on his neck still worked. The other three dropped to their knees in the heavy sand. He stuck his helmet on hers, pressed his forehead into the soft flexible material over her head. Ice like blades cutting into his forehead, he yelled, hoping their skulls would conduct enough of what he was trying to say to her. "You need to change your air bottle."

Her radio hadn't worked since they left the dome. Probably just a connection inside, or maybe the battery was dead. All of their radios were acting flakey out here. The low-powered transceivers were unable to deal with the scatter from all the particulates, he guessed, another line item for his people in provisions. Either way, he couldn't talk to her easily.

She yelled back through red eyes that still managed to find some tears in them. "We have to go back! Nils is out there somewhere."

"We can't turn back." He looked over her shoulder at the other two, Joe and Rory, were helping each other replace their bottles. Rory crouched in the sand, rubbing his legs and arms while Joe fumbled with his air bottle.

Keating pulled the parka up over his shoulders and reached inside Tamra's coat, finding the harness with the spare bottles on it. She just stared at him as he did, not moving to help. He glanced back into her hood, frozen tears stuck to her cheeks, her eyes expressionless. She was clearly in shock and that wasn't going to help them. "Joe, Rory. Your bottles changed?"

"Yah," Joe crackled back.

"C-cold," Rory said, teeth chattering. His blanket whipped around him in the wind. "My legs hurt. I don't think I can stand up."

He returned to work. He unscrewed the bottle on Tamra's hip and put it in the sand beside them. Then he knocked the fitting on her side with the new bottle and dropped it in, squeezed and turned. Grinding and a pop resulted as the bottle seated itself, the pressure gauge climbing back up to full.

His own now. He repeated the process with his own bottle and put the empties back under his parka in the pockets. His hands hurt from the cold and he balled them into fists. "We have to keep moving."

"I can't." Joe flopped down in the sand and pulled his blanket around him.

The smaller one, Rory, hauled on his arm. "Come on! We have to go!"

Tamra just knelt there in the sand. Her face turned and looked up, west. The pale grey sun reflected off her hood and she looked strangely peaceful for just a moment. The wind whipped up another cloud of dust and the sky darkened again, Tamra's face obscured under the flapping jacket.

Keating trudged back and hauled on Joe's arm, lifting him up in a cascade of sand. A divot appeared behind them where a sand slip fell away down the side of the dune. They were probably accelerating the dune's passage across the Tharsis plateau by walking along it, the shifting sands under their feet migrating on their slow journey across the surface. "Come on, Joe. Keep moving. Rory, help Tamra and link up. Let's go! We're halfway there!" He clapped his hands, trying to generate some energy in the lagging group.

He didn't know if they were halfway or even a quarter. He couldn't see the dome ahead anymore. The light and shadow of Ascraeus Mons in the late afternoon Sun made it hard to see anything. There was no contrast, only sand.

"Come on, Tam. Up!" Rory hauled on her arm and she just knelt there looking at him. Her mouth moved. She was saying something.

Still holding onto Joe's arm, Keating trudged forward and grabbed Tamra's other arm, lifting her up. "March." He knew she couldn't hear him, but he set out anyway, Rory linking up with Joe and pulling Tamra along behind him.

Four Martians, walking across the dune in the fading light. They only had another few hours of light left, but it was going to start getting colder in the shadow of the mountains.

They had to make it.

034

LIGHTHOUSE

The steady beeping of the consoles around the science station was grating on Greg's jangled nerves. He leaned over to Dan. "Can't we kill the noise?"

Dan looked at him like he'd suggested going outside for a swim. "No."

"This beeping is driving me crazy." Greg shook his head and returned to his station. His screen filled with code.

"What are you working on, anyway?"

"Image processing routine. Trying to clean up some of the surface footage we got on our last swath." Greg's fingers flashed across his tablet and the screen in front of him changed, bringing up a picture from their last pass over Ascraeus Mons. "Managed to get a little more detail out of the images. Might be able to get some more, but I'm at the limits of resolution here."

"Neat."

Dan's face went through a series of expressions, scrunching up and then turning into a frown.

Greg watched him go through whatever was happening inside of him. "What?"

"Nothing. Just... are you and Emma...?" He trailed off.

"Are we...?" Greg looked around. Emma was still in the biolab, looking for fruit.

Dan leaned in, whispering. "You know. Together?"

Greg shook his head, surprised. "No! I mean, we're friends, but...

she's got a boyfriend." He pointed up. "Jerem."

"I know. You just seemed pretty close the past couple of days." Dan passed a hand over his head. "Matching buzz cuts."

"Ah yeah." Greg laughed, sounding awkward in his own ears, then remembered the way she'd moved his hand away earlier. "It's nothing. Just a haircut." It was over.

Greg grimaced and returned to his code, cursing inwardly. He had let himself get too close in the past few days. Dangerously close the other night and that wasn't entirely his fault. It was just that there wasn't anybody else he knew on the station. There were people here, almost a hundred of them, but he rarely went outside the control deck. Still, he couldn't do that to Tamra. She was down there and needed him now that her father and brother were missing. The thought of betraying her for Emma made him feel sick.

He remembered what he was doing and looked at the image of the broken dome again. Tamra's dome and the dark streak on the eastern edge where it had suffered a blow-out. The image was sharper now, he'd managed to combine multiple images together across three frames to increase detail, largely eliminating the blur and distortion from the dust and atmosphere. The differences between the pixels combined to produce a higher resolution image. A single dot on the north side outside the airlock was Rover 2, parked there while they investigated the damage.

"We're coming around again. Will be in radio range in five minutes," Jill announced.

Greg switched windows and brought up the live view from the camera. He ran his program and another window showed a copy of the live camera running at one-third frame rate, about a second behind.

The spinward doors opened and Emma came bouncing onto the deck, a small bunch of green bananas in her hands. She dropped them down on the desk in front of Greg and flopped into her seat, making it spin. "What'd I miss?"

Greg pointed at the video screen in front of him. Mars was a bright red gradient in the early afternoon, the pockmarked surface of Terra Sirenum filled the screen, giving way to the highlands to the north. "I've got some image processing running this time. Should give us some extra detail through this dust."

Emma turned around and watched the red planet rolling through the big windows of the control deck, marvelling at the deep color as the surface dimmed, Olympus Mons to the north casting a long shadow across the Tharsis Plateau, Ascraeus and Pavonis Mons bulging on the horizon in deep red, racing towards them.

"Two minutes," Jill announced.

Sunil stood up from the Commander's chair and walked to the comm station. "Any transmission yet?"

She listened, shook her head.

"Domes coming into view," Greg said. Heads in the operations pit turned and lifted up to look at the main screen.

The radio was silent. Sunil looked like he was about to speak when the speakers came to life. "Lighthouse? This is ground control, do you copy? Over?"

"Aye, ground. This is Lighthouse. We read you, over," Jill relayed. "Looks like they were expecting us."

A slight pause as the station wheeled over Pavonis Mons, Ascraeus coming into view behind it. "Lighthouse. We have a request from Council asking for visuals from the impact site. Can you relay?"

Sunil looked over at the science station. "Is that a thing we can do with analog radio?"

Emma looked over at Greg, nodded to him and began working on her tablet.

Greg answered for them. "Yeah, we should be able to, if they've got the decoding equipment on their end. We'll have to work out a transmission…"

"Got it," Emma interrupted him. "We can rig up file transfers using X.25 and the Z-modem protocol. Tell them to patch their wireless in on a different channel and feed that to their computers. We should be able to send them a data packet on next pass."

Sunil grinned, turned back to Jill. "You got that?"

She nodded. "Pretty sure I can make that work." The old protocols were all still there, just rarely used. "Ground, on next pass we will broadcast X-ray-two-five payload, Zebra protocol handshake on frequency one-four-eight. Please acknowledge. Over."

The reply was swift. "Understood, Lighthouse. Over."

"Ground, we will begin transmitting in four-zero minutes. Over."

Greg, watching the output from his improved cameras, stuck up a hand and immediately felt foolish for doing it. "Commander, I've got something out on the dunes." He circled it on his screen in red, a dark smudge halfway between Domes 2 and 3.

Sunil walked over to him. "Are you sure?"

Greg shrugged. "Not really, hard to say. But it wasn't there on the last pass." He brought up the previous set of images and put them beside the new one. "There." He pointed at a dark smudge closer to Dome 3 on the older image. "It moved."

Sunil rubbed his chin and walked back to comms. "Jill, ask ground control to send their rover team back to that dune. There might be survivors down there."

"Aye." She relayed the instructions, then turned back to Sunil. "Funny, we're not hearing from Rover 2 anymore." She made some adjustments to her radio, then opened the mic. "Rover 2, are you reading us? This is Lighthouse. Over."

Static.

"We're here, Lighthouse. We didn't want to break in on your important conversation with ground control. Over." The radio crackled.

Greg. "I've got them. They're… shit. Almost ten klicks east of the domes now. They've been rolling."

Sunil picked up his headset, unable to contain himself any longer. "Rover 2, this is Lighthouse Actual. Please return to the dunes between Dome 2 and 3. We've spotted something moving across it roughly in the middle. Check it out, over."

A staticky pause, then. "Roger, Lighthouse. Ground Control, make a note of this in your logs. Rover 2 out."

"Ground control to Rover 2. We hear you. Over."

Greg whispered to Emma, "That sounded a little crispy."

Emma grinned. "Odd that the rover and ground control are having transmission problems."

Sunil overheard her. "Yes and no. Charged particles in the atmosphere can cause radio disruption. If they're aligned, they can deflect in unexpected patterns. It *is* a little weird, maybe check for solar activity."

Greg: "We're approaching Tharsis Crater. The impact site is coming up."

Eyes turned to the big screen above them again. The fading surface of the highlands rushed past beneath them at seven hundred kilometers per hour. The wall of Tharsis Crater rose up out of the sand, the other side obscured in deep shadow in the setting Sun.

A flash in the darkness, bright and hot, left an after impression on the imaging sensor. Static burst from the speakers as the room around him erupted in voices.

Sunil raised his voice so he could be heard. "Quiet, please! Greg, did we get that?"

The room settled.

Greg rolled the video back. Dan sat close beside him now, watching intently as the screen filled with bright white light. "Yeah. We got it."

035

MACHINE PARTS

Sean was walking back along the South Hall to Machine Parts, replacement screen and battery in the pouch of his hoodie, when a low rumble shook the floor beneath him, causing him to stumble. He reached out and steadied himself on the wall, a low vibration running through his arm.

The crowd gathered outside the cafeteria started babbling as the lights flickered in the long hallway. Sean jogged past the men and women, ignoring the request to pick up some snacks from the commissary and continued onto the door that would take him to Machine Parts.

Inside the room, his foreman Mike was talking to a man and a woman he didn't recognize. They were dressed like city officials, so he presumed they were management. They looked at him briefly then resumed their conversation. Mike ignored him, so he sat down on the floor and picked his tablet from his bag, and went to work, disconnecting the old screen and battery.

Man: "What was that? Another tremor?"

Mike shrugged. "You got me."

Woman: "The machines are still offline, aren't they? We need to send a cleanup team in there. Can you give us the access codes for control?"

Mike gestured at the board. "All offline." The lights flickered briefly. "I'm not supposed to…"

Woman: "Why is that articulator moving?"

Sean looked up as the others' heads turned to see one of the robotic arms moving along the tracks in the upper levels, carrying a block of metal to one of the machines. It released the block into one of the big shapers and the machine went to work on it.

Mike shook his head. "I have no idea. The board says the whole assembly's offline."

The man leaned over and looked at the board more closely. "Can we cut power to this section? We'll need to get in there when the emergency teams arrive." He looked back through the glass, squinting. He could just see the smear of red that used to be Steel on the third level. "We'll also need those access codes."

The woman pulled out a tablet and started tapping on it. "Power control is offline." She tapped at it again. A hiss erupted from inside the factory as a cooling valve opened up on the shaper, blasting it with a jet of cool gas.

Mike flipped controls on his console helplessly. "I have no idea what's goin' on in here. In three revs, I've never seen anything like this."

The man turned away and spoke into his wrist. "Uh huh... I understand... Here too. Just sit tight, we'll be there shortly." He turned back to his counterpart and said, "We have to go."

Mike threw up his hands. "Wait! What are we supposed to do?"

The man looked back at him, clearly uninterested. "Just stay here. We're still in lockdown. Get some dinner. Relax. The emergency crews are still working to gain access to Dome 3 but they promise that they'll be here next."

"As soon as they're ready," the woman said.

The man and woman regarded Sean on the floor as they walked past to the exit. He ignored them.

"Jesus. What the hell?" Mike looked back out over the Machine Parts floor as another arm rolled in on its track, passing its payload to yet another arm which swung down to one of the middle levels, dropping the pipe into one of the bending machines.

Sean was engrossed in reassembling his tablet, plugging in the new battery into its connector, then laying the soft gel insulation layer back over it and pressing the screen down in place. He flipped the power switch and the new screen lit up as the tablet ran through its boot sequence. A second later he was dropped into his home screen. "It worked!" The new battery had a fifty percent charge on it. That would last him until he could plug in. "Mike, can I get on the network here?"

"Sure kid. Any of the Machine Parts networks. Password's 'cadmium', all lower case."

"Nice. Thanks." He connected easily and tried bringing up his observatory. It was slow, taking over a minute to retrieve the latest batch of graphs. He suspected it was the local network connection at first, but then the graph of the past hour appeared. "Holy…"

The network was overflowing with traffic. What was usually a steady trickle of packets racing around the network was now a rough sea of noise at top volume, the graphs at 100% across the board. He scrolled back through the stuttering timeline and found the beginning of the spike. 0917. Roughly an hour after the tremors this morning.

The lights in the control hut flickered again.

Sean looked up and noticed Mike was watching him. "What is it, kid? You look like you just saw a ghost."

"There's something very wrong." Sean looked at his screen, watching the traffic crawl on his screen for a moment before his connection timed out again. He shut down the tablet, making sure to disconnect it from the network first. "Something going on with the colony's network. Big traffic spike." He didn't really want to explain how he knew this, not wanting to get in trouble for poking into something he wasn't supposed to.

Mike frowned at him. "What're you talking about?" He looked uneasy.

"I… run a network node. Traffic's maxed out. It looks like a denial of service attack."

"A what?"

"So much traffic, none of the network's able to deal with it. Used to happen on Earth all the time before the Collapse. Bad actors… Botnets could wipe out whole chunks of the internet by generating more traffic than the network could handle."

"Uh, you think someone's doin' that here? Why?"

Sean shook his head. "I don't know." Some of the local hacking groups might have been able to do this. It was possible someone wrote a worm and it got away from them, but most of the people he knew wouldn't do something like this intentionally. He would've caught wind of it sooner on the board. "No, this is different. I have to go." He stuffed his tablet into his bag and stood up.

"Wait! We're still in lockdown. You can't go anywhere!"

Sean looked at the machines on the other side of the glass working the material. New parts emerged and were carried off along the conveyor belts.

"I have to tell somebody. This could shut the whole network down."

036

CITY HALL

Henry Grayson entered his office, the lights rising to a soft ambient level. He waved his hand, the gesture picked up by the room's cameras and relayed to the controlling computer for interpretation. Three translucent screens rose up from his desk around his chair. He sat down, leaning back and surveying the displays in front of him. He had a full copy of the screens in the Control Room, with additional information superimposed by his personal systems. Callouts over the heatmaps with rolling identifications of the individuals clustered in locations around the city. Color-coded pixels representing City employees or monitored citizens. Inset into the corners, scenes from the streets rolled from the banks of security cameras scattered around the colony. Occasionally, one of the video squares showed only static from a failed camera.

Henry took a sip of water from his glass and placed it back on his desk. He leaned back, rubbing his eyes. He was tired, but there was no time to rest now.

Blinking twice rapidly, he said, "Feeds."

The screens shuffled and a new window appeared on the right-most monitor, showing the current trending topics.

Emergency at Dome 3 Lift
Power fluctuations
Tremors causing power outages
Pressure Warnings!
Food shortages?

… and so on.

He lowered the priority on these and bumped up some lower-rated topics. Pictures of babies doing cute things. Wedding announcements. An article about the MF calling for an end to the space program.

On the other screen, a new wave of Security personnel moved out from the station on Mechanic Street and headed south to the Dome lift. Soon, they would have the crowd gathered there under control. Henderson was still in command, quietly dispatching more Safety and Security Personnel to disperse gatherings near the hospital and churches. The callouts on those crowds contained a number of individuals flagged for agitation, others for aggressive behavior. This particular group outside the hospital appeared to be associated with the previous week's food riots. He watched the blobs converge with tired eyes.

Incoming call from Fred Darabont. A small window chimed for his attention in the lower corner.

"What is it?"

Frank's face appeared in the small screen. "We're getting more reports from outside the city. Our ground crew has found the breach on Dome 3. They're saying the airlock's been opened. Not sure about survivors yet."

"Fine. Keep me posted," Grayson grunted.

"Dan's asking what you want to do about Tunnel 10 near Hades?" This was the third time this morning Dan Perkins had asked to send a crew to investigate the collapse. Now he was using Fred as a proxy.

"We'll send a team when we have one available." Grayson regarded Darabont again. "Do we have any more available engineers?"

Fred shook his head in reply. "No. We don't."

"Alright. They'll have to wait."

He killed the window before they could ask him for anything else.

Grayson closed his eyes and took a deep breath. They'd been lucky. They'd managed to avoid a full-scale panicked riot in the city. What he needed to do was gain some modicum of stability, get people working again. He buzzed his assistant at her desk from his intercom: "Could you have Kaylee message me when she's available?"

"Yes, sir," came the clipped reply.

Christ, if Dome 3 was lost, that was going to impact their food supplies in a very real way. He looked at Dome 3's production sheet on his desk. Soy. Wheat. Corn. Coffee. Citrus. Potatoes. Spinach. Tomatoes. It was their most varied dome, the people who'd tended it had grown it into a high-density version of North American farm land. The others focused primarily on volume. Rice and soy.

Fucking spinach.

He needed two weeks. Just two more.

He sighed and cleared his desk screens. He opened a new message and began typing on the illuminated touch screen at his fingertips.

To: root@t5k-a0f5.mars

Subject: Promises

I just wanted to remind you about the terms of our deal. Don't forget me. I want to be taken care of.

While we're talking, I'd like a progress report. You caused a lot of damage with your little incident. People are losing their minds and I don't have the resources to contain a full-scale riot. I'm running some spin to try to keep this contained, but I don't know how long I can maintain that. Keep it clean until you're ready, otherwise the deal is off.

He hit send and exhaled loudly, took a breath. Notifications from people sending him messages filled up in his sidebar. He closed it and a little numeric icon appeared at the bottom of his screen informing him of them. The number kept increasing.

Grayson opened another window titled FABRICATION PRODUCT REQUISITION. He scrolled through a series of menus, tapping on entries. *Hardware > Tools*. He touched a gear-shaped icon and from the dialog that opened, tapped *Show Hidden Items*. He selected *Weapons* from the new entries that appeared. *Semi-Automatic > Handguns*. From the list that appeared, he selected an automatic handgun which accepted seventeen nine-millimeter rounds per magazine. He clicked order. He paused, then tapped the button another four times. Under associated items, he selected *Ammunition Magazine* and *Ammunition*. He ordered twenty magazines and 2400 bullets.

He clicked the checkbox labeled *Expedite*.

Order Ready. Complete? (Yes/No?)

Grayson tapped, *Yes*.

037

ROVER 2

Erika bounced on the couch in the crew cabin. Her discarded packet of bean stew flew off the pull-out table beside her. "Hey!"

Up front, Ray and Aden swayed back and forth in their seats as the big RV trundled on. They were making nearly twenty-five kilometers per hour on the uneven washboard surface of the plateau. Grey sky was visible outside as the Sun slipped into shadow behind the slope of Ascraeus Mons.

"I think we caught a little air back there." Aden grinned at Ray who looked like he might throw up.

Erika got herself repositioned on the couch. "Easy on the cargo, Reed."

"What cargo?"

"Me!"

The RV's lights flashed ahead, glimmering off the rising side of Dune 12. Ray leaned forward so he could look up the side of the hill, the ridge a hundred meters above them and running away towards Dome 2. "No way we'll be able to see anything up there in this light."

Aden slowed the big vehicle and took a look himself. "We can't climb that. Not on this side. We'll have to go around to Dome 2 and come up the other side."

Ray scratched his chest inside his coveralls and took a drink of water. He looked up the dune again and shook his head. "I dunno. I don't like driving in that heavy sand. We could get stuck."

"We'll see what happens. Got to get around it anyway." Aden turned the rover and pushed forward on the throttle. The big machine rolled ahead on its wheels, picking up speed. "Erika, you keep an eye up above."

"All ri–"

"Watch out!" Ray yelled, pointing ahead.

A cloaked figure held its arms out wide, blankets billowing around him like robes as the Rover barrelled down almost on top of him.

Aden locked up the wheels and the RV skidded to a stop a meter in front of the hooded wanderer. The lights flashed across and the wind whipped the young man's blanket aside, his face shining white and squinting in the lights of the RV under his clear, frosted hood. He wrapped the blanket back around himself and ran around the side of the rover to the airlock in back.

"Erika, give him a hand."

She was already off the couch, moving back as the airlock began cycling.

"He's just a kid," Ray said.

"Lucky we didn't drive right over him," Aden said, picking up the rubber hose on the console and shoving it between his teeth.

The outer door opened and the boy fell inside, shivering as the airlock's cleaning cycle blasted him with air. The dust and sand blew off him in a cloud to be sucked out of the vents in the floor. The cycle finished and the inner door opened, he fell inside and collapsed on the floor shaking uncontrollably. An empty air canister fell out of a pocket somewhere and rolled along the floor under the counter in the galley.

"Oh my God. I'll get you some blankets." Erika scrambled in the drawers under the couch, hauling out blankets and wrapping the newcomer in them. He nodded and tried to reach up to undo his hood, but his hands wouldn't let him. "Don't open it!" She held his hands in place on his chest. "You need to be brought back up to pressure slowly."

He gasped inside his hood, his face caked with frost. Burst blood vessels in the whites of his eyes and cheeks told her he'd been breached out there. "Can't... breathe."

"He needs air."

Ray crouched down beside them and dug around inside the blankets. The harness around his shoulders was empty. "You have any more air bottles for this thing? We don't have anything that'll fit."

The boy gasped, the bubble around his head collapsing down into his damaged face.

"I have to open this," Erika said. "He's going to suffocate."

Aden, still in the driver's seat, began rolling forward. "We gotta get him back to the garage. Ground control, this is Rover 2." He was yelling into his headset. "We have wounded coming in. Get a med team on site. Over."

Erika unzipped the seal on his neck and Nils took in a deep breath of air, filling his lungs. Then he stopped, gave a hard racking cough and blood trickled from his mouth and nose. He shook, arms and legs curling up around him.

"What's happening? Ray, do something!"

"What do you want me to do?" Ray looked at Erika helplessly as the boy choked on his own blood in front of them.

Erika wrapped the blanket around the thrashing boy and tried to hold him to keep him warm and prevent him from hurting himself. "I think he ruptured something in a lung." She did the best she could to hold him as Aden drove the RV forward. "Was there anyone else with you?"

"G-g-gh." Gasping for breath and more coughing took him and he had to wait for it to pass. "F-F-five. On dune."

"Were you ahead or behind them?" Erika waved to Aden, her reflection in the windscreen vying for his attention.

"D-d-on't know. S-s-separated." Another racking cough ripped through him.

Erika wiped the blood off his face. "Hang on."

Aden pushed the rover forward. "We're still going to have to go around this dune. We have to go forward before we can go back and get the others."

Erika looked at the boy in front of her: he was turning grey. "Stay with us." She continued rubbing his shoulders through the blanket. "I don't know what to do." She looked at Ray, silently pleading for him to do something. Then she turned to her monitor and rolled the floods across the face of the dune, sweeping the camera above and behind them, peering into the light. "Wait here a minute, Aden."

Ray stooped down and picked up the stray air bottle. He wiped some dust off it. The gauge read empty. "How much air does the rest of your group have? Those suits aren't meant for cross country."

A flash lit up the horizon off to the darkening east, the dust lighting up deep within.

038

THARSIS: DUNE 12

Tamra had given up.

She knelt on the cold sand, her jacket flapping around her in the wind. It was getting dark and the surface temperature was approaching negative eighty degrees Celsius. How could it be so far? It was only two kilometers between the domes but the sand and blowing wind made that seem an impossible distance.

She wanted to go to sleep. It hurt to think. Her limbs and lungs ached.

Outside her hood, she was vaguely aware of someone yelling at her, barely recognizable as a voice in the thin atmosphere and howling wind. She looked up. It was Rory, face white with frost, mouth jabbering. He was shivering, arms hugging himself.

Arms reached under hers and she was lifted off her feet. Rory and Joe dragged her along the ridge of the dune. Keating stooped down and picked her up. She was upside-down, arms dangling below her, sand and legs steadily pumping.

She felt like she was falling.

A distant flash off to her left. She turned her head, the world upside down. The dark ruddy cloud of dust swirled in a gyre.

Lights. Far off. Behind them. Flashing among the sands.

She remembered something about a flash. Emma had found something.

And Greg.

Greg and Emma had gone to the station, she remembered. Searching for something among the asteroids. Chasing the ships.

You could have stayed, Greg. Why didn't you stay? Everything would be different.

Everyone always left.

Her mom.

She was going to die out here in the sand. Out of air, covered over in icy granules, preserved forever until the wind uncovered her once again. She imagined herself as a desiccated husk wrapped in silicates.

She remembered going up to the domes that first time in grade school. Everybody went on a field trip up to the surface. For most people, it was their first time seeing sky and green growing things. On the day of her field trip, they'd had a break in the weather. It was summer, but there had been a late spring storm as the plains warmed up. Thermals heated the dry dust of the Lunae Planum and sent it over them. And then, that one clear day. The sky was blue through the dusty glass of the dome, and they ran around through the fields of wheat and corn, beans and barley. She could hear her mother calling her, smiling in her floppy hat as she worked the plants. This was her dome. Dome 3.

It sounded like someone was yelling. Lights in her eyes from somewhere far below.

Sand.

She was falling. Rolling. End over end, the world tumbled around her. Something hard hit her in the face and she felt a warm wash in her mouth. Her lip swelled and still she fell.

She landed in a heap. Keating had been carrying her, now he was beneath her, half-buried in the sand.

It took a great effort, but she climbed off him and got to her numb feet. She skidded down the remaining few feet to the base of the dune, almost collapsing. She was dizzy, but managed to stay up, her face throbbing.

Rory and Joe ran off ahead, arms flailing.

Red lights on the sand.

A rover.

Had they seen them?

She turned around and grabbed the man's arm. She pulled on him and he struggled free of the sand around his waist, climbing out. He took Tamra's hand and jogged forward, limping on one leg.

They bounded after the rover.

It was stopping! Now backing up. Flood lights turned and shone ahead of them, bright against the dusky twilight.

They were being rescued.

039

ROVER 2

Aden drove.

Black rubber tube in his teeth, the Rover rumbled across the washboard sand of the plateau, driving northwest under the shadow of the looming volcano.

"It hurts!" one of the kids wailed from behind, holding his head. Erika bundled blankets around his hands and squeezed, trying to warm them up but stopped when the boy started howling. The four they'd scooped up off the dune were in varying stages of distress. She'd tried keeping them sealed up in their suits, but they were all out of air. Releasing the seals on their helmets caused their temporary pressure suits to relax further, releasing the positive pressure they were barely maintaining against their skin. They all had varying stages of frostbite on their faces. The girl probably had a broken arm. Some described burning in their hands and feet.

Some had nosebleeds. One of them passed out, clutching his head. The boy they'd brought in first was breathing wetly.

"Hurry up, Aden!"

"Can't drive any faster in this sand. Keep 'em quiet." He chewed on his tube and it squeaked between his teeth as he turned the wheel, avoiding a patch of rocks in the track.

They were approaching Dome 1, bounding past the old rocket cones from the Ark ship that stretched up out of the sand like giant satellite dishes. Antenna spikes and loops had been mounted on the tops of the dead nozzles, to serve as radio relays for the ground station. Beyond the dome, their destination was the platform leading into the wall of the mountain. He tried the radio again.

"Ground this is Rover 2 on approach, requiring medical assistance on arrival. Come in, ground."

A bump jostled the inhabitants and the lights outside bobbed over the terrain as the big RV rolled across the uneven surface.

"Rover 2, what do you mean 'on approach'? You're supposed to be headed for the impact site."

Aden cursed inwardly.

"Ground, we picked up some survivors from Dome 3. We need a medical team on-site. They have pressure sickness and other injuries. Repeat, we are carrying injured. Over."

A pause and the line crackled with static.

"Roger that, Rover 2. What's your ETA?"

"About 5 minutes. We're coming in hot. Rover 2 out."

The RV sped across the open sand, crossing between the last of the dunes. Dome 1 loomed beside them, lights on inside casting indistinct shadows across the plateau. They could see the lights of the dock yards ahead, a gaping black maw in the side of the mountain big enough to drive ten rovers through side by side.

It was quiet in the RV, save for the plastic creaking of the interior, as they rolled over the terrain. Aden chanced another look behind him and saw a couple of the kids were asleep. They must be exhausted after crawling around on that dune. He wondered how long they'd been out there. Probably at least three or four hours. "Man, we're lucky we found them."

"We found you," the small dark-haired kid corrected him.

"Yeah, I guess you did."

Aden returned his attention to his driving. The surface was smoothed out from years of vehicles flattening the terrain with their wheels. A make-shift roadway funnelled them into the mountain's opening.

They drove inside, the lights illuminating their grubby machine and shining into the cockpit. Ray climbed forward into the passenger seat, getting out of everyone's way.

"You going to be in trouble for not following orders?" Ray's round, hangdog face peered over at him.

"Won't be the first time." Aden managed to smile back.

They rolled forward in the big open space, a dozen RVs lining the walls facing outwards, and the outer doors closed behind them. Smaller work vehicles zipped between the machines, yellow lights flashing on their roofs. Everything lit up in harsh, white artificial light.

Aden eased forward and executed a three-point turn. He flicked the rear camera on and backed the RV into its bay, waiting for the clunk that let him know they were locked in. He pushed the yoke forward and unbelted himself, turning around in his seat as the gantry pulled forward and made a seal on their airlock.

"Alright. Everybody sit tight and wait for the medics."

The girl in the group made an effort to smile at him. He found himself smiling back. "Thanks for saving us," she said, cradling her damaged arm across her stomach.

"Don't mention it, kid."

Erika, quiet this whole time, shook her head at him. "Like you did anything."

The doors opened. A vehicle tech stuck his head inside and checked everything out. Satisfied with whatever he was looking for, he waved a pair of medics in and retreated. They squeezed inside with a stretcher and loaded the first of them out. Erika had to squeeze forward behind the two seats up front while they helped everyone. The engineer, Don, refused any help and stayed with the girl, making sure she was alright. He seemed to feel some kind of responsibility for her.

"Man, you can't know what they've been through," Ray said after the last of them was removed.

The RV was jolted from outside and the lights flickered as they were connected to city power. One of the small vehicles outside pulled away, hauling their battery pack out in its square arms. Another one pulled up and slotted a fresh set into the panel underneath.

Aden shooed Erika away from behind their seats and stood up, making his way back to the airlock, getting ready to leave when the crew chief stuck his head inside, his body following it in.

The chief stood up, stooping under the low ceiling, gloved hand in one of the straps and looked at Aden. "Where do you think you're going?"

"I was thinking of going home and getting some rest. Shift's over."

"Oh, really? I guess you're ready to take that piss test you neglected to file when you came in this morning," the crew chief said, staring lasers into Aden's eyes.

Aden cursed under his breath. "You gotta be kiddin' me."

The crew chief held up a small jar. "I got the bottle right here. Jase's crew said they saw you at the Reef last night. You been drinking a lot of water today?"

"Fuck."

"Or, you could get back out there and do the job we asked you to do." The Chief punctuated this with a finger in Aden's chest.

Ray and Erika were quiet and Aden squeezed his eyes shut as he rolled his head around on his neck.

"You're kidding, right? We just put in a full day out there. We're all beat. We saved those kids!" He held his hand out, pointing in the direction the evacuees were taken.

"That remains to be seen. They're not your responsibility, anyway." The chief adjusted his hat on his head. "You need any more supplies before you leave? Inventory says you should still be full up on brotein in here." A hiss and a pop came from outside as the fuel line was pulled away from the intake.

"We're good." Aden stared at the man, barely masking the hate he felt for him.

"Alright, then. Shouldn't take you more than a day or two to get where you need to be. Have a good trip. Take lots of pictures." The chief smiled at Erika, then turned and crawled back through the airlock, the door closing behind him.

Aden turned around and looked at his stunned crew. "Buckle up. We're rolling out." He climbed forward, stepping over a smudge of blood on the floor left by the fallen dome worker.

040

HAPPENSTANCE

Captain Joseph Randall was leaning back in the pilot's seat, eyes closed, headset playing a recording of The Stone Engines' last concert in the park. His ship was traveling away from the *Terror*, further along Mars' orbit on a long loop towards the L4 Lagrange point, 200 million kilometers ahead. Once there, they'd be able to begin the series of spirals that would slow them down and bring them back to Mars. It was a long trip – over a month – made longer by the lack of rations they had left in the galley. Reggie and Vanessa, the auxiliary crew of the *Terror* had stripped them of all excess.

He hadn't eaten today.

He listened to the raging guitars on his headset, barely drowning out the banging from below. He considered turning the music up louder, but the noise was bothering him. He killed his music and set his headset beside his console, on its hook. He unclipped his belts and floated up out of the chair, stretching his arms and back.

Grace Fielding, his EVA and science specialist, was perched on the couch behind him. Her own headphones over her ears, she stared at her tablet intently. She looked tired. Her eyes were ringed with dark circles. She brushed one of the cups off her ears and looked at him imploringly. "You going to see what's going on?"

He nodded, his beard bunching under his nose. He rubbed his head, velvety smooth with new growth coming in. "I suppose so." He floated to the hatch and guided himself down the rungs of the ladder through the crew section, passing the bunks. Blankets from their newcomer's bunk were floating in the accessway, waving at him. Joseph batted his way through them, getting angrier.

He drifted into the galley, landing on the deck with a thump. Ration packs floated in the cramped, dimly-lit space. Water bottles and half-empty coffee bulbs hung in the air. Dark liquid globules floated away from one of them, the seal unclosed.

Tyron Fielding, the ship's engineer and second in command, was hammering on the door to the head. "Get the fuck out here," he yelled at the locked metal slab. He pounded again and his Captain pushed him back with a hand on his shoulder.

"What's going on here?"

Tyron pointed at the closed door. "This fucker's been in there for six hours and some of us would like to use the facility."

"Where's Stevens?"

"Down here, sir," came a voice from the equipment room below.

"Get the torch." Randall stepped between Tyron and the door, putting his ear to it. He listened for a moment, hearing groans from inside.

"Avery? You've got two seconds to unlock this door or I'm burning it open."

Winston Avery's voice was faint, weak and slobbery. "I can't. I'm sick."

Connor Stevens floated up from below, an arc welder on his back and black welding goggles perched on his forehead.

"Ten seconds, Avery. If you're sick, we need to get a look at you. We can help."

Retching. "You cain't." Coughing.

The Captain nodded to Stevens and he pushed himself back. Tyron Fielding backed up into the galley through the miasma of debris.

Connor put his goggles down on his forehead and the Captain turned away, squeezing into the galley with Tyron. "How long's he been like this?" The Captain was aware of the situation, but he could see his second was seething, agitated.

"Days. He's not right."

There was a blast of light as Stevens went to work on the door and hollering from inside over the hiss and crackle of the arc welder cutting through the latch. Smoke filled the cramped space. Then a snap as the torch was extinguished, and the lock clattered to the floor, cut away and red hot.

Stevens stepped back, making sure his torch was shut down as he pushed the goggles back up on his head. He sniffed, turning up his nose in disgust at his surroundings.

Captain Randall pushed the door open with a hard bang and reached into the tiny washroom, the only one they had. He pulled out a sweating, vomit-encrusted Winston Avery by the neck and pushed him against the wall. "What the fuck is wrong with you? You sick or just sick in the head?"

Winston started blubbering and tried to curl up, his muscles tightening him into a ball as his guts cramped up again, threatening to heave but he had nothing left in him. He smelled terrible.

"I asked you a question!" the Captain bellowed at him.

"I can't." Winston collapsed in a heap on the floor and started coughing again, clearly in agony.

"Ty, put him in his bunk. You two clean up that galley and the crew section. This ship is a disaster." The Captain looked down at Winston again, writhing. "If this piece of shit junkie gives you any trouble, I want him cuffed in the airlock where I can't hear him."

Tyron sneered at the lump on the deck. "Aye, sir. Come on, you." He grabbed one of Winston's arms and hauled him off the floor, still curled in a ball. "Shit, he's massy. Gimme a hand, Connor."

"I ain't touching him. He's covered in puke and shit."

"Fuckssakes, grab his feet."

The two of them maneuvered the convulsing ball up to his bunk and shoved him into it, Winston groaning the whole way.

Randall looked around his galley one more time before turning away from it in disgust. He floated down to the equipment room, deck plates lifted where Connor had removed the torch. He set them down again and floated over to the couch, space suits in their lockers looming over him on either end like sentries. He belted in his legs, then his waist and laid back. "Hap, lights down in equip," he said. The ship lowered the lights around him as he closed his eyes.

041

MACHINE PARTS

Sean approached a group of a dozen people surrounding the exit. Workers from Electronics Assembly and beyond massed in the concrete tunnel running along the outside of the building. Sean peered through the bodies at the heavy metal door to the outside: red light on the locks. A couple of them had facial implants and geometric tattoos on their necks and cheeks.

It was no secret there were a lot of Machine Worshippers in the Fab, but it was unusual to see their markings displayed so overtly. Sean kept his head down as he moved among them. It was bonus hour now and it felt like the group was getting anxious. Maybe he was just projecting.

"I hear there's a new project spinning up. Going to get some new toys."

"I wish they'd let us in on it. I got family outside."

Sean squeezed through the mob. They were bigger than him, all of them. Sometimes that was an advantage.

"Hey, you can't get out. We're in lockdown."

Sean looked at the man, coarse, unshaven. Bent nose. Pierced lip and tattoo over his right eyebrow. "I'm just going to try this." He leaned in and held his card on the door. It beeped and flashed red. "Nope."

The man laughed at him. "I said we're in lockdown."

Sean shrugged at him as comically as he could muster while he wormed his way back through the group. He traced his way along the wall of Machine Parts. This was one of the first structures built after the Assembly. The parts to build other machines were a key piece in the growth of the colony. He came to the commissary and wandered in. A few people were sitting there, bored, empty plates and wrappers on the tables in front of them. Sean went to the counter and grabbed a breakfast bar and some soy yogurt. He sat down at a table and flipped his tablet open. It took a second, but he could still reach the Machine Parts wireless network.

Rows of MARSnet notifications began scrolling by on his screen: trending articles and alerts about the pressure drop, the Dome breach, questions about the tremor. Tremor? He hadn't noticed anything, but he'd been inside the Fab all day. It must be really isolated. Maybe dampened. He took a few moments to scroll around and see what was happening outside. Another segment on the Mars Firsts popped up and showed a fiery clip of Zander Bale yelling about the wasted resources spent on the space program and how reliance on technology would end them all – his usual tirade but seemingly amped up to a higher intensity.

Looking around to make sure nobody was looking over his shoulder, Sean opened his shadow browser, an encrypted, tunnelling interface for accessing the dark net, the network within the network. It took longer than usual to start, but he gained access eventually and logged into Chicago, the underground message board he helped admin.

It didn't take long to see the top pinned thread. He opened it and a stream of comments filled his screen.

UNABLE TO ACCESS...
PORTSCANNED YOUR MOM?
WHOLE NET FRAGGED...

He skimmed, but it was a pretty common theme. High traffic all over the colony network. Denial of service.

Fingers tapping, he opened the messaging screen.

To: Hiro
From: Boots
Subject: WTF NETWORK
Something seriously wrong, as you've probably seen already. I'm locked in the Fab, but going to try to work my way out. Can you run some tracers and try to find where the attack's originating? Might be able to shut it down if we block source.
Will advise.

Slim chance, but Hiro and his buddies might be able to trace it. Turning around, he checked again that nobody was paying attention to him while he munched on his breakfast bar. The other people in the commissary were bored to the point of unconsciousness. He reached into his bag and pulled out the card writer he'd lifted from Electronics Assembly. He took a breath and stuck his ID card into it.

The whole Fab was segmented. Everyone had access to their section and an adjoining commissary. With seniority came access to other amenities like showers and bunk space. Sometimes you could move to another section, if you had need to, or if you knew somebody inside. The union helped enforce the boundaries, ostensibly, but not for physical security. It was for job security – you didn't want someone from outside your group taking someone else's position. People guarded their knowledge jealously and in order to move up, you did your time. Simple as that. Be a good worker, get seniority.

It had only taken Sean a few weeks after being assigned to Machine Parts to realize that.

He'd paid his union dues, but that was just the entry fee. He'd need to be here a lot longer than a few weeks to gain access to the rest of the Fab. He didn't have time for that.

It was time for a promotion.

His card writer beeped. The notification on his tablet read, *Writing Complete.*

042

CITY HALL

Bryce realized he was dozing off in his seat and checked the clock in the wall monitor. It read 24:16. Bonus hour. He stretched and looked around the table. Only four were left: Grayson, Natalie, Fred, and Kanan.

Did the lights just flicker?

Bryce blinked and stood up, stretching. "I'm going to head down to the control room, then walk over to my dad's place. Get a few hours' sleep."

Grayson waved at him from his seat at the table. Natalie was sitting close to him, showing him something on her tablet screen, a hand resting lightly on his arm. Bryce frowned and left the room, the cool air of the hallway refreshing after being stuck in the stuffy council chambers for so long. He reached the elevators and walked aboard, stabbing the button to bring him to the control room. It flashed red and beeped angrily. Bryce frowned and waved his card at the reader and tried again. No luck. "Screw it," he said aloud and pressed the button to bring him to the lobby.

The doors swung open and he walked across the empty oval room to the exit, the only sound was the bubbling of the fountains along the walls. A bored security guard nodded to him from behind his desk as Bryce passed. The doors opened onto the lawn. The city of New Providence was quiet, street lights on, the roof of the cavern dark above him. He walked across the lawn and, on a whim, turned left. He took the path through the park near the school. He thought back to his days before joining pilot school at the university: the friends he'd lost touch with when joining up with the shuttle group, the gatherings they used to have at the Social Club, parties at Prospect House. It seemed like such a long time ago.

He ended up on Main Street, somehow, and the lights of the Reef were a small pink and blue pool on the street in front of him. With no security on the door, it looked like a quiet night. Maybe he'd stop in for a drink.

Inside, the dim lighting illuminated empty tables. A few late nighters were assembled, but nobody looked too badly out of sorts. He pulled up a stool at the bar. The young waitress forced a smile as she wiped out a glass with a questionable hand towel. "Can I get you something? We're closing in fifteen minutes."

Bryce slid his card on the counter. "Yeah, just a vodka and soda."

She took his card and ran it. Satisfied, she handed it back to him and got him a fresh glass and made his drink.

The guy sitting next to him leaned over a little closer. "I don't know why they bother closing. Not like anybody sleeps in here."

"Maybe it's a good idea to give the folks the night off." He looked at the man more closely: stubbled, but clean, red-rimmed eyes, wearing a ground crew jacket. He extended his hand. "Bryce."

"Jayse." They shook. "You're the new station commander."

Bryce took a drink. "Yep." He tapped the pips on his jacket's collar with a finger. "Still fresh."

"Man. I heard one of the other teams was in contact with Lighthouse. Comms are all FUBARed out there. They say it's the storm, but I don't really buy that."

"You on a Rover team?"

"Yeah." The other man took a swig of whatever he was drinking. "It's a real mess out there. They've got us running double shifts tryin' to get the dome sealed up. You know anything about that?"

"Not much." He wondered what he should share, if anything, and decided he didn't care. "It lost pressure. Might have been a hundred people inside. It's not good."

"Jesus." Jayse scratched his neck. "My crew's on cleanup duty at first light. Not looking forward to it."

Cleanup duty. It had come up in the council room, Grayson ordering Henderson to have his teams recover the bodies for identification and then reclamation. He swallowed another gulp of his drink, silently toasting the fallen dome workers.

"You know anything about that meteor strike?" Jayse was looking blearier by the second.

"Not really, no." Bryce finished his drink and gave the man a pat on the shoulder. "Look, I gotta go make sure my folks are alright. Take care of yourself. Busy day tomorrow."

"Alright, man. Nice talkin' to you."

The girl behind the bar picked up his glass and leaned over to Jayse. "Time to go, pal."

"Come on. One shot for the road."

Bryce waited around for a second to make sure Jayse wasn't going to be a problem, and when he got up and staggered towards him, he nodded to the bartender and held the door open for him.

"You alright to get home?"

"Home? Night's still young. Come over to Pooky's with me."

"I can't. Sorry."

Bryce watched the man wobble off and pushed his collar up against the damp chill air. He made his way up Main Street towards Industrial. He was still processing the day in his head, imagining what had happened in the dome. It must have been chaos up there. His gut churned thinking about what the loss of pressure could do to a human body. Was it explosive depressurization? Slow leak? The street lights flickered briefly, distracting him for a second. The buildings along the street were dark inside. Empty windows with sleeping people. He came to Industrial Avenue and the looming wall of the Fab. A string of fanciful robots holding hands had been painted along the base of the wall: Machinehead artwork etched on the side of their temple to better living. It reminded him they hadn't always been entirely crazy. Their notions of freedom and artistic expression had been warped over the revolutions into sinister compacts with technology, their dreams drifting further from reality into a future devoid of humanity. *We are extinct, they would have us believe.*

He shuddered and moved onto Church Street, then up the alley to his dad's apartment. Keycard opening the front door, he hopped up the stairs to the second level. A short walk down the hall to his father's place on the padded hallway, he opened the door.

"Dad?" He tossed his jacket onto the couch and peered into the darkened kitchen. "You home?"

A note was propped up on the table amongst the gears and parts of his father's mechanical clock project.

Gone to see your mother. Back tomorrow.
Dad

That was unexpected.

043

ROVER 2

The Rover trundled along through the sand at barely ten kilometers per hour. The big wheels bounced on the rocks and uneven terrain, the suspension absorbing most of the impact and making a smooth ride for the occupants inside.

Erika Rin was sleeping peacefully on the couch in the crew section. Lights off, wrapped up in a blanket, she'd let the rocking cabin lull her to sleep.

Aden focused on peering ahead through the gloom, watching for rocks in their path that might damage the big vehicle. Ray sat beside him, ostensibly doing the same thing, but not really paying much attention. His real job was keeping Aden awake.

"I dunno. Think I'm gonna ask Cindy out. She's cool and I'm pretty sure she's into me." Ray tapped out a beat on the arm of his chair to some song in his head, foot tapping out the bass drum. "I mean, we get along pretty good. I messaged her the other day and we talked for a few hours. She even sent me some pictures."

Aden perked up. "Oh, yeah?" Obviously skeptical, he steered clear of a boulder that rose up in the gloom ahead of them. The lights pierced through the dusty darkness of the Martian landscape.

"Yeah. She made me promise not to show anybody though."

Aden smirked. "Ray, as the senior worker in charge of this vehicle, I command you to show them to me."

"I'm not sure that'd be a good idea." Ray fell silent.

The Rover picked up a bit of speed as they reached a flat spot on the plateau. Aden knew they had a good twenty klicks of relatively clear driving ahead of them and opened up the throttle, electric engines whining beneath them. "Come on, Ray. Now I don't even believe she sent them to you."

Ray stopped tapping the tuneless rhythm and let out a theatrical sigh.

"She probably never even talked to you, did she? You're just making shit up. As usual." Aden grinned. He knew he had him.

Ray dug out his tablet from the pouch beside his seat and thumbed it on. He tapped a few icons and brought up his chat window, holding it up for Aden to see.

Aden spit out the tube from his mouth and it bounced off the steering wheel onto the floor. "Holy shit," was all he could muster. He'd known Cindy for a couple of years now. Recently graduated from school, she was training for ground crew position, soon to be assigned to a team as a junior operations tech. There she was, on Ray's tablet, completely naked in her bed except for a strategically positioned bed sheet.

"She was, um." Ray took the tablet back and scrolled around some more. "It got pretty hot."

Aden refocused on his driving and they were quiet for a few minutes. It was a lot to take in. He'd considered Cindy as a potential addition to his team, but he didn't think he'd be able to look at her straight now. It was hard enough with Erika parading around in her underwear half the time. Ray was, well, kind of a schlub. Was she really into him or was she playing some other game?

He shifted in his seat, trying to get comfortable. He'd been driving all day and now it was after dark. He was going to have to stop soon, but if they could get another hour in, they'd be that much further towards their destination.

"Got any more?"

Ray grinned like he'd just eaten the last candy. "What do you think I should do? I mean, she's still apprenticing."

Aden thought for a minute, focusing on steering over the smoother sections of sand. "I think if you don't do something I'm gonna punch you in the face. She's really hot."

"Yeah." Ray took a sip of water. "I just don't know why she's talking to me, y'know? She showed up at band practice with a friend and then started messaging me on MARSnet."

"I guess she's into you. Can't imagine why." Aden paused, steering away from a dark patch that was probably rock. "Let me see again."

"No way. You said I was bullshitting you and I proved I'm not."

"As the senior worker…" A loud crack made them both jump as the steady hum of the wheels turned to a repeated mechanical thumping, heavy vibration running through the cabin. "Fuck!"

Erika bolted up. "What was that?"

Aden slowed the RV down to a crawl, the vibration turning into a steady drum beat. "Hit something under the sand. I think we broke a wheel." He slammed the throttle back and the RV came to a skidding halt.

"What do we do?" Ray asked, a hitch of nervousness in his voice.

Aden looked at the instruments for a second then slapped the generator on, a hiss and a whirr as the machine spun up. "Nothing much we can do about it now. It's two hundred kelvin and falling out there." The sound of the generator underneath the deck plates was momentarily obscured by hissing sand outside. "I say we get some rack time. I'm beat."

Erika looked disappointed, stuck out her bottom lip. "But I'm awake now."

Aden pulled the latch on the ceiling and dropped the upper bunk down, climbing up into it. "Serves you right for sleeping while we were on the roll. G'night!"

Erika got herself some water and saw Ray with his tablet in the front seat.

He noticed her coming forward and shut his tablet off hastily. "What? Nothing. Hi!" He put the tablet away in the pocket beside his seat and crossed his legs.

Erika made a disgusted sound and went back to the couch. She unfolded it into the bunks and curled up on her side, wrapping her blanket over her. "I don't know what you're up to, but you can stay up there."

"What'd I do?"

Erika shut the lights off in the cabin and rolled over. Aden started snoring in the bunk above almost immediately, barely louder than the hum of the generator and air compressors filling the tanks.

044

LIGHTHOUSE

Bonus hour. They were all still awake on the command deck, watching the monitors as they approached the site of the impact over fourteen hours ago. The lack of coffee was getting to Greg and he thought, might be the cause of his headache. He rubbed his eyes with thumb and forefinger and refocused on the screens in front of him.

"Approaching the impact site," Greg announced, rubbing his hands together over his terminal, getting ready to do the record-enhance-shuffle dance as they passed over their target. This was going to be their third pass today. Dust and sand had obscured the site earlier, but it appeared to be clearing now that the ground was cooling on the far side of the sun. They should be able to get an infrared reading off the surface and a few of their other instruments would pick up other parts of the radio spectrum.

"Thirty seconds," Dan advised, prepping their ground sweeping sensors aboard the station. "Coming up on Tharsis Montes." The station was passing northward on its sinusoidal path across the surface, the rugged, pockmarked landscape of Terra Sirenum giving way to the gentle dustbowls and lava flows of Daedalia Planum. They were nearing periareion just over Ascraeus Mons.

The surface of the planet was cold. Vague details on the high resolution cameras were visible in the optical band, but switching to radar and infrared, the surface took on greater depth. The deep striations of the rocky canyon had an etched quality under the nighttime imaging systems of the station, revealing structures invisible under normal light, but at lower resolution than the daytime optics.

Sunil had taken to pacing during these passes. It seemed to come with the position of Commander, whether merely acting or not.

Greg glanced over at Emma, hunched over her screens. She'd been coding up an automation solution for what they were doing, a system that would control the cameras, run the various processing routines and send the results to Jill in comms for transmission to the surface. She and Jill had been working on it together, Jill doing the coding for the comm systems.

Emma hadn't spent much time talking to him today. She probably felt as bad as he did about their recent encounter and was putting some distance between them. Just as well, he thought, looking at the screens that showed the rolling plains dotted with craters beneath them. He found his thoughts turning to Tamra, wondering what she was doing, if she was alright.

Greg brushed the thoughts aside and returned to the present. The sweep of the surface turned to the flatter, sandier terrain of the Tharsis Plateaus. Tharsis Tholus came into view at the edge of the screen at top right.

"Here it comes," he said. A new crater existed where none had before. Dark ejecta lay around the edges of the thin lip of the crater where the contents underneath the sand had been blasted up and outwards. Even in darkness, the crater's interior seemed to have a lightness to it, almost a glow. "Scanning…" He watched the histograms and waveforms from the surface scanners run through a wide range of activity then settle back down again as they drifted over the more mundane landscape of the plateau. "Definitely picking something up. Running the enhancement suite."

He ran the commands that would take their sensor inputs and pass them through noise filters and analysis. The software was all pre-existing, having been coded up over the hundred years the station and previous craft had been in orbit around Mars. It was just a matter of assembling it all into a package and making it do what they needed.

"Ready to go. Sending to Comms for relay." His work done, he could spend some time looking at what it was they recorded.

Dan moved over to see what the analysis software had done for them.

"Captured," Emma said and squeezed in beside him. "Wow," she said, looking at the spikey graph on Greg's display.

"Relaying data," Jill announced. "This bundle should complete in… five hundred seconds. Just enough time."

Sunil sat down, nodding. "Good work everyone. Feel free to grab some rest. It's coming up on one in the morning, and I want fresh eyes on this at dawn."

Everyone ignored him.

Greg pointed. "Lots of gamma radiation, banding in the five hundred to six hundred nanometer scale. This thing's radioactive, and hot. I think it's glowing, maybe even in the visible wavelengths." He brought up the wide-spectrum camera display on the main screen, and sure enough, after bumping the gain on the image, they could see a circular impression against the dark background of the surface.

"What the hell?" Dan asked nobody in particular.

"Are those emissions constant?" Emma asked. "If it were a bolide strike, it shouldn't be emitting anything."

They fell silent again.

Sunil swivelled in his chair. "Do those emissions pose a threat to the Colony or the Rover team?"

They shrugged, collectively. Emma tapped a few commands on her terminal. "It's really hard to say from up here. We saw a blip of a few millisieverts, but we're eight hundred kilometers up, and on an angle. There may be other emissions we can't detect from this altitude as well, like alpha and beta rays with quick decays. We're likely only seeing the longer lived byproducts." She frowned and looked at the display again. "Yeah, definitely dangerous without shielding, I'd say."

Sunil rubbed his chin. "Alright. We're almost through our passover. I want everyone to get some rest. We'll get Nelson and Ops to plot us a plane change to get us closer to the impact site by the morning. Everyone convene back here at 0600. Crew dismissed!" He stood up and started making shooing motions with his hands, physically tipping Greg and Emma out of their seats.

Greg stood up and Sunil ushered him towards the doors. "Hey!"

"I know you guys love a problem, but I need you well-rested and fresh. Go!"

Greg, Dan and Emma found themselves on the wrong side of the command deck doors in the hallway, curving away towards the crew section. Dim, orange lighting on the late-night program shone on the carpeted decking below.

Greg scratched his neck and yawned. "I guess it's bedtime. Good night."

He turned and started walking towards the cabins. "Wait up." Emma jogged to catch up, leaving Dan trailing behind. "You want some company?" She put a hand on his arm and he looked down at it, her big eyes looking up into his.

"Sure."

"I don't really want to be alone," she whispered.

They arrived at Greg's cabin and he opened the door, Emma stepping inside. Dan walked past them, his head down like he was trying to not look.

"G'night, Dan," Greg said to him on his way by.

It was not returned.

Greg stepped inside his cabin and closed the door behind him.

045

THE FAB

Before leaving the commissary, Sean loaded up as many maps of the Fab as he could find on his networks. The local file server contained crude maps of how to get around, stylized blocky wire diagrams with big YOU ARE HERE buttons emblazoned on them. These were not quite what Sean was after. It took him a while, but he managed to gain access to the Electronics Assembly computers and find some old schematics, complete with duct-work diagrams depicting the complex ventilation systems inside the Fab. It had never occurred to him before but the structure was completely sealed off from the outside, save for the outer access hallways. The whole thing was a concentric system of airlocks with completely isolated environmental controls.

It made sense, as he thought about it. Some of the facilities, like Semiconductor Production and some of the Materials producers had very specific air quality requirements. These were deeper inside, behind layers of locked doors and positive pressure. The clean rooms had their own isolated layers of protection.

Sean's goal was to get out, preferably without anybody noticing. He figured the easiest way to do that was through the big doors in Vehicle Assembly. The outer ring of the Fab seemed to be lined with workers surrounding all the doors. Even if he could somehow hack his way through one of the locks, he didn't think the union boys and girls would stand by and watch. In addition to the bay doors they could drive the vehicles through, there were lots of little access panels used to ship out parts and packages for delivery vehicles. It was a kind of shipping and receiving warehouse for the rest of the city.

He got up and stretched, set his tablet to record network identifiers, then tossed it into his bag. He did a quick tour through the commissary, loading up on soy milk, sesame snacks, fresh breakfast bars and a variety of dried fruits and nuts. His bag was more than doubled in weight, but it wasn't too heavy for him. He wasn't sure when he'd be back, or even if he'd be back, so this food had to last until he could get out.

He felt a twinge of guilt thinking about his baby sister back at his foster parents' home who'd be lucky to get enough to eat with his ass of a brother around. If he made it out of here, he was going to get her out of that hellhole. Himself, too.

But first, he had to get out.

He closed up his bag and slung it over his shoulder. Sean had never had any trouble blending in. Half the time, walking through the city, he felt invisible. In here, that might be a little harder. Everybody knew everybody. They were all Brothers and Sisters in the Fabricators Union. It was going to be hard. Who got to move freely throughout the Fab? The runners. People moving parts and equipment between different fabrication stages. Most of the parts were carried through on an intricate array of conveyors from zone to zone, but those that didn't fit or were requisitioned from a different area had to be delivered by hand.

He still had the old batteries for his tablet in his bag. Those might pass as parts if he got pressed.

Sean set out down the north-south hallway towards Plastics, the big materials division responsible for turning chemicals derived from plants and organic compounds into hardened resins and reusable materials. The actual chemical creation of the plastics was just the first stage. After that, an array of shapers, moulds, and forms was used to turn the raw polymers into the desirable finished product, be it containers or parts. Different plastics required different treatments. It was vast and he couldn't fathom a reason to be in there, so he would steer clear of it.

He went through a pair of doors, the worn sign reading MATERIALS TRANSFER CONDUIT 14S. He came to a set of metal stairs going down and descended to the level beneath the main floor. Two large flights of stairs and then another set of double doors opened onto a hallway. Metal tracks in the walls and floor, presumably for some kind of automated conveyor system. Above, a rail-line ran above the lights.

His modified ID card continued working without incident. He idly wondered about the locks in here and who was controlling the access to them. There was probably a computer system in here somewhere, maybe a server room. If he made it out, he might have enough information on his tablet to figure out where it was later.

The walls here were a different kind of concrete. More granular, rockier. Darker material from the rock leftover by the dead volcano. The air was heavier, too. It didn't feel like it was just a pressure differential: it was warmer and more humid. Mechanical noises reverberated through the walls and floor, deep subsonics he could feel in his bones.

He heard voices reverberating around an intersection in the sparsely-lit tunnel and he tensed up. It was late, well after the bonus hour now. He couldn't imagine anybody was still working. He crouched down and scanned the hallway for any alternate routes, but there were none. He edged his way up to the corner of the intersection and crouched along the wall under a conveyor track, listening.

"You think this batch is gonna be any better than the last one?"

"I dunno. They all look the same to me."

"I don't think the control boards are right. The movement's wrong."

"A little janky, but it found the target. It worked."

"Ah, what do you know? They haven't even been flashed yet."

Sean thought he recognized one of the voices. He snuck a peek around the corner. Sure enough, Perkins was standing there, vaporizer in his teeth, taking a hit, coveralls half-hanging behind him like a cape. He blew out a cloud as Sean ducked back around the corner.

"Better get back inside."

A drawn-out yawn caused Sean to stifle one of his own.

"Alright," Perkins answered wearily.

Sean heard them moving off and a door opened and shut. He stuck his head around the corner, looking down the hallway to a heavy metal doorway, before scurrying across the gap.

He continued on another hundred meters. He wondered if there were cameras following him – someone, somewhere in a vast control room, watching him on a bank of monitors. Hard to imagine they wouldn't have security cameras down here, but cameras were expensive pieces of equipment to build. Sensors and integrated circuit manufacture were one of the most delicate things they could produce here and required exotic materials. The sensor fab would be somewhere above him up ahead, near the center of the Fab.

Another pair of voices snapped him out of his train of thought. Another intersection lay ahead. A set of stairs in the hallway led down to another level. The sign read ASSEMBLY MACHINE ACCESS 3. The voices were getting closer, footsteps walking down the hallway towards the corner. In a moment they'd be right in front of him.

Sean took the stairs down another two flights, carefully stepping on the edges of the metal slats in an attempt to keep the staircase from creaking. Level Sub 3. He flashed his card on the door's reader and it paused for a few seconds, blinking at him. Then it turned green and the door unlatched.

He opened it and went through.

046

NEW PROVIDENCE

Bryce was awakened from a dream by music. The lights flickered then turned out, as did the music. Something from Old Earth. Had he imagined it? He had been dreaming about a girl he didn't recognize. Shouting from across an unrecognized street in a language he couldn't understand. Something echoed from across the city – not his city – bouncing off the walls. Was that a gunshot?

Confused, he sat up in bed and reached for his tablet. "Lights." It took several moments before the room lights came up in a staggered increase.

He rubbed his eyes and looked at his screen. An endless stream of notifications was rolling past, names he didn't recognize with subjects that made little sense to him. What the hell?

He cleared the screen and opened his messages. His path seemed clear to him now. He had to get back to the station. There was nothing more he could do down here. He'd delivered his message and asked for the people in charge to do what was necessary. Whether they did it or not wasn't up to him now.

To: Jun Nagaoka, Lori Harrison
  Subject: Assemble your crews
  Captains. I apologize for the short notice, but we have an emergency. I need a full ship's crew for the Banshee on station in case we need to launch. We have three ships in space, Terror is in trouble. Happenstance is inbound, and a third I can't tell you about. I am no longer comfortable with the situation down here

in the City. Watchtower is in need a refit. Lighthouse's supplies are running low.

Jun: See if you can get a shuttle fueled up and provisioned for launch today. Get your crew and be prepared to stay up there.

Harrison: Same goes for you. Get your crew together and tell them to be ready to stay on the station until needed. It could take some time, but I have a nagging feeling that we're going to need you.

I'll tell you more when we're away.

I will check back with you both soon. Expect rendezvous at Gagarin by no later than 1600.

Cmdr Bryce Nolan

He marked it priority, hit send, then brought up a new message. The lights in his room were flickering.

To: Robert Nolan
Subject: Get Mom and Meet Me at the Terminal
1600. Check in later. B.

He sent this out priority as well.

Bryce got dressed, grabbed his stuff and tossed it in his duffel bag and left his father's apartment.

*

The cool air of the city felt refreshing as he walked out of his father's stuffy apartment building into the alley behind Church Street. It was still early, before 0600, and the lights from the domes were still dark. He walked into the street and the multi-denominational place of worship stood tall on his left, looming over the ceremonial grounds of the First Founders, concrete and glass reaching up into the pillars, itself part of the vaulted ceiling holding up the sky. The cross on the north face shone out into the street, a crescent on the east.

The street lights were flickering. He could hear zapping sounds as the power fluctuated. All of the lights across the city were behaving irregularly, acting on their own seemingly erroneous inputs.

He set out at a jog, straight across to Prospect Street, heading south around the Fab to Industrial. People were lining the streets here, many in their nightclothes. The Fab was lit up along the roof, high above, shining against the vaulted ceiling high above them, bright and steady. Clouds of gas belched out of the roof and hung there like storm clouds in the sky.

This was new.

He jogged through the crowd, past a group of safety and security officers who looked unsure of what to do. A couple of them looked up at the glowing clouds above the Fab.

Bryce reached City Hall soon enough. Climbing the steps, he strode into the lobby, slightly winded from his run. A tired security guard at the desk stopped him.

"You know anything about what's going on out there? Lights have been acting weird all night."

"No. I'm hoping to find out." Bryce walked past reception to the elevators. He didn't feel good about lying to the man. Bryce was certain this was the object's doing, infiltrating their computer systems, bringing about the end of days. The entire city's automation was about to fail on them, or worse, turn against them.

The elevator arrived and he stepped inside, pressed the button to take him upstairs to the Council chambers. The light on the pad flickered and the elevator lurched into motion. Bryce held onto the hand railing and for the first time, felt like he might be in real danger as the steel box carried him up eight levels to the heart of City Hall. He realized he'd been holding his breath when the indicator read 8 and the doors opened onto the hallway.

He walked the short distance to the council chambers, the doors already wide open, lights glowing from the monitors and lights above the table. The room was quiet, empty except for Fred Darabont, snoring quietly on a couch along the wall. He had his jacket wrapped over him, his dark hair stuck to his forehead. It was still only 0630, so Bryce figured he'd let him sleep for now. Other people would be arriving soon enough. He'd like to get into the control room, but he still hadn't been granted access, and now likely never would be.

Bryce sat down at the table and pulled out his tablet from his bag, setting it on the smooth shiny surface in front of him. It took some time to access the network and another flood of notifications spewed across the screen. He swiped it clear and opened his messages.

An activity indicator was flashing in the lower corner of his screen so he tapped it, the log window opening.

Unable to send messages. Retrying in 30 seconds...

He watched the little spinner as another flood of messages arrived in his inbox.

He opened one at random.

Subject: HI S UPRME CMANDR
WE HOEP YOU LEIK THE SOHW.

047

ROVER 2

Aden jumped down from his bunk in the ceiling beside the fold-out cot in the crew section, jolting a sleeping Erika and Ray awake. He slammed the collapsible bunk back into its stowage space and crawled back into the suit lockers. He checked his suit out, made sure there was nothing in the boots and legs, then started climbing in.

"You need any help?" Erika rubbed her eye, wrapped in a blanket, bare feet on the cold deck.

"I might. I'll need a few minutes to see what the wheel looks like. Get Ray on the controls in case I need him to roll it."

Erika yawned. "OK. Do I have time to make coffee?"

"Fill yer boots." Aden reached up and pulled the chest piece down over his head, locking it into the waist. Once secured, he grabbed his helmet and gloves and put them on. He walked into the airlock, running the cycle. A thin film of carbon dioxide frost covered the edges of the airlock window. Outside, the Tharsis Plateau was a flat, blue sea of dirt running in all directions. The looming volcanoes of Ascraeus and Pavonis were just gentle slopes on the horizon from this distance.

The cycle finished and he pushed the door open, hopping down into the dirt. It was still dark outside, the sky black with bright stars overhead, lighting everything in dim blue light. Aden switched on his suit lights and walked through the tracks the Rover had left in the dirt on their drive last night. His suit was still cool but warming up inside. The temperature readout on his display read 155K. He could feel the heaters in his suit working in his backpack. Warm water ran through piping down the arms and legs, keeping his extremities comfortable. Later, when he'd warmed up, it'd run in the opposite direction, taking the heat away for cooling.

He walked around the rover, inspecting the rear wheels first, checking the body for damage. It was covered in dust. The statically charged particulates stuck to the hull of the big crawler. He reached the articulated front housing the cockpit and looked at the big right wheel. Four big steel spokes radiated out from a chunky round central hub, supporting the curved carbon and steel mesh tire that acted as both suspension and traction. The tires were designed to have a good amount of give to them, able to support a sizeable impact on the unpredictable Martian terrain, but sharp rocks were known to defeat them. The wheel came up to his waist and he knelt down in front of it. A sizeable hole had caved in the grooved tire treads, big enough to put his arm in, edges frayed where the woven lattice had been punched through. He grimaced at it, then banged twice on the side of the cockpit with one gloved hand. He looked up at the stars rolling above. A faint grey glow on the horizon to the east was obliterated by the lights coming on inside the domed bubble of the rover's cockpit.

"Ray, roll us back about half a meter, please."

"Right. Stand clear."

The wheels straightened out and then the big machine eased itself backwards and came to a halt, dust falling from the wheels.

Aden inspected the damaged wheel again, brushing dirt away from the wound. "It's not too bad. No sidewall or spoke damage. We can patch it." He did a quick inspection of the other front wheel, found nothing wrong with it before walking back around the side, opening up the storage compartment above the rear wheels. He reached in and pulled out a flat, one meter by one meter section of segmented carbon-steel mesh and carried it forward, placing it over the flattened hole. He bent the mesh down on either end, then folded the self-locking clips around the existing tire, teeth crunching into place in the dirty steel wire embedded in the sidewalls. He had to reach into the wheel well to attach the clips on the other side, once asking Ray to turn the wheel out so he had a better angle.

When he finished, he gave it a tug, satisfied that it would hold. He walked back to the storage container and slammed the hatch closed on his way to the airlock. He climbed up the short steps inside and closed the door.

Waiting for the cycle to finish, Aden nodded along to a Stone Machines tune running through his head. The sky noticeably brightened outside, obscuring the stars in the east. He didn't get to spend much time out here at night, but he relished it when he had the chance. On a clear night, you could look up at the stars and see everything, clear as if you were in space. The thin atmosphere didn't so much as make them twinkle. He sighed happily into his helmet, just glad for some quiet time before climbing behind the wheel again. He'd all but forgotten the fights he and Jayse were supposed to go to the night before.

The cycle finished, and the inner door let him in. He stomped his feet a couple of times in the lock before stepping inside the locker area, stowing his suit in its rack and pulling on his overalls.

He walked into the crew compartment and checked the counter. His coffee cup was full and waiting for him. He opened the top and took a sip. Erika sat on the couch watching him.

"Heard anything from control yet?"

"Nope." She had her own coffee in her hands and looked pretty pleased with herself.

"Well, I guess we should go say hi then." Aden walked forward. Ray got out of the driver's seat and clambered into the passenger's side.

"Wheel OK?"

Aden took another sip of coffee as he picked up his headset and put it on over his head. "Yeah, I think it'll hold. Pretty clean hole, right in the center."

"Good. Er. As good as it gets, I guess."

"Yeah." Aden flipped the mic on. "Control, this is Rover 2, do you copy, over?"

Slight static, then the channel clicked in. "Rover 2, Control. We read you loud'n'clear. Over."

"About time," he said to Ray before opening the channel again. "Control, we're about ready to roll out. How's the weather out there?"

Slight pause. "Rover 2, looks clear for the day. Be advised though, Lighthouse is measuring some pretty heavy radiation from the impact site. Advise caution. Check your rads before getting too close, over."

Aden and Ray exchanged a wide-eyed look. Erika got up from the couch and crawled forward to listen.

"Say again, Control? Radiation?"

Click. "That's right. Lighthouse sent down some readings last night. Looks pretty hot out there. Over."

Aden exhaled loudly. "How close can we get?"

A longer pause this time. Aden could imagine the eggheads in control arguing about how to answer this. "I'd say stop every twenty klicks and take a reading. Then once you're at twenty klicks out, stop and take another one every kilometer. Over."

"Jee-zus." He thumbed the mic. "Roger that, control. Rover 2 out." Then more quietly, with the mic off, "Fuck you too."

Ray brought up the instruments and did a check. "Normal here. Point seven millisieverts."

"Alright, keep that thing on. Let's roll. See how the new tire feels."

Aden pushed the throttle forward as he pulled back on the steering column, settling in. The rover rolled forward with the faintest of thumps as the driver's side wheel rolled over the new patch of treads. Throttle forward, the rover picked up speed and the vibrations smoothed out in the soft dirt of the plateau.

"Not too bad," Ray said.

048

THE FAB

You are in a maze of twisty little passages, all alike, Sean thought to himself. After crawling around inside accessways and conduits, he found a hatch in the wall of INTERMEDIATE SHUNT 17 and climbed inside the cramped space packed with pipes and cabling. It was warm here and he ate a snack of soygurt and bean stew by the light of his tablet. He poked at his tablet, organizing the network IDs he'd scavenged and tried to associate them with where he'd found them on the map, based on time. Before long, the steady hum and thump of the pipes lulled him to sleep. His dreams were filled with nightmarish, blood-covered versions of Perkins chasing him through tunnels. He jolted himself awake and hit his head on a steel pipe, confused about where he was in the dark tunnel. He fumbled around for his tablet and consulted his maps. He was approaching the center of the Fab now, three levels down, nearing the Assembly.

After some water and a breakfast bar, he checked the hatch and climbed out. His hands were dark, covered in dirt and grease. He imagined his face probably looked the same. He hoped it would give him a bit of camouflage, but might also make it harder to interact with anyone he encountered down here.

He stepped carefully to the end of the hall, ears pricked, listening for sounds of life. The hall ended in a pair of heavy steel doors. Sean put his head to them, listening for any sign of movement on the other side. No sounds, other than the deep thrum of the machinery all around him. He tried his card and was surprised again when it worked. Through the doors was a small room with another set of doors on the opposite wall: big slabs of steel with tiny acrylic glass windows set inside. The small metal room between the first set of doors and the second felt old. A hand crank on the wall beside the door conveyed some ancient purpose, labels long since scratched away, leaving only the faint suggestion of yellow and black warning hashes.

He went through the doors into a metal hallway, dimly lit with caged lenses in the walls. Steel plates on the floor made it difficult to walk quietly in his over-sized boots. Grooves in the walls and regularly spaced hooks and rings looked like attachment points for something mechanical.

Sean felt the deep resonance of heavy machinery through the floor and put a hand on the wall, feeling the vibrations. He heard voices up ahead. A doorway stood at the end of the hall with an intersection running between.

"We need another set of boards."

"Goin' through 'em pretty quick. Last batch didn't last a day."

"Almost done. This load oughta do it."

"Yeah, then we gotta program the damned things."

"Above my pay grade!"

Sean put his hands on the cold floor and found a ring. He pulled up and felt the floor plate rise. Sean crawled into the gap and carefully lowered the plate, just as a pair of boots rounded the corner of the intersection and walked towards him. It was dark in the crawlspace, but light leaked in from the edges near the walls. He had enough room to move. As his eyes adjusted, he saw the space seemed to run the length of the hall. He could feel cool air from ahead and hear liquid running through the pipes beside him. He reached over and touched one of the pipes, pulling his hand quickly away, the pipes coated in frost. Crawling forward, he saw a warning symbol and the word COOLANT in dark letters on one of the pipes.

"The fun part comes after," the voice above him said.

The door opened and closed with a bang above and behind him. He counted to fifty, waiting to see if anyone else was coming. When they didn't, he raised the floor plate again and climbed out into the hallway. He crept forward along the cold metal wall, listening intently. He crossed through the intersection and reached the door at the end of the hall, unlabeled except for the number 02.

He carefully opened the door. No card reader here. He just let himself in.

A large, dark space opened up before him. Dark blocks, a black cubist construct, descended several storeys below. He stood on a narrow gangway running along the outside of the cubic space, surrounding the machinery. Large conduits ran up and down, lengthwise and crossways through the structure, creating an additional tapestry of metal, carrying mysterious contents: parts and materials, liquids and gasses. The piping was all different sizes and thicknesses.

It was dark in the chamber and it took a moment for Sean's eyes to adjust. He could feel movement around him, and looking down into the gloom, could see the machines sliding about in geometric patterns. The whole environment changed shape, configuring itself to whatever task it was performing. He felt his way along the gangway to the corner along the right, hand against the cool wall behind him. If his maps were right, he needed to get through this construction room to the other side, the next section of tunnels should take him to vehicle assembly.

The noise was almost painful. It was loud. Not as deafening as Machine Parts, but steady, shrill and scraping, thumping and grinding. It was a bigger space and the noise had more places to go. It hurt his ears and made it hard to think. An indistinct cacophony of machinery merged into a single ear-splitting drone.

A nearby hiss and a cloud of smoke steam drew his attention and he edged along the gangway, leaning over the edge. Looking down, a dark shape emerged from one of the blocks and rolled forward along a conveyor belt, diagonally away.

"Hey! You there!"

A female voice, barely audible above the din, called from the level below pointing up at him.

Sean froze for an instant, not sure what to do, looking around nervously. It was a good fifty meters to the next exit along this gangway. He could see more dark shapes along the walls. More people.

He bolted, sprinting for the hallway that turned off to the right, boots clattering on the steel ramp. More boots from below, running up towards him, making the whole gangway shake on its bolts in the walls. Faces looked up, implants glinting in the low lights of the machines, some of them glowing blue. He wasn't going to make the exit before they intercepted him.

Looking around frantically, he saw his exit.

He leapt out into space, above the whirring, buzzing machines below.

He landed on the conveyor belt, round shapes ahead and behind him, moving up above the construction.

"He's over there. On the conveyor!"

"Go after him."

"No. We'll get him in Inspection. Get up there."

More running. Boots on metal.

Sean ducked as the conveyor brought him up to the ceiling, opening above into a dark tunnel. He didn't know where he was going – "Inspection," one of them said. They'd be waiting for him there.

He moved back to the ovoid machine on the belt behind him. There wasn't enough room to get around it, and it was full of sharp protrusions all over. The front of it was a maw of discs bristling with sharp teeth. What the hell was this thing? It was too dark to see and he couldn't understand it by feel alone.

He was trapped between these things, whatever they were. There was no space on the conveyor belt to move around or over them.

There was space underneath, though. The metal blob was raised up, squatting on what felt like a hinged, carbon-steel framework. Bars folded up underneath in a symmetrical nest, like the legs of an insect.

He crawled under the smooth metal belly of the thing and he hid there, waiting to find out where he'd emerge.

049

CITY HALL

Henry Grayson lay awake, not wanting to disturb the sleeping form beside him. Soft light from the clock on his nightstand drew a gentle curve across Natalie's back and shoulders, gently rising and falling, deep breathing of REM sleep.

She started, maybe sensing him watching her, and groaned, rolling onto her stomach, nuzzling into her pillow.

Henry put a hand on her waist, marvelling at the small size of her, feeling the curve and the dent of her lower spine, her ribs.

"Good morning."

"Stop it," she protested. "That tickles." She stretched her arms above her head, bunching up her shoulders in a satisfied sigh, pressing back into him.

Henry continued exploring her contours with his hand, watching her contented expression change to something else.

"Nat."

"What?" She shivered and pulled the blankets back up over her.

"Things are going to get... difficult."

"What do you mean?" She looked at him in the dim light, propping her head up on her pillow with an arm.

"I mean. This shit is happening. I don't know how bad it's going to be, but it could get..."

"Bad?" She reached down inside the covers, grabbing him, and he tensed up, then relaxed as she began stroking him. "How bad?"

"Really bad..." He caught himself before he lost himself in her grip and put his hands on her shoulders. "Come away with me."

She laughed. "Oh, where are we going? I hear Olympus is nice this time of year."

"The station… Earth."

She scanned his face, suddenly serious. "You're not joking."

"No. I'm not."

She seemed to consider this, was quiet for a moment. "What about Will? My kids?"

"Your family can follow along afterwards. When we figure out an evacuation plan."

Her eyes grew wider. "Henry. What are you talking about?"

He held her by the shoulders just then, and kissed her hard on the lips. "I need you with me. I can't do this alone." He kissed her again, before she could answer and he felt her melt in his arms.

*

The door chimed again. Henry was still getting dressed after his shower. "Just a second. System? Who is at the door?"

"Bryce Nolan is at the door."

Henry grimaced as he put on his shoes and walked out into his office, the lights coming up, closing the door behind him. Natalie was still in the shower and was in for a surprise when she came out. "Enter." The door unlatched and swung outward into the hallway. A harried Bryce Nolan stood there.

"Come in, come in. Just about to make some coffee. Want one?" He walked over to the bar and pulled three cups out of the cupboard. He arranged them on the counter and began scooping coffee crystals into a grinder.

"Uh. Have you seen what's going on out there?" Bryce was cut off by the loud ruckus of the machine.

Henry regarded him again. "Maybe we'll go easy on the coffee for you." He reached under the counter and pulled out the heated carafe, the induction burner having clicked on when the office system recognized his morning program. He dumped the grounds into a filter set over a glass receptacle and began pouring hot water into it. The smell of fresh coffee filled the room as he worked. "Do you take milk?" He waited for the filter to empty, then poured water over it again.

"No." Bryce shook his head like he'd just remembered something painful. "Henry. I can't stay here. I need to get a shuttle up to Lighthouse. I'm no good down here."

Henry placed the cups on the counter and filled each of them from the decanter. He slid one of them towards Bryce. He watched him pick it up, raise it to his lips and take a sip, wincing slightly at the hot liquid.

He poured his own and replaced the carafe on its seat under the counter, then placed the decanter on a small hot plate. Still standing at the counter, he took a sip and with a satisfied sigh, carried his coffee over to his desk. "System. Desk screens, please." He set his coffee down on the corner as three translucent monitors rose up from the old mahogany desk. Crisp, holographic displays showed the city from every angle: surveillance cameras and visualizations of activity outside the Fab, in front of the hospital, a new growing crowd northeast of the Fab near Church Street. "It's not even eight in the morning and everything's going to hell out there." Another screen was filled with rapidly-scrolling text. "You see these? System errors. They've probably been rolling out like this all night."

Bryce put his coffee down, untouched. "I told you. I told you we needed to reboot everything. The colony is in great danger." He looked desperate. "I need to get to the station."

Henry leaned back and sipped his coffee again, looking across the monitors at Bryce. "Yes. The station." Another quick sip then he put his cup back down. A wave of his hands lowered the screens back into the surface of his desk. "Who've you got on shuttle duty?"

Surprised, Bryce faltered for a moment. "Uh, Captain Nagaoka and his regular crew. I've already contacted him."

"Did you?" Henry smiled. "That's good. By my reckoning, *Banshee* should be just about ready to go too. You should contact Captain Harrison and get her crew together. In case we need them."

Bryce looked stunned. "I... already sent her a message."

"Splendid!"

The door to Henry's rooms opened and Natalie walked out, less formal than yesterday, drying her hair. "Did you see where I put my... ?" She trailed off, noticing Bryce in the room for the first time. "Commander."

"Have a seat, Bryce. Finish your coffee." Henry scanned his desk while taking another sip. "You might want to check your messages."

Natalie went back into the bedroom in search of her earrings.

050

LIGHTHOUSE

Emma walked into the mess hall with Greg just in time for breakfast. She'd woken them up early this morning, at 0530 after only four hours of sleep. Greg tried to linger, but she managed to get him up despite his protests.

The mess hall was half-empty. Engineering and ops members were eating rusks and breakfast bars. Chris the cook was looking bored behind the counter, so she walked over and picked up a tray, Greg in tow.

"Hey, Chris. Anything on for breakfast this morning?"

"Got some hashbrowns and whatever's left in the case – and that's goin' fast."

Greg reached in under the lights and pulled out a tub of soygurt and a banana. He held up the tub. "Seriously?"

"Don't give me any guff, kid. All the stuff we picked out of the biolab earlier is going into tonight's dinner. It's going to get hungry up here real soon."

Emma picked up a cup from the counter and was about to fill it with coffee when she saw the sign. HOT WATER.

"Some tea leaves in the bucket. Toss a scoop in that water and let it steep."

Emma did as she was instructed, putting a small scoop of loose leaves into her cup, then filled it with steaming water.

"Thanks, Chris." She picked up a breakfast bar and said to Greg, "Might as well get up on deck. This isn't exactly a sit-down breakfast."

"You can say that again."

"Watch it!" Chris said loudly from behind the counter.

Greg grinned and gave the cook a wave on their way out.

They walked in silence for a moment. Emma broke it. "What do you make of that?"

"I think we're going to need to grow more food."

Emma thought of Tamra and the domes, and hoped everyone had made it out alright. "Ugh." The sound escaped her lips unintentionally at the thought of sleeping with her best friend's boyfriend again last night.

"What was that?" Greg opened the doors and stepped onto the command deck, head turning to look up at the board instinctively.

"Oh, nothing." She looked out the windows as Mars rolled past, the sun just coming up over the horizon ahead of them. She turned to look at the monitors. MSS13, *Happenstance,* barrelling in towards them, about a week out. A dashed line for Jerem's new ship, MSS02H, the *Terror.* A slow arc, deeper into the system. A third dashed line for MSS03E, way out past the belt. Imaging had put it in an uncertain band of space, its position merely a statistical probability. "I was just thinking it would be great if we could get Tamra up here to help with the food situation. Then I remembered the domes and wondered if she's OK."

Greg looked at her. "Funny. I was just wonder how Jerem's doing." He inclined his head at the board above them. Emma felt her chest tighten up at the mention of his name.

They shuffled over to their station in silence and sipped their tea and water while munching on breakfast bars.

Emma chewed in silence, thinking about Jerem. She wished she could get a message to him to see how he and his father were doing. Maybe they'd get word from *Happenstance* when she got home. She wondered what he'd think of her if he knew she was sleeping with Greg. *Great job, Em. You've managed to screw over both of your best friends.* She shook her head, trying to clear it, when Greg spoke up.

"Nothing new on the scans last night. The crater's going to be coming into view in another forty-eight minutes."

She checked the time. "Sun's going to be awfully low still. Might get a look at it."

The doors opened and Nelson Ortega walked onto the deck with Sunil. They walked over to the science station, Nelson munching on a breakfast bar, crumbs already on his jacket.

"Hi, Nelson," Emma said. "What've you been up to?"

"Hardening our network." There was barely any expression on his face as he said it. He took another bite of his breakfast bar and spoke around a mouthful of dry cereal. "Sunil says you have some sensor readings for me to look at."

Greg spun around to face them. "Yeah, over here." He brought up the captures from last night, his automated recordings of each pass in a series of files.

Nelson leaned over, dropping some crumbs on Greg's shoulder and took a look. Without saying a word, he walked off the deck into the boardroom to spinward.

"Did you... want to talk about them?" Greg said, only partially under his breath.

Sunil brushed a crumb off of Greg's shoulder. "I expect he just wants to view the data without anyone else's interpretation clouding his judgements. You know how he is." He wandered over to the Ops team. "Mister Buchanan. How is the progress on our plane shift coming?"

Buchanan looked up from his station. "We're almost directly over the crater now. In another two orbits, we should be one hundred percent complete."

"Excellent."

Sunil strode over to his seat and climbed into it. Raising his screen, he began tapping on it, settling in with the morning's reports.

The knot in Emma's stomach grew. It wasn't unusual to execute maneuvers on Lighthouse. It was necessary to occasionally run the engine to make up for lost altitude or to avoid a stray piece of debris or even Phobos. The minimal atmosphere of Mars didn't present much drag on the station, and at the height of their orbit, it barely affected them. Plane-change maneuvers were infrequent and expensive.

Emma turned back to her station and brought up the new list of contacts from Watchtower. Four points of interest. No warnings. She sighed and brought up the New Mars Asteroid Catalog and went to work.

051

ROVER 2

The landscape brightened under the dawning sun, dark terrain resolving into blue-grey rocks and tan-colored sand. The surface rolled by underneath the rover's wheels. Sand absorbed most of the vibration from the makeshift repair work on the front right wheel. Aden's hands gripped the wheel as the machine rolled on.

"Should be able to keep a steady fifteen kph out here on the planes," Ray said from the passenger seat.

"Yeah. There's not a lot out here. Just keep your eyes peeled for craters."

"Right."

Climbing the wall of an impact crater out here could be a bad thing. Crater walls were rocky and rough, but the change in terrain could be gradual. The real danger would be going over the edge. A gentle slope or rocky hill might be concealing a big drop on the other side in the sand ahead of them. In the minimal contrast of morning twilight, you might not realize there was a rim until reaching the edge, and then you'd be in real trouble.

Aden glanced down at the map screen in the console. "Shouldn't be anything out here until the Badlands at least."

Erika yawned and stretched on the couch. "I might need another coffee."

"Yeah, I could use another one. If you don't mind." Aden reached back, holding his steel mug behind him between the seats. A hand took it from his and he returned it to the wheel. "I suppose we should check in. See if anybody misses us yet."

Ray nodded and held onto the hand rail in the dash in front of him.

"Ground control, this is Rover 2. We are approaching one hundred and one degrees west and making good speed towards our target. Over."

Crackle on the radio. "Rover 2, this is ground. We copy, but you may need to deploy a relay soon, over."

Aden cursed under his breath. "Roger that, control. We'll drop a spike in the next hour or two. Over."

"Acknowledged, Rover 2. Be advised, keep the channel clear in the next hour. Lighthouse is running a sweep and we're trying to keep the interference to a minimum. Over."

"Understood, Ground. We'll listen in. Rover 2 signing off."

Aden flicked off the mic switch on his wheel and an arm reached between the seats with a full thermos of hot coffee. Ray took it from Erika's hand and held it until Aden was ready to pick it up.

"Sounds like Lighthouse is control's new best friend." Erika slurped her coffee.

"Yeah. Maybe ours too."

They were quiet for a spell. The only sounds were the sipping of coffee and the bump and rattle of the RV as they rolled over the uneven ground. They hit a small channel in the dirt, partially obscured by sand and the rover slammed into the other side, all six wheels banging through the ditch. A tense moment followed as everyone listened for tell-tale signs of damage to the wheels and suspension, but there were none.

"Goddamnit." Ray wiped at the front of his jumpsuit, coffee stain spreading across his gut.

Aden focused on driving, his own coffee in its holder beside his seat. He had to bite back from telling Ray to be more careful, but didn't bother. He'd be planting their relay soon. Because of the curvature of the planet, ground-based VHF radio didn't work so well over longer distances. Dropping a powered transceiver relay gave them the ability to stay in contact with the ground station, provided they weren't interfered with. His thoughts were interrupted by a crackle on the radio.

"Ground Control, this is Lighthouse. We are coming into view of the impact site. Over." Slight high frequency squealing remained on the channel after they'd clicked off.

"Ray, see if you can clean that up, please."

"Yeah." He went to work on tuning the radio and the squealing went away.

"Lighthouse, this is mobile land operations. Prepped and awaiting transmission on side-channel, over."

Erika plunked down on the couch. "Ooh, fancy," she said, referring to ground's formal naming.

Ray snorted. "Ground think they're spacers now."

"Quiet," Aden said, still concentrating hard on the terrain ahead of them.

"Land ops, we are coming into view of the impact... it's..." The channel fizzled and went out with a pop.

"Lighthouse, this is ground. We did not receive last. Resend. Over."

A pause, the gap filled with static, then the voice returned. "... Shiny!"

Aden let out his breath.

"We're seeing some strong reflections off the surface. Shadows, too. There's some structure around the edges. Beginning side-band transmission. Over."

"Lighthouse, how are those radiation readings this morning, over?"

Aden and Ray exchanged a glance. Ray indicated the radiation meter on his console, unchanged from before. Gave a shrug.

"Ground, they are... reading much lower this morning. Like, a fraction of what we saw last night." A pause. "Hold on. We're getting new readings. Gamma radiation is spiking. Whoa..." The voice trailed off. "We saw a flash. Over."

Silence in the rover as the crew eavesdropped on the exchange. "Lighthouse, send us your data. We'll have our people down here take a look at it. Thanks. Over."

"Roger that. You should be receiving. Looks like the dust is starting to lift on Tharsis. Tell your rovers to be safe out there. Over."

"Understood, Lighthouse. Talk to you in a few hours. Mobile land out."

Aden steered the rover around another divot in the terrain, managing to avoid it this time, then took a sip of his coffee. A thin line of dust had appeared on the horizon, the sky almost imperceptibly dimmer as the dust took to the air around them. He pushed the throttle forward and built up some speed. Might as well make as much progress as they could before the dust got thicker and they'd have to stop to plant their relay.

052

THE FAB

Sean wasn't sure how much time he had. The machine he was hiding beneath was hot. The warmth reminded him of crawling inside the big bender in Machine Parts. His view outside was limited by lack of light and presumably, a lack of any surface detail, just smooth metal walls with a track running through it. It felt like he was climbing. Going up. He wanted to consult his maps, but didn't dare pull his tablet out under here. There wasn't enough room.

The conveyor levelled out and he craned his neck around so he could see ahead. A growing light shone around a bend, the machine ahead of him turned on the belt, disappearing momentarily. The machine he was under curved around the tunnel and the belt rolled into an open space. Racks of these machines lined the walls. Squat, insectile hulls, faces full of sharp cutting wheels. Camera lenses like the eyes of a spider.

These looked like mining robots, the original machinery used to carve out the tunnel around the city. Scavengers built to chew their way through rock and metal, harvesting raw materials to be turned into concrete and steel. What the hell were they doing with these?

"You think he made it up here yet?"

"Where are you, little grub? Come on out."

Sean tightened his grip on the robot's legs, lifting his back off the belt. Hooking a leg around one of the folded up steel appendages, he could practically crawl into this thing's undercarriage. He hoped it wasn't going to start moving. It could easily break a limb or crush him if it were powered up. He inspected the joint of one of the legs he was hanging from. Electric motors and hydraulics seemed to make the limbs move, the fluid pressure acting like a muscle, providing strength. The motors could propel the legs with more rapid motion, but with less power. Given enough time, he'd love to get one of these things and take it apart to see how the whole thing worked.

The belt stopped and the digger rattled forward on a set of rollers into the back of a lift. Three of the robots banged together in the load-carrying box of the lifter, almost knocking him out of the machine.

"He should be right here."

The lift smartly carried its payload to a rack. It rose up, raised the lift and dropped the first robot onto the shelf. The lifter shifted sideways and dumped Sean's robot onto the shelf next to another. The legs flexed as it shifted, picking up the weight of the machine's body and threatening to crush Sean underneath, but it stayed up. Then the last of the robots was dropped in beside him with a creak and a bang. Sean couldn't see outside, but there was enough space on his left to get out.

Sean disentangled himself from the machine's legs and slid out from underneath, along the back of the metal rack to the end of the line. He climbed down into the corner and crouched there, getting his bearings. A quick count of the racks in this room, four across, stacked four high, ran forty or fifty meters down the room, gaps for passing lift machines and people. Each one of these diggers was nearly a meter and a half around and a meter tall. There must be over three hundred by his estimation.

He could see one of the men following the lifter, carrying the next machine to its destination on the rack beside him. He scrunched himself up into the corner as best he could, partially obscured by the robot on the bottom shelf. The man watched the lifter dump the robot unceremoniously into place and looked under it, slapped it on the shell, then walked back to the conveyor.

"I don't know, man. You think he could've gotten off somewhere along the line?" The man with implants in his cheeks and temples squinted into the shelves. His eyes were bloodshot. Sean suspected he was a sniffer.

"There's nowhere to go in there. I had to clear a blockage last week and it's a straight line."

"Here, kitty. I've got a treat for you."

Footsteps. Sean could see a pair of legs walking up the row of shelves towards him. Between the lowest shelves, through the machines, Sean watched the man getting closer. Sean considered making a break for it. There was a door in the middle of the wall on his left, but a man stood in front of it, looking at his shoes, uninterested in the proceedings here.

Or, he could just stand up and turn himself in. He vacillated between these two options when the door opened and another man entered, interrupting their search.

It was Perkins from Machine Parts sauntering in pushing a plastic cart. From his low vantage point, Sean couldn't really what was inside.

"Oh hey. Those them?" the man with cheek and temple implants said to him.

"That's the last batch for a while. Sixteen," Perkins said.

"We're still short forty. When can we get another batch?"

Perkins shrugged. "I don't do integrated electronics. Ask them." He shoved the cart with his foot, sending it rolling towards Sean's corner. "Where you want these?"

The other waved a hand in Sean's direction. "Just dump 'em over there in the corner. We'll sort 'em out when we're ready to start flashing."

He'd be seen here. Sean climbed over the closest robot on the lowest shelf and squeezed in between them, his back pressed up against the wall, frozen still. He remembered Perkins, covered in blood on the Machine Parts floor, Steel's remains all around him and those dead eyes just staring straight back at him. He suppressed a shudder.

Perkins pushed the yellow plastic cart over to his former hiding place and dumped it out. Circuit boards inside poly bags tumbled to the floor of the shop. Perkins looked inside, making sure it was empty, and began pulling it away. He turned it around and headed back towards the door, the other men waiting for him.

He had to move before they remembered they were looking for him. Sean saw a moment where everyone was gathered together, focused on Perkins leaving. Crouching, he ran along the edge of the rack, back the way he'd come in. He stopped behind the inert lifter, parked in front of the conveyor belt and listened.

"… anyway, Pike says we should get started on this batch. We want them ready to go by tomorrow."

"That's not enough time. What if we have to debug them?"

"Get it right the first time."

Sean climbed onto the now still conveyor belt and crawled into the tunnel heading back down to the Assembly. The metal on the belt creaked, the shaft of the tunnel warping under his weight and he skittered forward, deeper.

"You hear something?" one of the men asked.

"Oh yeah, we were looking for someone. Looked like a kid down in Assembly."

Perkins' voice. "Boots."

Sean didn't waste any more time listening. He crept forward around the bend and felt his way forward in the darkening metal tube.

He hoped this thing wasn't going to start up again and bring him back into the inspection area. Without the machines on the belt, he had plenty of room to move and could half-slide his way down the thirty-degree incline. It didn't take him very long before he emerged inside the blocky mechanical chamber that built the robots. He waited a moment for his eyes to adjust to the dim lighting. There was nobody here now and the machines were quiet, except for the occasional hiss of a pressure valve and a blast of air.

On his perch, he took out his tablet and turned it on. He loaded the maps he'd downloaded and kept an eye on the network icon in the corner. It remained hollow, indicating there was no network access here, at least nothing visible. The Assembly wasn't even detailed on his map. It was just a black box on the third sub level. The legend told him the little red circles meant "no access," so the Machinists must have gained access somehow, probably using a combination of turned management and violence. As he'd seen, it wasn't hard to escalate privileges with the right technology.

It was easy enough to reorient himself. He'd come in from that door across from him. If he climbed down from the conveyor across that stack of machines, he could reach the ramp and leave from the door on the opposite side. Hopefully he wouldn't run into anyone on the other side of the door.

He turned off his tablet, stuffed it back in his bag and climbed down to the stack of machines.

053

CITY HALL

Bryce walked back down to council chambers in a daze. There was something completely surreal about the meeting he'd just had with Grayson. And Natalie, he supposed. Not only was he alright with a launch, it sounded like he was planning on joining him on the shuttle. Worse, it sounded like he was already aware he'd been in communication with Jun and Captain Harrison.

He rode the elevators to the eighth floor, wondering if he was doing the right thing. On the one hand, he was deliberately abandoning the city. It felt a lot like a flight response and that made him uneasy. People might need all the help they could get down here, and that wasn't necessarily a thing you could provide from the comforts of City Hall. On the other, what the situation needed was intelligence and science. If this was an attack, Lighthouse might provide a significant boost in perspective and data gathering, something that might not be possible from underground.

The doors opened and he walked out automatically, walking down the hall past the old space suits of Captain Cavanaugh and his first officer. The old Mark I space suits gathering dust in the closed environment. He checked his watch before entering the chambers. It was 0845.

The room had started to fill up. Tadeuz was sitting there in his brown jacket, white hair wild about his head, a tablet with a physical keyboard attached to it propped up on the table in front of him.

"Hey, Tad." Bryce sat down beside him and extracted his own tablet from his jacket, putting it on the table and flicking it on.

"Bryce." The old astronomy professor exhaled through his moustache. "It's getting weird out there. All the computer systems are going a little haywire."

"I know. I saw the lights on my way in." He looked around the room at the new additions. Fred Darabont, now awake and frowning at his screen. Maude Richardson, fidgeting in front of her tablet, tapping a stylus with a dissatisfied expression on her face.

"Network access has been spotty. Video transmissions aren't working and everyone's being bombarded with junk messages." Tadeuz cleared his throat. "Kanan's down in the server room trying to get things sorted but I haven't heard of any progress."

"We'll let him work on it." Bryce checked his own tablet and the flood of messages continued. It was draining his battery just trying to keep up with the raft of notifications. Skimming, he couldn't find any replies from his father or Jun or Captain Harrison.

He killed the power and stood up, walked over to Fred. "Fred, I need access to Central Command. I hear ground control is in contact with Lighthouse and I need to talk to them."

Fred frowned at him. "I'd give it to you, but our security systems aren't accessible. The room should be open if you need to get in there."

"Alright. Thanks. If Grayson's looking for me, tell him I'm either down there or outside. I have a few errands to run."

Fred looked at him like he was crazy. "Good luck with that. I'm not going out there."

Bryce raised an eyebrow, about to say something when he had an idea. "Fred, do we have any runners on hand? People who can get messages to people. You know..." He searched for the word. "Couriers."

He thought about it for a second, scratching his chin. "I suppose we could task some of the safety officers to deliver a message if it's important."

Bryce smiled. "It is. I need two messages delivered. Can you help me out?"

"Sure, go talk to Henderson when you're in the Command Center."

*

Leigh Henderson was going on thirty hours without sleep. He was standing behind his desk, staring at the screens, cycling through footage from the city without really seeing any of their contents. He knew if he sat down, he'd fall asleep almost immediately. He reached behind to his desk and picked up his cup, almost knocking it over in the process. His hand was shaking as he lifted it to his lips, taking a sip of cold coffee.

He had the shakes from the amount of caffeine he'd been taking mixing poorly with his lack of rest. His second in command, Davies, would be in shortly and he was hoping he'd be able to grab a few hours' sleep to take the edge off.

"Henderson?"

He almost jumped out of his skin when he heard the voice. "Wha?" He turned to the speaker and recognized Station Commander Nolan from the day before, looking unshaven and somewhat disheveled. "Commander."

"Sorry to interrupt, but I heard your ground control team have been in contact with my station. I need to speak to them."

He heard the words and took a moment to process them. "Right this way." He walked around his desk, down the steps into the communications pit and led the Commander to a console with three people sitting at it. Monitors on their desks showed different views from the surface. "Mister Taylor, this is Commander Nolan. From the station."

Taylor turned around and looked up at Bryce. "Sir. We've got some images from the crater. They look... interesting."

"What've they found?"

Taylor shuffled his display and brought up a still image of the surface. "This was taken just this morning after sunrise. You can see the shadows at the crater's edge."

Bryce leaned forward and Henderson found himself doing the same, leaning in to get a better look. The crater was perfectly round with a bright shine reflecting off it in the morning light. "What's the scale here?"

"Um, we think the crater's about eight hundred meters across. It's shallow though. Not very deep."

"And these shadows?"

"They appear to be some kind of structure in the crater wall. Kind of unusual-looking. Areology says it might be a product of heavy quartz crystals in the area."

"Why is it shiny?" Henderson asked.

"Same thing. Probably quartz?"

Bryce nodded, still looking at the image. "Anything else?"

"Um. They said it's radioactive. I sent the data over to the university so they could look at it."

"That's troubling. Make sure they get that data. You might have to run it over on foot." Bryce said. Then he clapped the comms tech on his back and said, "Nice work. When's the station coming back into view?"

"They just passed over. Should be here in a hundred minutes from now."

Bryce looked unhappy about this, but set a timer on his watch. "Good enough. I'll check back then." He was about to turn away, then put a hand on the tech's shoulder. "If I'm not back, tell them to expect a delivery sometime later today. Thank you." He turned back to Henderson and they walked back up out of the pit. "Now then, I need you to do something for me."

"What?"

"I need you to get one or two of your junior staff and get a message to some people. Shuttle pilot Jun Nagaoka, and Captain Lori Harrison of the *Banshee*."

Henderson blinked at him. "You can't just message them?"

Bryce narrowed his eyes and spoke more slowly this time. "Our communications systems are being disrupted. Messages aren't being delivered. Can you get these people a message for me?"

"Yes, sir."

"Good. Do you have any paper?"

Henderson looked at Bryce like he'd been asked for a piggy-back ride.

054

LIGHTHOUSE

Greg and Emma sat in the bigger of the two boardrooms. Nelson Ortega was already there, his tablet in front of him, red eyes staring intently into the screen.

Greg's stomach grumbled loudly and all eyes turned to him for a moment, before looking back to their respective tablets.

"Sorry. I'm getting a little hungry, is all."

"It's almost lunch time. We can see if there's anything new then." Emma struggled to contain her own hunger noises.

"I'm sick of soygurt."

Emma frowned, then sighed. "You could be eating hashbrowns and brotein."

"Oh man. I could so go for some hashbrowns right now. I should've got some this morning." His stomach growled again, more violently, and he found his mouth watering at the thought of the reconstituted potato bits fried in oil. They weren't exactly nutritious, but they were relatively plentiful. They tended to be popular among some of the younger citizens from the wrong side of town. "I'll skip the brotein, though."

Emma turned up her nose. "Who wouldn't like ground up grub protein in drink form?"

Nelson barely lifted his eyes from his screen. "Quiet. I'm trying to work here."

"Making any progress?" Greg asked.

Nelson lowered his tablet. "Not really. I can't figure out why the crater's emitting so much gamma. If the bolide had a high concentration of fissionable material, it might be hot, but not like this."

"Are you forgetting about the object?" Emma reminded him.

"No, I'm just trying to rule out any other natural possibility first."

Greg thought for a moment, adjusting his hat on his head. "What about something in the ground? Could the impact have set off some kind of reaction in some of the elements already down there?" He shrugged. "I don't know, like, uranium or thorium?"

"Or potassium? Very unlikely. They don't tend to cluster in large enough quantities, and only a millionth part of those elements are radioactive isotopes. We don't tend to get naturally occurring fission reactions on planets." Nelson corrected himself. "Not that close to the surface anyway."

"Oh." Greg thought back to his recent anxiety troubles and remembered Doctor Lau admonishing him on his nutritional lapses. He'd told him he had a potassium deficiency and ordered him to eat more bananas, something that was in limited supply here on the station.

Emma continued watching Nelson while absent-mindedly tapping her fingers on the table to some inner beat.

"Stop that." Nelson looked at the offending finger.

"Look." Emma stood up and walked over to the monitor, now displaying the image of the impact site. "Look at the surface." She pointed, staring at Nelson. "This is not a naturally occurring thing. The surface inside the crater is shiny." She swiped the view out. "These craters near Tharsis Tholus aren't. These," she waved a hand around the edge of the crater, "do not look like naturally occurring formations." She leaned on the table. "I think we can safely rule out natural phenomena."

"It could be quartz... fused silicates... salt?"

"Gah!" Emma threw up her hands and sat down.

"Mm. Salt," Greg said. "I could go for some noodles."

"Would you stop?" Emma swatted his arm.

Nelson powered on, ignoring them. "We've measured two rather intense radiation events. Sustained on first pass last night, then this morning, a short pulse lasting for several seconds, coinciding with a flash of light in the visible spectrum."

"Like, how many bananas of radiation are we talking about here?" Greg asked.

Nelson studied his charts. "Our detector picked up almost point two millisieverts per second sustained gamma and neutron emission." He paused while punching in some numbers. "That's nearly twenty thousand bananas' worth."

"Holy, that's a lot of bananas," Emma volunteered.

"Yes." Nelson nodded, not noticing Emma's smile. He continued, deadpan. "It takes nearly thirty-five thousand bananas to generate a lethal dose."

"I could maybe eat half of that right now," Greg said.

Emma giggled.

Realization crossed Greg's face like he'd been slapped. "Wait, are you saying that's what our detector was reading here? On the station?"

Nelson nodded. "That's right. I have to tell Sunil to move us back off axis. It's too dangerous for the station."

"Holy shit. Then, the dose on the surface must be…"

"Accounting for our angle at time of measurement, our altitude… At least two orders of magnitude higher. Yes."

Emma and Greg looked at each other. Emma stood up. "We have to warn the Rover team not to go near that site."

Greg followed her out. "We're still half an hour out. Let's see if there's any food out yet, then we can tell Sunil and Jill."

055

ROVER 2

Aden eased the big rover over a clump of exposed rocks in the terrain. Driving had become steadily more difficult now that they'd reached the long downslope of the Tharsis Plateau. The smooth surface of the previous two hours gave way to ancient lava fields, boulders and weird rock formations, eroded by wind blasting sand over the surface over the millennia.

They were entering what was colloquially referred to as the Badlands.

Some music was playing low on the RV's sound system, loud guitars and crashing drums. Aden was a keen follower of the throwback-styled "machine rock" movement and had the t-shirts to prove it.

Erika cleared her throat. "You'll want to swing north once we clear this rock field. Some big formations up ahead."

Aden nodded, brow furrowed in concentration. "Got it."

Erika turned around in her seat and looked back into the main crew space. Ray appeared to be asleep on the couch. The rover hit a bump and the cabin rocked side-to-side, Aden's steering column rolling him back and forth.

Ray almost fell off the couch, waking up with a start. "Cindy?"

"Sorry, princess. Little bumpy up here," Erika called back to him. "Who's 'Cindy'?"

Aden shook his head in a don't-go-there expression.

Ray got up and crawled forward, hunched over and holding onto the hand-holds along the overhead cupboards. He knelt down between the two forward seats and wiped his eyes. "See anything yet?"

"Just a lot of rock and dirt," Erika reported. "Dust's come up again."

Aden, without looking away from the terrain in front, reached down to the console and picked up the stubby section of rubber tubing and put it between his teeth.

Erika looked up her from her tablet. "Cut north here."

Reed cranked the wheels left, the cabin swaying.

They were only able to sustain a fifteen kilometer per hour speed in the clear sections, the big RV's six wheels churning in the dust and sand. Over the rocks, their speed dropped to barely a jog. Erika checked the clock on the console. They'd been driving for two hours straight and it was approaching eleven. At this pace it'd be 1800 before they reached their destination. The sun would be going down.

"How's our power supply?" Erika asked.

Aden looked down at the gauges. "Battery's down to around seventy percent. Solar cells are only giving us about sixty percent of optimal because of this dust. Genny's still eighty percent full and good for at least three charges."

The Rover had a range of about sixty kilometers, depending on terrain and battery health. The methane generator could charge the batteries in a few hours at rest, or maintain a charge level while rolling. Erika had no idea what state the batteries were in on this vehicle. After the swap last night, they'd run them down to nearly forty percent capacity before setting out this morning. Chances were, they'd be dry when they arrived at their destination and have to spend a few hours charging up for the return trip.

"Everybody done their coffee?" Becker's arm reached between the seats, taking Erika's mug from the cup holder.

"Thanks, Ray." Erika didn't want to mention that they'd be on the surface for potentially a day without the power to move. Becker tended to overthink things and she didn't want to put him in one of his quiet moods.

Erika scanned the terrain on her tablet, picking out a path between the walls on the high res satellite map. She couldn't really blame Ray for the way he was. He'd been given the job on the surface team after a tour in the mines. He was on the crew in Tunnel 14 when it had caved in. They'd lost eight people in that collapse and he was one of only two survivors. She shuddered at the thought of being trapped underground under tens of kilometers of rock for two days. The thought gave her the chills.

"Oh well, it's not like I had a date tonight anyway." She didn't. She was supposed to meet up with her family. Her parents were having her aunt Tilda over for dinner. Her cousin Geoff was probably going to be there too. They were older now, their childhood friendship now distant and awkwardly-remembered.

Aden ignored Erika's attempt at banter and turned down the music, Hammerdown crunching through their guitar solo fading to a quiet din. He held his earphone to his head and spoke into the mic, "Come again?" He slowed the big rover and turned his head halfway to Erika. "Signal's getting weaker. We're going to have to drop that spike."

"Not it." Erika grinned. "Eighty klicks seems about right." The dust outside was probably not helping their radios. "Becker. You ready to take a walk? We need to drop a repeater."

Ray got up from the couch with exaggerated heaviness. "Fine, fine. Can I get you anything else while I'm up? More coffee? A sandwich?"

Aden looked at Erika, with raised eyebrows. "We have sandwiches?"

She shook her head. "It's not lunchtime yet. Seems like all we do is eat in this thing." She patted her stomach, feeling squishy from too much sitting around.

Aden lifted the steering column away from him now that they were stopped, putting the big machine into park. He stood up and stretched. "Well, I'm going to see what we do have." He climbed back into the crew section.

"You won't like it." Erika looked at her nails. She had to keep them short because of the suit, but she still painted them when she could. The clear polish kept them hard against the moist interior of the gloves. A lot of people lost nails if they wore the suits too long. It made a real mess of their fingers.

"Goddamnit. Hashbrowns, brotein, tofu and bean stew."

"Told ya."

Ray made a lot of noise putting on his suit, taking longer than was strictly necessary. He trundled around the back of the RV, gathering up his tool belt and knocking Erika's helmet onto the floor in the process. Eventually, he got into the airlock.

Erika watched Ray climb out of the back of the rover and jump down into the soft dust and round rocks of the Badlands on her monitor. He lowered the steps behind the door then moved around to the side, just out of view. One of the panels flipped up in the edge of the camera's field of view, then he reappeared, dropped a hard shell case onto the dirt with a splash of dust.

Aden came back to his seat and shook up a bottle of brotein, then popped the top and took a couple of big gulps. "Strawberry's my favorite."

Erika turned up her nose at him. "I don't know how you can stomach that ground up bug powder. And we don't have any strawberries. It's synth flavor."

"Whatevs. Still tastes good." He poured some more of the thick shake into his mouth and ballooned his cheeks with it before swallowing. "Ray, why don't you check that wheel while you're out there? See how she's holding up."

Tinny voice on the radio. "Yeah, sure."

They watched him open the tabs and unfold the case onto the surface. A spike in the middle of the box stood up and Ray gripped it with his gloved hand, pulled upwards, extending the whip antenna three meters above him. The aerial flopped in the wind as Ray bent down and turned on the power. Red light flashed briefly then turned green as it acquired a signal. Ray brushed a glove over the little solar panels on the box, looked up and adjusted its position to get a better view of the sun, dim as it was.

"We're all set up out here, I think."

"Signal looks good, Ray."

Ray moved around to the front of the vehicle, disappearing from view, before re-emerging in the rover's bubbled windshield. "Wheel looks fine, Aden."

"Alright, get back inside."

Erika watched Ray looking around at the light brown terrain. The short, wind-blasted rock formations stood all around. The stones were worn smooth, sculptures carved over the eons, taking on mysterious organic shapes. Round rocks rested in curved nests, placed there like offerings by some long dead disciple.

Aden shook his head at Erika. "Come on, Beck. Get a move on."

"Right, right. Coming." He turned and made his way back to the airlock. Erika and Aden felt the bump as the hatch opened and closed, the whir of jets as the lock re-pressurized and ran its cleaning cycle.

056

THE FAB

Sean sat on the ramp in the upper support structure munching on a breakfast bar, crumbs dropping from the corner of his mouth and drifting down below, disappearing into the gloom above the dark machinery. He risked the glow from his tablet, shielded in his jacket, to consult his maps.

He placed himself in the center of the map. The dark box called "The Assembly" was an ancient vestigial component of the Fab left over from the *Exodus'* original framework. The boot-strapping component of the Fab, its purpose was to create a swarm of mining robots that would return core materials to build the rest of the Fab. Raw materials were transported to the smelters and turned into concrete and steel for construction. The builders rolled out into the newly-formed hollow and began building up the structures needed to house the next set of machines and so on until the humans arrived to take over.

Of course, it was never intended that the humans would end up operating the Fab. It was meant to be an autonomous structure, robotic assistance for the colony so the humans could make the most of... whatever it was humans did in a post-technological society.

Sean finished his breakfast bar and took a swig of water from his bottle. He traced his path back up to materials. The large open spaces contained vats of chemicals that could be combined to form various types of plastic and glass. Steel and heavier glass were shipped in via rail from the smelters.

He crawled along the ramp and made his way down to the outer walkway that circumscribed the cubical assembly area. The machines hissed and whirred below, awaiting instructions, finished with their mining robot construction. Sean wondered if they had a new job as the conveyors started moving again. A new batch of materials flowed into the room as lights activated on the machines around him.

Sean hurried, making his way along the ramp way to the door opposite the one he came in originally. No card lock here. He opened the door onto a metal hallway and had to verify that this wasn't the way he'd come in the first time. The number on the door read 01.

He made his way to the next intersection and heard voices on his left. The hallway led to a door and he could see metal stairs beyond it, pairs of boots running to the door.

He bolted.

Running hard, he reached the door at the end of the hallway and keyed his way through it, closing it gently behind him. He waited for a moment, listening to the door behind him as he steadied his breathing. Satisfied that no one was following behind, he crept forward to the metal stairs leading up and out of the Assembly.

He was losing track of time in here. It didn't follow the normal queues of the city, presenting different colored lights to indicate the time of day. In here everything was yellow-white and red. The stairway was illuminated by soft red lights. He emerged into a dark hallway at the top of the stairs. The lighting flickered on as he opened the door to a new hallway.

"Sub-Level 3," he muttered under his breath.

Another short hallway and another door leading to another set of stairs. Sean trudged up, ignoring the burning in his legs. His heavy boots, clomping on the stairs, sounded loud in his ears and he made an effort to stay quiet. He reached the end and found a door with a card lock.

He passed his card over the lock and pressed the door.

It took him a moment to realize the lock hadn't worked. There was no green light from a successful authorization. He tried it again.

Red light. The door would not open.

He began to panic. He thought he heard voices down below, on the other side of the door downstairs. He hauled his pack off his shoulders and began digging through the bag. Shuffling through the tubs of soygurt, brotein and breakfast bars, he found what he was looking for. Steel's card.

He slid it over the lock as he heard the door opening below and voices echoing up the stairwell.

Green light.

He opened the door and slipped through into a harshly-lit cavern. Bright, blue-white spot lights lit the concrete floor in front of him on sub-level two. Massive cylindrical vats lined the walkway in front of him, illuminated on all sides by massive floods. Stairs circled around their outsides, connecting them to a massive grid-work of ramps and conveyors, pipes and conduits. Part refinery, part chemical plant, the materials section took the inputs from the smelter and farms and converted them into plastics and more rarified metals. The temperature in this area was not as warm as the machine works below. Massive cooling towers and vents pulled off the excess heat and distributed it elsewhere throughout the facility.

Where were all the people? This avenue should be filled with workers moving between stations, vehicles delivering packages. Overhead, the network of rails and conduits was quiet. Immobile. Nothing was running.

Voices. Sean snapped out of it and started running, boots echoing off the concrete spaces around the towers. The door opened behind him and three men piled out of it. He risked a glance behind and saw Perkins at the head of the group. Their eyes locked for a moment and Perkins broke into a run, picking up speed as his strides lengthened.

One of the towers beside a cylinder blew out a puff of flame and lit the ceiling in orange, the dark undersides of the ramp ways suddenly shining in dim, shaking fire light. He scanned the ramp on his right, saw a small lifter parked on the side of the platform and ran to it. He jumped into the driver's seat, Perkins and the other machinists almost on top of him as he pressed down on the pedal. The engine whined and he lurched out onto the road, past the yelling men, spinning the steering wheel, throwing the cart into a squealing drift. He leaned sideways across the seat to keep the little buggy from tipping over as the men dove to get out of his way. He drove as fast as the little lifter would take him, soft rubber wheels gripping the smooth track.

Sean grinned. This was his first time driving.

057

NEW PROVIDENCE

Bryce ran down the steps fronting City Hall towards the gathering throng of protesters carrying Mars First protest signs. He pushed his way through the Safety and Security personnel barricading the front entrance to the building. A lady carrying a sign reading, "FEED A MARTIAN, STARVE A SPACER" saw the Lighthouse patches on his jacket and pointed a finger at him.

"Go back to space, leave our food!"

A cheer rose up around her. Bryce was suddenly unsure he was going to make it through.

Zander Bale, the head of the Mars First movement, stood on a makeshift podium erected in the middle of Hopper Drive, blocking all traffic in the street. Students and protestors lined both sides, filling the lawn. An amplified voice: "Please. Maintain order, citizens! We can do this peacefully."

"We are tired of living under the rock. Tired of giving up our best so a select few might hang onto their precious orbital museum." The voice of Bale echoed across the buildings and the high roof of the cavern. The assembled people cheered and the safety and security personnel looked at one another nervously. "We must strike out! Make new colonies on the surface. Risks be damned, fortune favors the bold. With God's help, we can succeed as our forebears did before us. The Valles is a temperate environment. The deepest canyons have pressure and warmth and running water. We can live there! Make a home for those of us willing to step outside the false safety of this autocratic cacocracy. Let them have their relics and their machines. We can make a new life! An honest life, unencumbered by the forced imprisonment of our men and women. We can be true Martians once and for all!"

The crowd cheered and pressed forward against the security personnel. Bryce faltered for a moment, frozen in place during the speech.

"Step back!" one of the black, armor-clad safety officers yelled, stepping forward with his stun stick.

"Excuse me! Let me through, please." Bryce pushed his way past the woman, further into the crowd, people turning towards him. He raised his hands up. "Please let me through. I need to…"

Stars. He stumbled forward, almost falling to the ground as the crowd cheered and pressed in around him. Had someone punched him?

"GET BACK!" Then a zapping sound and a pair of bodies fell beside him.

The crowd roared and Bryce stumbled back, the press of humanity charging towards him. Two of the security personnel grabbed him and pulled him back behind the line. "Get inside, sir. This is not safe," the officer said to him as he and his team deployed clear plastic shields, stun sticks held between the cracks at the oncoming wall of people.

Bryce scurried backwards, and made his way along the wall of security guards. A loud clattering of rocks and whatever else that could be thrown caused Bryce to duck down and cover his head with his jacket as the debris struck the wall of shields, followed by more zaps as the security officers stunned members of the crowd. Zander Bale, no longer on his podium, had seemingly vanished, no doubt whisked away by his followers.

"Masks up. Launchers," one of the lead guards ordered and an officer on the steps of City Hall fired a canister into the crowd in a long, slow arc. It bounced off one of the protestor's heads, dropping him to the lawn like a sack of cement. Tear gas burst out of the canister as a nearby man, wrapped in a scarf and goggles, bent down and picked it up, heaving it back towards the security line. The officer reloaded his launcher, dialled in his range and fired again.

The crowd roared. There were screams from the groups nearest to the erupting gas cans, unable to cover their noses, mouths and eyes in time, pressing through the crowd to get away from the growing cloud of irritants.

Bryce checked his head. No blood. He made his way back to the outside edge of the circle of guards. At the end of the line, Bryce tapped the shoulder of the last officer and pointed at her headset. She looked at

Bryce's jacket and then she took out her earpiece and radio and gave it to him. Bryce nodded thanks and clapped her on the arm, stuck the earpiece in his ear and cut out onto the side lawn.

The iron fencing separated him from a crowd surrounding the Safety and Security Barracks along Industrial Road. The protestors were running along the edge, further south on Hopper Drive as a male voice came in over his earpiece. "Get some barricades out here. North, west and south walls. I want a hard seal on this facility." Some ten-fours acknowledged the request.

Bryce rounded the building and saw another crowd running along Commercial Street, lining the west side of the Fab. Lights flickering on the streets were augmented by a yellow-orange glow emanating from the roof. He did a double-take, almost thinking it was a fire at first.

What the hell is going on in there? Bryce thought to himself as he skirted around the edge of Commercial Street towards Industrial Road. Protesters from the Mars First rally ran around the corner, fleeing the tear gas-infested front lawn and ran in among the Machinists standing alongside the Fab. The Machine Worshippers sent up a cry, seeing the sign-bearing protesters and began surrounding them.

"Security to Commercial Street. Some of the protesters are getting caught in some Machinehead group." Bryce spoke into his headset as he made his way along the back of the Security Barracks.

"Who is this?" The gruff voice of the lieutenant overseeing the security line at City Hall barked at him.

"Bryce Nolan, sir. I borrowed a headset from one of your officers. I'll give it back soon."

"Send a team to Commercial Street. Cover the back entrances in case of breach. Mister Nolan, you be careful out there."

"Copy that." Bryce rounded the corner at a jog, entering the back of the High School grounds. He switched off his transmitter and ducked through an alley to Jackson Lane, turning the corner around Turk's Provisions. More scattered noise on the radio as the lights flickered in the streets. Looking up at the apartments lining the small pedestrian road, people were hanging over their balconies watching the scene unfold in front of City Hall and The Fab. A woman on one of the lower balconies called out to him. "Do you know what's happening?"

"No, ma'am. Get inside," he said as he jogged past her.

He ran up the steps to his mother's apartment and carded himself in. Up the stairs. Down the hallway.

Banging on the door. "Mom? Dad?"

The door slid open and Bryce's mother Caroline stood there, looking like she was dressed for tea with the ladies. "Bryce! I'm so glad you've come. I was wondering if I was going to get to see you."

She gave him a big hug. He smiled and gave her a kiss on the cheek.

"Come in. Don't stand around in the hall like some kind of urchin."

Bryce's father, Robert, was sitting in the big chair, feet up on a stool, a mug of something hot beside him. "Son."

"Don't get up or anything," Caroline said as she whisked past him and sat down on the couch, patting the cushion beside her for her son to sit down.

"I don't have time to stay. You both need to pack your things. We need to get out of here."

The lights flickered and Bryce's mom tutted. "I don't know what is going on with the power, but I hope it's fixed soon."

"Mom!"

She looked at her son, shocked at his tone.

"We're under attack. The City's not going to be safe for long. You need to pack your things and meet me at the shuttle terminal in the next hour."

The voice in Bryce's earpiece was issuing orders for more units to be dispatched in front of the hospital. He hoped he'd be able to make it to the terminal, with or without the help of security.

"We can't go, Brycey." His father leaned forward in his chair. His face was a mix of regret and resignation. "We're staying here." He reached over and took his wife's hand in his.

"It's so nice to have your father back." Caroline smiled at Robert and she patted his hand before taking hers back. "He's agreed to move back with me."

"It's just, what are we going to do on the station? There's nothing for us there. Down here, we can help out. I can fix things."

Bryce's jaw dropped as he listened in on the radio, the voice warning security they were going into blackout in fifteen minutes and to secure their buildings in case the crowds panicked. He looked at them both with what must have been a stunned expression on his face. "You can't stay here! Things could get bad. Really bad. It's already crazy outside. There's a riot…" He couldn't tell them about the impact site. He didn't really know anything about it, but presumed all of the disrupted systems were because of it. It had to be doing something, infecting their computer systems.

"Space is a young man's…" Robert looked at his wife. "Person's game. We're too old to be any good up there. Take someone young."

"Mom, Dad… We have to go."

"We'll be fine, Bryce. Don't you worry about us." His mother smiled at him and looked perfectly happy in her blue dress and faux pearl earrings.

Robert stood up. "She's right. We'll be fine."

"I… don't feel good about this." Bryce gave his father a bear hug, not sure if he'd ever see the old man again. "You two take care of each other. Keep the doors locked."

Caroline stood up for one last hug and kiss from her son. "You be careful," she said to him, as if sending him off to school for the first time alone. "Remember to keep taking your radiation medicines."

"OK, Mom," he said, kissing her cheek.

The voice in his ear announced a new gathering of Machine Worshippers around the Network Operations Center in the northeast quadrant.

"You might lose power soon. I'll try to send an officer over to help you get to a pressure center if you need to move."

His father nodded at him. "Really. We'll be fine."

058

LIGHTHOUSE

Jill turned around, facing Sunil. "Everyone's inside," she said.

"Very good." Sunil addressed the team down in the pit. "Ops, execute plane change maneuvers."

"Aye, sir. Plane change commencing," Buchanan confirmed.

Emma half-expected a jolt or a shift in motion or a deep hum from the engines, but the big station felt unchanged to her, sitting at her console in the hab ring's command deck. Unlike an altitude change, a plane shift was performed by the station's lower-powered, lateral ion thrusters mounted along the spine. Ops programmed a steady burn that would translate their orbit south of the impact site by several hundred kilometers over the next couple of orbits.

"Might as well get one last look while we're still overhead." Greg had his screens up, watching the view from the big lens pointed down at the surface.

"Jill. Begin broadcast, please," Sunil requested.

"Aye." She turned to her station, hand on her ear. "All ground crew, this is Lighthouse. Please be advised, impact crater appears to be highly radioactive. Please exercise caution. Repeat, all ground crew..." She recited the message once more then set it to repeat.

Emma watched the screens in front of her and Greg. The ground rolled past below, a thin layer of dust partially obscuring the surface as they swept towards the blasted rock surface of Fortuna Fossae. The ground shimmered in the afternoon heat of the sun.

"You think we're in any danger up here?" Greg shifted uneasily in his seat. "From the radiation?"

Emma shrugged. "We're getting bombarded every hour we're up here anyway. This is just adding a few more days to our dose."

Greg held his stomach, trying to prevent another outburst of hunger noises.

Emma ignored it, frowning at her screen.

"Here it comes."

All eyes turned to the big screen above them. The shiny surface of the crater was now clearly visible in the mid-day sun, reflecting back up at them brightly like a pool of water. The crater flashed, a burst of static on the open channel to ground radio.

"Was that a reflection?" Sunil asked.

Greg shook his head. "Big gamma spike. Visible flash overloaded our optics for a second. Didn't last long."

It looked to Emma like there was a cloud of dust emanating out from the edges of the crater, a circular wave front radiating in all directions. She made a note to take a look at it in slow motion when they had their recording.

"Lighthouse, this is Rover 2, do you read? Over."

Jill glanced at Sunil who gave her a nod. "Go ahead."

"Rover 2, this is Lighthouse, we read you. Over?"

Slight pause. "Lighthouse, we're still about forty klicks from our destination. What do you want us to do, over?"

Emma thought the voice sounded concerned. The usually brash rover driver didn't like what he'd heard from their warning.

Jill turned around and looked at Sunil, unsure what to say to him.

Sunil stood up. He walked over to the communications station and sat down, picked up his old headset and put it on. "Rover 2, this is Lighthouse Actual." Sunil shook his head, continued. "Acting Commander Sunil Pradeep. Did you just see a flash from your position? Over."

Another pause. "Pleased to make your acquaintance, Commander. This is Aden Reed. Senior Ground Ops, Driver first class. Yeah, we saw the flash. Over."

Sunil closed his eyes and pinched the bridge of his nose. All eyes were on him now. "The pleasure's all mine, Aden." He looked at Jill, who was watching him. "There may be some additional dust kicked up from the impact site. My science team tells me the site is radioactive. It's fluctuating, so the level of danger is changing over time." He took a breath. "I can't ask you and you team to go in there. That's not my call. But it would be awfully nice to get some eyes in there and see what we're dealing with. Over."

The pause was longer this time. "We're drifting out of range," Jill said.

"How long between pulses? Over?"

Sunil turned around and waved Emma over. "Do we know? Hurry."

She shook her head. "We only see it once every rotation. About 90 minutes. We've seen two today."

"Not sure, Aden. We've seen two today so far, but we're not overhead. You'll have to keep count. See if they're regular. Over."

The channel filled with static then. "... again? Didn't get that. Ov.*"

"Rover, measure pulses. You have to see if there's a pattern. Over."

The noise obscured any response from the surface. Then a different voice broke in. "Lighthouse, this is Ground Operations. What pulses? Over?"

Sunil took off his headset. He said to Jill, "Tell them to expect new data. Begin transmitting." He walked past Emma to his seat and slumped down in it, leaving her standing there looking concerned. Jill went to work relaying the message and bundled up the latest data package for transmission.

Greg stood up. "I'm going to see if there's anything to eat yet."

Emma grimaced. "Fine. Go eat." She watched him go, still thinking about the flash from the surface. She was convinced now that this was the Object that had pursued their ships, or something like it. She brought up the signal analysis and compared it to one of the histograms she'd saved from the Object's propulsion flashes. It didn't match at all. She frowned and looked at her screen. What was it doing? Was this a beacon? A different power source?

She looked around, hoping to talk to someone and caught Dan Wilkins staring at her from beside his divider.

"Hi." He grinned at her.

She turned away, back to her station.

059

ROVER 2

The inside of the rover was quiet except for the whine of the electric motors driving the wheels. Aden was navigating between the rock formations at a steady ten kilometers per hour. Visibility was good, but the complex terrain of the Badlands was not. It was a maze of rock formations, canyons and outcroppings, all vying to take pieces out of their wheels.

"What was that all about?" Erika finally broke the silence.

"Keep your eyes open for flashes, was what I got out of it."

They might not notice it but it gave them something to think about, Aden thought to himself.

Erika scanned the surroundings with the roof camera, her tablet propped up on her knees. "How close can we get to this thing?"

"I dunno."

A slight bump as the rover found a rock in the sand. Aden peered out of the bubble at the wheel below him. The repaired section was still holding.

"Are we going to go all the way into it?" Ray snuck in and crouched behind the seats.

"I don't know, Ray." Aden scowled.

Erika fiddled with the radio in the passenger seat. "Ground ops, this is Rover 2, come in…"

Aden glanced over, "It's these rocks."

"Yeah. And whatever else."

"Do we need another repeater?"

"Everybody just shut up!" Aden gritted his teeth and banged the steering wheel with his hand. "Just stop talking. We'll get to wherever we finish up tonight and keep eyes on it overnight. We can ask Lighthouse about it on their next passes." He couldn't turn them around yet. He was worried he'd be demoted back to crew or put on maintenance if he turned around now. He liked driving the bus.

Aden looked down at his distance gauge and started grinning. He cranked the wheel, turning around a big outcropping.

"What, you're happy now? After snapping at us?" Erika's radio was forgotten.

"Nothing." He grinned wider.

"Come on." Erika picked up the smile. "What?"

"This is the furthest I've been out. New personal record."

Erika's smile faded. "Oh."

"Why? What'd you think?" He glanced over at his passenger. "Did you think I was thinking about you or something?"

Erika frowned.

Ray chuckled and flopped onto the couch and began fumbling around on his own tablet.

"Like, were you thinking that maybe we could go out sometime? Dinner and a movie kinda thing?" Aden kept pressing.

"Really?" A hopeful squeak from Erika. She immediately regretted it.

"Oh yeah. Get all dressed up. You can wear that little black dress you were wearing the other night."

Erika blushed.

"Then, you can come back to my place…"

Erika blushed harder, staring intently at the camera showing the view outside.

"… and you can clean up my kitchen."

"What?"

"Maybe my bathroom too. It's getting a little grimy. I've got all the stuff. You just need to hit it with some bleach and…"

"You asshole." She unbuckled herself and clambered back to the crew section, kicking Ray off the couch.

"Come on. Erika! We can do other stuff too. Like laundry!" Aden grinned and picked up the rubber tube on the console and stuck it between his teeth, squeaking noisily on it.

Ray climbed into the passenger seat. "You are an asshole. You know that, right?"

"I gotta do somethin' to keep my mind occupied out here." He chewed again, sucking some of the saliva out of the tube. "Seriously, though. This is the furthest I've ever been out here. Past the fifty-klick mark. You?"

"Yeah, me too. We're past pinger range now."

"All alone. Just the three of us."

The inside of the cabin was quiet again and they listened to the squeaks and whines from the suspension and motors.

"I'm sorry I snapped at you guys."

More quiet. Aden put the rubber tube down again.

"How about I make it up to you?"

Ray looked at him, an eyebrow raised.

"I think it's called… a *ménage à trois?* We can try it right here in the rover. Ray, you and Erika get started and I'll watch from up here."

A cushion hurled with considerable force struck Aden in the back of the head, bouncing onto the console between the two front occupants. Aden's rubber tube fell with the cushion onto the floor around his feet.

"Aw. My chewy." He bent down between his legs and fished out the tooth-mark riddled rubber tube and stuck it back between his teeth.

"Pretty gross, Aden." Ray shook his head at him.

Erika crossed her arms over her chest and sank deeper into the couch. "I hate you both."

060

THE FAB

Past the materials section, the road turned into a ramp, climbing back up to level one. Some men and women lining the hallway were moving between sections, carrying parts, or tools, or pushing carts. Nobody seemed to be paying attention to him driving the lifter. Most of these people didn't have the hallmark piercings and implants of the Machineheads.

They were probably all in danger and didn't realize it.

Sean pulled the lifter off to the side of the ramp and parked beside another one. He got out and took stock of his surroundings. The towers of material production behind and below were connected all around by snaking conduits. Ahead, a sign read VEHICLE ASSEMBLY and pointed down a hallway.

He was thirsty, he realized, so he dug out a bottle of water from his bag and took a big drink, draining half the bottle. He was also sore. The adrenaline from his escape had worn off, leaving him tired and achy from all the crawling around and running he'd been doing. He put the bottle back in his bag and pulled out a breakfast bar, tearing the wrapper open with his teeth.

Entering the tunnel to vehicle assembly, a wide hallway with tracks on one side for carrying parts from other sections of the facility, he munched on his breakfast bar, surprised that it was soft and chewy. The year-old, dried-out versions he was used to didn't really compare to these.

The tunnel ended in a corrugated metal door, the type that opened upwards on rails. A smaller door for humans in the wall beside it had a fifteen centimeter reinforced window inset and he peered inside. The space beyond was vast and filled with lines of machines and articulating arms reminiscent of the ones from Machine Parts. The door wasn't keyed. Anybody from below was granted automatic clearance here, it seemed.

He opened the door and dragged himself inside on tired legs, looking around at the conveyors moving a large vehicle chassis through the assembly phases. Three lines, one after another, ran close to a full kilometer across the entire north side of the Fab. Each one produced a different type of vehicle: diggers, haulers, rovers. Huge articulated arms hung suspended above each station, ready to attach whatever was required of them. The lines were quiet, save for the occasional hiss of paused hydraulics. Nothing moved.

At the end of the line, a huge set of closed doors that opened up to the outside, onto Mechanic Street. Freedom.

He began walking, not really minding his surroundings, when he heard a voice call out to him. "Hey! What are you doing in here?"

Sean considered bolting as he looked for the source of the voice. A man, wearing grey overalls, a hard hat and safety goggles was approaching him.

"This area's sealed off until further notice. No work."

"I, uh…" Sean faltered. "Got lost."

The man got closer and Sean read the badge on his pocket: *LUND, G. Management.*

"Do you know why we're sealed in?"

Lund blinked at him. "We had an accident earlier." He gestured in the direction of the lines. "One of our people got… hurt."

"Badly?"

The man looked upset at the memory. He scratched the back of his neck with a gloved hand. "Look, kid. I already answered to the union reps. They're investigating. Until then, nobody gets in our out."

Sean fished into his bag and pulled out Steel's bloodied card. "It happened in Machine Parts too." He took a gamble. Management seemed to be outside of the loop and he needed a friend right now. "I'm being chased. The union's been taken over by Machine Worshippers… Witnesses. They're building robots and I think they're going to use them. Maybe in the city."

"Kid. What the hell are you talking about?" Lund took the half-mangled card and turned it over in his hands, inspecting the brown stains on the corners.

"You have to believe me." Sean was all in. "We have to get out of here and tell people… Security, engineering, whoever! We can't…" This was too much for Sean. He wasn't a talker and he lacked the words to make his case.

"Look, settle down." Lund guided Sean over to a table and chairs and sat him down. "You want some water or something? You look like you been through a press."

Sean shuddered at the thought of being put through a machine designed to compress metal. Lund put down a cup of water in front of him and sat down at the table.

"Tell me what happened."

And so he did. Steel's death in Machine Parts. The machinery taking her apart like a piece of defective metal. Perkins, covered in blood, eyes staring out of a red face. The union reps meeting with Mike. Perkins down below talking about the new robots. Then running through the Fab to the Assembly. All of it. The robots. Perkins. The chase. Coming here.

"It's been over a day. And… I know there's something going on outside." He didn't tell him about the network observatory. "The network's been overloaded."

"Well, I don't know about any of that." Lund looked at him like he might be insane. "Just sit here for a minute. I'm going to call your manager."

"You can't."

"I'm just going to make a call." Lund got up and walked over to the wall and picked up a communications handset, held it to his ear. "Admin." A pause. "Hi. Lund in Vehicle Assembly. I've got someone here. Says he's from Machine Parts…" Another pause. He looked over at Sean sitting at the table, his empty water cup in front of him. "Yeah. OK." He hung up the handset and Sean knew he had to get out of there.

"Just sit tight. You want a snack or something?"

Sean bolted towards the first assembly line, between two of the gigantic arms holding a cage assembly to be fitted around the frame of a rover chassis. He jumped over the line and a buzzer sounded nearby, a proximity sensor triggered by his motion.

"Hey! Come back here! It's not safe in there!"

The machines hissed as he ran along the base of the line, heading for the doors that would take him outside. He passed rovers in increasing stages of completion, their frames covered in more and more finished parts. Six in all, the last one waiting for a glass bubble on its cockpit and hardware mounted onto the external hardpoints. *Why so many rovers?* he wondered as he ran past them.

He could see Lund's legs under the line and through the machines as he ran to the end. The line stopped and a rover was parked there, airlock hanging open, freshly completed.

The doors to Vehicle Assembly were closed. He wasn't sure he'd be able to open them without an override. Lund walked to the back of the rover, hands out. "C'mon, kid. Take it easy." He was breathing hard, not used to running. Beyond him, back where he'd come in, the doors were opening and more people walked in. Union reps wearing black suits entered, followed by another man in a half-open coverall. Perkins. He pointed at them and they began walking forward. Perkins broke into a jog, a metal rod hanging from his hand.

"That's him. He's going to kill me! You have to get me out of here," Sean implored the man.

"Just sit tight..."

Sean dove into the rover's open airlock and slammed it shut. He crawled forward into the cabin, the overpowering chemical smell of fresh plastics filling his nostrils. He climbed into the driver's seat and ripped the plastic covering the controls.

"Come on, come on, come on..." Hands banged on the side of the rover. He could hear the latch turning on the airlock behind him. Lever on his left, covered in plastic. He pushed it forward.

Nothing happened.

He looked around at Lund crawling inside, Perkins behind him in the door.

"Come on!" He banged the wheel and saw it was on a hinged yoke. He pulled it back towards him and the wheels spun, electric whine from the engines driving the big carbon steel wheels against the concrete at full throttle, pressing him back into his seat. He hung onto the steering wheel, trying to keep the big rover pointed at the steel doors in front of him. Perkins yelled as he tumbled out of the back of the airlock onto the floor.

An impossible crash. The doors crumpled in front of the rover, torn from their brackets, buckling outwards. Scars across the plastic bubble of the cockpit window as the doors scraped across it. The engines propelled the machine forward through the bent metal. He bounced across the road and through the fence, the rover crashing into a hauler parked in the lot across the street, flinging Sean forward into the plastic windscreen over the dash, cutting the power to the engines as the steering column flew forward.

He groaned and hauled himself up. Lund was half in the cockpit, blocking his exit.

Sean clambered over him back into the cabin. The couch and overhead bunk had come loose and were strewn across the cabin, plastic sheeting and bunk forming a web in the small space. He hacked his way through it, tearing it from the walls.

Perkins climbed up into the airlock, blood dripping from his head.

"You little shit. What do you think you're doing?"

Sean screamed at him. A yell from deep inside roared up and out as he threw himself across the space between them, crashing into the bigger man's abdomen like a cannon ball, propelling them back and out of the airlock into the lot of empty vehicles. The steel rod fell out of Perkins' hand, clattering to the ground with a loud ring as they hit the concrete surface. They rolled, Perkins landing on top of him. "You little fuck! What did you think you were gonna do, hey? You gonna run and tell your mom you saw some robots? So what? Nobody cares, you little shithead." He raised his hand, about to punch Sean in the face, his head pressed back against the hard, rocky surface, when a loud clank reverberated off the surrounding machines.

Perkins' eyes defocused as he fell sideways. Lund stood behind him, holding the steel rod in his hand let it fall to the pavement noisily.

"You alright?" He knelt down over Sean, who struggled to sit up, feeling his head for injury.

"I... think so?"

Voices. A man and woman in suits walking towards them. "You better get out of here. I'll deal with them."

Sean picked his bag up off the ground. "Thanks, Mr. Lund."

"It's Gary."

Sean smiled at him. "Sean." He ran.

061

CITY HALL

Bryce strode down the long hallway of the twelfth floor of City Hall to the double doors at the end. He was still picking up chatter in his earpiece from the Security and Safety personnel outside, trying to keep the mob contained on the front lawn. They seemed to have the building secured for now.

He threw open the big double doors onto a room bathed in bright lights. He squinted as his eyes adjusted. Grayson sat behind his desk, an aide beside him patting his face with a pad, applying a base layer. People were scattered about the room, cameras and towers of lighting panels blasting down at the man behind the desk.

"Keep those doors closed, please," a man with a tablet and a headset said to him. "You can stay if you want, just be quiet while we're shooting."

Kaylee Baker was skimming through a tablet of her own, mouthing the words she was reading, another makeup artist dabbing at her cheeks.

"We'll just be a moment, Bryce," Henry informed him, shooing his makeup person away.

Bryce approached the desk. "It's getting crazy out there, Henry. The S&S teams have the building locked down, but I don't know how long they'll be able to hold them off. The MF are out there."

Henry held up a hand. "That's what we're doing here. A little calm and peace gesture. Isn't that right, Kaylee?"

She acknowledged the Chief Councillor with a wave and a nod and continued memorizing her lines.

"We're almost ready. Places, people." The producer-director shooed Bryce away into the corner and he allowed himself to sit down on the couch beside Natalie, idly tapping at her own tablet.

"You were outside? What are the crowds like?" she whispered at him, not looking up.

"It's getting pretty bad," Bryce admitted.

She said nothing and made no indication she'd heard him, but kept poking on her tablet.

"We are live in three, two ..."

The man in charge of the shoot pointed at Kaylee, standing beside the Councillor at his desk, and on cue, she nodded and raised a microphone to her mouth. "Ladies and gentlemen, we are here with Chief Councillor Henry Grayson with an urgent message of calm for the citizens of New Providence. Mister Grayson?"

"Thank you, Kaylee," Henry began smoothly. The makeup made him look ten years younger. His face seemingly absorbed all the light in the room without a hint of reflection. "Citizens of New Providence. I urge you to remain calm. The disturbances and power fluctuations around the city are the result of yesterday morning's tremors causing imbalances in our city's aging electrical infrastructure. Teams are assessing the extent of the damage, but they have assured me that they will be cleared up within a day or two. I am also told that these fluctuations present absolutely no danger to anyone's safety. St. Joseph's Hospital has a separate power supply that is still stable."

"Mister Grayson. We are hearing reports of unrest. Earlier, Zander Bale of the Mars First movement was seen speaking just before a violent incident outside of City Hall. Would you like to issue a statement on that?" Kaylee's face was a mask of concern.

"I have just received the reports of the incident on the lawn. We were dealing with the power issues and, frankly, I was rather surprised that Mister Bale would choose a time of crisis like this to evangelize his pet political agenda. I will say now what I have said to this man in the past: Without everyone doing their jobs, this Colony cannot survive. If Mister Bale thinks he can take one hundred, one thousand or ten thousand people to die out on the Martian landscape, he is wrong, and he and his followers will be punished for inciting unrest. But it won't come to that if everyone disperses immediately and desists these unlawful and dangerous protests."

Kaylee's face darkened. "But these citizens are allowed to assemble in protest, are they not?"

"Kaylee, despite what Zander's been preaching, this is not a prison.

This is our home! If people want to get together to gather and protest, they are free to do so. We only ask that they keep it civilized and not endanger the lives of everyone here. If things get dangerous, the Safety and Security Officers are authorized to use whatever safe means are necessary to disperse the crowd. Safely!"

Kaylee pretended to consult her notes and after a brief quiet moment, spoke solemnly. "Mister Chairman, could you tell us how the recovery is going in Dome 3?"

Grayson frowned, his makeup doing its best to not crack. "Certainly. As you know, we lost pressure yesterday morning after the tremor. The losses in the dome were very large. All of the biomass up there, chickens, crops, amended soils… all gone. Worse, we lost nearly fifty people up there. It's the worst disaster since the Ascraeus Chasma collapse of thirty-eight. We are still assessing the impact it's going to have on us. I expect our food supplies are going to be somewhat leaner in the coming months."

Bryce had heard enough, but he was trapped here by the cameras. Surely they'd wrap this up soon.

"I heard there was a rescue on the surface. What can you tell us about that?"

"No names yet. We're trying to keep things quiet for them, as they've been through a pretty tough ordeal. One of our rover teams found a group of university students trying to get to another dome. They were almost frozen to death by the time they got picked up. A real close one."

Kaylee's face lit up with a smile. "And the others?"

"Right. There was another group found inside the dome's farmhouse. They'd built a shelter out of suits and blankets to keep warm. The engineers found them huddled in there. Apparently they'd been quite comfortable."

"That's a small bit of good news amid a very difficult two days here in New Providence. Any final words for the city before we let you get back to the business of running the Council?"

"Just one. I would like to thank each and every one of you personally for persevering through this. We're doing our best, but it wouldn't be possible without your help. Please, if you know of anyone that needs assistance, don't hesitate to ask. If you need help, please come forward to one of our safehouses or the city shelters. I understand the Fab is still locked down, but I understand they are dealing with the issue from inside and there is nothing to be concerned about. Peace be with you. Be safe."

"From City Hall, this is Kaylee Baker signing off. Over to you, Jim."

The producer-director silently counted down, pointing at the crew on each beat as Kaylee and the chairman held their eyes on the camera. "Cut. That's a wrap." Everyone visibly let go of the air they were holding and the camera and lighting crew began breaking down their gear.

Bryce stood up and walked over to the desk. Henry was already wiping the makeup off his face, a skin-toned stain appearing on the white towel.

"How'd I sound?"

"Uh, fine. Good speech."

"But did it sound natural? Believable?"

Bryce looked at the man as he turned on his tablet's camera and looked at his face in the screen, dabbing with a corner of the towel.

"Sure. Listen, it's really bad outside. I don't know how much longer the S&S can..."

Henry held up a hand. "We have to get ready." He stood, hands raised. "Everyone out, we've got work to do here."

Cases slammed shut as the crew packed away the last of their gear. Kaylee was talking to the producer of the show. Bryce overheard her say, "We have to get an interview with those kids. Get their names, Bob."

Grayson walked over to her and gave her a hug. "Thanks for doing this. You have everything you need for later?"

Kaylee nodded. "I think so. We should have enough for a few days."

"Good. I should be back by then."

Bryce glanced over at Natalie on the couch, staring daggers at Kaylee. He listened in on his earpiece as the sergeant on the line called for more tear gas launchers.

062

LIGHTHOUSE

Emma reflexively checked the navigation board. *Happenstance* was still on its inbound leg from L5. The *Terror* drifted inexorably towards Earth. The blurry outline of *Hope* wound its way back from Jupiter and beyond, out past the sparkling dots of the asteroid belt. The monitor was zoomed out to encompass these three distant contacts. All quiet. Painfully slow.

"Plane change complete. We're now twenty degrees off from the impact site as requested. Apoareia four thousand kilometers."

"Thank you, Mister Buchanan." Sunil, slumped in his chair in the center of the command deck, watched the view of the surface on his monitor. "We're coming around on close approach. Jill, see if you can raise the rover team."

"Aye, sir." She made the adjustments on her console and began hailing the ground team.

Nelson was at the science station, having relieved Dan of his post. Greg leaned over to him. "So where've you been, Nelson? You haven't been around much lately."

"I've been reconfiguring our network."

Greg regarded Emma with a raised eyebrow. "What do you mean?"

"I've reflashed all of our networking components with some new configurations. I locked everything down that isn't in use. External access points have been hardened and I've added an extra layer with intrusion detection between them and our internal network. Everything gets shut down in the event of an attack."

"Is that going to work?" Emma asked.

"I hope so." Nelson brought up the list of points of interest from Watchtower and began poring over them.

Emma turned her head to check on Jill continuing to hail the ground team. "Lighthouse to Rover team, do you read us? This is Lighthouse to Rover team. Does anyone read, over?"

Emma was about to turn away when a crackle began the reply over the deck's speakers. "*house, this is Rover … We read you, over."

Jill turned to Sunil in her seat, still listening on her headset. "It's noisy. Low signal strength. The additional angle and distance is making them harder to pick up."

"Can you boost our signal at least?"

"Already at max."

Sunil frowned.

"Rover 2, this is Lighthouse. Good to hear you. What's your position, over?"

Crackle.

"We are approximately fifteen to twenty klicks we… *" A loud keening replaced the driver's voice on the line and Jill turned the volume down on it, adjusting filters to try to clean it up.

"Rover team. Do you have visual confirmation of flashes from the site? You need to time the flashes if you plan on approaching. Over?" Jill sounded desperate.

A ratcheting sound like a zipper being pulled up and down fed back over the speakers covering Aden's weakening voice. "… again, z..house. Xxz not cvvvv lasssss*…" and then a pop accompanied by a flash in the windows.

Jill turned to Sunil. "Signal's gone, sir."

"Mark the time of that flash. Any view of the site with ground cameras?"

Greg rolled back to his station. "Checking." He tapped out the sequence to put the footage up on the big screen, replacing the navigational display. A video appeared of the surface rolling past. At their new angle, the view was much further away, the crater obscured by shadow in the late afternoon light. A single brightened frame was all they had, momentarily illuminating the hills around the impact crater. "Yeah. We got it."

Emma scanned the histograms from the pulse. "Radiation's much weaker on our detector now. Back down to moderate levels." She thought of the engineering crews who had to work on the ships outside and shuddered. They'd be taking double doses of antirad meds.

Mars rolled past the window as the habitat ring of the station spun away. They were drifting further past the impact site now, climbing back up on their outward path of the eccentric orbit. Sunil addressed Jill. "See if you can raise ground control. Send them what we've got. I'm going to get some rack time. Call me if anything happens."

"Aye, sir."

Sunil raised himself out of the chair with a groan and dragged himself out the anti-spinward exit. Emma looked up at the monitor replaying the ground video from Greg's station. The oblong crater looked like a dark grey smear against the surface from their new southerly position and then a bright flash obliterated the camera's sensor before it compensated for the sudden glare, the image returning to its former intensity.

"Let me see that." Emma pulled herself closer to her terminal and pulled up the video from storage.

She scrubbed through the footage, selecting a frame just before the flash and then one after the exposure had returned to normal a couple of seconds later. She zoomed in as far as she could, rendering the crater as a bunch of blocky pixels.

"What are you looking for?" Greg asked sliding over beside her.

"Just a hunch." She rotated and warped the second image so it more closely matched the orientation of the first one. Their position change had altered the shape of the crater as they'd drifted further away in their orbit. After a couple of minutes she stared at her screen, a frown creasing her forehead.

"What is that?" Greg leaned in closer, a hand on the back of Emma's chair.

Around the outside rim of the crater, through a fresh haze of newly suspended dust, the wall had changed shape, sections of it casting new blocky shadows across the surface of the crater that weren't there before.

"I have no idea."

063

ROVER 2

The Sun was sneaking behind the ridge of hills and volcanoes in the west against a beige-grey sky. The wind-blasted rocks took on increasingly bizarre shapes, some of them standing like towers that cast long shadows across the sandy terrain. The Rover rolled on between them, Aden carefully avoiding the rocks in their path, turning the meter-diameter carbon and steel wheels in the dust.

It had been hours since their last contact with the station. Ground control had been quiet. Aden eased back on the throttle, slowing the big machine down among the boulders in the shallow rocky canyon. Shadows stretched over the vehicle from above in the late afternoon light.

"We're almost out of daylight. Should we stop for the night?" Erika asked, tired and restless in the navigator's position in the cockpit. She had crept back into the seat after a bout of petulance on the couch, boredom eventually winning out.

"Yeah, might as well. We don't want to be too close to this thing anyway..." A burst from the radio interrupted him.

Fizzle. "... read us. This is Lighthouse to Rover team. Does anyone read, over?"

Ray bounced forward from the crew area and leaned against the back of Aden's seat. Erika and Aden looked at one another as Aden eased the big rover to a stop.

Aden flicked on his transmitter. "Lighthouse, this is Rover 2. We read you, over." He turned to Erika. "See if you can clean this up for us."

The Rover rocked as it settled on its suspension as they waited for a reply. Erika fiddled with the tuning on the radio before turning to Ray. "We might need to drop another relay."

After a few seconds, the radio crackled back. "Rover 2, this is Lighthouse. Good to hear you. What's your position, over?"

"We are approximately fifteen to twenty klicks west-northwest of our target, over."

A buzzing started breaking into their frequency and Erika adjusted one of the filters to try to clear it out.

"… visual on… Site…" the transmission fizzled out into high-pitched static.

"Come again, Lighthouse. Did not receive last. Please repeat, over."

More static. Then a brief instant of brightness in the shallow canyon, the shadows reversing for a split second.

They waited, but no more voices came back over the radio.

"Was that a flash?" Ray asked from behind the seats, checking the time on the dash. It had been two and a half hours since their last communication with Lighthouse.

"I guess that was it. We might as well park here for the night, anyway. We don't have great visibility in this dust and we're losing light. I could use a walk." Erika got up and squeezed between the two seats and Ray bunched into the wall of the Rover to make space for her. "I'll suit up and drop another relay."

"Not it!" Ray said, beaming.

"I just said I'd do it, Beck. God, you're bad at this." Erika shook her head.

Aden unbuckled from his harness and stretched. "Worth a shot. Not sure we'll be able to get any signal down in these rocks. I'm gonna hit the head." He pulled himself out of his seat and climbed into the back of the RV, stretching and twisting his back along the way.

Erika climbed into her suit and sealed it up, Ray helping her with her boots. "Maybe try to put the relay up high if you can."

"I don't think I'm going climbing in this thing," she said, referring to her suit as she closed the rings on her gloves, then picked up her helmet and pulled it on over her head. "Back in ten."

The whoosh of air as the airlock depressurized buffeted her suit. They were only allowed two of these every hour. It took that long to replenish the system's air from the atmosphere. Erika looked out of the visor through the scratchy porthole set into the heavy outer door at the bleak, rocky landscape beyond. The wind stopped and the light turned red, indicating it was safe to go outside. She walked around the side of the big rover, inspecting the wheels caked in dirt and sand as she made her way to the side panel above the rear wheels. She opened the panel, hauled out the black case and lugged it back behind the rover, looking around to make sure she was in the best position to give them a line of sight back to the previous marker.

The walls here weren't especially steep or difficult. Maybe she could make it up one of them. The wind whipped up some dust around her, sand pelting her visor like snow.

"I'm going up, Ray. Be a few more minutes. Keep an eye on me."

"OK." Pause. "Be careful."

Yeah, right. She was sick of being cooped up with these shit heads. Any excuse to get some time away from Ray's goofy staring and Aden's assholery was welcome. She began climbing up the rocky wall, the awkward bulk of the radio relay in her left hand. The shadows were increasing now as the sun settled behind the hills to the west, the sky darkening. She flicked her helmet lights on as she made her way up to a ledge. It was almost like climbing a steep set of stairs. Ancient winds had etched horizontal lines into the sandy stone. She was almost at the top when she felt the ledge she was stepping on begin to move under her weight. A crack and a hiss of sand fell out of rock and she tumbled backwards, down the cliff nearly three meters, crashing onto her back on the floor of the small canyon in a puff of sand. The case landed beside her with a thump, popped open.

"Erika! You alright?"

She tried to answer, but couldn't find her voice as she tried to catch her breath, the wind knocked out of her.

She wheezed wordlessly into her helmet microphone as she struggled to her knees. She looked where she had fallen. An outline of her suit's backpack surrounded a fist-sized rock poking out of the dirt. She hauled air into lungs noisily and then she noticed the hissing sound. Her gaze flicked to her O2 gauge reflexively. An orange line had appeared, indicating ten minutes of breathable air. A red flashing light showed her rebreather had a fault.

"Inside," she managed as she half crawled, half hopped to the rover's airlock. She scrambled up the steps and fell inside, pulling the door shut behind her. She reached out and slapped the button to begin the air cycle. Fifteen long seconds of getting blasted by jets of air, wondering if this was the time the airlock was going to fail. The light turned green.

She opened the inner door and flopped inside, opening her helmet seals.

"Erika!" Ray was turning her around checking her suit out. "You punctured your pack. Are you OK?" He looked at her face, hands holding her as he looked into her eyes, checking for petechiae and any other signs of depressurization.

She batted his hands away and slumped down on the couch, still in her suit, fumbling at her wrist seals. "This fucking thing. Get it off me." She wasn't going to cry. She wouldn't give Aden the satisfaction of seeing weakness.

And then he was in front of her, holding her gloved hands in his. "Let me help you."

She pulled away, more violently than she'd intended. "I can do it myself."

"Fine! I was just trying to help. You took a pretty big fall out there."

"I know that." Her breathing was coming easier now. She took a deep breath and let it out shakily.

Aden was still kneeling in front of her. Ray, off to the side, stared at her as she undid her gloves.

"I'd hate to lose you, is all." Aden patted her shoulder and crawled forward into the driver's seat, pulling out his tablet from its pocket. Music started playing on the rover's speakers. "Hey, Ray?"

"What?"

"What's for dinner? It's getting hungry in here."

064

CITY HALL

After the press conference, Bryce made his way back down to the council chambers in a daze. He'd always felt that something was off about Grayson – the man was an autocrat and made only the barest denials of it. He'd been running the City as the sole authority for nearly fifteen Earth years. But he'd never expected him capable of outright lying to the people through the press. He had good reason to, of course: he wanted people out of the streets, back in their homes and schools. Back to work. Still, it didn't feel right.

He sat down at the table. Fred Darabont was yelling into his screen about containing the Firsters. "I don't care where he's hiding, flush him out! That's your job!" He was talking about Zander Bale, their leader. Still eluding the S&S, it seemed. Bryce wondered idly if the MF had a mole inside. He listened in on his borrowed headset for a moment. Chatter about a crowd gathering on the north side of Mechanic Street deploying smoke bombs. The thought made him think the air scrubbers were going to be working overtime.

His tablet finally connected to the network and through the slew of notifications, he saw a message from Jun fly by.

Subject: Re: Launch
Just received green light for launch tonight at 1730. See you on the pad.
Jun

They were go for launch. He checked the time, 1500 and stood up from the table. He half considered leaving Grayson behind, but decided he should at least tell him he was on his way.

His stomach knotted on the way up in the elevator. He hadn't eaten anything today. Just as well, if they were going through a launch. The high-gravity maneuvers of leaving the ground were always a touchy thing, gastrointestinally speaking.

Voices from inside the office on the other side of the closed doors. Henry's booming voice and Natalie's quieter one underneath it.

"We don't have time for this." Henry.

"I can't just leave them. They're my boys." Natalie sounded on the verge of tears.

Bryce approached the doors and knocked firmly before entering.

The office floor was covered in boxes, some of them open, contents and packing material strewn about.

Grayson was standing behind his desk wearing a dull grey, form-fitting space suit of a type Bryce had never seen before. GRAYSON, H. stencilled on the chest. Armored shoulder and knee pieces gave him the appearance of a soldier ready for combat.

"Do you like it? It's the Mark III. My engineers have been working on it for nearly two years now. A little more modern than those old clunkers you've had to wear."

Bryce looked around at the opened plastic cases. Inside were more boxes. One of them opened, showing shiny metal cylinders arranged in a neat grid. He looked to Natalie Park-Shehan, hands together in front of her. "I have to go," she said and ran out of the room and down the hall.

"Pity," Henry said. "I'd hoped we'd get a little time away from all this. Together."

Bryce shook his head. "We have to go. Launch is at 1730 and it'll take us at least forty-five minutes to get to the terminal." More if they ran into trouble with crowds.

"I have a car waiting."

Bryce noticed the opened box on Henry's desk for the first time. A black mass of metal lay beside it. "Is that what I think it is?"

Henry followed Bryce's gaze down to the gun. "Do you like it? It's fresh from the printers. The first one in New Providence." Henry picked it up, hefting it in his hand. "Amazing piece of machinery. It's surprisingly heavy when loaded."

Bryce backed up. "Is it? Loaded? We haven't had a gun in the colony since zero-zero-one." He shook his head. "Why?"

"Look, what's coming next won't be easy. We're going to have to make some hard choices. Are you prepared to make them?"

"I don't... I have no idea what you're talking about."

Henry pointed the gun at Bryce. "I need you to reactivate the network on the station."

"What? I can't do that from here. Even if I could, I wouldn't do it. The whole city's been compromised by that... *whatever* the hell is out there." Bryce gestured out with an arm, his other hand in front of him as he backed away towards the doors.

Henry laughed and lowered the gun. "You don't know what you're talking about. All this," he waved his hands around in the air, "is a ploy by the Machine Worshippers. They engineered that bolide strike."

Bryce boggled at him while stepping back towards the door. He desperately wanted to get away now. "What are you talking about? Engineered a bolide strike?"

Henry sighed and continued like he was talking to a small child. "The Worshippers have been in contact with another power in this system. They made a deal with it. They arranged to have the strike coincide with their network attack. There is a new authority here and I'm going to negotiate a treaty with them." He pulled the slide back on his gun, a cartridge slipping into place. "Just not from here."

"What? Who? Earth?"

Henry pantomimed Bryce's confusion, then raised the gun and pointed at his chest. "I'm relieving you of your command, effective immediately."

Henry Grayson pulled the trigger, a blast of fire blaring from the muzzle of the gun, the bullet flying through the air as the spent casing flew from the ejector. In an instant, the bullet hit Bryce in the upper chest and he twisted backwards, hitting the door frame and falling to the ground in a mist of blood.

Henry looked at the gun with a raised eyebrow and a ringing in his ears. "Hunh. That was easier than expected." He marveled at it as he latched the safety and stuck it into his duffel bag next to a box of ammunition and zipped it up. He slung the bag over his shoulder, then picked up the case with his helmet and gloves and walked to the door. He stepped over Bryce's body, a pool of blood growing on the floor.

065

NEW PROVIDENCE

Sean slipped carefully between the heavy loaders and haulers parked in the vehicle yard on Mechanic Street. The lights from the cavern roof were dimming as the sun went down in the west, street lights dancing in stochastic confusion. At the edge of the yard, St. Joseph drive turned north to Memorial. Sirens blared as an armored vehicle rolled north towards the train station. The streets were empty here, people having returned to shelters and homes.

Standing there at the edge of the yard, looking across the street at the huge piles of ore tailings from the smelters looming like miniature versions of the mountain they were beneath, he realized he couldn't go back to the Stacks. There was nothing for him there anymore. He looked east along St. Joseph and saw a flash and another plume of smoke rising into the sky, a distant cheer from whatever was going on there. Another mob of rioters was taking advantage of the city's confusion.

No one was following him. He strode out onto St. Joseph and headed west, towards the hospital. More sirens as an emergency vehicle pulled up in front of the squat concrete building. Emergency workers jumping out and throwing open the doors, two gurneys pulled out into the lot and pushed inside.

It looked like Safety and Security personnel on the stretchers.

He passed Commercial Street, avoiding going closer to the Fab again, which he could see looming over the apartments here. Lights on the roof of the Fab were reflecting off the cavern ceiling. He had to tell someone what he'd seen in there. He didn't know what the

Machineheads were planning to with those mining bots, but they could do a lot of damage if let loose into the city. Hopper Drive was a mess. Safety personnel were trying to drive back a crowd of protesters in front of City Hall. The building was surrounded on all sides. Above, the last light from Dome 1 shone down through a kilometer of glass and mirrors.

Avoid the crowd. He went west again. Edison Drive. Teachers' apartments, quiet in the confusion. He ducked through an alley and found himself behind the university in the quad. He looked up at the doors across the lawn of the Nikola Tesla Science Building. Why not? At least he'd have access to whatever was left of the school's network.

He wandered up, tried the doors and surprised himself to find they opened for him. Why shouldn't they? He was a citizen here. He walked inside, not sure of which direction to go, so he went straight down the hall, up the stairs to the second floor. A small lounge area looked inviting, so he slipped inside and flopped down on a couch.

He dug into his backpack for his water bottle and took a huge drink, emptying it. He'd been walking and crawling through the Fab for two days. He could go to sleep right here if he let himself. The thought seemed very appealing right now.

He reached back into his bag and fished out food, laying the items out on the couch beside him: two tubs of soygurt, a bottle of brotein and three breakfast bars. He picked up a breakfast bar and setup his tablet on his knees, waiting for it to connect to the network. He peeled back the wrapper and took a bite, chewing as his tablet connected and a spew of notifications flooded his screen. Gibberish. Endless nonsense. He disabled the notifications and opened up the connection to the observatory. He had finished his breakfast bar by the time he'd connected to the network and absent-mindedly picked up the soygurt and peeled off the top.

The graph in front of him was a flood of red. Nodes bounced traffic in every direction, unable to keep up with the onslaught that was assaulting them.

Except for that one.

The node in the northeastern corner of his map was a large cluster representing the network operations center of the city. Whatever was generating all this traffic was coming from there. He thought back to his walk here and remembered the smoke bombs and cheering from over the mounds of ore tailings, and figured that must have been where it was coming from. Could the Machinists have taken over the NOC as well? It seemed plausible, given what they'd done in the Fab.

He fumbled around in his bag and dug out his spoon, then scooped a mouthful of soygurt into his face. "Strawberry".

He was about to try to send a message to his friend Hiro when he had the sense he was being watched. He turned his head and saw a large form standing in the entrance.

"What are you doing in here, grub?" The overly-large boy who'd attacked him in the park stood there, staring at him. "You don't belong here."

"It's Derek, isn't it?" Sean said, staring up at him.

"You gonna leave that there? Pick that up," Derek said, pointing at the breakfast bar wrapper.

"You want one, Derek? I've got a couple more. How about some brotein?" This usually prevented a beating at home. He wasn't sure how this bully would respond to it.

Derek blinked at him, confused. "Yeah? OK."

Sean handed the big guy both of his breakfast bars. "Here. Take them. You can have them all." He handed them to Derek, who tore one open and stuffed half of it into his mouth.

Chewing. "These are fresh."

"Yeah. I got 'em in the Fab. The commissaries get stocked pretty regularly."

Derek finished the first bar and opened the second.

"My name's Sean." He slumped. "I have a problem and I have to tell someone about it."

"What kinda problem?" More chewing, Derek staring at him, but not with the baleful look he had given him minutes ago.

"I found something. In the Fab." He hesitated, then figured what the hell, he might as well tell him. This was a new experience for Sean, talking to strangers. "The Machinists... Witnesses, have taken over the Fab. They're building an army of robots. I think they're also responsible for the network attack that's been going on." He gestured towards the lights and they flickered as if on command. "I have some data that might be useful."

Derek blinked at him. "Really? Can I see it?"

"You promise you're not going to break my tablet again, right? This is the only thing that can show these maps and I don't think I'm going to be able to repair it again."

Derek looked pained. "I'm sorry. I didn't mean to break your tablet. I... don't have one."

Sean brightened up. "Maybe when we get this sorted out I can show you how to build one. There are lots of parts lying around if you know where to find them." He picked up his empty wrapper and soygurt tub and put them on the table, moving over so Derek could sit down next to him.

"See, this is a map of all the access points I found in the city. I've mapped them out."

"How did you do this?"

"I borrowed some network analysis software from the archives, patched it up. It monitors radio frequencies used by the wireless radios."

"What's this?" Derek pointed at the green square in the upper right.

"That's the Network Operations Center. I think that's where the attacks are coming from."

Derek frowned at it. "Come on. I know who you should show this to."

Sean stuffed his tablet back in his bag, picked up the garbage and stuck it in the chute by the counter. He noticed his hands, still covered in dirt and grease, his knuckles skinned.

"Maybe I should get cleaned up first. I'm a mess."

"Don't worry about it. Come on. I think he's still in his office."

Derek proceeded to escort Sean down the hallway, pushing the occasional surprised student out of his way. They were startled by Derek but looked genuinely scared when they saw Sean in his dirty coveralls and big boots looking back at them. One girl recoiled, shrinking away. "Hi," he said. Derek rounded a corner and came to a door. The little rectangular plaque read, "Dr. Tadeuz Powell".

Derek knocked and the door slid open. A voice croaked from inside. "Yes? Come in."

The bigger boy pushed the door open all the way and they stepped inside. "This is Sean. He says he found something you should see."

Dr. Powell frowned behind his glasses, bunching up his mustache under his nose. "Classes have been suspended for today." His eyes widened when he got a look at Sean. "You're not a student, are you?"

"This isn't about school," Sean said as he stepped forward. He opened his bag again and pulled out his tablet, setting it on the desk. "I know what's causing the network problems."

Tadeuz raised an eyebrow. "Is that so? Show me." He waved a hand and dismissed the window on his computer screen that showed the operations center from City Hall.

066

ROVER 2

After an unsatisfying meal of bean stew, Erika went to work replacing the air system on her suit. The backpack making up the bulk of the rebreather system had sprung a leak when she fell on the rock and it needed to be swapped out.

"I hate how these bean stew things end up half cold and half nuclear hot." Ray Becker, always complaining.

"Would you rather have a brotein shake?" Aden was sitting at the folded-out table, one foot up on the corner, eating his dessert of strawberry soygurt. "Why's everything always strawberry-flavored? I didn't think we were growin' any."

Erika popped the damaged backpack off her suit and disconnected the air and power lines. She inspected the puncture, which was more of a series of cracks in the carbon plastic shell, a dent pushing through that had broken one of the circulation lines feeding into the CO_2 filter substrate. The back of her suit itself had a ring surrounding the now absent backpack where the Martian dust had stained it. She inspected the suit for any other damage, finding none, she began attaching the replacement.

A fizzing, crackling sound popped out of the rover's speakers, accompanied by a flash of light.

"What was that, about ninety minutes?" Aden checked his watch and looked outside. 1725.

"Yeah, I guess so." Ray put down the bag of bean stew and panned around outside with the external camera.

"Great. That means I've got ninety minutes to setup that radio relay. Plenty of time."

Aden sat up, taking his foot off the table. "You want me to go instead?"

Erika was surprised at how genuinely concerned he appeared to be. "Nah. It's my mess, I'll fix it. Besides, I want to make sure this new pack is working alright before we do our recon tomorrow morning."

Aden nodded, apparently satisfied by this. "Just be careful."

"Yes, Dad." Erika rolled her eyes but was smiling. She turned away before he could see.

She finished climbing into her suit. They were still fifteen kilometers from their destination. With good visibility, they should be able to reach it in an hour of travel.

"If we've only got ninety minutes between pulses, that doesn't give us a lot of time to get onsite, do our recon and get out again."

"We'll have to time 'em, should be able to give ourselves an hour on site if we leave early." Aden picked up his tablet and thumbed through the collection of movies he had stored from the archives.

"No guarantee these flashes are regular yet. We've only been counting three of them." Erika pulled her helmet on, not waiting to hear Becker's inevitable counter-argument. She powered up the suit and thumbed on her radio. "Radio check. Come in."

Aden reached around for his headset and popped it on his head. "We hear you."

"Alright. I'm going out." She went back to the airlock and stepped inside, closing the doors, waiting for the air to get sucked out. Red light. She slapped the button and the door swung open in a puff of dust. She jumped down into the soft sand and looked up. The sky had darkened now and the stars shone bright overhead. A thin band of light in the west against the mountains was all that remained of the daylight over the rocky ledge beside her. The days were still getting longer. In another six weeks they'd have another forty minutes of sunlight in the day.

A bright streak caught her eye and she followed it into the sky. It arced gracefully up towards her overhead, passing south of them, picking up speed and fading on its flight into space. "Looks like we just had a launch." She stood there for a moment, watching the light fade from the rocket, then kicked herself into motion.

"Station must be gettin' a package," Aden drawled back. The launches were normally pretty regular, but with the events of the past few days, she guessed they'd been on hold.

She recovered the box with the relay. One of the latches had popped open and she dumped the case onto its side, banging the sand out of it.

"Case doesn't seem damaged," she guessed. She looked up at the line of rocks climbing out of the sand beside her. "Not sure I feel better about climbing up in the dark."

"Just set it up here, it'll have to do," Aden replied.

"Roger." Relieved, she opened the other latch and flopped the black case open into the sand. She dropped the spikes and extended the antenna, standing it up. She pushed the big power button and the lights flickered on, pulsing as it looked for its frequency, then flashing orange. "Well, it's on. We'll see if we get any signal."

"Alright, get back inside. We can play some spades."

"Can do." She took one last look above. No sign of the shuttle rocket anymore, the sky filling up with stars. Orion stood in the west facing a setting Taurus. She waved and climbed up the steps to the airlock.

*

"Feels like we've been out here for a long time," Aden said, dropping a six of hearts into the pile.

"That's a low card." Ray ducked it with an off-suit jack and pushed the trick back to Aden. "Last night, though. Got any of that hooch left?"

"You afraid of the bags, hoss? I think ah might have some shine kickin' around. Might just be an appropriate way to finish off the trip." Aden's drawl was getting progressively longer as the night wore on. He reached into the cupboard behind him and pulled out a bottle of clear liquid, banging it on the table.

Erika and Ray put their water bottles up onto the table and Aden dumped their contents into the sink. He pulled the cork out of the bottle with his teeth, making a soft pop, then poured a couple of fingers into each bottle. He spat the cork out onto the floor and it bounced away towards the suits. "To a nice drive in the desert."

They all raised their bottles and took a drink. Coughing and wheezing fits filled the silence for a moment as the harsh vodka hit their throats.

"Hoo-whee, that just doesn't get any better with age, does it?" Aden laid down an ace of diamonds.

The rest followed, laying down their cards, eyes watering from the intense alcohol.

*

Erika couldn't sleep. Aden was snoring softly in the bunk above. Ray was breathing slowly on the fold-out bed beside her. She didn't want to wake anyone, but felt fidgety and uncomfortable.

As carefully as she could, she picked up her tablet and crawled around the bed towards the front of the cabin. Ray groaned and rolled over, pretending to be asleep, or he had a headache from the alcohol.

She ignored him and climbed into the passenger seat, perching with her feet up, wrapping her blanket around her, staring out at the brightening sky to the east.

The dashboard clock read 0330.

She looked out again and realized that wasn't dawn approaching: the sky was lit up in a soft pink glow.

"Ray," she hissed. "Come look at this."

Ray, no longer groaning in the bunk dragged himself forward, towing the blankets with him. "What is it?"

He looked out the bubble in front of them at the orange-pink glow. They were silent for a moment. Finally, he asked, "What is that?"

"I don't know." She flipped the camera on and started recording. The low resolution camera mounted on their roof wasn't any good in low light, it turned the surroundings into a glowing green sea of noise. "Do we have anything that can make that any better?"

"I don't think so. Suit cameras aren't going to be much better."

A bright flash interrupted their observations and they shut their eyes, an after-image of the rocks and landscape on the insides of their eyelids.

Ray rubbed his face. "Ah, I don't think that's good for the eyes." He checked the radiation meter on the dash. The needle hadn't moved.

Erika blinked and peered back into the gloom. Her face reflected back at her off the glass bubble of the windshield. "I don't think it's good for anything."

They sat there in silence again, Erika waiting for her night vision to return. After a half an hour, she wasn't sure if she could see the glow on the horizon or not. The green image from the external camera showed slowly falling particles on the monitor in the console, like seeds falling in the wind. Maybe it was just sensor noise.

067

LIGHTHOUSE

The ride up had taken longer than usual. The passengers crammed into the cabin aboard Shuttle 5 were suffering varying degrees of queasiness. Henry Grayson had taken a full dose of anti-nauseants before leaving the terminal and had passed them around to his security detail, Daniels and Xu. The rest of the passenger seats were filled out by the crew of the *Banshee*: Captain Lori Harrison, her second-in-command, Nadia Boroshenko and Vance Peters, mining and engineering specialist.

It was a little awkward meeting Captain Nagaoka in the terminal. When pressed on the expected arrival time of Bryce Nolan, the station commander, Henry had informed him that he wouldn't be joining them on this trip. The shuttle captain had questioned this, claiming he had been told to wait for him explicitly, but demurred when the chairman had given him a direct order.

The extra travel time had been because of the recent orbital shift the station had performed. Captain Nagaoka was surprised that Lighthouse wasn't in the expected location and informed the passengers that they would need to perform a couple of orbits to line themselves up – over four hours of weightlessness in an unpressurized canister. Officer Xu hadn't adjusted well to the negligible gravity in the cabin and was making horrible sounds on his headset until his Henry ordered him to switch off his comms.

That had helped.

Now they were docked. Grayson had little time to waste if he was going to do this the way he'd planned it. As soon as they were secured, he undid his harness and gestured to his two security officers to follow him. He pulled himself forward to the hatch and peered through the porthole. The gantry was still connecting when he unlatched the door and opened it out onto the open space of the docking ramp.

"Mister Grayson, you have to wait…"

Henry brushed the crewman aside and floated out to the hand rail, the gantry enveloping him as it extended to mate with the docked shuttle craft. He banged on the door of the airlock and a surprised technician on the other side opened the outer door, letting him and his two security detail inside.

The air cycled and Henry gave the indication to switch to secure comms. Green light blazing in his helmet display. Carrier locked.

"We need to do this smooth and fast. If anyone gives us trouble, I'll give you the nod and you will subdue them. We need to keep the senior bridge crew intact, but everyone else is a potential threat. Are we clear?"

"Yessir," the two responded.

"Alright, let's go."

The cycle finished and the inner door swung open. Grayson reeled at the enormity of the Central Hub, remembering why he hated coming up here. It had been nearly ten years since his last visit and he'd hoped then he'd never have to repeat it. That had been for Mancuso's appointment, the old fool.

He made his way past the startled shuttle tech, mouthing something to him inside his helmet. Grayson ignored him and rode the handrail to the end of the line, stepping onto the "ceiling" of the Hub, his two officers just behind him, struggling to reorient themselves to the spinning cylindrical interior. Grayson jumped down into a lift labeled 2 and the others followed him in. The hatch closed and they rode the elevator down the spoke to the outer ring, their gravity steadily increasing on their descent. He reached into his duffel bag and pulled out the gun he'd stowed there, placing it into the holster on his hip. The elevator stopped and the doors opened. Henry walked out into the reception area, taking a moment to adjust to the sensation of standing in the spinning habitat ring. He couldn't be sure, but he felt slightly heavier up here than on Mars. Four hours in a weightless, tumbling shuttle craft was confusing enough. His security detail were looking uneasy again and he worried Xu was going to start throwing up.

Suit lockers lined the walls and bathroom facilities were present for those who needed them. He strode past it all to the doors leading out into the hallway and took a left turn, past the crew cabins, marching spinward to Section 1, his security detail in tow.

The Command Deck.

He popped the seals on his helmet, the neck seal hissing as it released its grip and he pulled it off over his head with some effort. The neck seal pulled hard on his ears as he popped it off over his head. He flexed his jaw and neck, cursing the engineers who'd designed the thing. He'd have a talk with them when he got back, he started to think, then laughed at his foolishness.

He looked around the command room at the startled faces staring at him and ran a hand through his grey hair.

"Mister Grayson?" Sunil Pradeep stood straight in front of him with an expression of amazement and curiosity on his face. He spent a moment looking him up and down, casting glances at the two security officers with him. Grayson presumed he was marvelling at the Mark III suits. Sunil's eyes came to rest on the holster on his hip, then quickly darted back up to his face.

"Mister Pradeep, I presume?" Sunil began to step forward, raising his hand for a shake when Henry stopped him. "I'm relieving you of command of this station." He turned swiftly to the comms officer, a tired-looking woman with short hair and a pretty face. "Please activate the orbital network."

"I… sir?" Jill Sanchez looked to Sunil for help. He held out his hands helplessly.

To his own surprise, Henry pulled the gun out of his holster and held it to the comm officer's head. "I won't ask you twice. Activate the network."

"Y-yes. Alright." Her hands trembled as she entered the commands to reactivate the orbital network around Mars. The different satellites whizzing about the planet came online and lit up her board.

"Mister Grayson, what's going on? Where's Bryce?" a younger girl asked. She looked barely old enough to be out of school. He looked from her to the young man standing next to her, who wore a station cap in a ridiculous manner.

"Why are there children on my Command Deck? Lieutenant Daniels, see them to their quarters, please. Have them sent back on the next shuttle."

"Sir." He saluted, then grabbed Emma by the arm. "Come with me, please."

"Hey. Let go of me!" She wrenched her arm free and shot Grayson a defiant look that made him want to laugh, it was so adorable.

Greg stepped forward, ready to say something or maybe throw a punch, until Xu intercepted him and hit him with his stun baton. Greg collapsed to the floor in a twitching seizure.

"Have them removed, please. Anyone else?" Henry looked around the deck at the startled expressions on people's faces.

One of the men from the science station stepped forward. The patch on his overalls said WILKINS. "Commander. I would like you to know that these two have been interfering with the day-to-day operations of the station since Mancuso had them brought up here."

Emma looked at Wilkins with her mouth opened, stunned.

The doors opened and a couple of orderlies from medical entered, half out of breath. "What's happened?" The first of them stopped, looking at Greg's still-twitching body on the floor, then looked at Xu standing there in his armored suit, stun baton in his hand. Officer Daniels quietly asked them to help him and his friend out.

"Escort them to their cabins, please. Make sure they stay there."

Grayson looked at the remaining science officer: grey bags under his eyes, station overalls half unzipped over a dirty tee shirt. "What's your name, son?"

"Dan Wilkins, sir. Science Officer, first class. I fully support your command of this station."

Emma's eyes turned to ice as she was escorted off the deck. "You piece of shit!" she yelled at him as the doors closed on her and Greg.

"Thank you, Mister Wilkins. Good to have you on board." Grayson walked to the commander's chair and put a hand on the back, feeling the worn leather there, still warm from Sunil's body heat. "Comms. Tell engineering to get *Banshee* prepped for flight."

Hesitation. The female comms officer appeared to be in shock.

"Can anyone else operate the comms station?"

"I can, sir." Sunil stood there, no indication of defiance.

"Do it."

He relieved Sanchez and she stood up and left the command deck, tears streaming down her face.

Grayson turned and looked up at the navigation board, still rolling as always. His eyes settled on MSS03E, *Hope*, inbound for Mars, just inside Jupiter's orbit, her package in tow. He smiled.

068

ROVER 2

"Wakey, wakey!" A rumble and a jolt as the rover started rolling.

Erika groaned and peered up over the bulk of Ray beside her, who had gotten closer in the bed than she'd have liked. She punched him in the arm. "Get over on your side."

"Hey!"

Erika got up, taking her blanket with her, and put the kettle on. She squeezed around the bed in her bare feet and plopped into the passenger seat. "We saw a flash last night around three-thirty-five." She glanced at the dash clock reading 0600, doing the addition in her head. "Next one should be around six thirty?"

"Sounds about right." Aden chewed on his rubber hose. "Man, I slept like the dead last night. What were you doin' up at three thirty?"

"Couldn't sleep," she said.

Behind them, Ray folded up the bunk and padded around the counter, holding onto a hand strap in the ceiling as he waited for the water to boil. "We saw somethin' last night."

Aden looked over at Erika wrapped up in her blanket, still chewing, the hose squeaking in his teeth. "What'd you see?"

"Don't know. We saw something… glowing. It looked like sunrise." She trailed off, still half asleep. "Then the flash."

"Coulda been the sun." It was still dark outside, the sky deep blue and brightening in the east. A faint yellow glow spread across the horizon. Frost had formed along the edges of the plastic acrylic windscreen.

"I don't think so."

"Me neither," Ray opined, scooping coffee crystals into their thermoses. "I think it stopped after the flash. We sat there for about a half an hour and didn't see it again."

Erika wasn't so sure. "I think it was still there. Maybe just dimmer. And there were... it looked like particles on the camera."

Aden scratched his chest thinking about it. They were doing ten kilometers per hour, the rover rocking gently on its springs as they rolled over the soft sand. "We'll be more'n halfway there when we see the next flash. Sun'll be coming up. We can evaluate then."

The smell of coffee hit their nostrils before Ray handed Aden, then Erika, a full mug. She thanked him and took a deep sniff. "I mean, what are we going to do?"

Aden put the rubber hose down on the console. "About what?"

"Radiation. If this thing's hot..." She hesitated. "It's not like we have any equipment for that. We don't have any portable radiation meters. The gauge on the dash hasn't moved." She said, annoyed with herself for sounding petulant.

Ray nodded behind them, slurping at his coffee. "It's true."

"Well, what are we supposed to do then? Turn around? We can't come this far and just abandon it." Aden steered clear of a clump of rock, the edges of the small canyon dwindling into the sand. They seemed to be climbing now, the slow rise of Tharsis crater still far to the east. "Look, the rover's shielded. Our suits are shielded. We'll be fine. Try to call ground if you want. Maybe they have some instructions for us."

None of them really expected the radio to work, but Erika picked up her headset anyway. She put it on and spoke into the mic. "Ground Ops, come in, this is Rover 2, over."

Static.

"Lighthouse? Anyone? This is Rover 2, come in."

The static rose and changed pitch – a kind of warbling on the radio and then a loud snap accompanying a flash of light.

Aden winced and blinked, slowing the rover down as his eyes recovered.

"There's yer answer," he drawled, taking a sip of coffee.

Erika looked at the clock: 0610. "That flash was early. Maybe it's only seventy or seventy-five minutes?"

"Maybe it changes," Ray offered.

"So we've got somewhere between seventy and ninety minutes until the next one," Aden said, slightly perturbed now that everyone was getting edgy. "We'll keep driving, wait for the flash, then go outside.

Alright?"

Nobody answered.

"Alright? Come on, people. We have a job to do."

Mumbled assent.

"Alright, alright." Aden took a big slurp of coffee, reached for his sunglasses and popped them onto his face.

They drove in silence for a while. Erika stared out the front glass, watching the terrain roll by.

*

By 0730, the rover approached the five-kilometer mark. Aden pulled the throttle back to zero and pushed the steering yoke forward into the park position. He pushed his sunglasses up on his head and turned to Erika. "We wait here for the next flash, alright?"

Nodding from Erika and Ray. Ray was back on the couch with his tablet, probably looking at his picture of Cindy again.

"Now how are we going to do this? We want to spend as little time out there as possible. That's a given. We don't know what we're going to be able to see there, so we need our helmet cams on record the whole time. We're going to take samples of whatever we can, but we'll be storing our cases outside in the side storage compartments. Nothing gets inside."

"Are we all going?" Ray asked quietly. Erika looked up from her screen.

Aden nodded. "That's a fair question, I guess." He rubbed the stubble on his chin. "I kind of expected everyone to go. We can collect more samples and get more footage that way in less time."

Erika nodded. "I assumed I was going."

Ray was silent.

"I was going, obviously," Aden said. "I mean, my rover, my mission, right?"

Ray exhaled loudly. "Alright. I'll go."

"Great! Let's get suited up. Don't want to waste any time getting in and out of those things. Probably best to stay in them until we're clear of the site. Let's go."

They all stood up and filed to the suit lockers in the back of the RV, Ray first, since he was closest. He pulled his pants on over his one-piece liner, then lowered the torso over his head.

Erika stripped down to her underwear and climbed into her suit. Aden waited for them to get situated before he climbed into his own suit. He stood and supervised, making sure everyone was done up properly. "Now, I'm going to want everyone to do a full cleaning cycle before they get back inside the bus. I don't want anyone pulling any hot sand inside. If this site is radioactive, there could be all kinds of particles floating around that could kill us if they get into our food or water."

"Jesus, Aden," Erika said, sealing up her waist. "Worst pep talk ever?"

"I don't want to sugar coat this. Radiation's bad juju."

"Fuuuuck." Ray just stood there in his suit, staring at him.

Flash. The cabin lit up from the glass in front.

"Jesus. I swear I felt that," Ray said, clutching the front of his suit.

"That's just yer mind playin' tricks on you. Take a seat. Let me get my suit on." Aden patted him on the shoulder and stepped around him, reaching for his suit.

Erika watched him as he stripped out of his coveralls. He wore boxers and a Stone Angels t-shirt underneath. He grinned at her with his straight white teeth as he stood there. "Get a good look, darlin'. When we're back home I'll let you take it out for a test drive."

Erika blushed and turned away.

*

They drove. Full suits. Ray sat in the passenger seat manning the camera.

"Helmet cams on. We want a full record of this to show the folks back home what they're missin'."

Erika flipped her camera on, helmet lights coming on automatically.

"I wish we had rad sensors in our suits. Why don't we have those?" Ray asked.

"Because we've never needed them before," Erika answered. She watched the screen in front of her. A line of rock was growing larger as the rover approached. They were rolling up a slightly steeper incline than earlier, sand had given way to rock.

Aden brought them to a halt. "That's it. That rock wall's less than two hundred meters. We've got about sixty minutes out here, so let's hurry up. Don't forget your sample cases."

They got up in unison and headed for the airlock. Erika was first. She climbed inside and ran the cycle. Her stomach was a mess of knots and she realized then that she hadn't eaten anything for breakfast. She'd have something when she got back. Red light. Open door. Jump down onto the hard rock. Her sample pack hung on her hip and it flopped into her, the weight familiar but unusual.

The door to the RV closed and she thought briefly that this was another stupid prank and they were going to turn around and leave her here. She cursed herself and bent down. "I'm going to get a sample out here." She pulled out a hand pick and chipped away at the rock, then picked up another rock beside it and tossed it into a compartment in her field case, closing it up.

Ray bounced down beside her. "Hi."

"Don't waste time here. Start moving up the hill to those rocks," Aden advised from inside the lock. "I'll catch up."

"You heard 'im. Let's go." Erika closed up her case and started trudging up the hill.

It had become quite steep. The terrain was built up either from erosion or the impact itself. Erika's areography wasn't the best, but this area was still part of the lava flows from Ascraeus, the Labeatis Fossae to the north east, Fortuna Fossae to the south: depressions in the plains where the sand and dust had been scraped away by the wind, leaving nothing but solid rock for vast distances. The bones of Mars.

"Those rocks look funny to you?" Ray was panting beside her, his large frame heavy on this hill.

She snapped back to reality and looked at the line of rocks growing closer. They were sticking out of the slope at odd angles. Geometric shapes permeated the ridge. Cubes and tetrahedrons grew out of the rock. "Yeah. Kinda." She looked down at her boots on the rock, pebbles rolling back down the hill. "Maybe they're fresh rocks that just got fired up. They haven't been eroded yet."

"Maybe."

Aden jogged up beside them. "You girls havin' fun yet?"

"Oh yeah. This is a blast," Erika said. Ray wheezed.

"Come on, we're almost there." Aden jogged up the hill ahead of them. Erika picked up her pace to follow, leaving Ray behind.

"Check out these rocks," Aden said as he approached, excitement in his voice. Distance was hard to gauge out here, but as he moved further ahead of them, the size of the rocks became apparent to Erika. A huge black cube standing on one corner loomed above, some twenty or thirty meters high, the scale still hard to judge.

"Careful, Aden. Those might not be stable."

"Alright. I'm getting a sample." He bent down and disappeared behind a boulder as she struggled to catch up, Ray still panting in her ear.

"This rock is hard. Shiny," Aden said. "It's not like the sandstone and granites we're used to seeing out here."

Erika could see the sun shining off the face of the cube ahead as she approached the ridge.

"Wait'll you see this," Aden said, and she crested the hill and joined him behind the boulder.

Under the shadow of the cube, between the faceted rocks, she looked below at a field of glass stretching out in a gigantic oval ahead of them.

The walls rose up around it nearly a hundred meters high. The wall below them was shining orange in the rising sun.

"Would you look at that?" Aden whispered.

Erika boggled at it as they waited for Ray to catch up to them. "Aden, this is too weird. These aren't natural."

In the center, a large black spike was sticking up out of the glassy surface of the crater. Branches of smaller spikes stuck out from it at irregular positions around it.

"What the hell?" Ray managed to get out between breaths.

"I don't know. Let's get down there and get a sample of some of that shiny stuff." Aden went on ahead underneath the cube and over the ridge. He scrabbled down the hill on the other side as Erika edged down the slope after him, unable to keep up.

"Be careful!" she yelled after him, a dark cavity between the rocks catching her attention on her right. She approached it, shining her lights into the void. A tunnel descended down into the ridge wall, satin smooth. "I found a tunnel! A cave entrance, I think."

Ray followed her, out of breath. "Don't... go in there."

"I'm just going in far enough to get a sample." She slid down the crack in the wall, a triangular hallway split in the rock. The smooth curve of the tunnel gave way to more regular geometric angles. She bent down and chipped a piece out of the wall in front of her, dropped it into her case with a sharp click.

Ray's feet clomped down beside her. "This is... this looks like it was cut." He brushed the wall with his gloved hand, shining his light and camera onto the surface. "There aren't any grooves. No seams. It's... perfect."

Erika stood up. "I want to see where this goes."

Aden's voice crackled through their radios. "Don't get lost. Only thirty minutes until we turn around." Static.

"Alright, just a few minutes." She tugged on Ray's arm. "Come on."

They walked down the hallway nearly twenty meters and it turned, curving through the rock. An opening ahead revealed a round chamber, sandstone stalagmites climbing out of the floor like fingers. Square openings in the wall looked out over the glassy floor of the crater below like windows. Erika walked in among the structures, turning her head to record as much as possible on her helmet camera. "This is so weird. It's not like the tunnel." She checked her helmet gauges and her eyes widened in realization. "Guys, I'm getting heavier atmosphere in here. Heavy CO_2 and... oxygen?"

"The rocks aren't the same." Ray chipped a sample off one of the stalagmites and watched the surface recoil away from his pick. He looked up at Erika, who was still studying the walls, leaning out of one of the openings looking out over the crater. "Erika! This just moved! I think these structures…"

"I'm almost– surface." Aden's voice was clipped. The radio connection seemed to be losing strength.

"Aden, you're getting hard to hear. Don't go down there any further."

"Just… sample."

Erika felt her skin crawl inside her suit as she became aware of something moving in the corner of her vision. She turned, her lights shining into the dark cavern on the other side of the circular chamber. Nothing.

"Guys, I think we should get out of here." She felt queasy, like they were being watched. Her head was tingling like it was crawling with insects. She eased herself over to another one of the openings, looking down, and saw Aden far below near the glassy surface of the crater.

Then she saw it.

Outside, on her right, a small humanoid shape was standing there. A meter tall, made of something like glass, almost transparent with traceries of shiny metal running through it like veins or nerves. Its head was too large for its body and it stood there staring at her with black eyes. It raised a shiny arm and pointed a long slender finger at her as the air around her began to glow. A whooshing sound built from deeper in the tunnel walls.

"What?" Ray's voice.

"The… g…" Erika stammered, unable to make the words come out. The air seemed to catch fire and the surface of the crater began to ripple like water.

Aden yelled in their headsets through the keening static. "Everyone get out of here now!"

And then the world turned to fire.

Erika and Ray were blown back up the tunnel by the force of the eruption. Wind and dirt blasted them back, Erika knocked into Ray and it took them a moment to disentangle themselves. They scrambled back up the tunnel and out onto the ridge under the gigantic onyx cube. Down below, Aden was stretched out, skewered on a blade of black glass poking out of the surface. He glowed, like he was lit from inside by a great source of power, arms and legs outstretched in a pantomime of the Vitruvian Man.

Erika half ran, half fell down the slope to the rover, in a blur. She was only half-aware of a keening in her ears from the radio, a bright wordless noise of indeterminate pitch. She dragged Ray by the arm and somehow they made it to the RV and clambered up into the airlock, shutting the door.

Fast cycle.

They burst inside, Ray pushing past Erika to the driver's seat. He rammed the throttle forward and careered down the hill as fast the machine would take them.

069

THE TERROR

"Burn complete in five, four..." Captain Francine Pohl ran out the countdown, then cut power to the engines, pulling back on the throttle and locking down the ship's controls. "Navigation, how do we look?"

Vanessa Macgregor checked their telemetry. A new arc curved steeper into the system, now had them passing Earth in nearly four weeks. "Telemetry is looking good. Looks like we'll have a shot at orbital injection once in the Earth-Moon neighborhood."

Jerem snorted on the couch behind them, looking up from the tablet he'd borrowed from his father. "I still say we could shave off another week with a longer burn."

Vanessa glanced at her captain, still going over their telemetry, making sure their course was correct. She turned around and said, "Not willing to risk the fuel, kid. We're gonna need it."

"It's fuel or food. One way or another, we're coming up short." In the past week, Jerem had been busying himself with inventory in the galley and running calculations on arrival time. He didn't like what he'd come up with. "I think I've got an idea how we can save more time without burning fuel, though."

Francine turned around at this. "We'll have to talk about that. In the meantime..." She flicked on the intercom. "Ladies and gentlemen, please prep for gravity spin."

From somewhere below, Reggie's voice drifted up. "Give it to me, baby!"

"Is he always this obnoxious?" Jerem asked Vanessa.

Vanessa and the Captain exchanged a look. "You don't know the half of it," Vanessa said.

"Lateral thrusters coming online," Captain Pohl announced and adjusted the port trim. Pops and pings rang through the ship as the thrusters started firing and were replaced with a loud hissing that turned to a rumble. Jerem looked up through the glass windows in the nose of the hab module and watched the stars turning around them, picking up speed. Gradually, he felt himself become heavier. The gravity from their thrust program earlier had pushed him down in his seat, now the new spin of the ship was pushing him back against the wall.

Creaks and groans filled the ship. The repair work Hal and Reggie had performed on the struts seemed to be holding, but the negative stresses on the cargo module were causing previous indentations to pop back out with occasionally violent jumps on the hab. The struts holding the cargo module to the ship were now a complex framework of salvaged metal parts and jury-rigged attachments. The remnants of *Making Time*'s damaged hab module was incorporated into the nose of the cargo module, the remains of the ship's dome shield used for repairing the damaged cargo pod gave the thing a patchwork appearance. The remaining extra fuel pod was slung onto the cargo module, but not yet connected to the ship's fuel delivery lines.

The last two days he and his father had helped the crew round everything up that was loose and get the ship ready for gravity spin. The added mass on the cargo module, holding nearly sixty tonnes of ice added to *Making Time*'s broken hab, shifted their center of gravity well below them, allowing them to spin about the cargo module enough to generate a nominal internal gravity. The ship was already laid out with this as an option, it just wasn't used much in practice for the short trips the spacers made to the asteroid belt.

Jerem felt the sideways acceleration begin to ease up as the thrusters stopped firing. The rumble dropping back to a hiss, then light popping as they shut out altogether.

"Reading 0.2G on the accelerometers," Vanessa reported. They sat quietly for a moment. Francine's head cocked to the side, listening for any sign of damage.

"Vee, do you think you can get Spot out for a quick inspection?"

"I can get him launched. It's the docking that'll be the problem."

Francine said, "Don't worry about that for now. Spot can drift alongside for a few days if need be. Our ace remote pilot here can help bring him in if we need him to."

"Alright." Vanessa dropped her goggles and pulled out the controls for the remote sensor platform. "Dusting off."

Jerem watched the remote's screen between the two consoles ahead of him. The stars were spinning so quickly around them, the view made him dizzy. He focused on the one stationary star in the center as the drone lifted off the back of the ship and fell away at half a gee. The sky suddenly stopped spinning on the camera, causing his stomach to lurch and he leaned sideways. *Watch the screen. Ignore your inner ear*, he reminded himself.

Vanessa brought the drone around and pointed the nose at the spinning vessel. The *Terror*, patched and held together with welded steel and aluminum, was spinning at nearly a revolution every two seconds about the bulky mass of the cargo module and *Making Time*'s forward section.

"She's on a bit of an incline," Jerem observed. "The mass from the engine section is pulling the center of gravity down in back. The nose is a bit downhill."

"Not much we can do about that," Francine agreed. "Zoom in, please. I want a good look at the cargo truss. Make sure we're not leaking."

"Aye." Vanessa swept in and increased the magnification. She scanned the length of the ship, slowing the video down on screen so they could look at it more carefully. "I'm not seeing any sign of leaks. I think she's holding."

"Alright. We'll leave it there for now." Francine flipped the intercom back on. "All hands, meeting in the galley."

Francine undid her buckles and grabbed hold of her console. The arrangement of their gravity now had her suspended almost two meters above the new "floor" that Jerem was lying back against. Getting out of the cockpit meant climbing up the floor that had become a wall to the hatch that would take them between levels. The deck plating had plenty of hand and foot holds, but it was still awkward for the pilot and copilot chairs.

Jerem remembered the fall he'd had while trying to get out of his seat while *Making Time* was tumbling and shuddered, reflexively holding his bandaged arm in his other hand.

Francine, by way of holding onto the edge of her console and the base of her seat, managed to get herself onto the wall and climb up to the hatch, then flipped around and disappeared through it.

"You need a hand, Jer?" Vanessa winced as soon as she said it. She was half-turned in her chair, holding onto the back, legs crossed and locked around the seat.

He shook his head and undid his straps, clutching his bandaged arm involuntarily. He stowed the tablet in his pants pocket. Then, rolling back on the couch, he planted his feet on the wall that was now the floor and stood up, wobbling. He climbed up over the couch and carefully made his way up the wall, one hand-hold at a time. Reaching the edge of the hatch, he peered over the lip through the accessway that led between the bunks, now arranged along the outer wall below. Edging his way over the lip of the hatch, he turned around, back to the floor and hooked a leg around a rung of the ladder and hauled himself up the rest of the way, suspended over the bunks below.

Vela Banks, his doctor, was climbing out of one of the bunks, looking a little green. He waved down at her with his bandaged arm, then regretted it as the weight of gravity pulled blood down to the sutures holding him together.

Inside, the ship, without a view outside, it almost felt like he was hanging on the bars at the gym back at school. He shimmied his way down the line into the galley, then let his legs drop, lowering his feet onto a cabinet. He stood there for a second before negotiating his way down the cupboard to the new floor. The table bolted in above the cooktop. He found a seat and eased himself into it as the rest of the crew began climbing down from the hatch above.

The cupboards now ran in a curve up the walls of the galley, all the way up to the entrance, in a confusing Escheresque interior that made for convenient ladders but inconvenient seating.

"Well, ain't this just dandy?" Reggie flopped into a seat beside Jerem. Hal jumped down and took the other seat beside him as Vanessa helped Doctor Banks down the cupboards to a seat.

"Sittin' here, almost feels like we're inside a house that fell over," Reggie observed.

Vanessa grinned. "Reminds me of the Reef back home."

Francine was the last to arrive. She jumped in near the cooktop and grabbed the last seat, turning it around and putting a foot on it.

"Everybody OK?" she asked. Her gaze settled on Vela, whose icky pallor made her stand out among the spacers. "If you're not feeling well, feel free to go back up to the bunks."

"Are we still calling that up?" Reggie asked. "Feels down to me."

"Actually, it is slightly down." Jerem pointed out. "The ship's engines…"

Vela contained a gulp and reached into her pocket for an anti-nausea tablet.

"OK, we can all figure out how we're referring to directions over the next few weeks. Right now I want to talk about options." Francine looked around the table. "After our last burn, we now have a suitable course for Earth. We should make the Earth-Moon neighborhood in just under four weeks. That's twenty-eight days, so get comfy in here."

They all leaned into the table. Not so much out of interest in what the Captain was saying, as the curvature of the hull and the direction of spin inclined everyone that way. Except for Reggie, who managed to lean back and hook a booted foot on the counter somehow.

"First up, all EVA are now canceled while under spin."

"Woohoo!" Reggie raised his arms, his bandaged fingers and hands the victims of the past week's intensive repair work.

"Anything going out the airlock is getting ejected at pretty high speed under this rotation. So the airlock's off limits except for... ?" Francine looked around the table, waiting for someone to fill in with an answer.

Jerem obliged them. "Garbage."

"That's right. We'll still recycle whatever we can." Francine thumped the recycling bin above her to her right, halfway up the wall. "But any junk that needs to go, including human waste that isn't liquid, goes in the airlock."

Reggie raised his arms again. "New shitter!"

Vela gulped.

"Which brings us to the head." Francine pointed straight up, the door to the head facing them, a view of the toilet inside tilted down directly above them. "The head is off-limits while under rotation. Use your shower gels. We'll get some water setup here on the table for people to wash their faces in. You have your water bottles. Any water that doesn't get used goes back into the reclamation system as per usual."

Grumbles and mutterings went around.

"Captain?"

"Yes, Jerem."

"I said before, but I think I know how we can shave off a week or so of transit time. And save us water in the process."

All eyes turned to Jerem.

"Go on."

"We're sitting on sixty tonnes of comet ice in the hold. We can melt it, siphon off the liquid and run it up to the fuel tanks for separation. If we can get a loop setup, we should be able to burn our maneuvering thrusters pretty much constantly without losing any fuel. Not to mention, free water."

Hal rubbed his chin. "We can probably salvage the water lines out of *Making Time* to use as conduits. We've even got the spare fuel tank on the side of the cargo pod."

"That'll mean more EVAs." Reggie was unimpressed.

The Captain sighed and stood up straight, holding onto the back of her chair. "Are we forgetting that we have to get back to Mars? Earth is not our final destination here. We need to figure out how we can get back. We don't have enough food for the full trip."

The table quieted down.

"It's something to think about anyway. Jerem, I want you to run the numbers and tell us what we'll save. Work with Hal and Reg to come up with time to implement the fuel extraction. If it takes us two weeks and burns a lot of energy in effort, it's probably not worth it. But keep it coming."

Vanessa was looking at her tablet. She raised her eyes to her Captain. "When we do get to Earth, we're going to be in the wrong position to make a return. It'll be six months before Earth's in position for a return window."

"I am aware and have concerns about this, yes."

More grumbling around the table.

"Last thing, and this is the important one: food." Everyone shut up. "We are on strict rations from here on out. I know you men have been burning up a lot of energy with the EVAs, but that's got to stop. From here on out, the men get twelve hundred calories. Women get a thousand. Includes me. We'll be sharing ration packs for dinner."

"Aw, come on, skip." Reggie dropped his foot to the floor with a clunk.

"Sorry. No exceptions. You count calories. You write them down on the whiteboard." She slapped the fridge, picking up the marker. She erased the messages and doodles that were there and drew a grid, each of their names on it.

"Jerem, how many calories total do we have in our inventory?"

Jerem pulled his father's tablet out of his pocket and flipped it on. "Lessee... two hundred pouches of bean stew, a hundred tubs of soygurt, a few random bags of assorted dried veggies and mushrooms. Just under two hundred and forty thousand."

"Yeah. We're going to have to find some food before we can make it home."

The assembled crew looked around the table at one another. Reggie started grinning.

"No, Reggie. We don't eat people."

070

ROVER 2

Erika felt like she was on fire and freezing at the same time. All her nerves were raw. Her skin crawled. She fumbled with her helmet latches, barely able to find them with her numb hands, her gloves felt like balloons. She managed the releases and pulled her helmet off, a mass of hair coming with it.

She vomited, dry heaves from her empty stomach, taste of blood in her mouth like copper as her whole body became wracked with pain. It took a minute to recover, and she crawled forward, lurching as the rover bounced to a stop.

"Ray," she croaked. She didn't sound like herself and realized her ears were ringing. "Ray."

Nausea took hold of her again and she was helpless until the waves passed.

The interior of the RV was hazy, like it was filled with fog. She blinked and waved a gloved hand in front of her face and the brightness dimmed. She realized that it was her eyes that were filmed over.

She was going to die.

"Ray. We have to upload. Data."

She crawled forward. Ray was slumped in the driver's seat up against the wheel, preventing the RV from rolling forward.

Erika shook him weakly and his head rolled to the side. "Ray," she sobbed. She saw her face reflected in his visor and had to look away. She didn't recognize herself.

She was alone and she didn't know how much time she'd have left.

Her gloves wouldn't come off. Working at the rings, she managed to get one of them to shift and twisted the glove so hard she thought she was going to break her wrist, but eventually it turned. The metal and plastic were warped. The glove looked like a mutant appendage, the fingers fused together.

But her hand...

The skin was pink and peeling. Spots of red marked where capillaries had burst near the surface. Black patches showed where the skin had died. One of her fingernails peeled away easily and fell to the floor.

She laughed then, a horrible sound that turned to a scream before it stopped. Then more coughing and sobbing.

"Ray. I need to upload your camera footage." She pushed herself up onto her knees and carefully leaned Ray back in his seat. She lifted his head up and popped the data card out of his suit's chest piece. She leaned down close to the console so she could find the slot and carefully, her fingers shaking, pushed it in. It was hard. She had hardly any feeling in her fingers.

She pressed the OK button on the screen and it imported the files. When it was done, she popped the card out and dropped it on the floor.

Then she did the same for herself. She removed the card from her chest piece with numb, half-dead fingers and slotted it into the RV's console. "OK," she said as she pushed the button to import the files. "We don't have Aden's card. We had to leave it..." She trailed off, sniffing. She wiped at a tear on her cheek and her suit's sleeve came back red with blood. Her left eye no longer worked.

"Don't have much time. Need to set to broadcast on repeat," she said. Ray stayed slumped in his seat without response. No movement.

She reached over the passenger seat and pushed the controls on her radio rig to transmit everything in the rover's file system from the last two days. Then she set it to loop the transmission on their sideband data channel. She pressed SEND and squinted at the lights.

They were too far from the last good repeater they'd setup. Ray's headlong race down the hillside hadn't taken them very far before he'd passed out and died on the controls. They needed to travel west. They had no data network, so they didn't have positional data from the drive out. No autopilot. "We'll have to aim west and hope for the best," she said, her voice a harsh whisper.

"Excuse me, Ray." She pushed him back into the corner again, then fumbled at his harness. She pulled back on the steering column and the rover lurched forward again, almost knocking her back. She pulled back on the throttle and set it to five kilometers per hour. "That should be fast enough, shouldn't it?"

She tried to swallow, but her mouth and throat were dry.

Her vision was fading fast. She couldn't see far ahead of them, but she turned the wheel slightly and set a course north of where they'd come from, hoping they could skirt around the badlands and avoid some of the worst obstacles they'd driven through. She coughed. A horrible wet wheezing came out of her and she sprayed blood on the controls.

"We need to keep this wheel pulled back," she whispered. Ray's harness wasn't long enough to reach the wheel, even fully extended. She needed another twenty centimeters to close the gap.

Aden's rubber tube was still on the center console, teeth marks in the one end he liked to chew on.

She reached over Ray's legs into the pouch beside the driver's seat and fumbled around for the length of tubing. She unwound the black rubber and looped it around the wheel where it joined to the steering column and pulled it underneath. She had to squint to see what she was doing, but she managed to get the ends together and make a crude knot in it. It had to be enough. She unlatched the two ends of the driver's shoulder straps and ran them through the rubber tube, clicking them back together to form a chain. The steering column stayed back, the Rover crawling at a steady five kilometers per hour.

"You're driving now, Aden. You're the driver."

She smiled then and, with a great effort, managed to drag herself into the passenger seat. The rocking motion of the slow-moving rover lulling her to sleep almost immediately.

"We're going home now, Ray."

Acknowledgements

Now that the dust has settled and all the pieces are in place, I get to look back and thank the fine humans who made this possible. It's been just over nine months since Trajectory Book 2 was released. In addition to this book, I've completed a house move, a bunch of renovations, two short stories and a bunch of other stuff that probably isn't very interesting. Deb and I have setup the beginnings of a hobby farm and we've got space cleared for this year's round of pickling and vegetable harvests.

So first, thank you to Deb, my special collaborator and co-conspirator. You're not a very strict task master, but that's ok. You lit the fires when it was necessary or when it was time to burn stuff.

Mom and Dad, you're still cool. You were a big help getting us setup out here and we couldn't have done it without you. I am looking forward to some barbecues and fire bowls this summer.

Scarlett R. Algee did the editing on this one and was a real pleasure to work with. Professional and responsive and just a nice gal. I'm happy to have met you.

My writing crew over at the Bureau of Scifi Explorations have been an enormous bunch of help and support. Thanks for the laughs and virtual good times. Ralph for reaching out and making contact, I will be eternally grateful. Nathan, you are a force of nature and expect great things in your future. Josh, I appreciate your enthusiasm, humor and dedication, even when life is throwing you fastballs. Scott for his rugged manliness and get 'er done work ethos, I really respect what you do. You're all impressive talents and a continued source of inspiration. Thank you for all your help and knowledge.

Nick Bailey, who feels like a kindred spirit an ocean away. Thanks for your support and generosity.

Chris P and Eric, I owe you guys an email.

… as ever, thank *you*, dear reader. I really appreciate the interest.

I look forward to a time when we can all hang out and tell stories around the fire under the stars.

A word from the author

Thank you for reading Seedfall. I hope you enjoyed it. Feel free to leave an honest review on <u>Amazon</u> and on <u>Goodreads</u>, if you have a moment. Every review helps these books find their way to interested readers.

Please tell your friends!

If you'd like to stay in touch, here are a few of the places I frequent online. Like, follow and subscribe to them to stay in touch. I'd love to hear from you if you have questions or comments, or even just a hello.

<u>http://robcee.net/</u>
    <u>http://facebook.com/robcampbellbooks</u>
    <u>http://twitter.com/robcee</u>
    <u>https://www.goodreads.com/robcee</u>

Last, if you want the inside scoop and some free book deals, sign up for my <u>newsletter</u>. I'll write about progress, process and try to have something special for you to read once per month. I respect your time and privacy and promise I will never give your email address to anyone. This is just between us.

The very best,
    Robert M. Campbell

Further Reading

Explorations: First Contact

An exciting collection of First Contact science fiction stories, each set in the same universe. Join many of today's best SF authors as they tell you stories of explorations.

The Sphere ship appeared suddenly, damaged and dying. After making contact, Earth learned they weren't alone in the universe. The Sphere gave them knowledge of space travel, and co-ordinates to other races spread across the expanse. It asked them to continue its mission of exploration and contact, but also left them with a stark warning: Stay away from the Star.

Over the next twenty years, the United Earth Foundation formed, and their ships were built, their displacement drives giving them the sphere shape when engaged.

Their Mission: First Contact

Prologue - Stephen Moss
   Deja Vu - Peter Cawdron
   The Signal - Ralph Kern
   Status: Inactive - Richard Fox
   The Bottom Line - Chris Kennedy
   End of the Line - Robert M. Campbell
   Mercurial Rescue - Isaac Hooke
   The Mission - PP Corcoran
   The Last Command - Nick Bailey
   Sleeping Giant - PJ Strebor
   The Darklady - Scott Moon
   Triaxial - Stephen Moss
   Harbinger - Josh Hayes
   Epilogue - Empyrean - Jacob Cooper

Visit http://scifiexplorations.com to sign up for their newsletter and receive exciting book offers!